THE WITCH'S DAUGHTER

Sarah Smith

The Witch's Daughter
Published by Sarah Smith - https://www.storybridge.org
Email: sarah@storybridge.org

First edition: February 2026
10 9 8 7 6 5 4 3 2 1

The moral rights of the author have been asserted.
Cover design, typesetting and layout by Sarah Smith.
Cover illustration, all maps & illustrations by Sarah Smith.

ISBN: 1-76446-611-X
ISBN-13: 978-1-7644661-1-0

This is a work of fiction, and although the names of historical figures have been used along with dates in Irish history, most events depicted are entirely imaginary and bear no relation to actual fact. This was written because its enchanting to think what might have been.

A catalogue record for this book is available from the National Library of Australia

For all those witches accused of writing heresy.

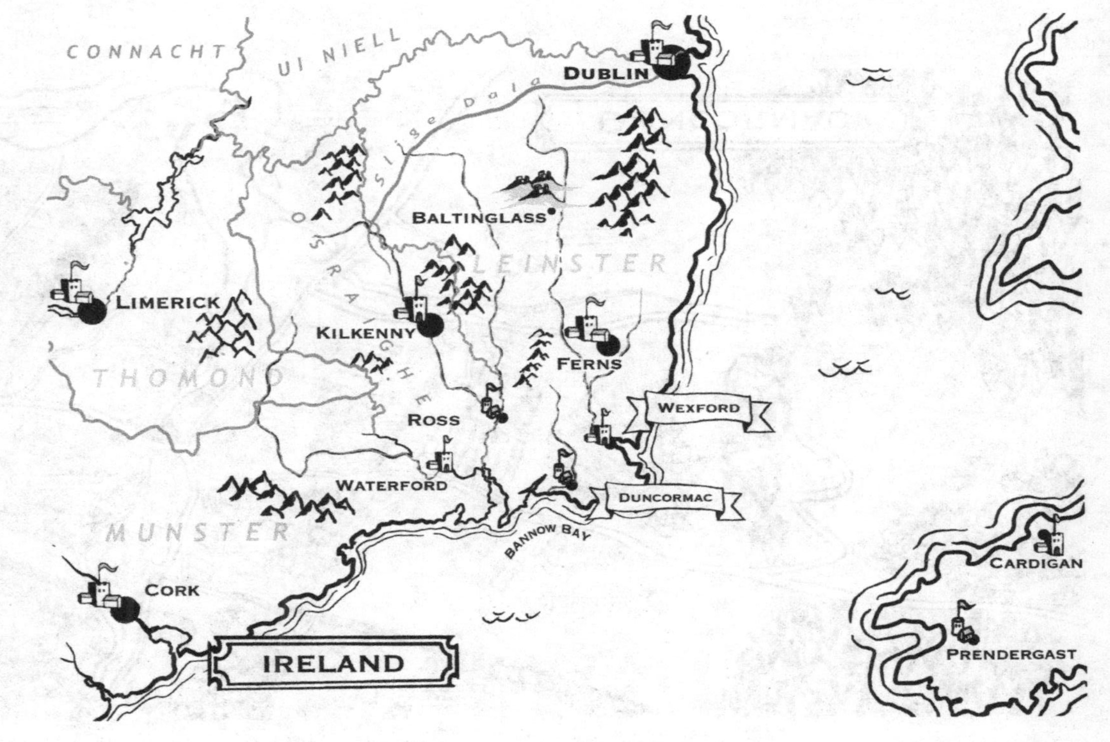

CONNACHT
UI NIELL
Slige Dala
DUBLIN
BALTINGLASS
LEINSTER
OSRAGHE
LIMERICK
KILKENNY
FERNS
WEXFORD
THOMOND
ROSS
WATERFORD
DUNCORMAC
MUNSTER
BANNOW BAY
CORK
IRELAND
CARDIGAN
PRENDERGAST

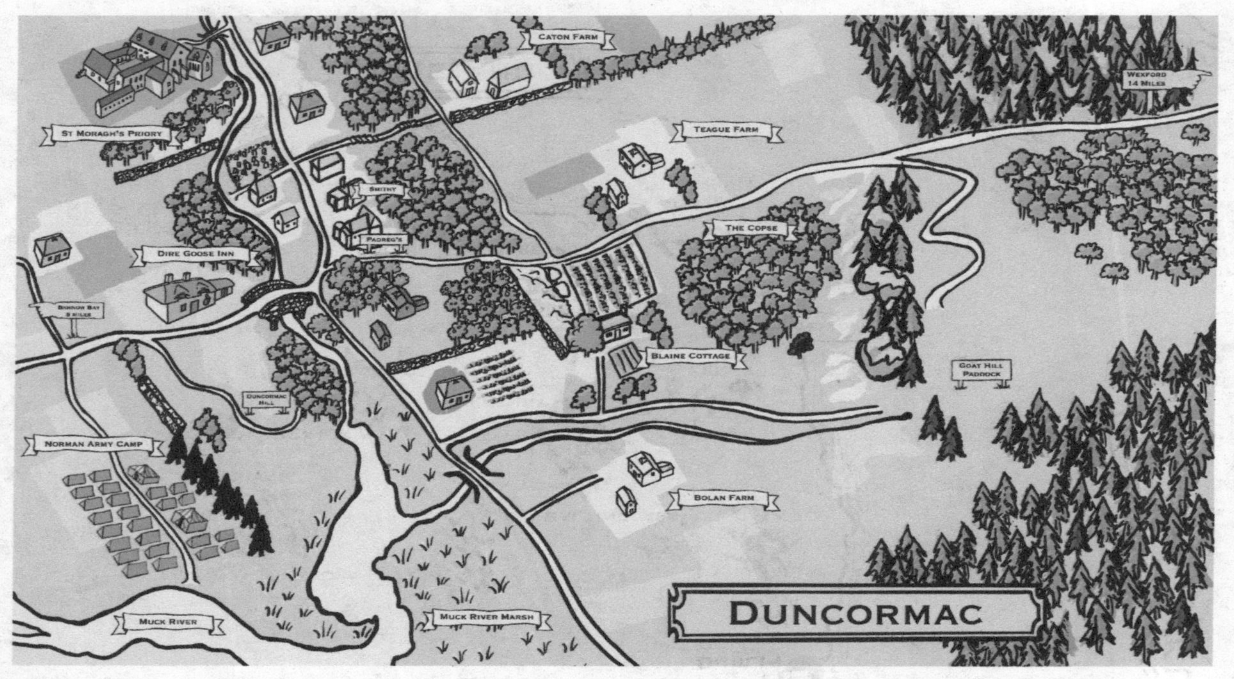

CATON FARM
WEXFORD 14 MILES
ST MORAGH'S PRIORY
TEAGUE FARM
SMITHY
THE COPSE
PADREG'S
DIRE GOOSE INN
BURROW BAY 8 MILES
BLAINE COTTAGE
GOAT HILL PADDOCK
DUNCORMAC HILL
NORMAN ARMY CAMP
BOLAN FARM
MUCK RIVER
MUCK RIVER MARSH
DUNCORMAC

1

Blaine Cottage

Hilde Blaine pulled her blanket over her head, and willed silent the unholy cawing from the other side of the thatch.

It can't be daylight yet.

She ventured an eye out from under the blanket and looked to the dormer window through the roof that sloped up over her loft bed. A glow already picked out the tops of the fruit trees in the smallholding outside.

A rooster crowed. Hilde let out a strangled noise of frustration.

She was only thirteen but it already felt like she spent far too much of her life doing chores when being warm in bed was nicer. Or, if she must get up then playing ought to be the cause, not chores.

Mother would already be up.

She rolled out of bed carefully to avoid the low sloping ceiling. Splashing a small amount of water from a jug into the bowl by her bed Hilde washed away the sleep. It was cold and her teeth began to chatter, so she quickly tugged on a pair of woollen tights, a smock and scarf.

Hilde bit her lip as she tip-toed. A quiet cough came from below the loft. She peered over the edge of the rough wooden platform. Mother sat in her rocking chair below.

She hasn't told me I have to do my chores yet. Dress up time!

Hilde yanked open the chest at the foot of her bed, and pulled out her favourite coat.

Supposed to be just for church? But I'm a princess! I'm late to attend the King of Leinster's court!

A disc of silver dangled from a chain hooked to the thatch and she twisted it so that she could see herself, as she put on the coat and tugged at her mop of unruly long hair.

Out the window Hilde's loyal subjects, the pigs and hens below in the yard, awaited her royal presence.

Hilde stooped under the rafters, looked in the mirror and admonished her hair, which was a birds nest. She battled against it with her long-suffering hairbrush.

The sun was high enough to limn the tree-line, and now it cast its unrelenting eye in through the window.

Her heirloom swung on its chain, shining in the ray of light. Hilde put her brush back carefully, so as to not bump it again. She peered down through a gap between the timbers. There shone mother's lamp at her elbow as she worked at the mending.

The precious heirloom cloak pin, had been put on a silver chain for safe keeping. Hilde put her hand to it and brought it carefully into the light. A beasts head open-mouthed disgorged the pin which closed the cloak pin. And its silver circle was a filigree glade, scalloped edges framing forest animals among leaves.

Hilde put the chain to her neck, so entrancing in the early light. Dust motes circled, magical faerie lights, around her head in the silver. For a moment the twigs of thatch behind her were a sylvan crown in her reflection.

Peering close, the pin bore Father's silver-mark 'AB'. Hilde stood mesmerised.

"Hilde!" Her mother Bronach glared up at her now, a baleful eye where the elbow had been.

Hilde jumped. "Coming!"

She clipped the chain closed at the back of her neck; and slipped the pin under her smock. Hilde held it there for a moment; with an aching in her throat.

She looked out as the rising sun peeked over the hills, lighting the laneway like a silver band. The way bounded by hedgerows led from their smallholding into town.

Father.

His ghost passed down the lane. A silhouette bobbing in the dawn sun, over the rise. Leaving them, just his hat on, and a small pack on his back.

Hilde squeezed her eyes closed.

In her minds eye his face formed, a tense smile, frozen in a time three harvests past.

Gone to a war, for a usurper King, mama said.

Hilde blinked and looked into the dawn, eyes smarting in the glare, fighting the tear forming in her eye.

The figure she'd seen down the lane was gone. Being maudlin was no good for a princess! Hilde started down the ladder.

❖

Dawn rose over the coast of Hibernia. An early lone gull soared in the sky, searching the inky ocean for fare. It let out a mewing shriek.

"Merde!"

In the half dark, in the boats below, a swarthy captain in light armour looked up, cursed the bird, and cursed the dawn, and then cursed at his soldiers to row harder.

"Rangée! Allez au Diable!"

Oars redoubled and dipped into the dark waters anew. The sun would soon rise above the coastal hills banishing the shadows that cloaked the soldiers approach.

Steam rose from the men's shoulders, muscles bunching as they pulled at the oars. The rowlocks groaned in the timber of the gunwales.

The gull came down like an arrow, and pierced the water with hardly a ripple. A mullet, the target of it's fell swoop, had no chance.

Guillaime Giffard turned from watching the bird, and stood up on the prow of his boat, placing a boot on the gunwale. Drawing a spyglass he extended it and held it to his eye, and a mirthless smile spread across his face. His ship was in front of the small flotilla, and would choose the landing then lead the army up the shore.

That is the bay. Those idiots better have found a good campsite or that Flemish bastard will not be happy. If I find any drunk, maybe I'll tattoo their belly with my sabre tip.

Their camp was not visible from the sea, which made sense. Giffard had campaigned with the hard men in these boats. Many from the marches, a few others like Giffard, sell-swords from England and France. Prendergast had led them to riches before, so the men would fight. Giffard put the glass to his eye again, and looked back over the other boats.

In the largest ship, just behind Giffard's, Prendergast bellowed orders, and the men got to work to get the horses ready for landfall. Giffard turned to train his gaze again on the sleepy mist-covered land and shook his head. Barding, ramps, armour, knights and trained hard men. Norman military technology. It would be like a wolf among lambs.

Even if the men had a skinful, sacking villages of the dumb Irish would be as simple as plucking a grape from a Toulouse vine.

"Tirer... Tenir!!" He waved the boats on.

Two dozen boats followed Giffard's into the surf near the shore. Pulling hard, then holding the oars up, they one after another crested a wave to slide down its other side toward their target; the shelter of Bannow Bay in the Irish coast.

High above the soldiers, the early gull returned with its prey. It passed the waves, crashing on the beach and flew inland into the grey rising morning mist. Its giant wings spread, riding the breeze, following the dawn light as it crept across the land.

❖

Verdant hills, and quiet waterways lined with willows, rolled under pleasant blue grey skies. Crisp clear air rose to puffy clouds on high, but mists rose from fens, curling mysterious wisps around alder and birch trees.

In a hidden valley a stones throw from the coast, drab canvas tents lay tucked into the dark below the willows near a brook, but brash pennants on their ridge poles caught the early dawn light.

Horses, stout destriers, and others ready to be laden with supplies, stood tied to a line of birches. Most slept but a few snickered awake, and nibbled at the grass.

An officer used the low bough of a spreading oak tree as a wash stand. By the reflection of his long-sword, he completed his morning ablutions. He scraped his face clean of whiskers with a dagger as long as his forearm. The man's warhorse, tied to the same tree, eyed him and blinked as if in critique.

"Bientôt," the officer mouthed back.

A thin lipped smile spread across his face as he wiped his weapon clean.

Soon we taste glory.

He hefted his sword high, admiring his reflection. His tunic nicely set off his FitzStephen jawline. He slammed his sword home in a scabbard at his belt, and the dagger into his belt. Many more soldiers now moved around dressing by lamplight, while others fed horses or adjusted and oiled armour.

A pained cry went up, sounds of a scuffle rapidly subdued.

Scouts led a few captured locals. Time to put on a show for the men. FitzStephen rubbed his hands, and pulled his tunic straight. Light torture and then execution would give the men the taste for blood.

A few soldiers stood lookout atop a nearby rocky outcrop, eyes toward the coast for the last of their number to approach by sea. On a hilltop on the opposite side of the hidden valley two more sets of fierce eyes looked inland, to land for the conquering.

High above the soldiers, the early seagull returned with its prey. Past the waves, crashing on the rocky headlands, and inland above the grey low-lying morning mist.

❖

"Hilde Maeve Blaine, what has befallen you child!" Bronach Blaine said, as she set aside her mending. She coughed, the acrid smoke from the tallow lamp catching in her throat as she raised her voice.

A parade of emotions crossed Bronach's face, a surprised smile at her daughter, shock of dark curly hair, best coat and scarf, earrings made of chestnuts; a smile that tightened to judgement. Then pained eyes and a furrowed brow.

"Ach, girl - you can't go out feeding pigs dressed in your best coat!"

"Mama!"

"At market I saw Chief Fiach. Do you know what he told me?" Bronach said, arching her brow.

"I can be really careful!" Hilde said, pouting.

"Listen, Brehon judges travelled here from the Northern towns. They told the Chief the dawn sun is near the Beltane stones! It will be May day very soon."

Hilde grinned.

"Wear nice things to dance the maypole. Alright? Until then no good clothes outside!"

"I'm doing it right away Ma. Promise!"

Hilde climbed out of the coat as she grabbed for the buckets of kitchen scraps by the front door. She slung the scarf over a hook on the wall, and chucked the coat over a kitchen chair.

Bronach gasped as the silver flashed around Hilde's neck.

"And not before you take off your beautiful necklace, my girl! You'll lose that in a second!"

Bronach tried her hardest to keep a stern face, and not to grin as she held out her hand to her daughter for the heirloom. Her hands that were pricked and bloody from mending soldiers uniforms.

Hilde gave the necklace to her mother, and looked down at her shoes, chagrined. As she went to race off, her mother caught her by the finger.

"And the second you're done, put your finery back up where it belongs! You hear me?" cautioned the weary seamstress. She pointed to the coat and scarf, picking up her work again.

Hilde paused in the door, turned her head and nodded sullenly to her mother. Behind her mother on the wall, figures of the sainted virgin, and of saint Brigit all judged Hilde.

Hilde sniffed, and turned to the outdoors.

Blaine land bejewelled by dew laden cobwebs awaited beyond the threshold. The pigs had their sty right up along the back wall of the cottage. Their eager snouts pressed up to the railing as Hilde walked out.

Not fair. Mother Mary, what will I be? Its alright if I'm not a princess. But surely more than this?

She sluiced out their troughs first, and then poured in the kitchen slops. The other bucket held acorns and chestnuts which Hilde carefully distributed across the top.

A gulls piecing cry set Hilde's teeth on edge. High above it wheeled in the sky. Against the glare of the Irish dawn sky she could see something in its greedy maw.

Picking up the old besom from the threshold she set about the next job, cleaning their pen and watering the hungry sows while they were occupied with food. Their muck made fertiliser and a good land girl wasted none of it. Hilde swept the pure into a sack to be put in the pit. Later it would go on the beans and potatoes.

Around the side of the cottage an indignant snort erupted, followed by a plaintive *hee-haw*. And at the rear of the property a chorus of clucking joined in. Sebastien, their donkey was normally very patient. So unlike him to be bickering.

Is he just looking for breakfast?

His nose quested around the end of the cottage, as far as he could reach from his stall. Hilde laughed, and started toward the grain cellar at the side of the house.

And Sebastien, I hope you are not wearing your Sunday best!

Hee-haw! Sebastien called, as if he really did hear Hilde's thoughts.

Sebastien followed that statement with a spluttering snort.

"What!" Hilde said out loud as she looked back.

Something is up with the beast. He had never been like this.

Was he sick?

Hilde set the buckets down and went to him, patting his nose. She fed him a chestnut, and a piece of turnip. He turned his head in the direction of the laneway and sniffed the air.

"Gobnait and her girls first, the cock and chickens; then you Sebastien," called Hilde to the donkey.

Hilde shook her head, picked up her buckets and went about her day.

Above the hedgerows by the lane a thin streamer of black smoke arose.

2

A Hidden Valley

"Mama! There's people up the lane!" Hilde gasped, as she burst through the door of Blaine cottage. She set down the two buckets, now clean and full of water from the well.

Two starlings fluttered up into the thatch, startled as the door banged against the jamb.

"Hilde, what are you talking about," Bronach said. Her face gave the lie to her dismissive words; with furrowed brow and glances to the windows. "Why are you always making up stories, my princess? Hmm?"

"It's not stories! I *could* be a princess in the court of King Diarmait mac Murchada when I get older. There's a picture of him on the wall in the Priory in his finery!" Hilde twirled around, smock flaring out, and boot tracing a dainty arc on the dusty floor.

Bronach went to the one window that faced out toward the lane and peered out.

"He hasn't been King for years! I don't suppose our High King Ruaidrí can be bothered to come to an old priory in

Duncormac to replace some pictures," Bronach said turning back and folding her arms. "Chief Fiach's heard nothing to say King Diarmait will return, sweetheart."

"Sister Gobnait told me that he's coming back! He's going to add even more chapels and study rooms to the priory," Hilde said, moving about the space to collect up their water jugs and the kettle over the fire for filling. "She has a story about him for me to read. I don't know all the words yet, but the pictures look lovely!"

"Hilde, did I hear you in the yard calling to our girls in the henhouse? Using the Sister's name?" Bronach asked.

Hilde answered with a rub of her nose and a barely suppressed giggle. "The big one with the fierce look. It's her, I swear!"

"Saints be! You'd better not let slip that you've named that big hen after your teacher. I'm in enough trouble for not going to mass as it is," Bronach coughed the words out. Then spluttered, several times, her eyes tearing up with the effort.

"But you've been ill mother. Your cough! Can't sing vespers with that. It could be catching," Hilde said, pushing the door shut, and wiping her hands on her smock.

"It's fine. Its just the smoke," Bronach said, turning to peer out the window again. "Sweetheart, even if old Diarmait came back the wars would not end. It won't bring your father back."

Hilde replaced her mothers jug, full of water, on the timber beam next to her mothers bed. Her fathers things were in a trunk next to the bed, and had not been touched in near two years. Hilde wiped dust from the top of the trunk.

"Mama, where is Papa's silver? Why don't we get it out any more?" Hilde asked, walking to her mother's side to put her head under her arm. She would soon be taller than her mother, and Bronach chuckled. She lifted her arm and held Hilde, resting her palm on the window sill as she gazed out.

"Hidden. Sweetheart, people think a woman on her own is fair game. We have to use our heads, we Blaine women," Bronach said, her speech slowing as she peered out and thoughtfully cupped her hand over her eyes.

"Mama, see that smoke?" Hilde said pointing excitedly.

❖

Hilde and her Ma had stood at the window straining their eyes for several moments. Now Bronach tensed.

"What did you say about people?" Bronach asked, a chill edge to her voice.

"In the lane! I saw smoke, so I peeked. I looked under the hedge and there's maybe ten?" Hilde said. Then she saw her Mama's face, visibly pale. Hilde's excited grin dropped from her face, and her brow furrowed. "Then I heard arguing. One man sounds really horrid."

Bronach moved quickly to the door, and dropped the bar in place.

"Hilde, pull the shutters! Tie them up as though for a storm!" Bronach said, her voice now an urgent whisper.

"Mama! What is it! What's happening!" Hilde looked from her mothers face to the window, peering out. The yard was strangely quiet.

"Grab your things! Out the back window, Hilde!"

This was impossible! Tears streamed down Hilde's face. She ran through her loft bed, and grabbed up an armful of her things, including her heirloom and her coat which had still not been put away.

There was a doll that her father had made the head for, and her mother the body. It broke when she was nine, and father had said he would fix it, but never did. Hilde held the head of little Dotty, and stared at her mother. Hilde's mouth was open but the crying inside her would not come.

Hilde climbed on a chest, and placed one hand on the back windowsill. Outside happy clouds scudded across blue skies and mayflies buzzed. The turnip pasture reeked of fertiliser.

"My brave girl," Bronach said. She turned.

Hilde ran to her and buried her face in her mothers apron. Bronach stroked her hair, then pushed at the mending, abandoned on the table. She emptied a drawstring muslin bag of soldiers uniforms awaiting repair.

"Your name - do you know where it comes from?" Bronach asked.

Hilde shook her head. She sniffed, and wiped her nose. Bronach took Hilde's things from her, and tucked them into the drawstring bag.

"Chief Fiach gave it to you. He doesn't like to talk of it, but his blood comes from the men of the icy north over the sea," Bronach forced a smile, but her eyes flicked to the shuttered window. "I want you to go out the back window, and not turn around. Run to Chief Fiach's house."

Bronach Blaine!

A voice sounded from outside.

"Mama!" Hilde's tears started again.

"Run Hilde!"

❖

It was mid-afternoon and the Norman army stood ready to march.

Orders in several languages and dialects, along with insults and laughs were traded between the men. Over by the line of birches, men lashed down tents and supplies onto the big draught-horses. Men hefted packs, bedrolls and stowed their helms, greaves and shields in strapping on their backs.

The only thing remaining on the trampled grass was a gibbet with the corpses of three men strung up, their intestines spilled on the ground below them.

On the ridge line of the hidden valley, a group of a dozen men stood in silhouette. Their simple leather armour and helms gave them a presence but their shifting weight, and turning heads betrayed nervousness.

"Tell him to come down here, dammit Giffard!" Prendergast said.

"He says he's the King of Thomond. He wants you to go up there," Giffard replied. He had a twist to his thin-lipped slash of a mouth, that didn't bode well for Thomond. From the rocky outcrop two dozen paces away a squad of archers had their bows at the ready.

"Thomond?" asked FitzStephen.

"A day's hard ride that way, the other side of Ossary," Prendergast added irritably. His horse skittered as Prendergast shifted his weight in the saddle and pointed. "Too many damn Kings in this place. Let's get this over with."

"Monsieur," Giffard said, touching his forelock.

"And Giffard, bring a squad with you. Quietly."

"What the blazes has happened to MacMurrough? That inbred sack of puke!" FitzStephen shouted, slamming a fist against his saddle, as he mounted up. Prendergast rode at a slow walk up the side of the valley.

❖

The army in the valley stilled and watched as the two rode slowly up the side of the valley.

"Let's hear him out," Prendergast said as they neared the ridge and FitzStephen drew level.

Out of the tree-line on the right, below the outcrop, Giffard led his destrier and a group of men moving quickly in single file through the scrub. On reaching the ridge-line where the outcrop broke line of sight from Thomond and his men Giffard mounted up. He grabbed up the reins and held up a palm to his men as they formed up.

"Treachery!" FitzStephen spluttered. He was a big man, with an aquiline nose, swarthy features and fierce eyes. His every move was a twitch, and his spiky black hair emphasised his erratic mood.

Prendergast was pale, and his blonde hair paired with slab-like cheekbones and an impassive expression made him look otherworldly. Nothing seemed to faze him. Everything that happened slotted neatly into the millstones turning in his mind.

"Thomond!" called out Prendergast as they drew closer. "Is that a white flag?"

"Letter!" the man shouted back. His long hair, beard and colourful heraldry made him look more like a court jester than a King. Either side of him were two serious young men with a distinct family resemblance, wearing light armour and similar heraldry.

The King did hold a white object in his left hand. He waved it again. It *was* a letter, with a seal. "From the rightful High King of Ireland Diarmait mac Murchada!"

FitzStephen shot a glance at Prendergast and burst out laughing. They reached the King, his cousins and his small retinue of soldiers, and a stiff breeze was blowing in off the sea. Two colourful banners streamed in the afternoon sun.

"My lords, welcome, welcome. I am King, and my cousins here are the Lords of the royal court of Limerick. My liege King Diarmait mac Murchada is detained. He has been fighting Uí Tuathail, the Uí Broin, and Uí Conchobhair Failghe north of Leinster, and…"

"Good gods man, speak so we can understand! Don't waste my time!" FitzStephen shouted, drawing his sword in a flash and then pointing to the gibbets. "Or the lot of you will join *those* lads, swinging in the breeze."

The Thomond men took a step forward. An arrow flashed and stuck in the ground between them, quivering. Giffard and his men rounded the rock and walked slowly toward the men of Thomond.

Prendergast swung his leg forward over his horse and hopped to the ground, and strode past the arrow, hand extended.

"Domnall Mór Ua Briain, King of Thomond, at your service," the King said, holding out his right hand.

Prendergast snatched the letter from the mans quivering left hand. He glanced at it, then back to the King.

"Quis que c'est?" Prendergast said to Giffard, jerking his head at the King. Giffard was now a few paces from the Thomond men.

"Donàl O'Brien, Monsieur," Giffard said sotto voce, leaning down from his horse. "A key ally of MacMurrough."

"My name is Maurice de Prendergast. And my lord, Monsieur FitzStephen and I were expecting MacMurrough," said Prendergast, turning to the King. He whipped out a dagger from his belt, stabbed the letter with it and extended it up behind himself to FitzStephen who remained in his saddle. "But we have you, King O'Brien."

With Prendergast's blonde haired calmness the royal deference was more chilling than a direct blade to the throat.

"Sir Prendergast, my liege MacMurrough is fighting the North Leinster men. He is cut off. He will meet you on the road to Wexford. With his army of five hundred men. As promised."

"Lies! Giffard, kill this idiot," FitzStephen shouted. Giffard's horse snorted and cantered forward a pace.

"You have his letter! MacMurrough's envoy rode all night on the Slige Dala to get it to me," the King said. He gestured to his cousins. "Instead of sending my lords, I did the right thing and came myself! My realm of Thomond, my people are without their king tonight! I am here as a sign of respect!"

Prendergast cleared his throat. FitzStephen held up a hand and Giffard halted his men.

"Well, the signets match. MacMurrough says 'Humble apologies…' ah, let us see, 'cut off in the Wicklow Mountains' umm." Prendergast looked up to FitzStephen, and raised his eyebrows. FitzStephen kept reading.

"… oh, and he'd like to meet us. How pleasant," FitzStephen said, shifting his bulk in his saddle, and twitching the reins to settle his horse.

"King Domnall, we are going to kill one of your cousins. And we will keep one with us. So you understand who we are," Prendergast said. He eyed the Thomond delegation. "And then we are going to send you back to your kingdom with a message."

Giffard walked his horse forward, and whispered something in French to Prendergast. The Thomond delegation began backing away, looking left and right.

"You tell mac Murchada we are waiting for him on the road to Wexford," Prendergast said.

FitzStephen pointed to the younger of the two men flanking the King, and signalled to the rocky outcrop. Two arrows hit the young man in quick succession, and he crumpled to the ground.

The other young man's face went as pale as parchment, his mouth fell open, and his knees knocked together. Prendergast signalled to Giffard and turned to walk his horse back to his men.

Giffard rode past him the still quivering Thomond cousin, and with one hand, pulled the lad up over his saddle like a sack of grain. He headed back down into the valley after Prendergast.

❖

The rich soil was in Hilde's nose and eyes, and her ribs hurt. Winded, it was a struggle to breathe and the drawstring bags contents was poking her in the chest.

Hilde rolled over and breathed. The window was high above, as the turnip fields rolled away down from the house on this side. So… the fall had been greater than expected. She picked up her things and brushed off the clods of dirt clinging to her legs. And ran.

Ahead at the bottom of the paddock the fence line to the left curved away toward the town, back up the rise, following a brook toward a spot where the water went into rocks and back under ground. To the right the fence line went toward the copses and up a hill. Beyond that low hill, another hill rose up with lines of barley in its lee. Hilde slowed.

The barley marked Chief Fiach's land. It would take forever to get up the hill, and over the stile. But once there barley would be a place to hide. The turnips were too low to provide any cover, but a row of beans on tall wooden stakes cast a shadow. Hilde bent over there and leant into the shade. Loud voices floated from behind, at the cottage. Several thin columns of dark smoke. Threatening raised voices.

Hilde ran again, and tripped, nearly losing her balance in the ploughed soil. Mud clung to her boots. She stopped, and bent over, her hands on her knees, panting for breath. Her ribs still hurt from the fall. There was a noise behind the row of beans. The stakes rattled and moved.

Saint Brigit save me!

Hilde ran pell mell. And crashed into the fence. She started to climb. And felt a push from behind.

18

Hee haw!!

"Oh Sebastien! You'll be the death of me!" Hilde said. She looped her head around the beasts neck and buried her face in his mane of wiry, dirty hair.

He spluttered.

"Who let you loose, hey?" Hilde asked.

From behind the raised voices carried again. Then a banging noise. Someone pounded at the door of Blaine Cottage. Other voices were raised making demands, an argument.

Run, Hilde, run.

She looked back to the hills ahead. And there on the ridge line, on the weather side of the hill, stood a rider on a horse.

A man with a mirthless smile.

3

The Copse

It was late afternoon, and darkening thunderheads gathered in the north, iron-grey shapes in the sky, as if ships hulls of a ghostly fleet floated high above the land. The army marched along a river from its mouth, the watercourse narrowing as the army headed inland. Their pack horses groaned under the weight of pillaged food and ale.

The river drove through a gap between two low hills clad in greensward. Here the water was clean and clear, tumbling over rocks into a pool. Not the briny undrinkable tidal water encountered when they'd picked up the river earlier in the day. The men slowed, shouted, a few pointing to the cold stream.

An outrider galloped from the front of the column of men.

"Sir, water hole sighted!" the outrider called.

"And sir, we have a lot of food now," said the two sergeants that walked up from the rear to hear the report.

"Bien sûr. Water the horses! Eat and enjoy!" Prendergast said. He walked his horse back toward FitzStephen.

"A stop? We've marched not half a day!" FitzStephen spat on the ground. He walked his horse out a dozen paces ahead of Prendergast. Keeping the coast then the river to their right hand, travelling north-east as arranged with the scouts was painful, but Prendergast and FitzStephen were in no tearing hurry. They needed to ensure they did not miss MacMurrough's men riding south. Still it grated.

A flock of blackbirds took to the wing, ahead of the army. As it rose out of the willow and alder trees along the river bank it formed into a wedge, their powerful wings beating against the freshening north wind.

"Omen!" FitzStephen shouted, pointing to the sky, as the formation flew above them, banked and headed inland. He shaded his eyes with his hand, as he tracked their changing flight, allowing the Flemish soldier to catch up. "See it?"

"Oh aye. What do you take from it?" Prendergast called back. His voice was carried away by the wind, but the question was stark on his face, as he dismounted. That damnable calm made him hard to read. Prendergast didn't share FitzStephen's fascination with the arcane, but was that face disdain or intrigue?

Prendergast led his horse, through the soft ground and sedge grass, toward the water.

"Ye'd do well to listen! It's good tidings," FitzStephen replied, cantering up to the Flemish man, a flash of anger in his eyes.

Damn him. FitzStephen scowled as he gripped the reins of his destrier. Prendergast was from a lesser castle in coastal Wales, ought to be a vassal to him in reality. The younger man was an upstart with no respect.

FitzStephen's squire moved to take his reins, a warning finger marking the soft ground ahead. He looked up for an order. But FitzStephen's eyes now were on a rider, coming toward them along a cow road through the hills.

"Certainment. Let's water here. Pray its good news he brings."

"What about him?" said the squire, nodding toward the abject figure of the young Ua Briain cousin. He staggered along, hands bound to a rope behind Prendergast's horse. Blood and grime marked his forehead where he'd stumbled and fallen along the way, and mud caked his fine clothes.

"Clean him up. Giffard speaks their gobble. We'll see if he knows anything useful."

Lieutenants barked orders and the men on foot broke ranks, sitting on lightning felled trees and river rocks to eat the food they'd taken.

❖

The sun was lowering in the gloomy sky, distant thunderheads more thick now. The dim outline of the moon, like a pale reflection, rose near the horizon. Between the low hills they were sheltered from a north wind that blustered.

In a patch of sand by an eddy in the stream, Giffard scratched a few lines. FitzStephen watched on with one boot up on a stone. Prendergast sat on a rock peeling an apple with a dagger.

"How far?" Prendergast asked.

"We can be at this town by sundown."

"Merde!" FitzStephen cursed. He idly threw a rock at the young Ua Briain, eliciting a sullen groan. "We should be near Wexford by now."

"Any sign of *mac Murchada* and his army?" Prendergast asked. FitzStephen glared at him.

How did that blonde haired ponce manage to utter their weird names so well. They sounded drunk when they talked.

"Rounded this big hill, good view of the village," Giffard said, pointing to a rough circle scratched in the sand. He drew a smaller circle. "Got to the other side, this small hill near the woods. No army."

"Those idiots can't be stuck in the Wicklow mountains still? Surely they'd send riders," FitzStephen said. "How far did you go?"

"That small hill had a good view east, but then there's thick woods," Giffard said, gesturing. "Saw the Wicklow's in the distance. I got seen by a big fellow, looked like an Ostman. A man of the North. That's when I turned back."

"Just him?"

"Him and two others. Not MacMurrough's men."

"The North Leinster men?" asked FitzStephen.

"Villagers I reckon," Giffard said. He scratched in a few more details to his map.

"Where do we cross this river?" Prendergast asked, pointing to a thick line running south to north through Giffard's scratchings between the two hills.

Two of Prendergast's men brought over barley bread, ale and salted fish they'd plundered.

FitzStephen looked up, grinned and waved them over. Prendergast gestured a mockery of hospitality, but the irony was lost on FitzStephen who grabbed at the food as if he hadn't eaten in a week. Giffard shook his head slightly.

Overhead a gull cried. In a gust leaves fluttered from the willows. FitzStephen belched.

"Narrow bridge in the town, near a tavern," Giffard said, pointing with his stick in the centre between the hills. He drew a line east-west, south of the two hills. "Or we follow the north banks of this river, and ford here, just south of the village. But I don't like it. The fens are soft and treacherous."

"Follow the river. We camp here, high on the west side of this big hill," FitzStephen said, indicating the big circle with the toe of his boot. "It's before the town. Good high ground, should be dry. A good defensive position. If those men were

MacMurrough's or the North Leinster men we'll see him coming."

"O'Brien know anything useful about the town?" Prendergast asked.

"A monastery lies North of it, west of the river. St Moragh's," Giffard said.

"Tomorrow we sack the town. Kill the men, have our fill of the women, the food and ale," FitzStephen said, as he straightened and put his thumbs in his belt. He nodded his head north-east. "Then we head for Wexford."

"You want to rule over these people?" Prendergast asked, folding his arms and straightening. He measured his distance from FitzStephen, shuffling back slightly.

"Quoi?" FitzStephen stopped, a piece of barley bread in his hand. Crumbs spilled from his lip. His right hand made for his sword hilt, but he fumbled with the fistfuls of food in his hands.

"Murdering our way to Wexford? Why?" Prendergast said. His blue-grey eyes blinked, implacable. The last light of the sun lined distant clouds in silver, as thunderclouds gathered nearer the coast. In the distance bats flew up in front of the rising moon shadow.

"You going native on me?" FitzStephen asked, looking for somewhere to put his food.

"You want to be a King here, so kill the Kings. Killing your new subjects, who will enrich you? It makes no sense."

Prendergast's men, Giffard included, all turned to look at FitzStephen.

"How about I start by killing an annoying Flemish turncoat."

"Calm down. I'm here for the gold. Pure and simple. Return to my castle a rich man. Not sport. Not kingdoms," Prendergast said, walking to place his hands on his men's shoulders. "My men too. Oui, mes amis?"

His men lined up beside him, arms folded.

"Bah!" FitzStephen spluttered. He pushed past Giffard, and walked toward his men. "Get ready to move!"

❖

At the top of the rising land of the turnip field, above the thatch of the cottage, several thin threads of smoke filtered up into the sky. Indistinct voices floated from there on the mid-morning air.

Hilde stood on the Back Road, leaning over the turnip field's bottom fence. The image of the hatchet faced stranger burned in her mind, but right now an obstinate donkey was a her biggest problem.

"Sebastien! Go back!" Hilde urged in a loud whisper, straining over the fence, pushing at him. "Go on now!"

The Back Road led from the town, past Pádraig's Goods and down along the border of Blaine land all the way to the copse and the Broken Hill. The hill was marked by black stone outcrops that rose up through the green like rotten teeth in a giants jawbone, and it marked the edge of their property.

Hee haw!

Hilde gave up pushing.

"Quiet!" she said.

This was no good. Someone would see her. In fact a bleating, and ruckus of hooves that'd been gathering behind Hilde up the lane to Caton's Farm, got louder. Hilde spun around.

"Gáethán!" Hilde greeted the young man at the head of the small herd of goats. She straightened her rumpled smock.

She looked back to the hilltop, but there was no sign of the stranger. "Did you see that man? On the hill?"

"My Da was up there a wee while ago. It'd be him," Gáethán said, nodding. He planted his crook, a stout wooden staff that bore a simple carved relief of Saint Brigid, worn smooth by years of use.

"No, the Chief is big. I'd never mistake him. This man was tall, but thin. With a horse," Hilde said. She frowned.

"Didn't see anyone Hilde. Had my eye mostly on them," he said, nodding at his herd. "A man? Filching turnips was he?"

"I saw him get off his horse and bend down, up there by that flat rock on the top of the hill. Not near our crops."

"I'm putting my girls to pasture up there. Come on," Gáethán said, he strode after his charges, already jumping and bleating toward the hilltop.

"Not using the Bolan's pasture on Duncormac Hill any more?" Hilde said, as they walked.

"One of best big girls got sick. Not sure what she ate," Gáethán said. He reached out with his crook, snagged the neck of a goat and pulled it back into the group.

"Oh no! Is she alright?" Hilde asked. He flicked a glance at Hilde and shook his head. Hilde chewed on her lip. Gáethán was very close with his charges.

"Her remains are up on the fence there. I need to get the tanner up there to finish the job," Gáethán said. Nothing could afford to be wasted.

"You know, that man was all in black and green. The way he moved. I don't know," Hilde shivered. They pressed on toward the hill.

❖

Gáethán brandished a large stick, and cajoled the beasts up the Back Road, on to the goat track toward the hill. Despite the ropes they bucked and pushed as they surged up the hill to the grass.

"Sainted Brigit!" Gáethán said, as one leapt on the back of another. He used his stick to seperate them. Hilde ran up the rise to join him. His long legs outpaced hers near twice over.

"Oh, I suppose I can come," Hilde said, breathless. As she drew near, one of the goats got its leg caught in the roots of a yew tree.

"Begorrah," Gáethán said, as he strained to lift the beast free, minding his language in front of Hilde.

She caught her breath and stood scanning the hilltops, hand over her eyes. She flicked a glance at the cottage. "Only, Mama said I have to find your father."

"He's in the village. Some sort of panic. He's calling the Tingmote," Gáethán said, herd on the move again. Below them the scrub in the copse covered the slopes down toward the forest.

Wild bracken and berries on the vine snarled over old paths. Hilde's Da used to hack these back but they'd grown over.

"Hilde! Somethings happening at your cottage," Gáethán said, as he shaded his eyes and craned his neck.

"Uncle Donegal says you're not supposed to call it TingMote. 'Town meeting' is what it is, he said," Hilde said, a scolding tone in her voice. "You Ostmen. I love your ways, but you can be so funny sometimes."

"Folks like my Da enough to keep him as Chief," Gáethán said, batting one of his charges with the stick as she darted out of the herd. "Hey, really Hilde, what's happening at your place? Tell me."

"Something bad," Hilde said. Her voice cracked.

She put her hands to her face, and tears brimmed again. She trudged further up the goat track to the hill top. "Really bad. Mama said to run, and get your father. But I have to hide too."

"What do you mean? What's that smoke!" Gáethán asked. "Hilde!"

"I don't know!" Hilde said. She burst into tears again. And nearly tripped. Metal snagged her boot.

She bent and pulled it free from the tree root it'd snagged in.

"Look!" Hilde said, holding it up. "A horseshoe. That man!"

"Calkins like this?" Gáethán said, taking it from her, touching the prongs at its ends. "That man is not from here."

"You have to tell your father!" Hilde said.

"You saw the man Hilde. Come back with me," Gáethán said, holding the iron shoe out to her.

Hilde wiped her eyes, and took the shoe back, and put it in her pocket. She started putting one foot in front of the other.

"Hilde! Where are you going?"

"Gáethán, I need to see Mama," Hilde said.

She broke into a run and headed through the turnip field toward her home.

4

The Witchfinder

Welcoming puffs of smoke rose from the chimney of Blaine cottage. The leaves of the the fruit trees in the yard and of the ivy on the back wall swayed gently in the summer breeze. As Hilde trudged up through the turnip field a lamp light glimmered, just visible through the back window. Surely all was well and her mother's desperate orders were some kind of game? In a few moments she'd be laugh with her mother about it, and they'd talk about the stranger she'd seen.

But as Hilde neared the back of the cottage, the sound of raised voices increased. Booming above them all was the voice of the man she'd heard in lane. Strident and sing-song his voice rose above the others. It had a dangerous edge to it. Hilde had heard the priests give sermons at the Abbey, but this voice was rude and strident. Boastful.

She made for the right side, where Sebastien's lean-to attached to the cottage wall. The left hand side was covered in dense trees and ivy and going around it would mean coming in on the laneway from the Blaine pasture where everyone would see her.

As Hilde rounded the thick back wall, she saw Sebastien's rump. The trusty creature was back from his jaunt through the turnip field.

"This stops now!" yelled the man. "Come out or we burn it down!"

Burn it! Get her! Witch! Demon lover!

"Mother Mary save me!" Hilde whispered. Her hands shook, as she put her hands to her mouth, stifling the scream she knew would doom her to whatever fate her mother had tried to protect her from. The donkey snickered loudly. He put his hooves on the bottom rail of his pen.

"Steady Sebastien," Hilde whispered. She walked behind him, running her hands down the donkey's sides. She peered between his legs, through the gate to his pen, but could not see much beyond the size of the crowd gathered there. At least a dozen pairs of legs.

The tall pear tree by Sebastien's pen grew up to shade the cottages roof. Hilde eyed its stout trunk, one she'd climbed a hundred times.

"I'm coming!" That was Mama's voice.

Shinnying up the tree, Hilde clambered along a bough that hung out over the yard. It was past spring and the tree was in full leaf, with pear blossom heady in the air. Bees and mayflies swarmed in the air around her. Below, the cottage door rattled, and Bronach opened the small shutter.

Hilde felt sick. It seemed like the world below swum in circles, the swarming insects and the gently swaying bough unhinging her from reality.

She coming out? Get her!

There were low mumbling voices, and shuffling feet among the crowd. A man in a long black robe stood at the front of the group, holding a long staff, and wearing an odd hat. In his other hand he bore a sheaf of parchments.

"I'm opening the door! Speak my charges! Then I'll go! That's our law!"

Witch! Set her to the flame!

Brehon law. That's the way. Another man's voice, not the man in black.

"I am the instrument of God! Ye of serpent tongue! Gods law alone will judge you, heretic!" the man in black yelled, banging his staff on the flagstones.

At chapel Sister Gobnait taught the heavenly world. Hilde had sat through classes of the trinity, of God and the angels. All the sisters and priests said there was no faeries, banshees or witches. At least to be a good Catholic Hilde had to not talk about such things. Even though so many in the village still put out food for the fairies! Even Fiach appeased old gods. Father Stephen himself often mixed up Mother Mary and Saint Brigit.

Mama said the figurine on the wall inside the cottage was Brigid the goddess, but never to tell that to Father Stephen. None would dare come out in front of churchmen and talk of faerie circles, goddesses or witches. It was all fine as long as no-one mentioned it in church. Adults were very confusing.

So who was this sing-song man of God, talking about witches? A few in the crowd joined a chorus after every word the man in black said. But others mumbled quietly, shuffling their feet. A few mentioned the Brehon judges.

It seemed like everyone was very confused. Except for Jezabel. She weighed something in her hand.

A rock hit the wooden shutters, and another. From the front of the crowd a torch flew on to the roof of the cottage.

"Brehon law! Read my charges" Bronach's voice came through the stout wooden door. "And I will do as you say!"

A few in the crowd sighed and nodded. The mood lightened. For a moment.

The still burning torch rolled down the thatch and landed with a thump on the flagstones at the mans feet. The group leapt back, a woman screamed.

"Demons! Hell fire!" shrieked Alice.

"Witchcraft!" shouted Emma. Panicked voices yammered.

Mother, don't go out!

Hilde crawled further along the branch, trying to glimpse her mother through the cracks in the shutters.

"Bronach Blaine, I have your charges!" the man said, brandishing a rolled up parchment.

From the cottage came the sound of the draw bar being removed. The small crowd stepped back and gasped. Two women near the front grasped the man in black's sleeve.

Mother!

❖

A jackdaw settled on the end of the bough on which Hilde clung. The bird tipped its head on one side and eyed her balefully. It snapped up an unlucky insect that crawled on a pear blossom, its wings disturbing the leaves as it gulped down the morsel.

Down below the crowd was regaining its bravery and shuffled forward. Hilde could almost reach the thatch of the cottage if she lowered her foot but if she did any of the group who looked up would easily see her. Hilde shifted her position carefully looping her feet over the limb of the tree.

A man walked up to the torch that had fallen.

Father O'Connor!

He picked it up and smiled. "The torch we threw up! Falling as naturally as an apple from a tree."

Bronach stood in the door way of the cottage, her face hidden from Hilde by the eaves. She brandished the besom that they kept near the door. Emma and Jezabel hung off the sleeves of the man in black. They peered around him as though he were a shield from a gorgon that could turn them to stone at any moment.

Oh my what a pair of squawkers. That Jezabel is the worst of the two. How does Uncle Donegal stand her?

Their screeches stopped when Father Stephen cleared his throat.

"Now let's all keep our heads. God is watching us! Bishop Ahearne, that's right isn't it?" the preacher announced.

Dónal O'Rourke stood behind Jezabel. Everyone called him Donegal though he'd lived in Leinster for years now. He looked as if he wished the ground would swallow him up. He had drunk too much again. He staggered to one side, as Jezabel raised her fist.

"Witch! Heretic! Not so clever now!" Jezabel shouted, she threw a rock, but Donegal bearing on her to keep his balance threw off her aim. The rock clattered against the cottage wall, and the pigs began a fuss. "Your fancy cottage and your silver won't save you now!"

Fergus Keenan, the blacksmith!

He stood at the rear with his hammer, wearing his apron. He was unmistakeable although his face was obscured by the pear tree leaves.

Is he with the man in black? He's been here for dinner! Please don't be against us?!

The jackdaw was joined by two of its friends and their wings blocked her view even more. Carefully and slowly Hilde moved some smaller branches and crawled out further onto the bough.

Fergus looked straight at her!

He held a finger to his lips. Too late, as the shock of being seen made Hilde jump a foot in the air. She banged her head on the branch above her and scrambled to hold on to her perch. The jackdaws squawked and flew up over the cottage toward the pasture.

Ahearne doffed his hat - a strange high crowned, wide-brimmed affair. Strangest priest ever! But perhaps that's what Bishops looked like.

"We see your magic! Fiend! Your demons flee you now!" called the man in black, Ahearne, shading his eyes as he tracked the birds flight over the cottage roof.

"Steady. Just jackdaws," Fergus said. Several of the group laughed. "Bronach's no witch. Surely this is a misunderstanding?"

"Bishop Ahearne. We are god-fearing folk here in Duncormac. Good Catholics. People here can get excited at times. Just a few old birds! No witches flying around here," Father O'Connor said, smiling. "Chief Fiach has called a town meeting we really should be at. So perhaps we should all go to the long house? Yes?"

Bronach lowered the broom and leaned on it. Fergus sneaked a smile up at Hilde.

One by one the group started to turn toward town.

❖

There was an oppressive calm in the yard of the cottage. Fergus the smith, Thomas the innkeep, walked slowly toward the lane that led to town. But Jezabel, Emma and Alice were in deep conversation, Jezabel gesturing vehemently. The other villagers stood in a knot between them, next to the vegetable patch, waiting to see if it was over.

Hilde didn't dare move, and her whole body hurt now from gripping the bough of the pear tree. A mayfly bit her and she itched fit to burst.

Bronach swept the rocks and the debris left by the torch, and rocks thrown. She gave out that she had no care, but her knuckles were white on the besom's handle.

The man in black walked toward the side of the cottage, until he was directly beneath Hilde.

She daren't breathe. The bark of the bough dug into her palms.

Oh Brigid your white flowers are everywhere, can you protect me from this cruel man?

He motioned to Father O'Connor.

"Your wife Alice invited me here, father. You should be helping me."

"What *is* this Callum?" Father O'Connor said. "Our church, our God does not teach these fears! These are my people, good people! What is this insanity? I have never heard of such things from a man of God. Heretics? Witchcraft?"

"Refer to me as Reverend! I am a bishop!" Ahearne said, through gritted teeth.

"Reverend, you were my novice at Cill Chainnigh only a few summers ago, and struggling with your reading. Then like magic you were gone. I heard later, to the Cistercians." O'Connor raised an eyebrow.

"Jealous I have outstripped you?" Ahearne straightened his cloak.

"Surely you're not a real bishop in that time? What is your diocese? How do you get on with the noble blooded bishops?"

"How dare you," Ahearne said, drawing himself up to his full height.

The conversation didn't make sense to Hilde, but it seemed like Father O'Connor was taking on the taller man, and winning. Hilde closed her eyes and tried to breathe as quietly as she could.

Ahearne stared at the ground, a vein pulsing in his neck. He pulled his hat out from under his arm, and gripped it with both hands.

"Did the King of Osraighe throw you out of Cill Chainnigh? Is that it?" the priest said. He pushed Ahearne's shoulder, to force him to face him. "Why are you dressed like a troubadour, with that ridiculous hat?"

"I was with the Cistercians." Ahearne paced up and down, then rested a fist against the trunk of the pear tree. "But the Abbot chose *me* to travel. *Me* to represent the order to the Pope himself."

"He wanted to get rid of you! Probably thought the Sicilians would kill you in France," Father O'Connor said. "Tell me, when you came back to Ireland, your bed was gone?"

"It is no matter! I am a warrior bishop now! The Abbot died and the new one did not recognise the debt I was owed. But the most important event in Christendom happened, and I was there. Pope Alexander defeated the anti-pope, and declared a war against the heretic," Ahearne said.

"You are no bishop, and you should not be in my village," O'Connor said.

"I have joined that war! You need to join, or get out of my way." Ahearne put on his hat again and Hilde could no longer see his face.

"I will be civil, as we have been brothers, but you leave! Gone by dawn tomorrow," O'Connor said.

"Perhaps it is you who is the apostate! Do you still give the full mass?" Ahearne jabbed O'Connor with a finger. "Or are you working with the druids and faeries out here by the sea?"

"You're ignorant of the Catholic faith and Irish belief. Go back to France," O'Connor gave a dismissive wave of the hand and met Ahearne's gaze.

❖

"Reverend!" Jezabel said, breaking the awkward silence. She ran to him, tugged on his sleeve, and jabbed a finger at the parchments he carried. "Wait everyone!"

Father O'Connor folded his arms as the two of them walked back to the group. Ahearne nodded to Jezabel, and patted her arm.

"We have proof! Proof! Of heresy and demonology most perfidious!" bellowed Ahearne. He held a parchment up high, his black robes flowing. With a grand gesture he let it unfurl. "Tell them child!"

"She made me barren! I lost my baby!" Emma walked the crowd, and screamed at the preacher and the blacksmith, pointing back behind herself at Brónach. She put one hand to her belly. Thomas the barkeep walked forward and patted his wife on the arm, with a worried look on his face.

Ahearne shook the parchment. "This is brave Emma's testimony!"

"Read it to us!" a voice from the crowd called.

"It is true!" He waved the parchment again before furling it. He turned to the crowd, and unctuously nodded as he placed his hand on Emma's shoulder. "I have examined this child of God and seen the work of demons upon her."

"I saw the demon!" Alice cried out in a fractured voice. Father O'Connor closed his eyes, tilted his head forward and a muscle in his jaw worked. Alice, eyes red-rimmed, chest heaving, turned plaintively to the Bishop, then to the priest, her husband.

"Callum, show them the demon Alice saw!" Emma said.

"Faint of heart beware! Avert your eyes!" Ahearne said. He unrolled another parchment and held it out to the villagers. Gasps ran around the crowd. From the sunlight shining through the vellum it appeared to be a drawing. Fergus turned back and peered over the heads of the others at the drawing.

"And crops have failed! Rónán, Cormac! Is it true!" Jezabel announced in a sing-song voice, as if expecting a sing-along response. She took two steps and shoved Rónán forward.

"Aye. Whole crop went bad," Rónán said. Jezabel looked daggers at Cormac.

"Oh aye, my barley failed with the blight. Terrible," Cormac muttered.

"And I saw her casting spells! Cavorting with demons!" Jezabel said. She spun around to point at Brónach.

"She has cast aside the faith! She spurned our Church to indulge in witchcraft! Heresy!"

Witch! Witch! WITCH!

The refrain went up around the crowd. A few abstained, grumbling and hushing to no avail as the group took the chant to a cacophonous roar.

HEE HAW!

Sebastien kicked over the front rail of his pen, and ran out. The timber crashed to the ground. His hooves clattered on the flagstones as the poor frightened beast tried to find a way out past the crowd. Screams went up, Cormac waved a stick.

"Sebastien!" Hilde called.

Demon!! God save me!! Panicked villagers tried to run from the donkey, trampling the garden, and running in circles.

At Hilde's voice, Brónach spun toward the tree.

"Go! Run!" Brónach desperately shouted at Hilde. "Run!"

The villagers started yelling. *She calls the beast! My soul!!
Mother Mary save me!*

"All right! I'll go!" Bronach said to Ahearne.

"Take her!" Ahearne said.

"Nothing happens to her until the Brehon arrive! You hear
me? Nothing!" O'Connor said.

"Rónán, Cormac! The sack!" Jezabel screamed.

The two burly farmers looked at each other then shrugged.
In an instant Rónán put a sack over Bronach's head, and
Cormac threw her over his shoulder.

5

Summer Rain

The King of Thomond spoke true. The Uí Conchobhair Failghe fought across their lands from the north-west of Laigins Tir to Dún Alinne.

But beyond Failghe's reach, east of their realm and west of the mountains, nestled in a valley of lush green lands cradled by the River Slaney, kings from long before lay at rest under ancient stones. For now, no war came here.

On a hilltop here overlooking the town of Bealach Conglas a bitter cold wind and sheets of rain lashed the tombs and ruined forts of Rathcoran. Wild scrub bent over from long battles with the elements. Heather and tussock dotted the hilltop, now trampled by an army and their horses.

A man in a helm and leather armour resolutely stared from the hilltop into the distance to the north-east where the shadow of the Wicklow mountains laid like sleeping beast, its lower limbs shrouded in rain-soaked mists. He was stocky with a full black beard, and he chewed on a bone, then threw it in the grass.

For an age he'd looked for soldiers coming after them through the mists. But there were none.

Another man, slim, and made of sinew walked up to the stocky man. With weathered hands the slim man pulled his collar up against the rain, and straightened his leather helm over his ears. The beginning of watch, and already the weather almost soaked him through. Flinty eyes gazed out up the valley.

The stocky man clapped the other on his shoulder, turned and walked toward the top of the hill, where a group of tents sheltered between the tombs of old Kings, and walls that may have protected soldiers now long dead. A place of peace, after days being pursued by the damn Failghe men.

The wind drove the rain into Bran's tent, the flapping of canvas drowning his words. The low ridgepole forcing him to sit, he used his pack to raise himself from the sodden ground.

"Sir!" the stocky man said, as he bent into Bran's tent.

"Nothing from the mountains?" Bran asked. The stocky man's face said all he needed know.

"Nay sir."

"Alright, get some food then spell the men watching toward the town and the abbey," Bran said.

"We're low on food. You mac Ghiolla Phadraig men, how are your supplies?" said one of the other two men in the tent.

"Low too," Bran replied. "The abbey, I can just about smell their roasting ovens from here. I'm about done waiting."

"Aye," said the other man. "My men are done with salted fish. Surely we trust the monks! They must owe our King enough to feed his soldiers?"

Bran turned back to the map spread on the tents floor. "Diarmait told us to wait here. We've done that. I say if by dawn..."

"...sir!" a man said. His a weathered hand on the tent flap, his words carried away by a strong gust. It was the lookout with the flinty eyes.

"What?" asked Bran.

"Sir! Men from the north!" the lookout said.

"Enemy?" Bran asked, spinning about. The lookout stepped away and shaded his eyes, toward the north.

"Soldiers?" Asked the other man, leaning on the map to bring his ear closer.

Drums and horns sounded outside from the camp, shouts came, feet running. Horses neighed in protest. Then cheers.

"By their banners, its King Diarmait mac Murchada sir!" the man said. A grin spread across his face. "And he's carrying food and ale!"

"Thank the holy mother!" said Bran.

The sky was dark now, iron grey clouds gathering above the faraway hills. A line of bright sky remained in the distant north, and the wind picked up.

It was many moments after the gaggle of villagers had left led by the triumphant figure in black, and Hilde breathed a sigh. They'd be well down the lane by now, near the Main Road into town. Hilde flexed fingers numb from clinging to the rough bark of the pear tree.

Her heart, hammering in her chest since the two men, Bishop Callum Ahearne and Father O'Connor moved under the tree she hid in, began to slow. Her stomach ached, so tense with the effort of remaining still.

Not a real bishop, Father O'Connor said, so who had given him the power to rule her mother a witch?

Jezabel. Uncle Donegal's wife.

Her voice, had been the last to disappear as she listened for them leaving down the lane, raised shrill above Fergus, the blacksmith's; above Father O'Connor's.

The jackdaws had returned to the tree. One squeezed out of the pecking order moved along the bough and eyed Hilde, an intruder in their tree.

What of all the parchments? The accusations? If Bronach Blaine is banished, what of me, her daughter?

Hilde sat up on the bough, and massaged her limbs. The jackdaw hopped a handspan away only, and eyed her again. It cawed at its fellows, insistent on taking its turn feeding.

There came a scent of wood smoke, acrid and wet. The pigs snuffled at their trough. Faintly the clucking of Gobnait and the other hens came to Hilde's ears.

Sebastien!

He'd run into the pasture. The poor beast was terrified. He poked his head around the hazel trees that stood between the pasture and their vegetable garden. Since Da had gone in King Diarmait's war, all this had become Hilde's work. Inside the cottage only that morning she'd hung a string bag of freshly picked apples.

It's alright little man. Hilde will feed you an apple.

Her mind spinning and tears welling in her eyes, Hilde climbed down from the pear tree. An automaton, she picked up a bucket of well water and topped up the pigs troughs. Maybe if she did her chores and went inside, Ma would be sitting there ready to chide her for taking too long.

Back on the flagstones by the cottage Sebastien walked to her, batting his long lashes and baring his teeth like a naughty child. He didn't protest as she led him to his stall, and lifted the fence back into place.

Good Sebastien. I'll get you that apple.

Hilde touched her cheek to his, and closed her eyes. Hilde scratched the donkey on his forehead, and he pushed himself against her fingers spluttering his gratefulness. She tied the gate to Sebastien's pen with twine and went to the cottage door. But stopped in her tracks.

On the door of the cottage a parchment was nailed, penned in a florid hand. Not all the words made sense.

Bronach Blaine. Witchcraft. Forfeit and sealed.

At the bottom of the screed was a name.

The breeze picked up more, and all the trees rustled. The jackdaws cawed.

The smoke was stronger. Even the putrid sweet smell of the pigs ordure didn't stifle the acrid odour. Hilde stood back from the cottage, scratched her head and put her hands on her hips.

A red ember floating drew her gaze up. It came from the thatch, where the torch had landed.

Saints save me! Mother!! Our home!

There were two buckets of well-water inside. Hilde pushed open the door hesitantly as if the parchment might come to life and accuse her too. She pulled the parchment free of the nails that held it and laid it on the stool by the door.

There were the buckets. Hilde grasped the rope handles, but they were heavy. It was impossible to climb to the roof with them. She took an apple from the string bag, and forgetting what she'd intended, took a bite.

The kitchen table bore candles and food bowls as it always had, ancient oak, her father had jointed with pegs so tightly, it seemed unmarked by time. The Goddess Brigid had been moved from the wall, and now sat on the table. In front of her lay an offering of food and a candle now snuffed.

The window shutters were still roped shut. Her mother's rocking chair stood empty and the hand knotted rug she kept over her knees lay on its seat as though she'd vanished from her place and it'd settled there.

Hilde's throat tightened and the impossibility of everything welled up in her chest.

Feed the pigs. Dance the maypole.

Mother's words from only the morning floated in the air. Hilde's knees weakened and she slumped to the floor, apple in one hand, the other resting on the buckets of water.

What can I do? Will the cottage burn? Would Da know that we tried?

After so much silence Hilde wailed. And then her tears overtook her.

Her sobs racked her chest, her cheeks wet with tears rolling down in an unstoppable stream. Hilde wrapped her arms around her knees and rocked, her smock no guard against the hard cold stones of the floor. What would it matter being cold when the flames consumed all?

After a time, when exhaustion stemmed her tears, she shuffled over to her mother's chair, laid her head on the rug and closed her eyes.

❖

Starlings chittered loudly on the oaken table. Hilde startled awake, and put her hands on the arms of her mother's chair. She'd crawled up, put her feet on the seat, and clasped the hand-knotted rug to her face. Now the rug fell away and with it the dream of her mother smiling, tending a pot that was bubbling on the fire.

"Shoo!" Hilde said, flicking at the greedy birds with a corner of the rug. They flew into the rafters, leaving behind the food bowl which lay in front of Goddess Brigid, and knocking over the candle with their wings.

Outside a steady hissing and spattering sounded. Not a bubbling pot, but heavy rain.

Hilde jumped to her feet and ran to the shutter, untying the rope. Then she remembered the villagers, the man in black, Callum Ahearne. She cracked the shutter carefully, and peered out. The pigs snuffled in the mud, water cascading from the thatch into their pen. No one there.

The rain pelted down. The fire was no more. Embers extinguished.

Thank the Goddess Brigid!

Hilde refastened the shutter. She smiled, a let go a sigh of relief, as she walked to lean on the kitchen table.

Thank you!

Brigid had moved. She lay on her back, looking at the roof.

Hilde picked up the small statue, Brigid's back a solid block, the Goddess carved in relief with her spring flowers around her. Up close her eyes were just holes.

It was the starlings that had moved it?

It didn't matter. Brigid was looking after the Blaines.

We have to use our heads, we Blaine women.

Hilde's young smooth brow furrowed. Her mother was not gone. Everything Bronach had built in Blaine cottage stood fast at this moment, not yet taken.

Many in the village lived on dirt floors, and envied the Blaine's for a stone floor like that of a church. Here in Blaine cottage the pots swung over the fire on irons. A high roof and solid rafters, as good as any abbey. Smoke left up a clever chimney that masons had built for them in return for silver. And three pigs was a fortune.

Hilde had never, ever thought of herself as better, but the sour tones of Jezabel's voice echoed now. Sly glances had met her and mother, when she went into the village after Da had failed to come back from the war.

Fair game.

The silver. Hilde rushed to the trunk that stood at the end of Bronach Blaine's bed. It stood on its end, as the cottage was too small to keep it. She laid out deerskins, lowered the chest, and opened it. Dozens of waxed cotton pouches with silver brooches, mirrors, chains and clips glittered still, in the lamp light. Oil had kept away much of the tarnish.

Before the mending work came in there were many nights of being hungry. No meat, only turnips and parsnips; some berries and mushrooms from the woods. Some pouches of silver had been emptied those first hard winters after Da had gone. Still many remained.

Hilde was only young, not big enough to help around the small-holding, and Ma had spent many nights staring into the fire holding Arran Blaine's things, keeping his place at the table set. But as soon as she was strong enough to carry the water pail with two hands, her working day had started before dawn. That winter mending came from a Blaine cousin in Ferns, and Bronach ceased setting the table for three.

Hilde was eight when they first went to Ferns to sell silver, and although young Hilde knew when her mother was scared. But she'd done it twice more.

The mending. A wicker basket against the wall held several bags of finished tunics. A horseman from the Leinster palace would come for them soon. The empty canvas bags piled next to the basket were made of fine woven hemp from Connacht. They were worth a days work each. The soldiers garments inside them, worth much more.

Hilde sorted through the mending basket. She pulled out a tunic and tried it on. It fitted. She twirled and laughed. Imagine being a soldier for the High King. Food laid out every day, nothing to do but sharpen a sword and die in a field.

When the King's men had come to the cottage, to tell Da to join the war, he hid in the cellar. But it was a short lived reprieve, he was caught coming back from a trip selling his work, and pressed into the army.

Your name was given you by the Chief. Run to Chief Fiach's house.

Ma had left the house after Da had gone. Now it was Hilde's turn to find the courage.

❖

Hilde kept hard in against the row of trees on the Back Road, as she walked up in the direction of the main road. There was no shelter as sheets of rain pelted down from the storm blackened sky.

Because she was seeing the sisters at the priory Hilde wore her best coat. It was thick wool, and they'd bought it in Ferns last year. The lamb grease was strong in it, and draping it over her head kept some of the torrential rain off her head.

Hilde sucked her finger where a large blood blister swelled. It throbbed and a splinter in it felt like fire. She'd seen Ma moving the boards off the cellar so many times, but it was harder than it looked. The space was at the rear of the cottage, where the ground fell away and rarely used because Ma and Da's bed had to be moved to get to it. Still, it was worth it — now their silver was safely hidden under stone.

She also had her heirloom in a pocket, wrapped in wax cloth, a bag full of apples, a skin of water, and bag full of all sorts of things from the cottage. Inside her coat, also wrapped in wax was the parchment that the man had left, the words 'Witchcraft' emblazoned on it burning through her pocket it seemed.

The Main Road ran along a ridge line, and as Hilde trudged through the mud of the Back Road it seemed steeper with every step. Then up ahead a shape. Head and shoulders. The head turned, and jumped off its shoulders.

Then spread its wings and flew. It was a crow resting on a stone. Hilde's heart was in her throat.

48

"God save me!" Hilde said out loud.

Ark ark ark.

The crow flew up through the trees and was gone. Hilde sighed deeply and shook her head, laughing weakly. She stopped and re-adjusted her bags. She was wearing the uniform trousers of some soldier, and his tunic as well. It was so warm compared to her smock. Especially in the rain.

She would return it to the mending pile once everything had been straightened out with these awful accusations.

What is that noise?

"Hey!" a voice came from behind her, faint through the rain fall. "Stop!"

Hilde jumped a foot in the air. Her apples spilled and she shrieked.

Through the spattering of the rain, the noise resolved into the sound of bleating goats. Gáethán.

"Careful of your apples, they'll eat them all, quick as look at you," he said.

"Gáethán, what are you doing?!" Hilde said. She lowered the coat from over her head, and bent to pick up the apples. One of Gáethán's charges lunged toward the fruit, and he gripped his rope hard as he fought a tug-o-war with it.

"Doing? I'm getting my girls in. And I've been trying to catch up to *you*. Hardly recognised you," Gáethán said. He gave her a searching look, and held out a hand, palm up. "Hilde! What's going on!"

"A man in black came. A Bishop. Gáethán they took Mama! She's gone!!" Hilde would have cried but the cool rain on her face slaked her grief. Her face contorted, and her fists tightened on the straps of her bags. "Our cottage is forfeit! This is all I could carry."

"What are you talking about" Gáethán said. "My Da will fix it. You're going to him, right?"

"He's at the Tingmote! Besides he won't interfere with a man of God," Hilde said. She straightened, and put the apples back in the bag. She pulled the waxed packet stuffed with the Bishop's parchment partway then thrust it to the bottom of the bag. "Gáethán, the Bishop left a page on the door. It says my Ma is a Witch."

"No! That's mad!" the young man said. He swatted two of the goats with his staff, Saint Brigid giving the beasts a hefty jolt. He yanked on a rope to reel in a third. "No-one's a witch, Hilde!"

"Jezabel was there. She called Mama a hare-attic," Hilde said, drawing out the strange word. "I'm going to see Sister Gobnait, to find out what that is. It's bad though. Father O'Connor says we have to wait for the Brehon."

Gáethán turned his flock back down the hill, toward Catons Road.

"I don't know what the Tingmote is for. But it must be done soon. They never go beyond nightfall," the goatherd said. "Promise me you'll talk to the Chief? I have to go!"

"Alright," Hilde said. "Gáethán, please don't tell anyone where I am. Not even your Da."

The young man paused a beat, then nodded.

"And tell him to talk to Father O'Connor?"

"Righto!" Gáethán said, not looking back, already skipping around his flock. Then he disappeared into the rain.

6

Pádraigs Goods

This was all of a day, near to evening and Hilde'd not eaten. Above her through the leaves of the oak, bats ventured out into the wet. There was a faint glow in the black clouds near the horizon, perhaps the moon.

It was late in the day, but after waking at dawn this morning to do her chores only to have her home threatened and her entire world upended it was still hard to grasp that all this had been in just one long day. The events of the morning belonged to another lifetime.

Up here at the main road through Duncormac, Hilde's idea to simply walk to the Priory was beginning to feel like a ill-considered journey fraught with peril. It was still pouring with rain, but several townsfolk were on the road. It could be busy, even quite late. As well as locals, folks from other parts came through, walking in through the South Gate having travelled from Carrick, and headed over the bridge, up to the Wexford Road and north-east.

Gáethán had not recognised her at first, so she might pass for a traveller. But not if a local looked her in the eye. How had she thought idly so lightly of this scheme. Stopping here at the oak was bad — as the light faded her courage did too, and every deepening shadow harboured imagined threats.

Also the Priory lay on the west side, a good distance from the main road. She had to cross the bridge, then pass from east to west into the Priory's lands. Before today every time of the many happy times she'd gone there it had been with other village children, laughing and telling stories. One or more parents corralled them, or drove them in a cart. It'd seemed no ills of this world could touch them.

It was bad luck to be on foot at night.

Today everything had changed. After hiding in the pear tree, with that man in black so close she could've almost touched him, just walking on this familiar road felt crazy. To be sure, just breathing it seemed it risked a terrible fate.

A pair slogged through the mud toward her, in the distance, just visible now in the gloaming light, in the mists as they crested the arch of the bridge over The Muck. Neither looked up at her, as she huddled under the big oak that marked where the Back Road ran down from the Main Road to the farms on the East side of the town. It was too late now to climb the tree, as that would only draw more attention.

Voices in the distance almost drowned out by the rainfall, sounded to be drawing some business to a close at Pádraig's Goods. Surely they'd walk up to the road and not glance here.

Hilde's stomach rumbled. She put a hand to her griping belly. Of course no-one could hear that. But she pulled her jacket about herself, and her hat down over her face. At least in this weather others had their hats down too, and no-one looked beyond the toes of their sodden boots.

The voices stopped, and footsteps trudged in the mud. Shapes of three people resolved in the mist of the rain, sheltering at the eaves in front of Pádraig's. The pair crossed the bridge, glanced at the three but no greeting passed between them.

Saints be praised. Don't fancy sitting in the rain waiting for folks to chit chat.

All while a glance could expose her. But it was alright, the two had moved off out of sight, and the three walked onto the roadway.

I at least thought of food.

Hilde pushed herself up against the gnarled trunk of the old tree, and pulled the bag off her back and took an enormous bite of an apple. She allowed her legs, suddenly leaden, to fold. She sat in the wet, and devoured another apple after the first. She'd slept for a short time, laying her head on her mother's chair in the cottage, but now tiredness hit Hilde like a wall. The crying, and the running, the climbing all had taken its toll.

I can get to the Priory and hide there. Just need to get there. Maybe I can sleep in the graveyard. And talk to Sister Gobnait in the morning.

Up on the roadway, just a stones throw away, the group from Pádraig's parted ways, two south, one north. The two — a woman and a man — chattered quietly sneaking glances back at the other.

The one walked north onto the bridge. As he crested the bridge, a dark silhouette against the watery moon, he pulled out an odd shaped hat and put it on his head.

Hilde gasped. She shoved her fist in her mouth to stifle the noise, her eyes wide.

The man in black, the witch finder. His cloak flared out behind him as he stepped over the crest and was gone.

❖

Hilde sat perfectly still huddled agains the trunk of the oak at the small crossroads. She clasped her knees to her, and her hands gripped the half-eaten apple like a sacrement. Clouds, grim and wet drifted across the briefly glowing moon and the roadway was dark again.

The man had left.

Breathe Hilde. Don't fret.

She shivered uncontrollably now, and jumped to her feet. The man in black had been right here. And of course, he was not the one that had to hide. He had his supporters, so many townsfolk carrying torches for his cause.

The rain was easing. More bats took off from the tree, their leathery wings thudding against the night. In the distance echoed drunken shouts from O'Briens Tavern.

The couple had walked off. Why were talking to the man in black, Ahearne?

They could have been Jezabel and Donegal, or Father Stephen and Alice. Or Emma and Thomas. No, not those last two, as the man did not have Thomas's paunch. And not Father Stephen as he'd go north to his home by the church, where the couple went south.

Actually if they were Jezabel and Donegal, it explained the shout she'd heard. They fought over him going in for a drink. Uncle Donegal was always fighting with her, mostly about his drinking. Bronach used to just shake her head, in a sisterly way, and mutter under her breath and call him by his real name.

Dónal. Dear oh dear.

Hilde felt a catch in her throat, and struggled for breath as the image of her mother flashed in her minds eye like a bright sunrise. She stood up, and breathed, trying to get a grip on herself. She brushed off some of the water, and stamped her feet in the muddy grass.

My brave girl.

Many had carried torches, but not all thought as Jezabel did. Uncle Donegal for example, he would never have Bronach Blaine hurt. He was not strictly Arran Blaine's brother but they'd both come from the North, and were close as brothers. He'd never hurt Bronach or Hilde.

And Father Stephen arrived with the witchfinder's party too, as had Fearghas. They both were not supporters of the new Bishop. Fearghas — the smithy was right next to Pádraig's! Ah - its late he'd be closed up.

Actually, this late in the evening, Pádraig's was closed. So why were Jezabel and Uncle Don here?

Unless.

Hilde ran from the moon-shade of the willow toward the store. She clapped her palms to its stone foundations and looked up the wattle-and-daub walls to its roof.

She's here!

She ran to the left, racking her brain for where she'd seen it. And then suddenly there it was. A small structure like an afterthought, built onto the left-hand-side of the store. Its round base joined the stone foundations and its solid walls blended with the stores' but it had a seperate roof of solid timbers, like the lid of a well. She ran her fingers across it's rough mud brick surface.

The gaol. A tiny lock-up, and the towns only suggestion of law. Rainwater dripped off the eaves of the store, and splashed on the flat timber roof the tiny round-house. As the clouds parted, with the lifting rain, moonlight silvered the walls above.

Hilde had never heard of the Chief using it. And when he'd been driving the cart to the Priory with her and his son Gáethán he'd never answer any questions about it. Mama had said the Chief preferred to settle things in the old way, when it came to anyone doing a wrong, at least a wrong that didn't fall to the Brehon or the Church.

Gáethán told stories about his father, the Chief, dealing with drunks and fights in his way, and telling of it in the Tingmote when it warranted it. He'd never use a windowless cell like this.

This — a pimple of a building on the side of Pádraig's — had been here a long time. Hilde could not see any window, and the door was of solid wood, no peephole even.

A man who would go to a town to find witches would use this.

"Mama! It's me, Hilde!!" she called.

She rested her head against the door, and listened.

❖

Hilde waited an age, as her voice echoed in the crossroads.

She held her breath but the Ó Néill's lived out the back, in a seperate house.

They didn't hear. It's alright.

And no-one stirred on the street. A few faint voices from the Tavern. Hilde allowed herself to breathe again.

Stupid! We have to use our heads!

She went around the side of the gaol, where the ground fell away to the side of Pádraig's toward the Smithy which lay on the banks of the river below. It was slippery in the grass, but Hilde grabbed onto the stone of the foundations. There, high up close to the eaves was a slit window.

Hilde scooped up some stones.

She clambered on to the lip of the foundation, then reached a foot up and dug her toes into a small fissure where the wattle-and-daub had flaked away. The window was narrow. Hilde pressed her face into it and waited for her eyes to adjust to the gloom.

A figure lay there. Curled up on a pile of straw, face turned away. Breathing slowly.

Hilde threw a stone, and it skittered across the floor. The figure stirred.

She threw another.

"Mama! It's me, Hilde!"

It was her. Bronach turned to her daughter, and across her face raced a torrent of emotion.

She opened her mouth to speak, but sobbed. Her browed racked with fear, she clasped her hands in front of her and muttered a prayer.

"It's the daughter! Grab her!"

It was Jezabel. And Donegal. Jezabel pushed Donegal toward the gaol's wall, pointed at Hilde.

"Jezabel, don't you touch her!" Bronach's voice rose from the cell.

"Hilde, dear, you can't be out at night like this," Donegal said. He slurred his words slightly, but his honeyed bur struck at Hilde's heartstrings. He stopped and reached toward her. "Come along with us."

"Hilde, run! Go to the Chief!" Bronach called. Her voice dry, cracked into a half-shriek.

Jezabel pushed her husband again. "Grab her!"

Hilde leapt for the eaves of the gaol. The fear in her mothers voice drove her, feet digging in to the rough wall. One toe on the window sill, she grabbed the protruding timbers of the roof, scrabbled with her feet against the outside of the gaol and got herself half onto the timber surface.

"Come down Hilde, you'll hurt yourself," came Jezabel's voice. Hilde could hear Donegal grunting as he reached for her swinging legs.

"Hilde!" Bronach called from inside the cell.

She swung her legs to the side, built momentum and then clambered on to the roof. Her heart hammered in her chest, as she got to her knees. The thatched roof of the store was the only way to go.

Hilde jumped onto the roof and like a crab ran across it, in the direction of the Back Road.

7

The Chief

Thunderheads hung in the sky above Duncormac Hill. Trees reached up to the lowering moon, their spindly black fingers swayed into a permanent lean by the prevailing north wind. Two men slowed their horses to a walk as they climbed the hill toward the sea.

Waves crashed on the nearby shoreline, a long spit with scrubby vegetation. The light breeze carried a fresh, salty tang of sea air, and it mixed with the scent of rain on fresh earth rising from the cropping fields north of the hill. The river snaked around the sand flats east and south of the hill in a narrow delta before turning west to run along the coastline.

The men's arrival near the crest of the hill disturbed angry crows that had already settled in the dusk. The lane the men were following ended at a cul-de-sac, bordered by a rock wall, and marked by a wooden trough. A plough and oxen harness leaned against the wall.

"Wait," Bran said, holding up a hand. He patted the heaving flanks of his horse.

Bran swung from his saddle and tested the water in the trough. There'd been heavy rain and the water was fresh. He led his horse to it.

"We ride like mad men all day, for what?" the other man said, shifting in his saddle.

"We'll stop here," Bran said. "The horses can't take much more tonight anyway."

"But there's no sign of the foreigners," the other man asked. He strained his eyes out over the sea. "What if they didn't come?"

"They'll be here," Bran said, his voice testy.

"Sir, pardon me for asking. What signs do you see?" The man's flinty eyes lent him the look of permanent suspicion. Wariness was good trait in a lookout, irritating in a companion. The man jumped from his horse. He ran his weathered hands over the horses flanks.

Bran stood next to the shorter, sinewy man, and pointed west. "Their ships'll be in Bannow Bay."

The other man turned his eyes in that direction, squinting into the dusk. "Can't see anything."

"Fin, King Diarmait sent us. Speak up if ye think ye have something better to do," Bran said. He filled a leather bound tankard with water. He kicked at the tall grass growing in the lee of the wall. "Pasture here looks good, eh?"

Fin, nodded. Bran let his horse feed on the lush greenery. The man was irritating but he knew his horses and pasture.

Fin checked the horses feet. He brushed his mare as it watered and joined Bran's in grazing. He dropped his weapons to the ground, and unstrapped his kit from his horse. Fin took a big swig of water, then struck a pose with one sinewy arm braced on the rock wall, looking back in the direction they'd come.

"I don't like it! Nothing about this feels good," the smaller man said.

"They're supposed to follow the coast, so they have to come past here," Bran said, climbing a stile onto the top of the wall, and pointing out along the starlit coastline below the hill. "I'd wager they got King Diarmait's letter, and they're taking it slow. We've reached the coast, no point in riding further. We're doing the right thing stopping."

"It's not that," Fin said. "It's these men the King has fallen in with. They don't understand us."

"Aye. They speak another language, to be sure," Bran said. He rubbed his face.

"They're ruthless mercenaries! What's to stop them taking any village they like?" Fin asked. He gestured toward the town they'd just passed. Fin pulled off his helm, and scratched at the back of his head.

"What are ye talking about, man. The King asked for mercenaries, to get his throne back. What do ye expect!"

"They're not here. Maybe they're sacking your home town or mine," Fin gestured to the town again. Then he lowered his voice to an ominous whisper. "How much gold has the King promised them? I hope its enough."

North of them, mostly hidden behind the row of trees the sleepy village's chimneys sent innocent wisps of smoke into the night sky. Duncormac it was called. The ride from Baltinglass followed the Slaney, then the road passed west of the town, west of the river. It was the quickest way to the coast.

It looked as idyllic as any Irish village. These were farmers. They'd fall before the Normans as a field of wheat before the scythe.

"Aye, ruthless," Bran said. "But they like gold. And they'll get plenty once King Diarmait mac Murchada is back on the throne of Leinster."

Fin made a rude noise. "They're sons of the conqueror! Our army must be half a day behind us at least. What happens if these lads just decide they'll take land, women *and* gold?"

"You know our first stop is Wexford. Maybe its not just gold that's been promised. Let's just say I wouldn't want to have family in any town that sided with the High King Ruaidrí Ua Conchobair."

Fin sucked his teeth. "Or with Tigernán Mór Ua Ruairc that put King Diarmait off his throne."

"Fin, they're Englanders. They want to go home to their castle in Wales, with their riches and plunder," Bran replied. He carried his kit over a stile to a flat, higher piece of ground to make camp.

Fin walked off shaking his head, and went to check on the horses. Bran piled some dry rocks to form a fire-pit and put together sticks piled up near the wind break built by some farmer clearing his land. Bran added tinder from his bag.

Fin returned. "Horses are sleeping."

He stretched a canvas out from a tree to make a tent and shook out his bedroll, while Bran continued to work on the fire.

Fin went to his kit bag and pulled out bread, wine and cheese. He grinned and held it up to show Bran. "Praise be to our King!"

"They'll be here. We just wait," Bran said.

"Diarmait's not seen them has he? Tell me honest sir," Fin asked.

"We light a fire, and keep watches," Bran said. "What else can we do?"

"Fair," Fin said. "I'll take first watch."

❖

The roof of Pádraig's Goods was slippery from the rain, and as she fought for grip, digging her hands into the tightly bundled thatch, it ripped at Hilde's skin. Pausing here, keeping down low to the roof, there was a chance they'd lose sight of her and give up, but down below Jezabel and Donegal's voices continued.

But holding still hurt as much as moving. A whimper escaped her. Hilde gripped with her feet, and elbows to free her hands. She closed her eyes tight, balled her fists, and sunk onto her knees.

Enough. Giving up, sliding down from the roof into the hands of the two, that was the only sensible thing. Hilde's arms shook with exhaustion. It would be easy, it would be an end to this wet, this cold and pain.

Jezabel, don't you touch her!

Her Mama's voice echoed in her mind.

Jezabel had never liked either of the Blaine women, and now it was plain that the gloves were off. This man in black, she'd brought him here. This wasn't Donegal's doing. He was no match for Jezabel once she saw what she wanted.

"Come down! You little wench! Devil spawn child!" Jezabel's screams floated up from the roadway. "Do you think I mind if you die of cold up there?"

Jezabel could look upon another's happiness, and see poison. What other folks had around their hearth to her was either bad, or something she ought to have for herself. She was one with a jaundiced eye. Bronach had never said as much but now Hilde understood hints her mother had made. It was clear now.

A scraping sound echoed from the street. More voices, Jezabel's chiding; and Donegal's mollifying. A bang, and a curse. They were up against the building now.

It was hard to turn and look down, but Hilde did that now, her fingers gripping into the thatch. Hands appeared at the eaves, on the edge of the thatch.

"Hold me! Dónal Ua Ruairc! Begorrah!" Jezabel said, the top of her head appearing at the eaves. She lurched to one side, disappeared and then resurfaced.

"Don't curse," came Donegal's voice. "I'm trying, woman!"

"Was no curse! Want to hear a curse now?" Jezabel's hands were on the roof trying to lift, but could not.

Donegal grunted, and Jezabel appeared head and shoulders.

His strained voice came up from the roadway. "Well?"

"She's gone!" Jezabel shouted. "Scrawny gammon rasher that she is!"

"What?"

"Damn you to the blackest hell child! Run off then," Jezabel shouted. "You and your pox ridden witch of a mother!"

Hilde hid around the other side of the ridge-line. Thankfully a makeshift ladder had been left here and she rested on it, full-length, exhausted muscles shaking, breathing hard.

"Bringing you down!" Donegal said.

"Your mother is going to burn!" Jezabel shouted. "Burn like the heretic she is! Burn! Burn! Burn!!"

Hilde clung to the rails of the ladder. Her mouth contorted through anguished silent howls.

Mama, I'm sorry.

Heat of shame rose in her neck, and throat. Torrents of emotion flushed her red-eyes, and emerged in stifled sobs.

❖

Hilde took a deep breath, shook her aching hands and stretched. The stars were out now. Although dark skies still gathered and the rain might come again, beautiful sparkling constellations stayed, a glittering smile from the Gods.

Hare attic. That word again. The sisters would know. Don't say it was Jezabel, don't admit.

The willow she had sheltered under earlier reached its branches over the road, nearly to the roof of Pádraig's, but it made no sense to try to climb there. The branches would make noise, give away where she was, and even drunk as he was Donegal just had to stride to the tree and pick her up.

The only way off was down. And into the arms of the waiting Jezabel.

Throw something? Draw them away?

Hilde sat up on the rooftop ladder, and patted her pockets. Nothing in her jacket. She reached into her dress.

The horseshoe.

Hilde ran her fingers over its cold surface, in the pocket of her smock.

I have to give it the the Chief.

Chief Fiach had big bushy eyebrows, and cheekbones you could hang your coat on. His voice was so deep and commanding that it felt he could order up her soul from her body and she'd have no will but for it to jump into the palm of his outstretched hand. Honestly terrifying. Even as tall as Hilde was now, the leader of their town towered twice over her.

But there was nothing for it — she would have to try to find him. Going to see the sisters would have to wait. Gáethán would be home by now, and that made seeing the Chief loom less large in her mind. He was pretty nice for a boy, although not very clever.

Mama's call from the cell 'Hilde, run! Go to the Chief.'

Jezabel and Donegal's occasional mumbling voices floated up from the Back Road, just below the big oak. It'd been some time and they had not moved. As if waiting for her to follow her mother's instructions.

So I do the opposite! We Blaine women have to use our heads.

Taking care to be extra quiet, Hilde retraced her path over the roof, back to the top of the round house. Her breathing came fast, and her arms hurt like fire from the strain of spider-walking on the rough thatch. She paused for a few pounding heartbeats.

Hilde peered over the edge. The roadway was clear. The bridge and verdant tree growth along the river stood in silhouette against the starry sky and moonlit clouds. No man in black, no travellers on the road.

Like a rat, creeping on all fours she moved onto the roof of the gaol, and then dropped to her arms length from its back edge. The blood blister she'd gotten from moving the floor boards to the cellar smarted as she gripped the roofs edge. It was a longer drop here, into the dark, as the ground fell away.

Hilde let go.

She grunted as she landed and rolled. It was pitch black here. The land sloped down the hill, and she came to rest on a pile of leaf mulch. She lay between saplings of elm and full-grown whitethorn bushes forming a thicket that ran down toward the Back Road. The O'Neills were well into the old ways and would never cut it down, to the chagrin of Fearghas the smith.

Now it was the perfect cover as Hilde ran bent over down the gap between the smithy and the store to Caton's Road. She was bigger now and had to squeeze but the ways she and the other children had found through the thicket still remained.

Hilde didn't stop to see if anyone followed. She just ran.

❖

The Chief's house was one of the few in Duncormac as salubrious and decorous as Blaine Cottage. It was long, almost like two cottages end on end, and of a strange design. It was fully dark now, and Hilde carefully mounted the steps by moon and starlight. Then paused.

In the distance shouts travelled on the night air, but then the fracas fell silent.

An owl uttered its haunting cry. The sounds of its wings came, and went.

Just go up, and rap on the door!

The sleepy call of a nearby nesting bird, a low clicking in its throat, sounded so otherworldly in that dark night that Hilde shuddered, rubbed her shoulders and dashed up the last steps to knock on the door before her courage failed her.

"Who is it!" boomed the voice from inside.

"Hilde, sir," she squeaked. "Hilde Blaine."

The door was snatched open as if the occupants fully expected a prankster to be running off. But Hilde stood her ground shivering. Gáethán, his eyes as wide as dinner plates, stood in the doorway with his mouth open.

"Hilde! My god, come inside!" Gáethán said. His father appeared behind him, standing there in a thick woollen sleeping robe. He held a lamp, and a long piece of willow bark poked from his mouth.

"Father! Let her in!" Gáethán urged.

Fiach Caton stood to one side. He took the willow bark from his mouth and gestured with it for Hilde to come inside. Then he looked at the bark, put it in his pocket and scratched his head.

Hilde ran inside, and embraced Gáethán. And for a time did not let him go. Gáethán pushed her back just a little, enough to cast his eyes up and down her scratched, leaf mulch covered exterior.

"Come on you both. Let's find some food," Chief Caton said, his mouth curling into a smile. "Strangest creature to have washed up on my shore."

"Hilde, let me go," Gáethán said. Hilde did so, and went red when she realised her state.

"Get her something dry to put on boy," his father said. He shut the door and barred it. "Follow me Hilde. And tell all, what is going on?"

The house was strange. The entry door was in the short end wall of the house. The big single room, went a long way back, haze from the central fire pit obscuring the back wall. Hilde tried to form words but her teeth chattered so much she couldn't speak. The big man shook his head.

"Eat first," he said. He smiled, probably in a way that was meant to be reassuring, but was terrifying.

Hilde suppressed an urge to go to the back of the house with Gáethán. A pot hung on a chain from an iron rod over the fire. By the fire-pit a low table had the remains of a meal on it.

Blaine cottage had a chimney which had cost Arran Blaine a fair sum, but meant the air was clear of soot. But here in the Chief's house an opening in the roof was all the chimney they had. The floor at the door was packed earth, around the fire-pit the floor was stone. At the rear a large bed stood on a floor of wooden boards and a wooden loft floor jutted from the wall above it.

Fiach picked up a ladle and stirred the pot, scooping out several spoonfuls, and then gestured to a bench lined with furs and skins. He held out a bowl to Hilde. Lumps of fat swum around the watery broth. Hilde made a face.

"Sorry. Since Riane died, I do what I can," Fiach said.

"Sir, thank you. Saints blessings on you," Hilde said, smiling.

She devoured the food. Gáethán descended the ladder from the loft and came over with a cotton shirt, breeches and a woollen cloak. He held out his hand for Hilde's wet things, and she slipped into the boys clothes while the Caton men looked at the ceiling.

Gáethán went to the earthen-floored end by the front door, took water from a wooden pail, and cleaned Hilde's plate. Then he made them a small pitcher of spiced mead each. In that time Hilde explained everything that had happened since arriving at Blaine Cottage and hiding in the pear tree. When she related the part about the torch thrown on the roof Fiach frowned, leaned back and folded his arms.

Fiach and his son both leaned in over the fire-pit as Hilde described how the whole event had nearly dissolved when Father O'Connor spoke, only to have Jezabel appeal to the man in black. The two both shook their heads slowly at Hilde's description of Bronach being carried away in a sack, only to be found later in the gaol. When Hilde finished, they all sipped their spiced mead in silence.

"At least the priest spoke true. There's nothing to do until the Brehon arrive," the Chief said. He ran a big meaty palm around his beard. He slapped Gáethán on the back, and waved toward their bunks at the end of the house. "Time for bed my lad."

"Brehon? But Jezabel says Mama is going to burn alive! It's so unfair! How can that beastly woman know that!" Hilde said.

"She's trying to scare you. The Brehon won't be swayed that easily," said the Chief.

"My Mama is never a witch," Hilde said, pressing her palm on the Chief's forearm. "Nor a hare attic either. Chief you have to help me! Get her out!"

"What?" the Chief asked. "Hare attic?"

"Don't know!" Hilde said, holding her palms up, and shrugging. "The man in black said it. Bishop Ahearne."

"This is bad Hilde. Sounds like church business. I can't help you if its the church," the Chief said. He got to his feet, and helped himself to some more spiced mead.

"Mama told me to see you. She said you named me," Hilde said. Her eyes brimmed with tears, and her voice caught.

"I'll keep you safe Hilde, but I can't be leader of this village if I am renounced by the church," Fiach said. He got down on his haunches and gripped the seat Hilde sat on, to look her in the eye. "I'm sorry."

"That's so silly! Who else could be chief!" Hilde said.

"Father O'Connor and I see eye to eye on most things Hilde. But I'm an Ostman, and some look at me strange already," he stood leaned against a stout post that ran up to the ridge beam. "I love this town. But its not enough, if I'm thrown out of the church."

"But Father O'Connor says Ahearne is bad, he is not a real Bishop. I heard them argue," Hilde protested.

"There you are. I hope he can work it out Hilde. He's on your side," Fiach said. "Listen, Hilde, there's some very important things going on. Dangerous things."

"Father, what is it?" Gáethán asked. "Is it the riders?"

"We had a tingmote and the elder folk of the village and I are doing what we can. We have the reports but I can't get them to believe its real," Fiach said. He motioned with both hands for Gáethán to be quiet. He folded his arms and looked down. "I will do anything I can for you Hilde, but it seems this thing with your Mother is up to the church right now."

"Can she stay here tonight father?" Gáethán asked.

"Hilde, stay here in our barn. I'll get you some blankets and I'll bring your things out when they're dry," Fiach said.

"Chief Fiach?" Hilde said. She reached in to her pocket, and held up the horseshoe. "I found this. On the hill the other side of our pasture."

Fiach tightened his fists, and his jaw set like rock. He shook his head slowly, and walked toward Hilde like a man possessed. "That's real as cold iron. It's time. Even if I must do it alone."

"Father, what are you going to do? Don't go!" Gáethán said. "Please!!"

Fiach bent to Gáethán's ear, and put his arm around him. A few words passed between father and son. The boy's face reddened and his eyes filled.

Hilde stood up as the Chief walked toward her, and held out the horseshoe to him. He took it wordlessly. From a hook by the front door he took two large axes, walked out the door and slammed it shut behind him.

8

Porridge

"Keep those men in formation!" FitzStephen bellowed, peering eastwards, up the road, into the dusk. The snaking line of torches wound out of sight, one or two ragged breakers of rank detouring through the undergrowth. He yanked the reins of his warhorse, moving around the bole of a large ash tree that jutted out into the roadway.

His sergeant, moonlight glinting off the steel of his helm, raised a mailed fist in acknowledgement. The sergeant's crisp orders joined tramping feet and the rattle of bows on the night air. One of the men returning to rank copped a blow from the flat of the sergeant's sword.

It was only a short time since they'd left the waterhole and already the march was a damn mess. Still, they'd be at camp at the place Prendergast's man Giffard had found them in time for compline. If luck was about to change perhaps that lying drunken Irish King mac Murchada would be there to greet them with supplies.

The Norman knight stuck out his square chin, and straightened in the saddle of his destrier to present the best profile to his men, as he tugged the reins around to check on the tail of the army. The salt sea air more brisk in the late hour, stirred tendrils of dark cloud across the face of the moon. An owl coasted silently across the deep blue black of the heavens, the passage of its mighty wings marked only by stars winking out and back.

As he passed the ranks of archers, and neared the tail, the men at arms footfalls sounded heavily in the silence of the Irish coastal evening, their grumbling advance losing its rhythm as they straggled along in the narrow roadway.

The tail of his army here passed a cross roads of a sort. It widened the carriageway as small logging trails hacked into the underbrush led away north and south. A stone marker stood here also, graven with some message long covered in moss.

In the distance, past the knights who kept up the rear of the column, a shout went up. Prendergast's men.

Damn Prendergast — where the hell was he? His lot were an ill-disciplined rabble.

More shouts, and hooves.

One of Prendergast's knights breaking rank? If Strongbow hadn't pushed for that damn eerie irish-loving derelict to land with him the whole mission would have been so much simpler.

The sound of hooves on the muddy roadway got louder and the knights called out an alert. The Thomond prince staggered along sullenly behind, his hands bound in a tether, and a rear-guardsman pulled him out of FitzStephen's way.

A figure appeared from the side of the second column, riding up into the gap between the two armies. The Norman knight urged his horse forward. His men made way for him to pass alongside the column, and he rode out into the open area of the cross roads.

The other rider bought his horse to a halt, and the knights of his army, still marching forward, split and went around him.

Infernal damnation! What is that God forsaken annoying Flemish dullard playing at.

"Prendergast! Do you want my sword to your throat!" FitzStephen called, as the mounted soldier approached, pushing the tree branches aside as he squeezed between the column of soldiers and the overhanding greenery.

"Je suis Giffard, Monsieur!" the man responded.

"Where on earth is Prendergast?" FitzStephen bellowed.

"You act innocent now! You are the back stabber! You threatened his life earlier! Now our commander is gone?" Giffard called. His Norman-English patois degenerated and his southern French accent grew strong as he shook his fist. "Hand him over now!"

"My army is three times yours! French idiot!" FitzStephen yelled. His sword was half drawn from its scabbard.

"Allez!" Giffard shouted. The columns of Prendergast's knights either side of FitzStephen moved to surround him. "Not at this moment, Monsieur! His body or your life!"

"Alright! Listen, on my honour!" FitzStephen sheathed his sword, and held up his hands. "I know nothing of his movements. We only left the river moments ago."

Giffard's mount cantered to FitzStephen's side, his horse rearing up as the Frenchman scowled and yanked the reins. He was an expert horseman by his demeanour in the saddle. The Norman hadn't even seen the man draw his sword, but now it was weaving a pattern before his startled face. The whole time Giffard's eye was fixed on him. When the Frenchman's horse settled he put his sword to its scabbard and ran it home with a singing of steel.

"Perhaps your brains were addled by your stay in that Welsh prison," Giffard said. He turned and called to the army behind him. "About face! Back to the camp!"

The order rippled through the ranks. Giffard wheeled his mount around.

"You cannot be serious!" FitzStephen called. "We must march now!"

"It's late. We will return and camp. I will await my commander. Wait for us before you cross the river. At the spot we agreed," Giffard said.

"This is an outrage! You should be put to the sword for deserting!" FitzStephen shouted.

"Put to the sword? If Captain Prendergast is not found, we may be speaking again Monsieur."

❖

Funk from a dozen animals was the first thing that assailed Hilde's senses as she woke. Their snuffling and lowing from the floor of the Caton's barn was muffled a little by the straw she'd slept on up in the loft above. That and an insistent tapping and calling.

"Hilde!"

She rubbed her face and crawled to the edge of the hay loft. Gáethán was just raising the pitchfork to rap the loft again.

"I'm awake," Hilde said.

"Got breakfast for you," Gáethán said. He held up a bowl. "It's been light for ages!"

He was right, judging by the light streaming in from the door. Hilde ran a hand over her hair, and loosed several pieces of straw. She stood and grabbed the ladder.

"The Chief. Is he back? I need to talk to him," she said as she descended the steps. "How long have I slept?!"

After the rains and grey skies clouds had given way to clear blue sky, and wisps of mist rose from the muddy yard as the suns rays played across it.

The animals should all be out in pasture by this time. It looked as though the Caton heir was behind on his duties.

"Come and eat Hilde, and we can talk about it," Gáethán said.

"He's not back?" Hilde pressed.

Gáethán put the pitchfork against the wall of the barn, and walked up the steps into the long house.

She ran looked around the yard and peered up the road, as if Fiach Caton would step around the bend with his axe over his shoulder, despite Gáethán's statements.

"Gáethán!" Hilde ran up and followed the boy inside.

❖

She found him eyes closed, leaning on the low table with both hands. The bowl and a wooden spoon sat on the low table next to him. She bit her lip, and slowed her pace as she walked to the boy, and put her hand on his shoulder.

"He's gone scouting. That's what he said. But I think its war Hilde," Gáethán said, his eyes wet as she turned to look at her. "Right now? I don't even know if he's alive."

"Scouting what?" Hilde said.

"Don't know. They won't tell me," he said. He gestured to the chair opposite.

"They?"

"Fearghas, the blacksmith for one. And Father O'Connor," Gáethán said. "They know but won't say."

"The man on the hill. The horseshoe! Foreigners! It has to be!" Hilde said. "You know Mama should be in the know too. She's an Elder. How can they be thinking of doing this to her at a time like this!"

Gáethán blinked, and wiped his nose. "I hadn't thought of it like that. Listen, Hilde, father would help you both if he could. Interfering in a church matter - its dangerous."

Hilde eschewed the chair, and curled up on the floor next to the low table, close to Gáethán. She spooned the grey mix into her mouth tentatively at first then with gusto. "Oh, Gáethán, this is good!"

A smile stole across the boys face.

"Hilde, what would happen to Blaine Cottage if your mother was gone?" he asked.

The smile fell away and a serious frown replaced it. He scratched the back of his head.

"I would have to learn how to cook gruel as good as this!" Hilde said.

"Hilde, think about it. You're thirteen," he said.

"Oh," Hilde said, brows shooting up. She put the spoon back in the plate, got up and began to pace. "The priory. They'd send me there, the Elders."

He leaned back, looking coolly at her, then stood and took her plate to the bucket to wash it. He leaned against the bench and folded his arms.

She stood looking at the boy, wheels turning in her head. "Uncle Donegal. It would fall to him. And Jezabel."

"And all the pasture? The fields?"

"Oh, he would never farm it. He's supposed to be a soldier, but he's never done any of that since he came back. Just drinks," Hilde said. Close to Gáethán two windows looked out across the Caton's fields at the rear of the long house. She walked close to him and stared out.

"So he might sell it, for cheap. And who would want those fields?" Gáethán asked, jerking his head to the side, out the window. Two farms only lay in that direction, between Caton land and Blaine Cottage small-holdings.

"Oh gods! You're right! Saints preserve me! Rónán Teague, that rotter! And his cousin Cormac Bolan, ready with the accusations and the sacks over Mama's head", Hilde said.

"Its so obvious," Gáethán said, washing the porridge pot, and stacking it under the wooden bench.

"I can't believe it Gáethán! Who could hate someone enough to do this! It's one thing to want a property, but getting a person burned alive? And crowing about it?" Hilde said. She found a mug and ladled some water into it from the pot above the unlit fireplace.

"Greed. Not hate. And envy. Jezabel has long been saying bad things about you Blaines, and trying to make a joke of it," the lad said.

"But why Alice and Emma? How? And this man in black — where did he come from?" Hilde asked, pressing her palms together and looking up at the thatch.

"The man of God?" Gáethán asked, with a wry grin.

"Father O'Connor said all sorts of things to him. And about him. I couldn't follow it," Hilde said. "I think I need to see the sisters at the Priory."

"Good thinking. Hilde, I'm afraid you can't stay here. You should ask them if you can stay at the Priory," Gáethán said.

"What? Why not?" Hilde said.

Gáethán looked down, and his lip quivered. He crossed to the ladder and shinnied up it to the loft.

"Oh - sorry, I shouldn't have asked," Hilde said. "Gáethán?"

Rustling sounds and muttering issued from atop the loft.

"It's alright. I'll ask sister Gobnait," Hilde said, straining to try to see what Gáethán was doing.

His face appeared.

"Catch" he said. And then he dropped a boys tunic, chemise, scarf and pants into her hands.

"Oh, good idea," she said. "I'll put my hair up."

"There's a few strangers on the road at the moment. Keep your hat down and no-one will notice." He swung down from the loft.

Hilde walked toward the door, her mind a whirl. People from her own village attacking her just to get their hands on her family home was horrifying. It was like demons lived among them. They'd never been safe.

"You'll be fine Hilde," Gáethán said. "Don't go the Back Road. They might have people near the gaol. Just go out the front gate and straight up the hill to the Main Road."

Hilde turned and grabbed him. She pressed her face into the rough material of his tunic. An overwhelming "ahuh" noise in her throat surprised her, until she realised it was a sob she'd tried to choke off. There was no time for sobbing, but the feeling of pain and fear, so strong, broke through.

His hand landed lightly on the back of her head, patted her twice.

"I'm so, so far behind with my chores," he said. Hilde let him go slowly. He was gazing at all the animals as though seeing them for the first time since last night.

"You'll be fine too Gáethán. It's going to be alright," Hilde said. She gave a little smile but felt it start to tremble. And before more feelings broke through she strode off up toward the Main Road.

9

Secrets and Lies

Deep in the moist green cleft — a rocky forest valley, framed on all sides by oaks — the couple walked as wild juniper and bilberries gathered about the cloister of boughs like bunting at a banquet. Lazily a butterfly chanced through a ray of early morning sunshine that filtered down between the leaves, the woman pointing it out and laughing. Motes circled it, an escort of fae sprites, until it floated under the canopy and out of sight.

The couple walked slowly, the man scuffing up leaves, the woman tugging at his sleeve sharing a jest that didn't need words to say. They rounded a bend in the gallery of moss-covered rocks and willows, and stretching in front of them lay a small carpet of bluebells.

"For you my darling," he said, stooping to snatch up a few in a bunch to present to her. His blonde hair caught the sun too, and she reached out to touch it, a look of wonder on her face. She caught herself and took the flowers.

Her long curly black hair shone with red lights, in the morning light. Silver combs that pulled her locks back from her face on each side glinted in the hazy light of that glade. Her long velvet red gown against pale skin, dark green cloak fixed with an ornate silver pin; all against the green palette of the forest made her almost luminous in her appearance. Prendergast's mouth opened, and then shut again.

"My Lord Prendergast, so generous that you give me my kingdoms own flowers," she said, mirth curling the corners of her mouth. "Say 'darling' again; I love your strange way of speaking."

"Darling, its not your kingdom yet," Prendergast responded, snapping out of his reverie, and nodding his head toward the motte-and-bailey manor away to their left through the trees. "Unless daddy dearest passed away in yon castle overnight, and I hope not given he and I have more business in the future."

He traced her jawline with an index finger, then settled his hand on his sword, his slab-like cheeks and impassive expression at odds with his tender gestures.

Prendergast tried to move toward her, but she poked him with a finger in his shoulder, finding a gap in his leather armour. A darkness passed behind his eyes, for a moment, but then passed. "Let me kiss you. Don't walk so fast."

He batted away the hand she'd raised to him. "Not in front of all the guardsmen."

"What guardsmen," Prendergast said. He was deadpan, but his eyes flicked to figures moving in the forest parallel with them. "Come here."

He put his arm around her waist and thrust his pelvis against her. Laughter filtered through from the undercroft. She shot glances into the forest.

"Maurice, I must tell you something, and the guards must not hear," she said. She acquiesced and he pulled her into his arms, and leaned back against the trunk of gnarled oak. He kissed her, and nibbled at her ear.

"I'm with child," she said.

"Mine?" he said, eyes as wide as dinner plates. He pushed her back, and stooped to look into her eyes. "Éadaoin?"

She laughed.

"Éadaoin inghean Mhic Gilla Patráic, of Osraighe?" he asked again, something that might be called a smile slitting the angles of his face.

"You're getting better. With your Irish," Éadaoin said. She nodded. A grin spread across his face.

"A son, perhaps! God, please," he said. "How do you know its mine?"

"My Lord, I'm sixteen! My father has commanded my virtue. He won't let me near anyone, and as you can see his soldiers are effective in ensuring his wishes," she said, nodding to the shapes moving in the undercroft.

"We will have to hurry up the wedding then," Prendergast said. Prendergast's eyes became distant, and he stroked his chin. "That hot-headed idiot FitzStephen. He may not be satisfied with just what Diarmait has promised him."

"My Lord, you mustn't take risks with this. Its dangerous," she said. "Wexford places great faith in its walls, I hear."

"There will be no bloodshed on either side at Wexford," Prendergast responded. He walked for a bit, pausing as they reached some hanging moss. Éadaoin trailed her fingers through the green-grey curtain.

Éadaoin looked at him, one eyebrow raised. Laughing, she pulled the moss to herself, pressing it so it hung from her chin like a beard. "You can count on me. And I know I can I count on you Prendergast. When the time is right?? Young man?"

"My God! Spitting image of your father! I thought he walked here with us," Prendergast said, without a hint of a smile.

"Are you sure you'll be safe?" Éadaoin asked, suddenly serious.

"Yes, they will surrender, as long as we handle it right," Prendergast said.

"You men and your secrets. I thought it was all about swords," Éadaoin said.

In the distance a small group of people stood, near the edge of the forest, on the other side of a stile. Horses stamped their feet. Prendergast quickened his pace.

"Listen my sweet; I should not have stayed so long. This FitzStephen is suspicious. All for the wrong reasons, but now in my foolishness I've given him more to be angry about," Prendergast said. He waved at the group ahead.

Pages moved to put a bridle on one of the waiting horses, several hands taller than any of the others.

"I came all the way to Ross from our lovely Kilkenny to see you. I couldn't have you leave after father monopolised absolutely all your time talking about boring old bishops."

"Éadaoin! You were listening! No mention of that to anyone!" Prendergast urged.

"I was waiting for you. I didn't mean to over hear. I'm sorry," a catch came in Éadaoin's voice, deep-set brown eyes filling like forest pools with Irish rain.

"Éadaoin, oh, I'm sorry - I'm a fool. But pay this fool no mind. I will see you again soon, and you shall be my bride."

Two soldiers moved out of the tree line to stand next to the princess of Osraighe. They crossed the stile into a large pasture that surrounded the Manor Castle at Ross. A road bordered the pasture to the east. In the distance the Blackstairs mountains rose like a dark sleeping giant.

Prendergast strode to his horse and without a further word, spurred the beast into a canter then a gallop. Soon he was a dot on the horizon in the south-east.

❖

Along the main road in Duncormac several strangers to town walked on their various business. As was often the case this early in the morning a sea fog rolled along the River Muck and clung to the trees and low roads. Locals nodded and mumbled greetings to those they knew.

Overhead a gull wheeled in the sky a black ink mark against the blue, with scudding white clouds. The sound of metal striking metal rang out from the blacksmith. The River Muck was high after the rains, and chattered merrily as it passed under the bridge.

Indretach the physic carried his bag back toward his wagon. He'd pulled up the wagon in the same spot every April. Some villagers swore by his liquors and cures, others cursed him for a fraud, but every April he was there again. Now slogging south through the mud he fixed his eyes on his shoes, as he neared the main bridge to avoid Father O'Connor's glare. The priest had warned the villagers off Indretach, and preached faith in god, and clean living as a better medicine. Father O'Connor walked north up toward the church clutching a pail of milk and a bag of cakes, and although the physic irked him no end, there was no use accosting Indretach here on an empty stomach.

Meanwhile a young man in an ill-fitting tunic, with a flop hat pulled down over his eyes, and pants that were rather too big tied at the waist with twine, crossed the road into the shade of the trees that lined the roadside, avoiding both the priest and the physic.

A crow swooped down to the willows near the bridge to noisily challenge a rival and they pecked and dived in a raucous display. The young man jumped a foot in the air, and then looked around furtively - because of course it wasn't a young man at all.

Hilde pulled the flop hat down even further, detoured into the shadows of the trees, and marched as quickly as she dared up the road toward the Priory.

❖

Of all the buildings in the Priory Hilde had only ever been in the chapel, and the hall that they used for study. The room that she'd been led to was right at the back, away from the entrance, and adjacent to the dormitory cells where the nuns lived, and worked. A hard wooden bench sat underneath a portrait of a stern woman in a severe black shapeless dress. The image had her head surrounded by a glowing aura, and she gestured to others, tiny in comparison.

The portrait was so like the ones of the saints that Hilde wondered if she should recognise it but nothing came to mind. It had seemed simple, to just come to the Priory and ask to see Sister Gobnait and her friend Sister Luiseach. If she knew where they slept she could probably just get up and run to their room.

All around the sounds of quiet industry echoed through the halls. The short corridor Hilde waited in joined two dormitory blocks, that were at right-angles to each other, and black swathed figures glided past constantly, in the gloom of this ancient thick walled building.

So many nuns.

Two nuns turned the corner and strode past Hilde, talking quietly, their hands tucked demurely into their sleeves. One turned, and put a hand to her ear. A wooden door opposite the bench had a plate fixed to it with lettering that reminded Hilde of the books they used in study.

Mháthair-Uachtarán.

The other woman shook her head, and they hurried off, disappearing down the hallway.

"Are you here to see me, young man?" a nun said. "And you should take your hat off when you speak to me you know."

"Oh yes! Begging your pardon, ma'am," Hilde said. "My head its terrible with the lice. Is it alright if I leave it on? I don't want to take up any of your time."

The woman was slight, bony shoulders tenting the black wool of her tunic. Her back bowed, and her lined face bore two gimlet eyes, that seemed to bore into Hilde's soul.

"Reverend Mother, is how you address me. You *sound* too young to be out by yourself. How old are you lad?" she said, bending down to peer under Hilde's cap. "Come in to my office, the lights better. Damn my eyes, can't see a thing in this hallway."

"Reverend Mother, sorry again. I'm just ten years old. But I have a message for Sister Gobnait, or Sister Luiseach who is at this Priory. It's really important."

"Really. What on earth would a ten year old boy be doing delivering a message in a place full of busy sisters of God? We have lots to do young man! Gobnait is doing her chores, and Luiseach is in Carlow for a few days on an errand."

"Well, its because I... I mean, Sister..." Hilde paused, racking her brain. She gripped the handle of her bag until her knuckles were white.

"What? I can't hear you."

"Well, I...Sister Luiseach..." Hilde stuttered.

"Speak up! Are you wasting my time? And what is that on your face? You're filthy, like a beggar!" the Mother Superior said, wiping a finger on Hilde's face. Soot came off it leaving a white mark. "I should have you thrown out,"

"Luiseach is my sister. She's my sister. And I have to get her an urgent message. Our father got killed in the war. And our mother is taken away." Hilde began to cry. A little sob first, that caught in her throat, then hot tears that made tracks in the chimney soot from Chief Caton's fireplace that she'd smeared on her face.

"Oh. Oh, I'm sorry my lad. God bless you, poor wee chap. How have you been making do?" Mother Superior asked, as she started fingering the cross that hung around her neck.

"I'm a chimney sweep. Since Father left. Its dirty work. Sorry Reverend Mother." Hilde sniffled. "I better not take my hat off or go in your office, as I'm just going to make it all dirty."

"Alright, alright. Look, you're only ten years old - it won't do you any harm to stay here until Luiseach gets back. When Sister Gobnait is free she can find you a spot in one of the outbuildings to sleep."

"That'd be so wonderful. Thank you Reverend Mother," Hilde said.

"Sister Debforgaill!" Mother Superior called out to a nun who had just passed them in the hall. The woman stopped, and smiled, bobbing her head to the Reverend Mother. The spare old matriarch pointed a bony finger down the hallway. "Take this lad to the common room and get someone to fetch Sister Gobnait will you?"

"Reverend Mother," the woman bobbed her head again, and peered at Hilde. "This lad?"

"He's to stay in the barn here tonight, so we might as well feed him. Find some chores for him to do, to pay for his supper. Chin up lad, terrible news for you and your family, but God has a plan for all of us."

"Thank you Reverend Mother," Hilde said, jumping to her feet and starting down the hallway in the direction the Mother Superior had pointed.

The old lady clucked her tongue as she disappeared into her room. "War. Terrible business."

❖

The common room was nearly empty, rows of bare wooden tables, worn smooth in places from decades of use and diligent cleaning. High narrow windows ran along both sides, but in the corner where Hilde sat the morning light did not reach.

"Mother Superior really does need help with her eyesight, calling you a boy," Sister Debforgaill said. "I can see you're a lass under all that black."

"My father is dead in the war. My mother gone. Just need to talk to my sister," Hilde said. On the other side of the common room, two nuns sat down at a table with steaming bowls, and wooden spoons.

Debforgaill gasped and put her hand to her mouth. "Oh, I'm so sorry. And your sister is here?"

Hilde nodded. She sniffled and rubbed her nose. "Is there any food? Been on the road."

"Of course. Please just stay there," Debforgaill said. And moved off toward the servery.

From the other end of the common room, a figure strode in, silhouetted by the light from the high windows.

"Sloth and gluttony in one act, sisters?" he said, as he reached the table with the two nuns. One stopped with the spoon raised to her mouth. The other leaned back and looked the new arrival, her mouth open in amazement. "Not even midday and you're already avoiding your chores for God's house?"

"Bishop!" said one.

"Does Mother Superior know you are here, your Grace?" said the other.

Under his arm he carried a distinctive hat. He turned and Hilde saw his face clearly. The witch finder man. He looked around the hall.

"There is some lad here already? Why should I not visit your common room?" His eyes rested on Hilde, and her blood turned to ice. She willed her eyes to move, her face to turn away but she was frozen. Her hands shook.

"Feel free to wait here Bishop, and I can fetch the Mother Superior," the woman said, getting to her feet.

It sounded as though the nuns had called whatever bluff he was making.

Hilde could almost feel his eyes on her again. But she smiled at Sister Debforgaill who had returned to the table with a steaming bowl of gruel.

"Hmmph. I have my sermon to prepare. Thank you, but don't disturb Mother Superior," he said.

"Very well your Grace. God be with you."

"But I do think discipline here might better follow the Lords teachings" the man said, half to himself. And the sound of his measured footsteps receded into the distance.

<h1 style="text-align:center">10</h1>

<h2 style="text-align:center">The Priory</h2>

"Mercy me," said Gobnait, as she hurried through the corridors of the priory. She stole a glance back at Hilde's soot covered face, and patted her chest where her crucifix hung. "Dear oh, dear oh me. Hilde, what have you done?"

Hilde rushed to catch up to the taller woman's long strides. Away from the grand stone chambers of the house of God near the front of the Priory, they now walked down low-ceilinged, clay-brick halls and dormitories. In a long building that had a single door at each end and open wooden stalls, each with a pair of bunk beds inside.

Gobnait stopped at one, drew aside a sackcloth curtain of hemp and rummaged about in a pile of papers that lay on a small stool next to the bottom bunk.

"Mother Superior said it would be alright to stay in the barn," Hilde said, one hand on the top bunk bed.

"I don't know why I don't take you down to the main street and have the Chief throw you in the gaol! The state of you! Don't you dare imagine for a moment staying in my cell here with me," Gobnait said, seizing on a slim pile of manuscript with a leather cover.

"Oh, yes! The barn. I'm sorry! I'm sorry, Sister. I tried to explain," Hilde said. She stepped into the narrow space between the bunk beds and the wooden partition. Nuns in the other stalls peered around the ends of their cells at the sounds of raised voices echoing off the common wooden ceiling.

"To me you did. But what about all those lies you said to Mother Superior! What on earth have I been teaching you all this time, Hilde Blaine!" Gobnait said in an urgent whisper. She stood up, and brushed off her long black woollen tunic. She held up the leather-bound manuscript. "You know I have this book at last. I've been making just for you. Why did I make it when you don't care for the truth one bit!"

"Mama is in gaol! She was taken for a hare-attic! That's true! And my Da, he's gone too!" Hilde said, slumping to the bed. "God knows I didn't mean to lie."

"You didn't mean to? What about pretending to be a boy, a chimney sweep! It's all quite mad. I know you've been through a lot, but this making up stories is not helping, Hilde."

"Sister, it's true! I was chased by Jezabel. She told me that Mama is going to be burned. I didn't know what to do. What if I'm going to be burned too? She called me a Devil spawn! Who can I trust?" Hilde's voice fractured at that last, and she slumped to the bed, tears running down her soot-covered face.

"Hilde. Alright," said Gobnait. "You can trust us in this place. Why would you not trust in the Lord God? This is his house and we are his servants! Why lie to Mother Superior of all people?"

"The man in black! The Bishop! He is here! I saw him in the common room," Hilde said, her voice hoarse with crying. She reached for Sister Gobnait's sleeve, and pulled her closer. "Sister, is he really guided by God? Can he take me too?"

"Oh. I don't know. Hilde, I can't make sense of all this. I don't think I can help you," Gobnait said. She pulled a curtain across the end of her cell, and sat on the bed next to Hilde, ducking her head under the bunk bed above. She put the leather-bound manuscripts on the bed next to her. "I don't know. You are a mess child. Listen, this Bishop is dangerous, I agree. I don't like him, for sure…"

"Father Stephen says he's not even a Bishop! I heard them talking. When they didn't know I was hiding. In the pear tree," Hilde said, sniffling between sobs as she tried to get the words out. She burrowed her hand under Sister Gobnait's on the rail of the bed and blinked through her tears.

"What? Not a Bishop?" Sister Gobnait clapped her hands to her face. She smoothed her tunic and stood, searching Hilde's face. Hilde nodded fiercely. "That would explain a lot."

"That's what Father Stephen said. He knew him. From Cill Chainnigh," Hilde said. "I couldn't understand everything they said. But Father Stephen doesn't like him."

Sister Gobnait, peered out of the cell, down the hallway. She gathered some parchment, quills and a bottle of ink and put it in a satchel along with the leather-bound manuscript.

"We need to get you to the barn. Sister Debforgaill went to tell the Reverend Mother on this Bishop Ahearne for being in the women's common room. I don't think he's here after you Hilde, but we'll go the back way," the nun held out her hand to Hilde, and pulled the soot-stained waif toward her. She put her arm around her shoulders.

"Okay," Hilde said. She blew her nose on her sleeve.

"I don't think Reverend Mother likes him either. Why he had to come into the women's part of the Priory I do not know. Just stay behind me," she said, slipping the satchel inside her tunic.

❖

The morning sun smarted Hilde's eyes, and she shaded them with a hand. The countryside of Wexford was laid out for them, as she and Sister Gobnait walked the perimeter of the Priory. Rolling fields of cabbage and barley, big oxen pulling at a plough, and a miasma of mayfly hovering in the heat above the earth. Vines and apple trees lay to the south, screening the priory from the township.

"It's so beautiful here," Hilde said.

"It's hard work here, my girl," Gobnait said, a wry smile on her face. She picked up the hem of her long black woollen tunic as she threaded her way along a muddy dung-covered pathway. She led them over a yard pock-marked with oxen hoof-prints, toward a long wooden building. Like the rest of the priory its roof was red washed, and its timber walls imitated the masonry and stone of the other buildings. Its large double doors were thrown wide and several nuns worked inside and out with carts and animals, moving grain. The air was thick here with insects buzzing, and the sickly stench of animal excrement.

"Oh, it really smells bad," Hilde said, wrinkling her nose.

"Born with a silver spoon, Hilde Blaine? Well you'll learn how to earn your keep," Sister Gobnait said.

"Who's this young lad?" called one of the workers, a stout woman in a smock and boots. She held her hand over her eyes as Hilde and Gobnait slogged across the mud.

"Hallo!" Gobnait said, shooting a quick glance at Hilde, still in her boys breeches and cap. "New worker! Chores for two nights keep."

"Oh aye. He can have the loft on the right." said the woman. Inside the barn, left and right were hay lofts. The woman pointed through the doors. "See Sister Gráinne for chores!"

A women working with ropes, a basket, and a cartload of hay lifted her head at the sound of her name. She nodded at Gobnait and returned to her tasks.

"I'm sorry Sister Gobnait. I really don't have any other clothes," Hilde said, pulling her cap over her hair. "They nearly set fire to our cottage. I only have what I was wearing and that got ruined in the rain. Actually I don't mind boys clothes!"

"And you are tall and strong, for a girl. Maybe its easier if we just go with it for now," Gobnait said. She slogged a few more steps, bowed slightly to Sister Gráinne, and then pointed to a ladder that led up to the loft. "I can understand you being scared of this Bishop Ahearne, but our scriptures say a false witness will be punished. I hope you can soon speak the truth."

Hilde climbed the ladder silently. At the top she turned, to find Gobnait following her up into the loft.

"Oh! I thought I'd just drop my bag and then report to Sister Gráinne," Hilde said.

"I bought my parchments for a reason. I need to understand and write down everything that happened. Especially what you can tell me about this 'Bishop'. And no more stories," Gobnait said. She indicated a bale of hay, and sat leaning against it, her writing tools spread out before her. "By the way, I made this book for you. Well, for all my students, but your adoration of King Diarmait needs to be tempered by some facts."

Hilde took the slim leather-bound bundle of pages from Gobnait, and sank into a spot in the hay nearby. There were several beautiful illuminated letters showing King Diarmait, and Hilde recognised his name along with several other words. The black flowing script filled line after line, and Hilde turned the pages in wonder.

"Sister, its beautiful! Did you make all of this?" Hilde said. "I want to show it to Mama! And The Chief!"

"Yes. I made it after you became obsessed about Diarmait. And you cannot show it to anyone! I guess you saw him as the patron of our Priory, on the foundation stone in the transept, and his pictures?" Gobnait asked.

Hilde nodded. She leafed through the book, tracing with a finger words she recognised.

"I'm going to use it for a few lessons perhaps — so you won't get to keep it!" Gobnait said sharply. She carefully smoothed a blank piece of parchment on her lap, and set up a pot into which she poured a small amount of ink.

"I can't show it to anyone?" Hilde said, in amazement. She closed the book and hugged it to herself.

"Hilde, women aren't meant to write. That's why we are hiding out here in the barn to do this," Gobnait said. "I've been copying books and I'm good at it, so Reverend Mother tolerates me, and excuses me from working in the fields. But no-one is allowed to know. We do our best to teach, the people our knowledge goes to will think whatever they may so we have to be careful here at the Priory."

"You can't write? And you have to lie about it?" Hilde said. "Do you pretend a man wrote the hymns you make?"

"It's not lying!" Sister Gobnait said. She pulled a face, and grinned. "I guess its leaving something out."

"I'd love to write one day," Hilde said.

"You'll have to finish learning to read first," Gobnait said, laughing. "Now, start from the first thing yesterday, and tell me everything that happened. Not too fast. And no lying!"

❖

"Stop, stop," Gobnait said, her quill flying and spots of ink marring the page. "I've broken another quill. One moment."

Hilde got up from the hay bale and stretched. Here in the loft the scent of the beast's winter food supply was sweet and heady. Down below she could see Sister Gráinne returning with the hay cart. The mud in the yard was so thick she had to descend from the cart, and help turn the wheels as the donkey pulled.

"Well, that's about it anyway. After I got wet from the roof of Pádraig's and my smock and stockings were full of holes I was lucky Gáethán had some clothes he'd grown out of."

"I see," Gobnait said, her finger tracing the lines of text. "And you're sure they said Bronach was a heretic?"

"Yes. That word exactly. They talked a lot about witch craft, and those lies I told you about. Demons and such," Hilde said. "What does it mean?"

"It's a very bad word Hilde," Sister Gobnait said. "Do you know of Saint Patrick? And Saint Brigid?"

"Yes! Saint Brigid is my favourite!" Hilde enthused. She walked to stand behind Gobnait as she paged through the three sheets of parchment she'd filled with ink.

"They bought the word of God to our fair land. And they were never too hard on the folks here, as long as they came to church on the Sabbath," Gobnait said. "But some in the church, especially in the lands far east from here, don't understand our traditions. They say it's a mortal sin to get anything wrong about how we follow the Lord's teachings."

"Following our old ways is being a hare-attic? A mortal sin? How can you be burned alive just for doing things how we did since forever?" Hilde asked. She sat down and held her head in her hands. "Sister, you told me not to lie. And I need your help. So I'm going to not leave anything out."

"It's heretic. Not hare-attic. So you have something to add? Go on," Sister Gobnait said, picking up her pen again, face grim. From below voices came. Gobnait yelled in response. "Down in a minute!"

"When torches were thrown on the roof, I thought our house was going to burn down," Hilde said in a tense whisper.

"Yes, I have that here," Gobnait said, flipping back a page.

"But it rained! And Mama had put out our Brigid, on the table, with an offering. And Brigid bought rain, to save us. Does that mean Jezabel, and the man in black is right? Mama followed the old ways. Is she a… heretic for that?"

"No". Sister Gobnait wiped her pen with the hem of her tunic, and started putting her things back in the satchel. She stood and leaned over the rail, to call down below. "Just a few moments Sister."

She turned to Hilde and motioned her to her feet, then held one finger to her lips. Hilde turned her ear expectantly, eyes wide.

"In this book, I have put the stories of my Mother. Hilde, she was Abbess of Kildare, and thirty-three years ago King Diarmait came with soldiers, and took her very sorrowfully from her Abbey," Gobnait whispered, her lip trembling. "And he killed one-hundred-and-seventy of her sisters and brothers from the abbey and the town. After he took her, so foul was he in how he used her, that afterward she had a child from him against her will."

"Oh!" Hilde's head was spinning. This was not the valiant King she had lodged in her head, as a child. Not the gallant courtesan and diplomat she had imagined.

"This is the Abbess of Kildare! Sacrilege! Taken bodily from the same Abbey that Saint Brigid founded centuries ago," Gobnait said, her voice choking off in a half sob.

"Yes!! Just a *moment*!" Gobnait called down, in response to more grumbling. A small tribe of sparrows disturbed by the shout flew along the ridge beam of the barn, and out a window.

"He took her? Against her will? And killed the sisters of the abbey? How could he do that?" Hilde stared, slack jawed at the leather-bound volume she held. "And it's in here?"

"Words have power, when written down, Hilde. That's why the men don't want us writing. That's why my mother was attacked by King Diarmait. My mother visited me here years ago in secret to made sure I could write, to pass her power on to me" Gobnait said, a lump in her throat. Her face flushed, and she stared up into the rafters, rather than see Hilde's young face racked with worry.

"Oh my! Sister Gobnait!" Hilde said. "I didn't know!"

"Hilde, power is why your man in black has those two scrolls. If we are to help your mother, we need to make some words of our own. We need to counter what he has written," she waved impatiently at the ladder.

Hilde was in a dream as she climbed down the rungs. The scene in front of Blaine Cottage played in her mind now, framed by the boughs of the pear tree she'd hidden in. There was Bishop Callum Ahearne in his fancy hat holding the proclamations at arms length, haranguing the small crowd.

It was almost as if he was the one casting a spell.

❖

"When we get to the Inn, I want you to do the counting off," Sister Gráinne said. "Only, my eyes are terrible. Can you do that? Do you know your numbers? We use tally marks anyway, but make sure you don't miss any."

Hilde nodded. She accepted the slate Gráinne gave her. She turned and looked back into the cart, careful to avoid capturing Gráinne's searching gaze.

"Was that a yes? Shy one, aren't you," Sister Gráinne said with a chuckle. "Sister Gobnait explained you chimney sweeps don't clean up too easily, and I'll pay no mind to that. But best you keep to loading the goods, and let me deal with the Innkeeper, alright? His name's Thomas O'Brien."

Hilde clasped her hands in front of her in a gesture of thanks. She continued to make a show of counting the goods again. Had Sister Gobnait really just said she'd help? All the revelations raced around Hilde's head like a murder of crows pecking at a flyblown beast.

Writing was the important thing, and Hilde had not a clue how to do it. But if she could get Sister Gobnait to help, maybe others would too. Hilde shook her head and tried to focus on the load as the cart bumped over another rut

Four hogsheads of ale, two bushels of oats and two of barley, and a wooden pail of apples — it all matched the slate and the tally marks. With free labour and lots of land it was no wonder that the Priory was doing so well for itself — this was a small fortune in goods.

The cart slowed as it mounted the top of the curved stone arch over the River Muck, the poor donkey straining at the harness. The Dire Goose Inn lay in front of them, several beasts tied up in front even at this early hour. And standing out the front was Emma O'Brien, throwing a few pails of slops into the grass.

The Innkeeper's wife, picked up her buckets, scowled at the approaching cart, and walking with the pained gait of one much older went inside the Inn.

11

The Dire Goose Inn

It was the grandest building in Duncormac. The road from Carrick and Bannow Bay led through a saddle between Duncormac Hill and Priory Hill and then quickly dipped down to the bridge over the River Muck. In a prime spot there on that saddle, O'Brien's Alehouse stood ready to greet weary travellers and locals alike. Its two guest rooms, in the loft above the barrel room, each had a window that looked down river to the sea. Two windows peeked through the thatch like heavy lidded eyes. Red painted shutters over them closed demurely today as a light breeze pushed rain clouds down from the north. With the open front door it looked a sleepy mop-headed yokel of a building in some ways, but its chimneys with friendly wisps of smoke, marked it almost as grand as a castle.

But as Hilde and Gráinne drew close, the face of the alehouse didn't seem friendly to Hilde. Gráinne jumped down and tied the donkey to the rail outside. The small stables, and storehouse next to the inn had its double-door closed, but it was only for guests horses, and the O'Briens goods. The Inn's white limed walls made it stand out sharply against the green of the crop fields and church yard copse. A stand of lavender and hawthorn covered from the back of the stables all down through the land that sloped from the Inn to the river.

Out the front a red disc of wood as tall as a man swung in the breeze, painted with the fearsome design that gave it the name locals knew it by, the Dire Goose Inn. It's gloomy interior belied the dazzling white of the morning sun on its walls, as low rafters and smoke from the fire gave the barrel room the air of a murky hideout. Hilde hesitated at the cart, then pulled down the first barrel that Sister Gráinne had listed on the slate. No-one looked up as Gráinne stepped through the low doorway, low rumbling conversations continuing by the hearth and near the bar unabated, but Hilde tugged her hat down over her eyes just in case. Rough tables and benches, the floor all blended into grimy-grey with a patina of the ages. The sickly-sweet scent of ale hung in the air stronger than the smell of hay on a threshing day.

"Usual place Thomas?" said Gráinne, stepping up and slapping the counter. She jerked her head at Hilde, who dragged her barrel up to the threshold. As eyes turned to her, Hilde pivoted her back toward them, and bent to her task.

Thomas O'Brien, the Innkeeper and owner stood from a pail of water where he washed a couple of earthenware tankards, and wiped his hands on his apron. He looked for Emma, and saw her back as she disappeared out the rear door with buckets of slops for the pigs.

"Aye," he said. "Leave it there next to the empties, lad. The rest round in the barn."

"I need your mark here, and an accounting," Gráinne said. "It's past due."

Thomas groaned, the two talked, and Gráinne waved a slate, and stabbed a finger on a piece of parchment. She put the parchment on the top of a barrel near the door, and folded her arms as Thomas bartered. Hilde gritted her teeth and hauled on the hogshead for all her worth. The barrel was only half her height, but difficult to grip, and weighed like it was full of rocks. Emma came back in. Hilde's heart jumped in her throat, but Emma only had eyes for the two guests sitting at the back of the room, who looked well heeled.

"Lad! Grab that empty when you go back to the cart!" Gráinne called, she rapped the top of a barrel then pointed at it.

Hilde pulled at her cap, the way she'd seen men do.

Gráinne, nodded, and resumed arguing with Thomas about the worth of his pigs and the quality of the beer, stabbing a finger at tally marks on the slate; and showing him the parchment again.

Not far from the door, as Hilde's eyes adjusted to the gloom, two men carried out their own debate. One sullen, red-eyed and gesturing with imploring palms, the other half-standing his palm on the table, one foot on a three-legged stool, as if trying to leave but importuned by the other.

Emma nodded, and stood coquettishly in front of the other occupants of the room. But they both sat quiet — a small-framed but wiry man, and a bigger man, both dressed in soldiers breeches — likely from out of town. Emma would be pressing them for news. They had the remains of a good breakfast in front of them so must be good payers.

Feigning a need for a rest that wasn't much of a fake in actual fact, Hilde paused with the empty barrel near the door. She listened carefully to the red-eyed man, and realised as she did so, that it was Donegal. She risked a glance toward him. He was angry now, gripping the other mans forearm.

"The storms wrecked our crops Donegal, we don't have work for ye," the other man said. He pulled away, and Hilde saw his face. It was Cormac Bolan. Uncle Donegal was pitiful, drunkenly reaching for Cormac's purse at his belt. Cormac pulled away and straightened his coat, swatting Donegal's hand away.

"That's no way to treat an old soldier!" Donegal drawled.

"Pah! Soldier?" Cormac said, straightening up, and slinging his bags over his shoulder. "No point in paying ye to harvest storm ravaged crops, man! Soldier or not!"

"That's my sword! Mine!! And my helm! I fought for you! This town!" Donegal said, waving at a tarnished shaft of metal on the wall behind Thomas. A cracked leather helm sat on a small shelf next to it. Tallow lamps guttered in either side of the dust and cobweb covered display.

"Ye gave it to Thomas for drink!" Cormac said, shaking his head. "And was it yours to bring back from the war anyway?"

"Will ye speak to him," Donegal drawled, suddenly tearful, pointing a shaking finger at Thomas' back. "Promise him I'll give him silver?"

"I'm leaving now. Have a care for yeself, man." Cormac said.

At the word of Cormac leaving, Hilde quickly grabbed the barrel and dragged it out the door to Gráinne's cart, so fast that her muscles burned with the effort.

❖

Hilde peeked up and down the Main Street, as she rolled the barrel up a plank onto the back of the cart. But no-one was in sight. The bridge and trees along the river hid the view from the rest of town.

It had been a rough few years for farming. Last spring the barley and turnips had gone in as normal, but bad weather in summer had ruined much of those barley crops that livelihoods depended on. Bolan's farm had been particularly hard hit. When the tides were high from summer storms their fields got bad water from sea water coming upstream.

Cormac Bolan slogged off over the bridge and up the road, head hung, hands deep in his pockets, Hilde watching his bobbing head from her vantage point on top of the cart. He turned for a moment, cocked an eye up shading with his hand, perhaps at the rain squalls approaching from the north, then disappeared.

Standing on the back of the cart, Hilde located the next item on the slate, a small hogshead of fortified wine, and began dragging it down the plank. The donkey snickered and brayed at the movement of the shafts with Hilde's weight, and a pair of thrushes flew out from under the eaves of the Dire Goose Inn at the ruckus.

"What are you?" a slurring voice came from behind.

Uncle Donegal. He'd recognise me for sure.

Hilde turned up the collar of the oversize jacket, half covering her face, and caught a strong whiff of goatherd's funk. She dragged the small barrel from the plank on to the flagstones in front of the Inn.

Hilde turned her head, hoping he wasn't looking, to check. Sure enough, propped in the door, swaying slightly stood Dónal Ua Ruairc, soldier, vagabond, and now a wretched drunk.

Uncle Donegal. What's happened to you.

"Skinny, ain't ye. Gimme that barrel," he said. He reached out a hand and made to take a step, took a few but swayed, staggered, and grabbed the wheel of the cart. "I'll help ye."

"Can't." Hilde grated, in a hoarse whisper, trying to hide her voice.

"Help an old soldier, with no work. Just a dram," Donegal said.

Hilde turned her back to him. "Why the bad crops?"

"God!" Donegal said looking at the sky and shaking a fist, one arm now braced around the carts frame. "The tides and the storms."

"Lad! Stop your chatter and get that barrel in here!" Gráinne called. She was wrapping things up with Thomas, who stood with a side of bacon.

"Darling," Donegal said, looking past Hilde. "Ye come in time! This lad took my wine!"

An ice cold hand ran down Hilde's spine. She looked toward the bridge and there over the rise came Jezabel.

❖

"In the stores with that one, lad" Thomas said, pointing to the door out the back, that led to the barrel room. "And mind keeping your filthy paws off my goods. State of you."

Hilde tugged at her cap, turned her soot covered face away and bobbed her head. Her back and arms ached from pulling at the heavy barrels, but she hefted and dragged the small hogshead across the floor with all her might. A shadow fell across the room, as Jezabel appeared in the door. She had Donegal by his hair, and his head twisted down to her waist. A steady whining noise came from him.

"Where's that girl?!" Jezabel screeched, peering into the gloom.

Hilde rushed out the door, to the back of the Inn. Outside, on the left was a haphazard stair, hand-adzed by O'Briens a generation or two previous, that led up to the guest rooms. Hilde moved to the right, dragging the barrel for all she was worth, to get away from judgemental gaze of the innkeep and tugged at the back gate to the stables.

She could hear Thomas mumbling something apologetic. The gate to the stables wouldn't budge, it was stuck. Or there was some trick to it. Hilde stood the barrel up and tugged at the gate with both hands.

"Thomas, out of my way!" Jezabel's voice came screeching from the Inn like a banshee.

"It was Cormac he was talking to, not a girl. Ye can't be going up to the guest rooms. Settle lass," Thomas said, now pushed right up to the back door.

"I know he was talking to Cormac! It's that skinny little demon child I'm looking for! She was just here! Out of my way!"

"Jezabel, ye can't. We've guests! You work here! You know you can't... " Thomas said.

The door to the stables came free, and Hilde dragged the barrel inside. Thomas stepped out the door, and turned to Hilde, rolling his eyes. "On top the other barrels lad, and don't go near the cheeses!"

Thomas turned as Jezabel's hands reached past his shoulder. "Wait, what are ye on about?! Demon?"

"Bewitching child! I'll see ye burn too girl!!" Jezabel screamed. She pushed her way past Thomas, as Hilde peered out the crack of the door to the stables. The woman's face was a mask of rage, red as a beetroot and eyes popping.

"Jezabel!"

Hilde slammed the door, just as a big weight hit its other side. The door opened a crack with the force and Jezabel's face appeared like a rabid wolf at the door.

Hilde's eyes adjusted to the gloom. A collar harness, and tack hung from the wall, straw in the corner for a donkey stall, and against the wattle-and-daub tavern wall stacks of barrels, jars and shelves with cheeses stood.

Another thump against the door, this time it opened wide enough that Jezabel got her shoulder in. Then a retching, gagging and gasping sound.

"Aww, that's disgusting!" Thomas' voice. "Jezabel, ye got to to take him home. There's no girl — he's been with Cormac Bolan the whole time!"

"Thomas! Open this door!" Jezabel screamed. She pulled her leg out of the door. "Has that witch's spawn cast a spell on you? Have ye no eyes in your head?"

There in the corner to the right of the door was a bar. It was covered in dust, clearly not used often. Hilde pushed the gate to as fast as she dared, and slid the bar into place. She leaned on it and waited for her heart to stop thumping in her chest.

Outside noises and conversation between Thomas, Jezabel and a very sorry sounding Donegal continued. Hilde put the barrel on top of the others, and went to the front doors. She looked through the crack. Gráinne was sitting on the jump of the wagon, casting this way and that, with a look like thunder on her face.

Hilde tugged at the front doors of the stable. Barred.

The back gate rattled, and Thomas' pleading along with Jezabel's accusations raised in urgency. "Oi! Open up!"

The shafts of light from the north side of the stables came through gaps in the thatch and lit patches on the floor, but didn't reach the front of the stables. Hilde groped in the darkness along the surface of the doors. The bar had to be here. A big iron spike jutted out.

Found it.

Hilde grabbed it, slid it across and opened the doors.

"Come on, we've more deliveries to do!" Gráinne said, one hand on her hip, the other on the donkey's traces. The cart was already facing down the road. "What on earth were you doing?"

"Drunken patron. Had to lock the stable," Hilde said, making her voice as low as she could.

"Oh my. Skinny ten year old lad dealing with a big old drunk?" Gráinne said, clucking her tongue and shaking her head. "Will have to have words with that Thomas. He should throw 'em out before they have too much. Have ye got my tally marks?"

She shook the reins and walked the donkey cart out of the yard and onto the road.

"Aye, Sister," Hilde said in a hoarse whisper. Hilde passed her the slate, and Gráinne harrumphed in an approving tone.

"Can't have our nectar doing the devils work now, can we?" Gráinne said.

Shouts came from the front door of the Inn.

"Sister Gráinne! They're coming after us!" Hilde said, hands to her mouth. "Hurry!"

Sister Gráinne turned, gave Hilde an odd look, and waved at Thomas as he appeared in the front door. "Bye now! Watch your patrons Thomas!"

"Here!" Thomas called, waving at them, and taking a few steps after the cart. But he waved dismissively and went back to the door. Jezabel appeared, propping up a staggering Donegal. She pushed Thomas' shoulder, and gestured at the cart. She made shooing motions as if he would chase after them. She shouted and waved a fist.

But Thomas shook his head and guided the two of them away from front door. He pointed up the road.

Hilde bent, and rubbed her face, breathing a deep sigh. The cart bumped over the ruts as they headed East along the Carrick road.

"So who are you really, young one?" Gráinne asked. "You're not a boy. And not ten years old either."

Hilde's eyes went wide, and she stared at Gráinne. But the sister, with a matter-of-fact shake of the donkey's traces, geed the beast up and they continued to trundle down the road.

12

The Road to the East

"I should throw you out of this cart right now, for telling lies," the nun said through gritted teeth, eyes flashing and hands tight on the reins of the donkey cart. "Why play such a horrid trick!"

The freshening breeze caught at Hilde's hat as they climbed up the saddle between the peak of Duncormac Hill and Priory Rise and cleared a stand of birch trees that marked off O'Neills and O'Briens pastures. Crows circled and screeched on the far side of Duncormac Hill, over some prize out of view from the town. Perhaps carrion, like the dead goat that lay like a discarded plaything at the side of the road.

A muscle in Gráinne's jaw worked and her eyes became flinty gleams. She reached under the carts seat and slowly pulled out a whip, laying it between her and Hilde. Up in the sky the darkening clouds echoed Hilde's mood, as she pulled up her collar against the breeze, and huffed as she tried to quell the tears that threatened to steal her words. She daren't look at the woman next to her on the carts narrow bench.

Gráinne was firm but a decent and pious woman. Being accused by her stung, and Hilde willed the words to come that would show her innocence. But those words stuck in her craw. Gráinne pulled the brake on the cart and folded her arms, moving away from Hilde on the seat of the cart.

Oh my.

She parted her lips as if to speak but seemed similarly at a loss for words and instead reached for the whip.

"Sister, I... I..." Hilde stuttered. Gráinne shook her head, and blinked.

Then a new distant expression came on her face, and she looked past Hilde, craning her neck. She shaded her eyes, peering in the direction of the crows, past the trees and over the stone wall of the hilltop pastures.

"Your eyes — can you see anyone through the trees?" Gráinne gestured with the handle of the whip. She furrowed her brow.

Hilde screwed her head around, and shaded her eyes, but couldn't see anyone moving where Gráinne indicated. There were a lot of birds circling though.

"No?" Hilde said, turning back to Gráinne. The woman looked confused for a moment then looked at Hilde's face.

"Can I trust anything you say?" Gráinne asked. She gripped the whip and held it up to shake it in front of Hilde. Fury overtook Gráinne's face.

Hilde blanched white, and reached a placating hand out toward Gráinne. Gráinne slapped the whip back on the seat.

"I'm not going to hit you. Yet." she asked. She put her hand on the whip. "Why did Sister Gobnait give you to me? And why did she say we must do this delivery to the Dire Goose first? Hmm? Seems like I have two tricksters having a lend of old half-blind Sister Gráinne."

"It wasn't like that, I promise!" Hilde said. "Sister Gobnait is my teacher. I needed help so I went to her."

"How old are you, girl?" Gráinne asked, leaning forward until she was inches away and peering at Hilde with one eye.

"Thirteen," Hilde said.

"And why shouldn't I take you back to the Priory and chain you up in the scullery?" Gráinne said, gesturing wildly.

"My Mama is Bronach Blaine. She is already chained up in the gaol!" Hilde spluttered.

"Gaol?" Gráinne asked, eyes widening.

"If I'm imprisoned too then *neither* of us have a hope of proving her innocent before the Brehon come," Hilde said. She stuffed her hand in her mouth, and clapped her other hand over it. It'd been much more than she intended to say. Hilde bent over, and braced her fists on the seat of the cart.

"Daughter of a convict? I'm definitely taking you back to the Priory," Gráinne said.

She clucked her tongue and geed up the donkey with a shake of the reins. Just ahead lay the crossroads where the road north to Carlow branched off, and looking both ways Gráinne began bringing the cart around to go back the way they came. She patted the whip. "And don't you think of getting off this cart young lady. I might be half blind but I'm quick with this whip."

"Mama is not a convict! That Bishop - Jezabel got him to say my Mama is a witch, and a hare-attic. But its not true!"

"Bishop? You mean Callum Ahearne?" Gráinne asked, her mood changing. She sat up on her seat, and held the whip with both hands. "What's he doing accusing people in our parish of heresy?"

"That's what Father O'Connor said! He said that man is not a bishop at all," Hilde said, plaintively. She reached a hand tentatively to Gráinne's arm, but thought better of it. "I'm sorry sister, I really am. But some terrible wrongs are being done. There's evil afoot."

The cart gathered speed as it headed down the saddle again. The Dire Goose Inn looked quiet and there was no sign of Jezabel and Donegal. Emma was out the front picking lavender, no doubt to freshen the rooms with. The sky really began to look like rain, with squalls out toward the horizon. Gráinne concentrated on guiding the cart up to the bridge. But at the mention of evil, Gráinne shot a look at Emma.

Emma walked inside the Inn, and shut the door. Gráinne bit her lip, then tore her eyes away from the woman at the front of the Inn and hurriedly corrected the course of the cart. One of its wheels mounted a stone at the edge of the bridge carriageway and they jumped a foot in their seat.

"Sister Gráinne!" Hilde exclaimed. "You know something!"

Gráinne fought to get control of the donkey, which started braying and bucking. Hilde looked back at the Inn. One of the upstairs shutters opened.

There in the window, was a figure. Hilde shaded her eyes.

It was Emma. She looked out at them expressionless as Gráinne guided the cart up the road.

❖

It was some time before Gráinne spoke again. The cart trundled slowly up the Main Street, leaves from the big oak blowing down around them in the stiff breeze to land in the rutted, muddy roadway. Iron striking iron rang out from Fergus Keenan's smithy, and townsfolk moved to the sides of the road to let the cart past. It seemed a pall hung over the town, one that mirrored Gráinne's black mood.

Ahead a few cottages were spaced along the roadside. O'Meara the carpenter, and O'Neill the cloth maker lived opposite the churchyard but Hilde didn't know them beyond a curt greeting at church on the odd Sabbath. Looking at their

113

closed shutters and barred doors now it seemed like the town was preparing itself for an unfriendly time ahead.

"You say she's back there in the gaol we just passed, right now?" Gráinne asked. She looked steadfastly ahead, the donkey plodding slowly with the road being shared.

"Yes, I saw her in there last night," Hilde said. "And Jezabel says she's going to burn! Like it doesn't even matter what the Brehon say!"

"Jezabel is the one who's going to hell. Nothing surer," Gráinne said. She reached into her pocket where she had a few nuts, put one in her mouth and chewed thoughtfully.

"Sister, Jezabel wants me gone too. It's why I'm in disguise," Hilde said. "I know it was wrong to lie."

"Why would Ahearne accuse your mother?" Gráinne asked.

"He said it was… heresy? Sister, I don't understand that. They said she was a witch. Let me tell you what we talked about at the Chief's house," Hilde said. "Yes?"

"Go on," Gráinne said. She waved a fly away.

"Father O'Connor challenged him, the Witch Finder," Hilde said, as she pointed to the church of St Mary, a humble building but clean and white. "But Jezabel stepped in, and the next thing Ahearne was like a conjurer, at Beltane. He said fancy words and showed us parchments," Hilde said.

"Parchments?" Gráinne asked.

"Him in his dandy hat, with these parchments of the things Emma and Alice said," Hilde pulled a face, and waved the slate around, making grandiose gestures.

"Oh, aye. That hat is a bit odd," Gráinne said. A grim smile stole across her face at Hilde's performance. She pulled on the cart's brake. Old man O'Connor crossed the road with his walking stick right in front of the cart. The old man, the priest's elderly father, lived in a tiny house on the Teague farm and at this time of the morning was likely heading to the Alehouse.

"And what did these papers say, to put your Mother in the Gaol?" Gráinne asked, turning and looking back over her shoulder at the round house attached to Padreg's Store.

"Emma was barren from a spell. And Cormac and Teagues farm had lost crops from Mama being a hare-attic. I mean a witch."

"Is this true? This is an outrage for a man of God to suggest such a thing as a witch that casts spells. Maybe he should be the one in the gaol," Gráinne said, half to herself. Hilde cupped a hand to her ear, but Gráinne went on. "Tell me what the Chief said."

"At the Chief's house I told them both — him and his son. The Chief said its up to the Brehon to decide. But then he had to leave. That's when Gáethán said Jezabel wants our land."

"Saints preserve me. What a horrible woman," Gráinne said. She let the brake off and urged the donkey on. She waved to Father O'Connor who appeared at his front door of his manse to meet the older O'Connor and usher him over to the church. "And she'd be having your silver too, Hilde."

"You believe me!? Will you help me?" Hilde said. "Sister Gobnait said she would help. Oh please."

"Hilde, what you've done — lying to the Reverend Mother — you will have to right that wrong. But its true, you *have* been wronged. This lie about Emma..." Gráinne began, then put her knuckle to her lips, and flicked her eyes toward Hilde.

"Lie?" Hilde said, eyes wide.

"I can't say," Gráinne said, she gritted her teeth.

"What is it Sister?" Hilde put her hands on the seat and leaned to within inches of the Sister's face. "What do you know?"

"Hilde, sit down. Let's get you back to St Moragh's. And I have a bone to pick with Gobnait," Gráinne said, as she flicked the reins and urged the donkey up the Priory rise.

❖

Near the river, on the road east from Bannow Bay, the dozen knights laughed and joked, as they dawdled over morning ablutions at the waters edge. Drooping willows dappled the early light as pages attended to their horses. Rows of tents furled by the archers, and bundled into packs, put a wet earthy scent in the air. A portly soldier filled his water skin while another donned his leather breastplates.

Crows and others lower in the pecking order swooped to the fire places now extinguished, diving in for morsels the small army left behind from their leisurely breakfast. The crash of waves in the distance picked up tempo as the winds changed, heavier clouds moving over green canopy.

A cry went up from the western end, the back of the assembling formation. Fingers pointed.

"A rider!" called one of the mounted knights.

Giffard swung up into his saddle, and cantered toward the approaching figure. His face darkened into a scowl as he recognised the man on the horse.

"Giffard, you fine bastard. What a glorious day," Prendergast said, in French, a broad grin cracking his normally impassive features. He gestured with largesse around the camp, the portly soldier shooing away the birds to claim a roasting bird that still had meat. "I see my absence hasn't tested you too sorely."

"FitzStephen will be ready to murder you," Giffard said, resting one wrist on the pommel of his saddle, clutching his reins. He pushed his helm up with a finger, searching

116

Prendergast's face. He rested that hand on the hilt of the sword at his waist. "Perhaps I will just murder you myself."

"Come, come. Is that anyway to treat the man who has just secured the victory at Wexford?" Prendergast said, walking his horse past Giffard, his grin not dimming for a moment. "A lovely day all around."

"What is wrong with you? The weather looks foul!" Giffard pulled his horse around and followed Prendergast. "And from what I hear the walls of the Wexford port will not be simple to breach. We'll need to plunder some villages for supplies in case of a siege."

"There will be no siege. Keep it to yourself, but I have some bishops and a king, all ready to make their moves on my command, my dear Giffard." Prendergast walked slowly past the now rigidly at attention phalanx of archers. He gave them a salute, and slapped his small shield with his sword, as he reached the knights. A broad grin spread across his face. "There will be no blood, and no siege. They will lay down their arms and welcome their new rulers."

"I'm really looking forward to watching FitzStephen carve you up, after he's beaten out of you whatever the damnation it is you've been up to."

"Hah. Even that dour, old block of stone can't darken my mood. Get the men ready. We march to victory! Giffard, old man, we will be kings and princes!"

"Form up! Rear guard take your position!" called Giffard. He grinned at Prendergast and shook his head in wonder. Then he cantered up the line. "Archers! By the right! March on!!"

The two reached the front of the column and two knights fell into position either side, as they headed toward the East.

❖

Etienne d'Courcey had checked FitzStephen's tent, the river and nearby fens. No FitzStephen. It was now finally time to ask those slovenly reprobates from the damn Irishman's army where in the infernal levels of hell his leader was.

He looked up at the horizon and sure enough the wretched sun was a good stretch up into the sky, and the men had been ready since dawn. A flock of crows squawked above, picking at worms that had crawled away from their fire-pits and latrines.

But it was the remnants of the party that King Diarmait mac Murchada had bought that the crows fought over most viciously.

The Irishmen finally arrived on the hill late last night, with the Norman Captain ready to murder them. They'd circled around and come up from the west. FitzStephen was ready to have the archers loose arrows, when the Irish King's man Bran who'd been waiting for their arrival ran over screaming like a man possessed, not to shoot. Then the Irish King and his men produced two whole hogs, and six barrels of wine along with a cartload of bread. The Captain demurred and postponed the Irish Kings murder to the next day.

Of course by the time that lot had been consumed, the Captain and Diarmaid were chums. Now it seemed the plan of setting out to take Ireland by storm with just his own forces, had evaporated from Captain FitzStephen's mind; along with the good Captain himself. What a mess. Nothing for it but to stand

"Fall out! But no leaving the camp!" d'Courcey said, walking his horse past the ranks of archers. "Anyone doing so will be hung as a deserter!"

The men broke ranks and casting querulous looks at each other, began walking back toward the camp.

Yesterday evening FitzStephen had been swearing the men should be up at dawn and ready to fight. Who exactly was unclear. It made no sense at all. The tents were still up, as there'd been no order to strike camp; let alone march.

Then the sound of retching echoed across the slopes of the hill. It rivalled the crashing of the waves in the distance for the depth and gushing richness of it. Searching the fens in the direction of the noises, he saw heads and strode down the hill toward a small group near the marsh's edge.

"Aye man, get that out of ye," said Diarmait mac Murchada, a tall, rangy man in armour fit for a king, holding FitzStephen's head over a log near the damp sedges.

"Oh, what did ye do to me!" FitzStephen bellowed, straightening up and wiping his mouth. The lantern-jawed Norman swayed, then focussed on Bran who stood next to his King. He wound up a roundhouse punch, but the Irish lieutenant stepped out of the way, with a gracious nod of his head.

"Captain! Have a dram of this, hair of the wolf," Bran said. He held up a drinking horn.

Etienne d'Courcy had not come all the way from Cardigan and his nice comfortable manor house to follow a damn crazy man. Nor a drunk.

"That's not a good idea! I think he's had enough!" d'Courcey said, as he drew close to the men.

FitzStephen took two swipes before he managed to seize the horn and downed it. He passed the vessel to d'Courcey upside down and it dribbled down the lieutenant's arm.

"My head! Who beat me!" FitzStephen said. "Big huge man!"

"You were in the marsh sir," said Bran. "No-one out there. Nothing in that direction but sea and river."

"Was going to Wexford. To the fight! Its along there!" FitzStephen said, pointing over the marshes and up the coast. "And that tough bastard blocked my way!"

"Captain FitzStephen, remember me? Your lieutenant? When you are done cavorting with the Irishmen, we have near five-hundred men-at-arms awaiting your orders!" d'Courcey said. "What do I tell them?"

"Tell them I'm having a lie down," FitzStephen snapped.

Diarmait slapped FitzStephen on the back and then turned toward his marquee tent, one that the Irish had had the hide to demand and thus which d'Courcey himself had been forced out of. The whole operation was descending into farce.

Bran bowed graciously to FitzStephen, and doffed his leather helm. "The King of Leinster bids you a good rest, Captain."

"Who was I fighting then!" FitzStephen said to Bran, groping for his sword. His lieutenant put his hand on the hilt.

"Sir, you did a lot of damage to a tree." Bran said, hands demurely behind his back. "Found you passed out near it."

"Dermott, what in God's name d'you Irish put in your wine!" FitzStephen said, oblivious that he was talking to Bran and not mac Murchada. He started toward the camp, with a firmer stride than he'd had before. "Damn powerful stuff."

"Sir what are our orders?" d'Courcey said.

"Shut up man, my head is pounding. Don't you see? We can't do a damn thing until that great ponce Prendergast gets here," FitzStephen said. He strode toward his marquee, and opened the flap.

"What happened to taking on Ireland with your five-hundred?" d'Courcey said.

"And leave that rogue de Prendergast to stab me in the back? No. I want him to my right hand, where I can see him," said FitzStephen.

"He must be here soon. He knows Ireland, I agree we are better off fighting with him," d'Courcey said. This made more sense than FitzStephen's earlier plan, but the paranoia was not a good sign. The lieutenant put out a hand to guide the captain as he wove unsteadily up toward the camp. "We'll be welcoming him and asking why he was delayed very soon when he arrives. I'm sure of it Captain."

"And when he does I'll run him through, nail him to that damn tree," said FitzStephen, nodding to tall spruce behind the camp. "And then I'll command his men myself."

13

The Prioress

The midden pit at the back of the Priory stank with a putrid foulness that bit at Hilde's nostrils so strongly she felt she might succumb and tumble into the pile of fecal matter, food scraps, broken plates and old earthenware bottles never to be seen again. High above circling crows and gulls looked for an opportunity to get at its stinking bounty through the wattles screening it from the sky. Hilde mumbled a prayer for Saint Brigid to call the wind and bring her clean air to breathe.

"Don't stop, you have another barrow to shovel!" Gráinne called. She stood above the pit, near the wall of the dormitory wing of the Priory. She pushed a wooden barrow with her foot, and gestured to the back of the pit. The breeze changed direction and gave a short reprieve of fresher air for Hilde, but Gráinne winced and held her nose, and looked for a spot on the rim of the midden away from the worst of the smell.

"This is the last of it, Gráinne! Will you talk to me now?" Sister Gobnait said, approaching Gráinne around the corner of the dormitory, carrying two large wooden pails of broken earthenware bottles and jars.

"Girl, put your back into it!" Gráinne called, turning away from Gobnait. Hilde bit her tongue and continued emptying the barrow with the flimsy wooden spade and spreading the material over the mound in the midden. Perhaps it was lucky she had not eaten. Her stomach alternately growled and then gagged.

"Look Gráinne, I'm sorry. But you have to listen," Gobnait said, setting the buckets down. She lowered her voice, and looked around to confirm they were alone. She produced a small sheaf of parchments to Gráinne, and swatted them with the back of her hand. "Hilde is being pursued by this Jezabel woman, her drunk of an Uncle, and this Bishop. She is only thirteen years old. I have her whole story here."

"You shall not bear false witness Gobnait! We have to go the Reverend Mother," Gráinne said. She studiously avoided looking at Gobnait, motioning to Hilde who'd emptied the barrow and now started back up the steep path out of the pit. "How can I listen to liars?"

"Talk about liars! There is something very off about this Bishop. How did he arrive out of the blue and set himself up at the Priory? What does he think he is doing? This is not his diocese anyway!" Gobnait said. "I followed him while you were away, and the way he looks at the nuns scares me."

Hilde rubbed her aching arms, and wiped her hands on her borrowed pants. Gráinne pushed the barrow again with her foot and nodded at it.

"That lot too," she said to Gobnait. The nun rolled her eyes and poured the broken and useless earthenware on top of the barrow load of waste.

Hilde stared at the pile. It was only late morning but she already felt like falling in bed and sleeping. Some of the bottles and jars were from ale, beer and fortified wine. She blinked and tried to remember how Gráinne had told her to dispose of all the mess. One or two were medicine bottles, with their distinctive long necks, likely from the Priory's hospice. There was a specific spot at the back of the midden for these.

"Hilde, focus! Please tell Gráinne. How did Father Stephen cast our Bishop?" Gobnait asked, sighing and gesturing with her book.

"I told her already! Sister Gobnait, she *knows* how awful the Bishop is, and what a *rat* Jezabel is," Hilde said. She dropped the handles of her barrow, and picked up the new one. She looked pointedly at Gráinne. "But Gráinne, you know something *more*! You know about *Emma*!"

"Gráinne! What is it!" Gobnait asked.

An anguished look passed over Gráinne's face. She chewed her lip for a moment, then turned scuffed her foot on the path, then without warning sped off.

Gobnait stared slack jawed at Hilde. Hilde gestured at the her retreating figure, but Gobnait shrugged.

Soon Gráinne was past the fruit trees and out of sight.

❖

In the common room, a dozen nuns sat in near silence, eating gruel, and pulling pieces of bread from a few loaves in the centre of the large wooden tables. Hilde walked in timidly, and only just stopped herself from curtseying, as she did on entry to her bible study school.

In a corner a pair of nuns stood over a large pot, and Hilde got a helping, thanking them with a touch of her boys cap that she wore. As well as her grubby soot stained face, she now reeked of the midden pit so both nuns squinted and waved her away, her disguise still unchallenged.

124

Tucked in a corner on a long bench a familiar figure gnawed on a piece of loaf, and chased a few remains around the bottom of her bowl with a spoon.

"Sister Gráinne," Hilde said, sliding in beside her. Gráinne looked up, and her eyes flashed, a panicked look forming around her eyes as she realised she was cornered. "Please listen."

"It'll be midday not long! I have chores to do!" Gráinne said.

"We don't have long sister. You must tell me!" Hilde said. "Whose secrets are you keeping?"

"I've already told the Reverend Mother about you!" Gráinne said, gripping the rim of her bowl, and shifting in her seat.

"I'll take my punishment. You preach against false witness though! Why are you allowing these sinners to spread their lies!" Hilde raised her voice, and the others in the common room turned to stare.

"Keep your voice down!" Gráinne said. An anguished look came over her face. "Emma was with child. And I think it were the Bishops."

"What!" Hilde said, louder than she'd intended. She bumped her bowl and gruel spilled on the table. Gráinne gripped her wrist, and brought her face close to Hilde's.

"Quiet! Don't you see how dangerous this is!" she said, a hoarse whisper in Hildes ear. "I helped her! She begged me, and begged me. Lord save me, but I helped her in the end."

"Emma never had a child! She said she was barren! That my Mama cursed her with a spell to be so." Hilde said. Her face was red now, her hand on her forehead, mouth open in disbelief.

"Emma and I grew up together. That's how we know each other. She handles all the business at the Dire Goose. When I deliver there we talk. Then the Bishop arrived to stay at the Inn. Emma came to me, ready to kill herself. She was late."

"With child?" Hilde said.

"She knew it was Ahearne's. He forced himself on her. Do you know what I mean girl?" Gráinne said.

Hilde's eyes were wide as saucers. She nodded.

"So you helped her?" Hilde said.

"Indrechtach, the physic. His stuff is near poison, but Emma said she didn't care if she died. I went to his cart," Gráinne said. She released Hilde's wrist, and looked up at the ceiling. Her eyes filled with tears. "She was sick for a couple of days. And I told Thomas it was woman's problems. I visited every time I made deliveries."

"Oh Gráinne! Its right what you did," Hilde said, holding the nun's hand.

"Don't touch me! You have no idea. You're a child," Gráinne said. She clasped her hands to her face. "I had a child in me when I came here first. The Reverend Mother disappeared it. The nuns have always been there, when a child is not wanted."

Hilde stared into Gráinne's eyes. They filled with liquid, brimming, and the flickering lights of the tallow lamps reflected in them. There was much the nun was not talking of. Hilde could see the shapes of dark thoughts moving behind her eyes.

"Do you think those children get adopted? Our new Sisters join a life as brides of the lord and never see their child again? How could that work - children showing up wanting to see their Mama at the convent? You learned here Hilde. Ever wonder where all the children of the nuns went?"

"No, sister. I..." Hilde stammered.

"But we never talk of it. Thou shalt not kill. But we do it in secret anyway. It's an evil thing Hilde. Its our shame."

"Gráinne. I'm sorry," Hilde said. "But what of my Mama! She didn't curse anyone to be barren! You cannot let that lie stay in those writings that the man in black made."

"There's nothing I can do about that. You know the truth now of what happened to Emma, but I cannot speak of it. And the Reverend Mother won't hear of it either. Ye'll have to find your own path there."

Gráinne shooed Hilde out of the way, and she slid along the bench.

"What happened to Emma?" Hilde asked. She got up but put a hand on Gráinne's shoulder.

"Miscarriage," Gráinne said, scowling at Hilde, as she reached to pick up her bowl.

"Saints be. Was there a burial?" Hilde asked.

"No," Gráinne said. Hilde followed her, stopping at the door to the common room. "Unless you count the midden pit as such. Now leave me alone."

❖

Standing at the south door of the common room, hand on the latch, Hilde felt she'd forgotten something. Something big. After Gráinne stormed off, even though her voice had been low, the intensity of her expression had drawn stares from the others in he room. Gráinne had said so much, and it swirled around in Hilde's head.

Back at the table at the end the two nuns served gruel to a couple of nuns who'd just arrived. Thankfully, because they'd been stealing glances in Hilde's direction since Gráinne left. Hilde had taken their bowls back to their table, hat pulled down over her face and nodded her thanks, hoping that was why they'd been eyeing her, a rough, sooty-faced boy leaving dirty plates on the table. But there was something else. Something Gráinne had said.

Hilde took one last look around the room, and opened the door to leave.

"Stop there please. Young lady," came a booming voice.

A nun stood in the doorway opposite, nearly filling the frame. She held a cane in her hand.

Hilde shook, and her hands went cold. Gráinne had said she'd *told the Reverend Mother*, the Prioress. That was the thought she'd been trying to recall. The old lady she'd met seemed kindly, but all of the stone walls around them now stood or fell on her order, her word was law here.

And now the game was up. As a dead person walking, Hilde slowly crossed the room. Next to the statuesque nun who'd summoned her was Sister Gobnait. So small was she in the nuns shadow, Hilde only noticed her now. She looked white as a sheet, all the air sucked from her lungs.

Walking the corridors to the Reverend Mother's office it seemed a dream, or a nightmare. One cross hallway they passed a group of nuns turned to watch, in front was Gráinne, a scowl on her face.

Now the blood was pounding in Hilde's ears. She was too frozen to cry, throat swollen with rigour, and the tall nun's hand on her arm squeezing her so hard her sore muscles spasmed in pain. But the end was in sight. The open door stood ahead of them.

And outside of it, stood the man in black.

❖

In the Reverend Mother's office a small window opened on to the internal cloister. It was sheltered enough that it didn't need shutters to keep the rain out, and delicate ironwork screened it from the outside. The light from it dappled Hilde's face, as she sat on a chair and daubed at her skin with a wet cloth that the Reverend Mother had given her.

The small birdlike woman's gimlet eyes warily regarded the witch finder, as he bloviated about his religious theories. Hilde could not understand a word of what he was saying, so much of it in latin, so many fancy words. But she could see from the Reverend Mother's posture, and her hands that she did not believe a word of what he was saying.

Hilde finished the cleaning, folded the cloth and handed it to the large nun who'd escorted her to the musty book-lined office of the An Mháthair-Uachtarán.

Several times, Ahearne returned to her desk, and stabbed a finger on a parchment that lay there. One that looked like a letter, with a seal upon it. Finally the Bishop - if he was such - finished, and looked at Prioress Aíbinn with his hands at his side. He flicked a glance at Hilde.

He moved toward Hilde and went to grab her by the shoulder. But the Reverend Mother made an almost impercetible movement with her hand, and the statuesque nun chose that moment to place the cloth on the desk, cutting Ahearne off. He went to move around behind her, and she moved back, demurely placing her hands inside the sleeves of her tunic.

Ahearne's face reddened and he opened his mouth, raising his hand.

"Thank you Bishop. That will be all," the Prioress said. She grabbed the much taller man by the back of his raised arm, and steered him toward the door.

"What! You can't... Ah!" Ahearne cut off whatever he wanted to say, with a cry of pain. He stepped forward to release her iron grip, missing the stone threshold and stumbled forward into the hallway.

"We will let you know all our findings," the Prioress said with a smile. And as his expression grew more outraged, the tall nun closed the door. The Prioress moved so the light

illuminated Hilde's face, and bent toward her peering and
squinting. "Now, let's see. Who do we have here?"

14

Grasping at Straws

"What is to be your punishment, that's the question," the Reverend Mother said. She smiled and somehow was more terrifying for it. Although she was a head shorter than the Bishop, her iron grip and inexorable manner had overpowered and unmanned him completely. The spectacle of the Bishop being bustled out of her office by the Prioress' quiet ferocity still played out in Hilde's imagination.

The tall nun who stood in the corner like an ancient standing stone, had initially struck Hilde as an enforcer of sorts but after witnessing the Prioress handle the Bishop it seemed she didn't need one. The old lady's bright black eyes darted around, lighting on a pile of manuscripts on her desk, then glancing out the window at some passing residents, and then arced up to the vaulted ceiling to thoughts of the Lord. Or of other matters she was not leaving to divine providence, but taking into her own capable hands.

"Don't for a moment imagine you're going to escape judgement, young lady. Your lies would make a sixty year old sinner blush. The cheek of you."

The Reverend Mother crossed to the door and peered out through the crack. A quick glance and then she held it open for the taller nun, and jerked her head to one side. The statuesque lady crossed the room and left the two of them in silence. A crow cawed out in the courtyard.

The Prioress had an ear cocked toward the hallway. Her hand steepled, she placed her fingertips on one leather-bound pile of parchments on her desk.

"I have Gobnait's version. Now I want yours," the Prioress said. She blinked at Hilde. There was a subtle change in the Prioress' manner that made Hilde stop, feeling for the right frame for her words. It seemed that appealing for mercy was a hopeless cause, and opening her heart, given it was entirely unclear what was going on in the Prioress' mind might actually be the best chance at saving her Mama.

"Your grace, Reverend Mother. You said punishment? Jezabel said I should burn. For just being born to my Mama," Hilde said. She leaned forward in her chair, and took her cap off. She tucked her hair behind her ears, and clasped her hands in front of her. "That man? I don't think he is a real man of God. He is trying to get people to follow him. He is not pious. The things he says about witches and demons? Its not right."

"Start from the beginning child," Prioress Aíbinn said. She sat in a chair next to Hilde with her arms folded. "Maybe you'll be condemned when the judgement comes. But the Lord sees all. Leave nothing out."

Hilde closed her eyes for a moment and then speaking fast, recounted everything that had happened since she woke up yesterday morning in Blaine Cottage. At the mention of Father Stephen and his conversation with Ahearne under the pear tree, the Prioress shook her head slowly and a grim smile stole across her face. She gestured for more, and Hilde described the Bishop's performance in detail before going on to describe the bundling of her Mama up in a sack, the night in the Chief's barn, and her morning working for the Priory.

"Good lord," the Prioress mumbled. "So at this age you're thrown out of your home? You'll have to sharpen up your tale girl, to impress me. I was eleven when I was taken from my home. It's do or die in this world."

Hilde opened her mouth but found herself just staring. The meeting with Gráinne in the common room flooded into her minds eye, the woman backing into the corner as Hilde pressed her. As determined to relate the truth as she was, these dire secrets caught in her throat. Should she keep talking and expose Gráinne's secrets?

But the Prioress' eyes misted, and her knuckles whitened as she gripped the arms of her chair. The older lady pressed her lips firmly together and a muscle in her jaw worked. It seemed she'd heard enough and whatever her course, it was set.

"Do or die," the Reverend Mother said.

The older lady stood up. Her eyes drifted to the door.

Hilde rubbed her face and put her cap back on. She wrapped her arms around herself against the cold. They'd been talking for some time and old stone of the cloisters sucked every last bit of warmth. Hilde sat up straight. The older lady crossed to the desk, and looked down at the parchment with the seal. The one the Bishop had jabbed with a finger. She picked it up, and took it to the window, holding it in the light.

"Do you read?" the Prioress asked.

"Yes, your grace. A little," Hilde replied.

"What do you make of this," the older lady said. She moved the parchment back and forth trying to find an angle where it was illuminated most. Hilde stood, and peered over her shoulder.

"There's something funny with it," Hilde said. "It doesn't look right. Like one person made it. And another changed it?"

Aíbinn nodded. She opened the door and called out. She turned back and put a hand on Hilde's shoulder, as if measuring her. Hilde's sum, the strength of her back, the trueness of her spirit all seemed catalogued in the Reverend Mother's book of ages.

"You have done some work, some penance already. And you will face much more. But in secret you will help us unseat this false bishop. You will speak of none of this," Aíbinn said, guiding her to the door. "You stay here. Do you understand young lady? If anyone asks, you refer them to me."

Hilde nodded. Everything was a blur. It seemed that at any moment the Reverend Mother would sentence her to the stocks. But for now at least, what she knew about the Bishop seemed to have bought a reprieve.

The tall nun arrived.

"Find Gráinne and tell her to get this scallywag doing more chores. Gobnait is to ensure she gets another meal."

The taller nun nodded, and took Hilde by the shoulder.

The Prioress stood with her hand on the door. "And she stays in the barn tonight. In irons."

Hilde spun around. The door to the Prioress' rooms slammed shut.

❖

In the yard Gobnait worked on liming the walls of chapel. Another nun armed as Gobnait was with a small besom on a stick worked on a patch of the wall a stones throw away. It'd

134

been a few moments since the tall nun left Hilde here and there'd no acknowledgement of her presence.

"This is because of you, you know!" Gobnait said, not looking at Hilde, as she crossed to a wooden pail to drop the old, heavily caked broom into the lime-wash. She stretched and massaged her hands.

"I know! I've never worked so hard either!" Hilde said. "I mean, I worked before. Of course. You know Gráinne said I had a silver spoon? But I muck the pigs and work our farm every day. It's just that I never had to clean a latrine before."

"Why would I care about that! Just because I taught you, you think you can come and upend everything?" said Gobnait. "I'm as good as any monk!! I should be working on books! I have so much to do."

"But we don't have to!" Hilde said, a conspiratorial gleam in her eye.

"Bah," Gobnait said, looking to the section of wall, still to be painted.

"Sister, there is more happening. Reverend Mother said I had to see you and stay in irons," Hilde said. She gestured at the walls of the Priory, evoking the Prioress and her tall silent assistant in one sweep. "But I was left here with my hands free."

"You are a scamp," Gobnait said. "Do you think this place would be a house of God, a place for worship if everyone did as they pleased?"

A pair of monks, pates shaved into a tonsure, walked along the path below the towering white walls of the chapel and smiled briefly before resuming their learned conversation. Hilde and Gobnait paused their conversation, and bobbed their heads in greeting, as the men passed.

"I feel like we are supposed to do what is *needed*. Not just what we are told," Hilde said. "I know there's work to be done. But somethings happening Sister Gobnait. I feel it."

"Oh, you feel it?" Gobnait said. She held out the handle of a brush to Hilde.

"I prayed to Saint Brigid when I was being brought here. The Abbey of Kildare? You told me, it was sacked? Things are happening Sister Gobnait, as big as that. Our village is in the path of it. The Chief, I saw him readying for I know not what."

"What rot Hilde," Gobnait said. But she stopped, and listened. The brush dripped on the ground.

"We are caught up in it Sister. There is a part for us. The Lord has work for both of us," Hilde insisted.

"Hilde," Gobnait began. She lowered the brush.

"You need to be picking up your pen Sister," Hilde said. "Your pages? The Prioress *read* them, and I think she plans to unseat the Bishop with them. We cannot stop now."

"Lord save me. Why did I ever listen to you child," Gobnait said.

"Reverend Mother said you were supposed to make sure I stayed in the Priory," Hilde took Gobnait by the arm. "She means that you must write the rest of my story."

"Story?" Gobnait shrugged, shaking herself free.

"It is as you said, Sister. Words have power. I don't know how yet, but we need to get what Grainne knows into your story. And then it may be enough to free my Mama," Hilde said. Her eyes were wide and she gestured to the countryside and Blackstair Mountains beyond the Priory as though they were the very liberty at stake.

"I've already given it to Prioress Aíbinn," Gobnait said. She shook her head.

"The Prioress wants you to finish it Sister. I know it. I think with it you can win the Reverend Mother's favour. Maybe put away your brush for good."

"Alright. But its noon, and I'm hungry. I will find something to eat, and then to the barn," Gobnait said.

"I will find Gráinne. Then meet you there," Hilde said. She rushed off toward the dormitory wing.

The other nun came back to her pail of limewash and dipped her brush. She scowled at Hilde and Gobnait, then returned to the unpainted stretch of wall.

Gobnait laughed. She stacked her bucket next to the one the other nun had just left, and hurried off toward the common room.

❖

The donkey cart stood next to a fence in the yard outside the barn, and the beast was happily chewing on a feedbag when Hilde intercepted Gráinne. Hilde dragged Gráinne toward the loft.

In response to Gráinne's protestations, Hilde repeatedly invoked the name of the Reverend Mother and referred to her time in the Prioress' office as though she and the Prioress were old acquaintances.

"I still have the afternoon's deliveries to do! Why are you not in irons, or at least painting walls?" Gráinne protested.

Hilde responded by holding a finger to her lips. "Sorry. Reverend Mother swore me to secrecy."

"You and Reverend Mother have secrets? Rubbish. Child, are you mad?" Gráinne said.

"There's no time. Gobnait is here in the loft," Hilde said.

"Some of us have work!" Gráinne said. But she stopped resisting Hilde's urging. Curiosity apparently winning out over her exasperation.

Raised eyebrows greeted them from the other nuns working in the barn, as they climbed the ladder. Hilde ignored them, and bolted to the top. Gráinne begrudgingly followed Hilde up the rungs.

"It'll make sense, I promise," Hilde said, talking at the top of Gráinne's head, and steadying the ladder with a hand. Gobnait looked up, an exasperated look on her face. She leafed through her materials.

"Hilde!" Gobnait said. "I don't have my other pages. This is going to be tricky. I'll have to just start writing from a fresh page."

Hilde led the bewildered Gráinne to the area of loft behind a pair of hay bales, tied up tight with twine, that Gobnait was using as a makeshift desk. Her quills, ink and parchment lay on the bed of straw. As Gráinne approached, Gobnait picked up one of her quills and wrote the date at the top of the page.

"Can we start with what you told me Gráinne?" Hilde asked brightly. But Gráinne's face was twisted into a mask of anger, getting redder as she stood staring at them both.

"To hell with you! Damnable child! Is that what you dragged me up here for? What I told you, that was in the deepest, most heartfelt confidence. One woman to another. D'you think I'm going to have it committed to writing for anyone in the world to see?"

"Gráinne, I'm sorry! But its the truth! It can set my Mama free!" Hilde sat on a hay bale and tried to look small. Gráinne backed away. "Gobnait can write words that will counter the parchments that the Bishop has. You don't want him to win, do you?"

"How dare you put this on me! I helped Emma. Now I'm to forever be punished for my good deeds?" Gráinne turned, and nearly tripped as she groped for the ladder, tears in her eyes. "How dare you! I trusted you!"

"Gráinne!" said Gobnait. "What do you mean you helped Emma!"

But there was no stopping the solidly framed woman. Hilde tried to put a hand on her arm, but Gráinne shook it off. Hilde took a few steps after her, but Gráinne was already on the ladder.

"Get away from me!" Gráinne said.

"Gráinne!" Hilde said, taking another step.

"Ah!" Gráinne screamed. She missed a rung and tumbled to the floor of the barn. Hilde started to the top of the ladder. "Ah!! No, get away! Stay away from me!"

"Leave her Hilde," said Gobnait quietly. Hilde turned to the other nun, sitting quietly shaking her head slowly, quill in hand. "Leave her."

Hilde turned her anguished face to see Gráinne's back as she headed quickly toward the Priory, hobbling slightly, her arms ramrod straight and hands in fists. She kicked the door to the barn, and it slammed shut behind her.

"Hilde, what did she mean, she helped Emma?" asked Gobnait.

"My Lord, what have I done," Hilde said, not hearing Gobnait. She walked back to where Gobnait sat, in a daze. But the nun gripped her quill and the nib was flying. Several lines had already appeared on the parchment. Hilde looked on in amazement at the words flowing. "This is all true about the Bishops evil, but how can we prove it now?"

"The Lord God favours those who help themselves Hilde, and I have an idea, but first tell me exactly what Gráinne told you. I know its a secret, but we don't need to bring her into it if my idea works," said Gobnait.

Hilde related the story. Gobnait tut-tutted when she got to the part about how she baled Gráinne up in the common room. When she talked of how the Reverend Mother had sworn her to secrecy, Gobnait gasped, then her eyes gleamed as she urged Hilde on, writing down every last detail.

15

Dormitory of Secrets

A zephyr carried scents from the orchards and herbariums nearby through the large doors of the barn. The subtle breeze and fragrance thankfully dissipated some of the funk of donkey hide, old straw and stale feed troughs. Hilde stood and filled her lungs of the fresher air.

The noises of the working day filtered up to the loft more strongly now that both Gráinne and Gobnait were gone. The impressions in the hay bales that Gobnait had used as an impromptu desk conjured an image of the scholar's garret that the bookish nun wished for. A smile crept across Hilde's face as she imagined a young Gobnait at the skirts of her mother, the Abbess of Kildare dreaming of the books, ink and parchments that may one day be hers.

I have a plan Gobnait had said. A very unclear, but promising statement.

Hopefully it meant that Gobnait was minded again to help Hilde toward getting her Mama released from the witch finder's accusations.

Hilde stood at the top of the ladder, one hand on the top rung, as thoughts raced through her mind. The bed that the Reverend Mother had offered her in the barn lay behind her, not yet slept in, the mattress of straw still folded against the wall. It was only early that morning that she'd arrived and so much had happened, she'd not had a chance to even rest, let alone sleep.

Hilde pulled a piece of charcoal from her bag, taken from the Chief's fire and began applying her disguise again. There was no sense in leaving anything here. Who knows where she'd sleep tonight?

Time was racing past. When she and Gráinne walked over to meet Gobnait the sun was high enough already despite the clouds that noon threatened. Bronach might still be languishing in the round room attached to the General Store that stood as Duncormac's only gaol.

Surely they must feed her? It made no sense to have even a show trial with the main attraction starved to death just as the Brehon arrived to judge her.

It was all very nice that Gobnait had her plan, but the hints she'd dropped before leaving pointed more to research than action.

Let's see how well they all have agreed on their story shall we?

What exactly Gobnait meant by that mysterious statement remained locked up inside the studious nun's head. In stark contrast, the imminent threat posed by the Reverend Mother's crystal clear direction hung over Hilde's head like a hangman's noose.

I lied, it's true. Luiseach is not my sister, but I tried to say Sister Gobnait and Sister Luiseach are my teachers! Honestly!

Hilde's cheeks reddened at the thought of the mistruths that had tumbled from her mouth, when she'd first appeared at the Prioress' office this morning, her face blackened and disguised as a lad. The consequence of having a secret and wearing a disguise can be that you tell a mistruth with just an inflection. She'd never meant to be caught in such a tangled web.

Hilde sat on a bale of straw, pulled the cap onto her head, and began tucking all her curls up underneath it. She wished for the small silver mirror that hung on the wall in her home. Blaine Cottage, its solid walls seeming to be so safe one moment, only to be a trap the next. Bronach's warnings to run, to avoid Jezabel and the clutches of her enablers by heading to the Chief's had been apt advice.

But right now Hilde's heart ached for the familiar walls of her place in the loft above their old hearth, the dry familiar scent of the clean thatch overhead. The pigs would be unfed! And the hens!

Hilde's fists tightened, and her jaw set. Her mother, their home, their farm, all which now lay abandoned. For liars and cheats to take. Hilde's eyes narrowed and a lump rose in her throat, rage competing with grief to overtake her.

It is so unfair that so many can keep secrets and tell lies, and go about behind a mask, such as Emma and Gráinne; such as the Bishop even. What was that letter that the Reverend Mother had shown her? Why had she asked Hilde to use her sharp young eyes to examine it in the light?

I'm thirteen and must not make up stories, but for adults it is fine?

Rage began to win out.

If there was any justice in the world, the Bishop's lies would catch him and trip him up. And if Hilde could take the unspoken challenge that the Reverend Mother had given her, meet it, and shine a light into the man in black's well of secrets then maybe that fate would come for him earlier rather than later.

Hilde slung her bag over her shoulder and put on Gáethán's outsized coat. She kicked at the straw to cover the spots of ink, and foot steps that the three of them had left, then started down the ladder.

❖

Hilde kept to the shadows as she threaded her way back through the hallways and skirted the cloisters of the Priory. Following the outside wall past the large chapel, the sun shone brightly on the limed walls and it seemed the eye of the Lord God himself looked down on her. A dark dot, a lie in her borrowed boys clothing, face blackened, against the white.

The small dormitory that the monks and visiting men occupied must be along here. Hilde had seen two monks leaving it when they limed the walls. Ahead a tree shaded a row of columns that opened on to the north facing pastures. That had to be it. As if in answer an older man, his monks robe tatty at the hem, and a younger man carrying two wooden pails turned the corner ahead and entered the loggia.

Hilde hurried, and joined behind them. Soon they were in a small common room, a third the size of the one on the other side of Priory. Hilde's heart leapt at the sight of a tall man, shrouded at first in shadow until her eyes adjusted to the gloom. It was not the Bishop. The tall man was a balding monk, chatting to another in the corner.

Gráinne had bemoaned the Bishop's habit of hanging about where he ought not. Loitering in the women's common room, and bothering the younger nuns. Hopefully that meant she would not run into him here, as she put into effect the next step in her risky half-baked plan.

"Excuse me young man, are you lost?" the old man croaked.

Hunched over and leather-skinned the old monk peered up at Hilde, his coal black eyes twinkling. He smiled at Hilde, his rheumy eyes blinking, and put one hand on a table to steady himself. The younger monk at his side, shifted from one foot to the other, as the weight of the buckets took their toll. He bent and placed them on the ground, showing the tonsure shaved into his otherwise lush locks already tanned from working in the fields.

Hilde smiled back, playing for time. The younger monk groaned, and a made an odd gargling sound. As he stood again, he turned his face. Hilde leapt back, startled. His face was disfigured by a deep fissure down through his nose and top lip. He made another noise, and the old man put his hand on the other's shoulder.

"Oh it's alright Brother Reynold. I'll carry a bucket when we clean the latrine. But my back, you know that its broke," the old monk said. He leaned toward Hilde, who pulled her cap down further. The old man whispered to her. "Don't worry young man, poor Reynold has a cleft palate."

The old man gestured with his fingers to his own face, and made a sorrowful expression. Hilde nodded.

"But he is a good boy. He can't speak, and I can't see. Haha! Together we make a fine pair," the old man said. "Now. What are ye here for?"

"I'm looking for Bishop Ahearne, on an errand for the Reverend Mother. Or if he's not here I can leave a message at his door?" Hilde said, whispering back to hide her voice. She patted her jacket pocket, as though something of import lay there.

"Hah. Bishop? If that man is a bishop, then I'm a plum pudding," said the man, straightening up with difficulty.

He laughed at his own turn of phrase and then coughed, clutching his ribs as the rattling spasms of some dread malady of the lungs gripped him. He pointed a bony finger down a short hallway that led from the common rooms south-east corner. Eyes turned to the group from around the room, as the old monk held up a placating palm. Hilde took her chance before the old man asked her more questions, and ran toward the hallway.

❖

The wooden handle was worn smooth, and cold to the touch under Hilde's hand. There was nothing stopping her from stepping inside, but her gut tightened in knots as she fought with the accusing harpies in her mind.

This was what the Reverend Mother was asking her to do, surely. It was why she'd said that Hilde should be clapped in irons, and yet was roaming free. As a free agent, an accused outsider, already proven at getting herself into places she ought not go, the Prioress had seen how useful Hilde could be — but taking this last step of breaking the sanction of the closed door and entering the Bishop's room chilled her inside. A shiver overtook Hilde, shaking her from head to foot.

Voices raised from the common room at the other end of the short corridor. Only two rooms lay down the passage and one was empty, no bedding, clearly unoccupied. This was the Bishop's door. Steps sounded on the stone of passage, echoing as two approached.

She raised her knuckle as if to knock, make a pretence of looking for the Bishop. But then found herself barging in. Blood thundered in her ears. Hilde shut the door behind herself.

Smaller than the Prioress' office the room also had a window onto the cloisters. It must be a room set aside for visiting luminaries, or high office holders as it had a sconce for a lamp, and a small desk of oak. A wooden chest stood in one corner, vestments and cloaks spilling out from the shelves that filled the inside.

145

Along the sill of the window dozens of bottles and jugs were stacked. Below the window, piles of books and papers stacked to knee height. Stacked along the wall wooden boxes and sacks gave the rooms contents the bulk of a house lot, or certainly more than a monkish life would have awarded.

Was this a man who'd had his circumstances uprooted? Why would he at his age have his worldly possessions stacked inside a monkish cell, even one as nice as this?

A chair by the low single bed held a bowl and jug of water, and a tiny silver mirror. There was no way to put anything under the bed as its sides were timber panels that went to the floor. The bed itself was covered in clothes. Nothing about the room told of a man of rigour and piety. It was the den of a vagabond.

A stack of books sat next to the chair. The words were obscure, but an illuminated capital on the passage opened on top showed Augustine, whom Gobnait had taught Hilde about, and in the black letters of a monk's tidy hand the latin word for "sin" appeared in large letters.

Hilde put her hand to her beating heart. Out in the corridor the sounds of the footsteps approached. They'd either find her or not. No point in stopping now.

The desks contents were piled high, ink wells, and parchments in a wanton disarray. A quill that had been left in an ink pot to go dry lay abandoned. Other quills lay used and not cleaned. Gobnait would have cried at the mess.

The desk had a lid. Gripping it carefully with two hands, one holding the piles of parchments upon it in place, Hilde lifted it and looked inside. There was a stick of red wax, a candle and flint, and a woodcut seal. She braced the desk lid against her front and grabbed the woodcut.

Hilde moved to the window, and held the wooden rod up to the light. The seal was elaborate, a crest and flourishes. But oddly the detail was indistinct. Arran Blaine had made silverwork seals, often a signet ring, or cloak-pin that was worn. But this wooden rod had been carved with a design that would only be rendered faithfully in metal. So strange. Hilde pocketed it and a frisson of illicit delight lit up her face.

Voices raised in the hallway got louder. The sounds of Brother Reynold's guttural expressions and then another man's low rumble. The Bishop.

There was no way out. And nowhere to hide.

"Well I must go on," the witch finder said, his low voice unmistakeable outside the door. The door creaked slightly.

All across the windowsill the bottles and jugs emptied of the strong liquor stood as a tally of the mans dissipation. The window's shutters were open a crack. Hilde stared at the glimpse of the noon day light over the cloister, as the doom of the rooms owner approached behind her.

"You must allow us to clean up Bishop! Or do it yourself, as our other guests do!" The old man's voice. "We have strict instructions from the Reverend Mother."

Not all the bottles in front of Hilde had held strong liquor. A different scent caught Hilde's attention. That one had a longer neck, and a different design stamped into the fired pottery.

The sickle and skull logo of Indretach. This was poison, nothing surer.

Hilde snatched up the bottle. This could be it!

What if Gráinne had obtained it for Emma, and the Bishop had been preying on her, he had forced her to take it. Crammed the poison down her throat.

"What on earth! Stop there!" The voice was Ahearne's.

Hilde put a foot on the pile of books, and launched herself toward the window. She forced open the shutters, and scrambled over the sill, bottles and jugs flying. No use in looking back.

Slithering through the gap of the window with all her might, Hilde kicked as her oversize coat caught on the frame.

"Stop thief!" the voice of the Bishop bellowed behind her.

A hand came down on her ankle. Hilde kicked hard, and found purchase. She rolled forward out the window, and fell onto the unforgiving ground.

❖

The wind knocked out of her lungs, Hilde lay gasping on the hard flagstones of the cloisters. Stars revolved around, everywhere, and the legs that were beneath her felt disconnected from her body. And yet urgency screamed in her head to get up. Move.

From inside the dormitory buildings the sounds of sandals slapping against stonework, and raised voices came. Indignant, outrage, and doors slamming. The eastern side of the priory was an roofed colonnade that opened to the hills beyond, but that way was blocked by a gaggle of nuns. The chapel gave onto the front of the Priory and Hilde headed straight for it.

That fluttering in Hilde's stomach wasn't fear any more. It was a fierce, joyous anger. And it gave her feet flight. Hilde's knees were rubbery but she walked smartly — trying to avoid raising the nuns curiosity — across the quadrangle of grass, toward the chapel.

"Hie! Stop thief!! Stop him! There he is!" came a bellowing demand. The Bishop accosting some slow moving monk. "Get out of my way, fool!"

Hilde ran for the chapels double doors, clutching her prizes in her pockets as they started to bounce with her stride. The wooden rod, and the stoneware jug both heavy and awkward, but the rod punishingly so, jabbing her thigh as she picked up her pace. Hilde pulled out the rod, and put her hand on the pocket with the jug. Hilde's jacket flailed behind her and her hat flew off as she ran full speed toward the doors that led into the chapel.

The doors creaked. A tall figure appeared there, filling the door frame, silhouetted by the candles of the chapel behind her. She put her hands out wide. It was the Reverend Mother's assistant nun Maida, face implacable.

"Stop him! He's taken things from me!! Thief!!" Ahearne bellowed, his voice rasping as he lumbered to a half-run.

On some wild instinct now, Hilde changed direction, running along the north interior wall of the cloister. And there, just above head height a window opened. The Reverend Mother peered out with a huge grin on her face. She clapped her hands in glee like a young girl at the Beltane fair. Her eyes gleamed as she drank in the spectacle of the dubious Bishop, his robes flying as he flapped like a wounded jackdaw across the quadrangle.

Hilde had no plan now, if she ever did. But now the fates had intervened. She stood on her tip toes and handed the rod to the Prioress, the end with the seal facing her. The older woman's eyebrows shot up and she held the rounded design into the daylight. Even with her bad eyes, it was clear the shape was a match for the one on the letter she'd shown to Hilde.

The Prioress' grin hardened into a knowing smile.

A hand descended on to Hilde's shoulder.

"It's alright Maida, gently now," said the Reverend Mother out the window. Hilde turned and the tall woman who had her hand on Hilde's shoulder nodded.

"Gracious me," Ahearne puffed as he slowed to a walk, and approached. "You've caught the lad! I'll be having my things back now."

Ahearne grabbed at Hilde, and caught her coat sleeve. He pulled, and she ducked, moving to hide behind Maida. The coat came off and the jug flew from the pocket to land on the grass nearby. Ahearne rushed to grab it, flailing with Hilde's coat at first and then tossing it aside as he reached for the earthenware vessel. As he saw what it was, a thunderous scowl crossed his face, and he shot a poisonous stare back at Hilde, Maida and the Reverend Mother.

A group of curious nuns arrived in a half-circle, craning their necks to see the cause of the shouting. The older monk and his younger apprentice Brother Reynold with the cleft palate walked over from the mens wing. Brother Reynold carried Hilde's hat.

"Brother Walwyn, our visitor has inspected the grounds and an old discarded medicine bottle. Please take it and dispose of it safely would you?" the Reverend Mother said, from her vantage point at the window. Her voice although not raised filled the space with authority.

Ahearne spluttered, as he looked around. The old bent-over monk approached with a wooden pail full of old leaves and rags from his cleaning duties. He extended his hand for the earthenware vessel that the Bishop clutched to his chest. The dark look on the face of the old monk made it apparent he'd been the one rudely shoved aside.

"And Bishop, after you give that flask to Brother Walwyn" the Prioress said, pausing with gravity as she tapped the wooden rod against her bony knuckles, "please join me in my office immediately. We have something important to discuss."

"But this thief," the Bishop began. Hesitantly, he handed the empty flask to the monk. He blinked as he saw Hilde without her coat and hat, her long hair spilling down her shoulders. The normally confident man in black cast around looking for the 'boy' who'd stolen from him, then his lips parted as the truth dawned on his face.

"There you are young lady!" Gobnait said, running up to the group, a bright expression on her face. She put her hand on Hilde's shoulder. Brother Reynold passed Gobnait the hat, now covered in grass.

"Sister Luiseach's family are not to be wandering the grounds, Sister Gobnait. Please escort her out the front would you?" the Prioress said, pushing back from the window sill. She addressed the man in black. "I will hear your story about some lad that you say has been up to no good in the grounds. But after our business. Come, now please."

"I've been wronged! Stolen from!" the Bishop said, his teeth gritted, and eyes narrowing at the realisation it was a mere girl who'd given him the slip.

Gobnait took Hilde's shoulder and hustled her to the archway through the colonnade that led out of the cloisters. Hilde glanced back, to the knot of people in the quadrangle who'd erupted into a babble of voices. Speculative gasps and glances flew as more nuns arrived demanding to know the gossip.

"*Now*, Bishop, if you will," the Prioress' thunderous voice boomed from her window, amplified by some trick of the cloisters shape. And with that she slammed the shutters closed. Maida approached the Bishop and gestured toward the Chapel door that would lead to the Reverend Mother's office.

And as Hilde and Gobnait turned to exit the priory Brother Walwyn, with his wooden pail of garbage and all the evidence Hilde needed went in the opposite direction.

16

Saint Mary's Church

The stiff breeze had a blown apart the banks of grey, and the summer sun glared down accusingly over a tall stack of puffy white cloud.

Gobnait had not stopped clucking her tongue at Hilde since they left the Priory, but a sly smile crept across her face that gave the lie to her disapproval. She handed Hilde her hat with a final shake of her head.

In the town below them, down the gentle slope of the priory hill willows shaded the main road, but here Hilde and Gobnait stood by the Priory bridge with no shade, and no shelter from the blustery summer winds. Hilde pulled her hat down hard over her hair, as the wind threatened to pick it off and whipped at their coats. Gobnait put her hand to her coif as a gust caught it.

"Are you sure seeing Father Stephen is a good idea?" Gobnait asked.

"He always was friendly to my Father. Mama didn't take me to church much. But I'm sure he'll help. He does not like that Bishop at all. And he knows a lot. I hope he will. I have to see him," Hilde said. She shaded her eyes against the glare of the sky.

"I'll have to leave you here, Hilde," Gobnait said, raising her voice. She put her hand on Hilde's arm. "But listen carefully. You must say nothing about the Bishop. Nothing, do you hear?"

"What do you mean?" Hilde asked, leaning close to be sure she heard Gobnait. It seemed wrong to be protecting this false churchman.

"And nothing about what Gráinne confided in you either!"

Hilde half laughed, disbelief written on her face. As much as she respected Gobnait as a teacher, she struggled to make sense of this. If only she hadn't lost the flask with Indretach's stamp that she'd found in the Bishop's chamber. It would be hard evidence to show Father Stephen.

"And he just gets away with it?" Hilde blurted out the question.

"That is not for you to decide. And Gráinne is really upset and scared. Hilde, I'm surprised at you. It will be dealt with, but you must let the Priory handle this," Gobnait said. Her eyes narrowed, and then she looked down.

"I never meant to corner her like that. Honestly! She has to understand. My Mama's life is on the line! What she knows is so important!" Hilde said. She gestured back toward the Priory, where in Hilde's imagination she now saw the older nun downcast in her cell.

"You're just a girl! You have no idea Hilde!" Gobnait shook her head slowly.

Gobnait drew her woollen habit across herself, and folded her arms. She turned back toward the rickety wooden bridge over the Muck River, toward the Priory, toward her duties. Hilde spluttered a protest but it was lost to the winds, and the nun had already turned, not seeing her beseeching hands.

Hilde put her fists by her side, shook them and clenched her jaw.

The clumping of the nun boots diminished as she crossed the mud spattered timbers of the Priory bridge. The dark silhouette of the Priory's walls as the sun moved overhead toward the west seemed to absorb the figure of Gobnait as she crested the bridge and disappeared.

It seemed Hilde's hopes of absolving her Mama of the crazy accusations of Emma, Alice and the rest shrank to a dot as well. Gobnait being upset with her was a bad turn, her writing seemed the best chance of countering the doubtful Bishop's fistful of parchments. How did she let the clay vessel with its potent symbol slip from her hands?

Hilde turned her feet down the mild slope from Priory hill toward the town.

❖

Cooler and quieter down among the riverside trees of Duncormac's shallow valley, Hilde paused a moment.

Saint Mary's church steeple raised its modest wooden spire against the noonday sky. The front door was open, and a heavy set man loitered on the front steps. There was no sign of Father Stephen. From Hilde's best memory a small door opened on to a ladder at the back but it was for the seldom used wooden bell-tower, and likely latched from inside.

There has to be a way in. Hilde checked her disguise and walked on.

The graveyard's stone memorials stuck up from yellowed grass and trampled mud, like the teeth of an old sage, testaments to centuries of lives and deaths. A seldom used lane ran between the graveyard and the main church building, ruts left by the last time a casket arrived here. The lane petered out as it ran down through lupin and hawthorn to the willows that marked the rivers edge below.

Angry starlings flew in a small formation swooping and banking between the trees, eventually settling on the eaves of the church after bickering for a time.

Hilde slowed her pace as she drew close and the man continued to hang his head. The clay plastered timbers of the church's walls towered higher as the ground fell away toward the river at the back, the only public door being the large one in front that the burly chap occupied. Hilde touched her face. The grime of the charcoal still in place, Hilde took a deep breath and straightened her boys tunic, and pulled her cap down over her curls.

Tiernan O'Rourke looked up as Hilde approached, and moved to block the door. He wiped a rheumy eye, and blinked at Hilde. He'd always smiled at her in a weird way during the yearly village fair, and nodded at her and her father when they went to church. But the years had not been kind to him, and now he was more guarded. Hilde shivered despite the warm day.

"Confession?" he asked, leering into the bright sky.

Hilde shook her head.

"Well, lad, I'm next to see Father Stephen," Tiernan said, as he glanced back into the church, and then folded his arms. He peered at Hilde, turning his head as if his good eye might discern more. "You'll have to wait. Whatever it is ye seek."

Hilde's face reddened, under her grimy patina. She tugged on the front of her cap and ducked her head, in acknowledgement. She marched quickly away from the stairs, and around the side of the church toward the vestry. It lay in the same modest building as Father Stephen's rooms, apart from and behind the church proper.

It seemed O'Rourke's eyes were boring into the back of her head as she walked. And with no plan but to escape his interest Hilde went straight toward the vestry's steps.

❖

An older man's wheezing laugh came from inside, and halted Hilde in her stride. The door to the vestry stood open, and while a row of pegs with coats and a line of boots on the floor blocked her view she saw the legs of a man spread out at his ease. A shrill cackle followed, from another, then the faint sounds of movement. Two pairs of feet sounded on the floor, and a woman's voice. Hilde moved down the slope a little, behind a stand of hawthorn.

The room was supposed to be for Gods work, meetings of the group that kept up the yards, gravestones and buildings; for prayers and bible study. Adults doing what was needed for the good of the village. But it sounded unless Hilde's ears were mistaken like the clink of stoneware cups. And it was only just past midday.

Hilde looked up the slope toward the road and the front of the church, but it seemed as though O'Rourke had gone, perhaps to confess his sins, and no-one watched on. The back of the vestry, behind the coats, had a narrow privy. It was a tiny room with a simple board that sloped to the outdoors and a bucket to provide for the modesty of church folks instead of going outdoors under a tree as Hilde was used to back at her cottage.

"Ha ha!!" the older man's voice echoed out the door again. The man's legs moved and he unsteadily got to his feet. "Another!!"

As though a staff between her shoulder blades propelled her forward, Hilde found herself marching to the door and straight up the entry stair, going to her tip-toes as she mounted the wooden steps. The sounds of the man's unsteady gait echoed through the building. It was built on a pad of stone, and like Blaine Cottage had timbers where the floor went over a cellar, and now Hilde heard the unmistakeable sound of a trapdoor opening.

Pushing silently past the coats Hilde moved into the privy, and pulled the door closed.

"Who's there?" A reedy, slurring voice came from the next door room. "Are ye of this world?!"

Hilde's heart jumped into her throat. Daring not a breath, she listened for all she was worth.

"I conjure ye!" That was Alice. Her incoherent voice rang out again. Father Stephen's wife, yet she was far from being a pillar of the moral rectitude expected of the pious. Such a flair for the dramatic.

"Speak if ye be fae or infernal!!" She sounded drunk.

Hilde held the privy door closed by the rope handle inside. Feet moved but no-one walked. A room or so away, the sounds filtered of earthenware vessels clinking in a cellar.

Alice had spoken briefly that day but Hilde would never forget her fractured voice joining the accusations when the witch finder came to take her mother. Hilde's fingers tightened about the door handle, knuckles white, rage beating out fear, her breath coming hot in her nostrils. The privy stunk, and flies buzzed over the board at the back, but all served to sharpen Hilde's purpose hardening it to a bright edge.

Hilde leaned her head against the thin partition wall of the privy. Alice cleared her throat. This was getting her no closer to Father Stephen, but perhaps something else might come of it.

"What're ye yelling about Alice!? I found 'em!" came a voice. The steps were uneven, and quieter on the flagstones of the vestry. "My son is getting low on his ales, I had to dig right in the back to find these!"

That had to be the priest's elderly father. It seems he got a spring in his step when it came to drinking.

"It were the demons again Fearghal," said Alice, in her plaintive tone. "They won't let me alone."

Fearghal. He'd crossed the road earlier that day a frail old man, but when it came to drinking and gossip he was unstoppable by the looks.

"Ah, my poor wee lass. Get that into yer," he said. A clunk, then a slurping sound, burps and Alice's cackle. "Now which demon or faerie has been bothering you?"

"Two of them little ones with the wings. Black coats, red tunic, terrible little faces like a sinner," Alice said. Slurping sounds followed. "Ugly enough to crack a silver plate Fearghal," Alice said.

Hilde gritted her teeth and stifled a cough. The acrid biting ammoniac stench of the midden pit outside rose up into the privy as the wind changed, and Hilde's eyes watered.

"Up there?" Fearghal's voice. Hilde wished she could see them as well as hear.

"They've wings, yer daft old man!" Alice screeched. "Come to drag a god fearing woman to hell!"

"Oh, la di dah! God fearing! Ha ha ha!!" Fearghal said. "Least ways it wasn't the big demon with the horns and hoofs."

"Nay, don't torment a lady. That one, without a word of a lie, he had some evil intent for me. My virtue, I could feel it slipping from me. I'm never going up by Duncormac Hill again! Long's I live! His brown eyes, leading me to sin, Fearghal!"

"Wait until God's good man *Father* Stephen finds out we've drunk half his cellar! Then there'll be hell for both of us! Drink up my lady!"

More slurping. The both laughed uproariously.

Good lord. It was the starlings she was talking about. It had to be. Red tunics? She was quite mad.

❖

Back out in the noonday sun, and well away from the vestry Hilde gulped in fresh air, fresh, astringent and sweet smelling from the blossom on Pádraig's fruit trees. She rubbed her eyes as she climbed the slope to the front of the church, and realised too late that she had smeared her grubby disguise.

Threads of Alice and Fearghal's delirious conversation refused to resolve into sense, and they were still in full swing when she snuck out of the privy. Alice retold fragments of her story about the demon she'd seen, and admiration she felt toward the Bishop for his blessings after her traumatic supernatural encounter.

But one moment the Bishop was a young beau she'd danced with around the Beltane many moons ago, and then next he was confused with her husband, Father Stephen. Her mind skated from one figment to the next, but all with a turn of phrase that belonged to a minstrel not a madwoman. How did Father Stephen bear having her as a wife?

Hilde climbed the steps of the church and there was no sign of Tiernan. There was only one space for confession, and it was a simple curtain in the corner. As Hilde's eyes adjusted to the light filtering through the high unshuttered windows, a pair of starlings flew across the space between the rafters, and then disappeared into the thatch. The thick walls, wood plastered with clay, deadened the sounds of the outside world and Hilde found herself stilling her breath in respect for the sanctity of the space.

"Can I help you, young man?" The voice of Father Stephen came from behind, to her left. "No more confessions today, I'm sorry. I'm busy."

"Father Stephen, its me. Hilde Blaine," Hilde said, taking off her cap and holding her hands in front of her. She turned.

Father Stephen carried his vestments over his arm, and a bible in his hand. His eyes flicked toward the right, to the vestry. To where his father and his wife sat in their cups. How can a man of the cloth manage such a corrupting force as demon drink while shepherding his flock to Gods grace. What a burden he must bear.

The expression on his face when Alice had spoken up, made sense now. She'd spoken as Jezabel and the Bishop prompted her on the morning Bronach was taken. There must've been drink promised. That look, it was on the priest's face again. For a brief moment her turned to Hilde and he summoned a half smile.

"Not now child," His eyes were far away. He went to move past her, but then slowed. "And what happened to your face?"

"I'm hoping people won't know I am the witch's daughter," Hilde said. She dabbed at the grime on her skin with the back of her hand.

Father Stephen stopped in his tracks and gasped. He blinked and put a hand on the back of a pew.

"Hilde..." the priests eyes darted toward the vestry again. Clearly the task of tearing them away from his dwindling wine supply was not one he relished.

"Father, you do know your Da and your wife are drinking your wine? And talking about demons?" Hilde said. "I don't think they are going anywhere. I just need a little of your time."

"Save me," the priest's eyes clouded over. He put his fingers to the bridge of his nose, then slowly he sat down. He sagged as if the air had been let from him like a pie crust sagging. He patted the pew next to him. "Shut the door and sit Hilde."

"I found out some things Father. And I really hope it means you can help me," Hilde said, as she pushed the door of the church to. She lifted the latch into place. "Please you have to help my Mama."

"You always were a bright girl Hilde. Now look at you. So tall, and clever to boot," Father Stephen said, glancing back at her over his shoulder then shaking his head in wonder. "Where did you get the clothes? Gáethán?"

Hilde sat down on the pew a few feet from him. "Yes. Gáethán. I asked the Chief for help, like Mama asked me to. But Chief Fiach said its a church matter. It can't be up to the Church, Father! Jezabel is saying my Mama will burn for a witch!"

"It's got nothing to do with me, Hilde. The Brehon will come. Monday they are due. That's only the day after tomorrow," Father Stephen said. He clucked his tongue and patted her on the shoulder. "I'm sure they will throw out the whole thing and your mother will be free."

"Its that Bishop! Jezabel and him are working together. She says my Mama will burn! Will, not might!" Hilde said.

At the word *Bishop*, the priest snorted. He slapped the bible in his lap.

"I went to the Priory, and spoke to my teacher. Sister Gobnait. I found out that the man in black, the witch finder is not what he says. And I heard what you said. I was hiding in the pear tree."

"Pear tree?" the priest's mouth hung open.

"At our home. I heard everything. You know something Father," Hilde said.

"Hilde, I have to be very careful. Saint Mary's is under threat from him. He's looking for a diocese. You won't know what that means but…"

"He is a fake Father! Reverend Mother has a letter, but its not from the Archbishop at all! The man in black made it up himself," Hilde blurted.

A conversation ensued where the priest continually found himself alternately in wonder at Hilde's exploits and in despair at the circumstances that surrounded them. When Hilde got to the story about her mad dash across the cloisters he burst out laughing.

Hilde paused when she reached the point of her time as a fly on the wall in the vestry. She bit her lip and looked down.

"So you came looking for me, and overheard Alice and my father talking?" the question was more a statement. Father Stephen got to his feet and paced. He shot a dark look at Hilde, and his eyes were moist. "I am at a loss. What has she been doing with the Bishop?"

17

The Portents of War

Lieutenant Etienne d'Courcey had had just about enough of this damn soggy Irish hillside. And the sortie they made on Irish soil just kept getting longer and longer between landing and the glory they'd been promised. He eyed the approaching blonde-haired lordling walking up the dale with a baleful stare. It was bad enough the idiot Irish King was late to his own party. Now their own compatriots wander about the countryside like lost goats. That was definitely the Flemish man. At last. Now how to deal with him.

He came from Wales, where he'd been a marcher lord. But allegiance to King Henry had not bought de Prendergast here. That man came for gold, and land. Power. Whatever he had been, this de Prendergast is a mercenary. Certainly the shadowy Giffard — the Frenchman who followed him — was mercenary through and through.

"Tell Captain FitzStephen that de Prendergast is here," the lieutenant said to the page standing hesitantly to the side of the knot of fighting men beside d'Courcey. As d'Courcey peered harder it seemed the man in the distance was carrying something, dragging some burden. "Sergeant, go with him and make sure the Captain is here. On the double!"

As a lieutenant he fitted his Norman uniform well enough, but d'Courcey had an aquiline nose and thin lips that gave him the air of a mortician, more than a fighter. Some of the men did not like the fact that he was FitzStephen's right hand man, but this animus suited d'Courcey just fine. FitzStephen's young page nodded to d'Courcey's request and headed off followed by the barrel-chested, bald-headed sergeant in charge of FitzStephen's personal guard.

FitzStephen was right about de Prendergast's appearance. His blonde hair and fair looks were unusual. But the Captain was wrong about his measure. But there was steel under his skin. He'd not blinked when FitzStephen ordered the man from Thomond murdered in cold blood for no other reason than to send a message. Clearly FitzStephen assumed Strongbow had made him the leader — him the older, more experienced man, who spoke a smattering of Irish. But de Prendergast by his posture as he swaggered up the grassy pastures toward their tents, he had never accepted that mandate.

He needed watching. The Flemish soldier was like ice, like the cold in the far north. A slow killer, that had its hands around your throat before you woke to its presence. But the mettle of him was more than just cruelty, it was methodical and it was economic.

The Flemish mercenary stepped over the cow dung and tussocks of the hillside without looking down, his eye surveying the camp and the skyline as though on a Sunday walk but with a morbid coolness. He took in the two camps of men — de Prendergast's own, and FitzStephen's. It was a gaze the like of which d'Courcey had seen in those who'd manned the walls in the long hours of a deathly siege. As if sure that death would certainly come and be a welcome friend when it did.

And now de Prendergast walked with that cool fatalistic air, although he dragged two men, by their collars, one in each hand. The sorry figures bumped their feet over clods, across the grass in front of the men. The troops stood in front of their tents, one or two with food in their hands, others in the midst of sharpening weapons, or not fully dressed, mouths agape. Their eyes were on the whip looped over de Prendergast's shoulder, blood still dripping from it.

Not a big man, the Flemish man's muscles were whipcord and his frame iron. He looked nowhere in particular but took in every man in that line. Giffard who walked behind him, clothed in his characteristic black and green, seemed insubstantial compared to the mercenary captain. De Prendergast in a his captains uniform, a study of casual authority, drew all the eyes on that hillside toward himself. His own seventy men, and FitzStephen's near four-hundred men in the adjacent formation all looked.

"Giffard, get someone to clean these two up," de Prendergast said, loudly enough for all to hear. He waved vaguely at the line of men. "I want them fighting fit tomorrow."

"Oui," Giffard responded.

With the manner of a spy more than a knight, Giffard moved as though he were de Prendergast's shadow, oily and slick. He paused to check briefly for signs of life in the two. Then he motioned to a sergeant at the front of FitzStephen's men arms, a solid man with a scar down his forehead, and no neck to speak of.

What the hell were de Prendergast and his man Giffard playing at. The lieutenant stepped forward. The Flemish man must answer to his captain, he was the leader of the mission despite this display of one-upmanship, ordering about FitzStephen's men.

"Sir, Captain FitzStephen has asked for you," d'Courcey shouted, his voice echoing across the camp. "He is waiting over the hill."

A rumble of voices ran through the ranks of the men. From FitzStephen's camp a few voices were raised, and steel against steel echoed. The sergeant moved forward.

"These are *your* archers! *I'm* to get them ready to fight!" the sergeant said, looking from Giffard to de Prendergast. He bent and prodded the supine body of the closest soldier, eliciting a pitiful groan. The other injured man tried to roll onto his front, to relieve the pain of his bloodied shoulders.

It was a good question. Is de Prendergast and his few men really needed?

Etienne d'Courcey shaded his eyes, peering, trying to discern some intent, some emotion in the mercenary captains face. The man kept walking as though on a Sunday stroll.

The Irish were a bunch of wretched drunks, and judging by MacMurrough's men the garrison at Wexford would be an afternoons work for just Captain FitzStephen's men alone. They didn't need this spiteful de Prendergast and his paltry seventy men who seemed about to revolt against him anyway. Spies and schemes were not part of a battle fairly joined.

"I'm talking to you, de Prendergast!" the Sergeant said, his beady porcine eyes flaring as he moved his hand to his sword hilt.

Crack!!

"Merde!" The sergeants arm jerked as Prendergast's whip snaked around his wrist in the blink of an eye. A stream of insults bit off, as he stumbled into the Irish peat.

Is this how the mercenaries treated their men? Etienne d'Courcey shook his head in disbelief. In Cardigan there was a nice garden and his plans for a small grapevine waiting. This was madness, the man was an unpredictable snake.

"Captain Prendergast," d'Courcey began. "Captain FitzStephen was very clear. You've been away. He…"

"Not now d'Courcey," de Prendergast snapped, not taking his eyes off the sergeant in front of him, as he walked toward the prone figure looping his whip back into coils. "Sergeant, you seem a decent man. You want to get home, gold in your pocket, yes?"

The man struggled to get to his feet again. But de Prendergast yanked the whip, the sergeants hand went from under him, and the man's face dropped back into the wet grass. Nearby the two abject figures who de Prendergast had dropped stirred. One younger fellow, tall and thin, in uniform pants, his shirt hanging from his waist crawled toward the line of tents, toward his compatriots.

"Sir, forgive me," the sergeant removed the whip from his wrist revealing a deepening red welt. He pointed to d'Courcey. "The Lieutenant ordered that no-one leave the camp. But our lads, under the leadership of your good self, had no such order."

"The very good Lieutenant here is in charge of the camp. Is he not?" de Prendergast said gesturing behind himself at d'Courcey, who shivered and stepped back, eyeing the whip.

"Sir, we didn't know where you were!" the Sergeant said. "I mean, we thought something could have happened."

"What did Lieutenant d'Courcey say Giffard? Hanging? For anyone leaving the camp? Especially ones who wore civilian clothes and went out looking for local taverns," de Prendergast stood over the Sergeant now. The man was half again the bulk of de Prendergast, but his face was white as a sheet and he quivered at the Captain's feet. "We are all Normans! We fight together! Obey orders! Honour our uniform. Our purpose! No-one likes a deserter Sergeant!"

Using the coiled whip to mock a noose, de Prendergast looked around the ranks of his men, nodding, and laughing at his own joke. Nervous laughter passed through the ranks. The men nodded with him.

"I offered these men of mine choices. They *chose* this," de Prendergast said, gesturing to the two men he'd dropped. "They *chose* the lash. I'm a fair man, sergeant. They chose well, I think."

A tear born of pain rolled from the sergeant's eye, and he gritted his teeth, biting back a cry. Blood trickled from the welt on his wrist.

"So get these men back in uniform. Yes?"

"Aye, sir," the sergeant said. He stood, brushed grass off his uniform and massaged his wrist.

"And talk to your troops. There will be no more men taking their chatter out of the camp, yes?"

❖

Down by the salty marshes of the River Muck delta, old logs and banks of silt spread in a curve, as the bight of the watercourse wound west in a hook turn to follow the coastline. Over the long spit that lay on the other side of the river bank sea birds patrolled in the salt-laden moist grey sky and the sound of shallow breakers joined their raucous calls. A few last traces of morning mist lurked in the shadows of the marsh reeds.

"Here man, tell me. Don't spare me the gory truth!" FitzStephen shouted. He grasped a brace of wild rabbit, their guts spilling from their bodies in a red curtain of gore.

On a log, the animals entrails spread, skewered on a branch at one end, stretching to the bodies butchered beasts in FitzStephen's grasp at the other. Two knives covered in blood stuck in the wood.

The other man, clad in a woollen cloak that seemed to come from the mists, kneeled at the log his face daubed with ochre and blood. He held up the flat of a placating hand to the burly Norman Captain. With his other hand he waved a jagged bone, white with teeth and twisted it over the grisly tableau. From a pouch he drew powder and tossed it to the winds, some of it settling in places on the rabbits intestines.

The kneeling man pointed without turning, and FitzStephen dutifully laid the animals carcasses at the side. FitzStephen leaned over the display, his eyes wide.

"What do you see!" FitzStephen demanded.

"Ye've been betrayed!" the mans voice cracked and shrieked. His broken face and toothless jaw raised to harsh light of the early afternoon sun seeming translucent, as he turned to FitzStephen. "A fighter has gone to be a lover! Laid with the enemy!"

"Never mind the traitor! Do I win! Do I become a king?!" FitzStephen shouted. He grabbed the mans skinny shoulder, digging his fingers through the woollen cloak into the mans flesh.

"Sire! Sire! You will be king," the man said. Spittle gathered on his lip.

FitzStephen grinned, and he reached for the knives yanking them free. He wiped the smaller one on the grass, then on his tunic.

"The walls you lay siege to will open before you," the man said, pointing to a shape in the pile of guts that lay before them.

FitzStephen nodded then walked a few steps away up a slope, his bloody hands dripping. He pulled a handful of leaves from a lupin bush, and squelched momentarily in a patch of boggy ground. He wiped much of the blood from his hands with the damp leaves.

"Captain!" A voice raised over the distant din of the surf and cries of the sea birds. "Captain FitzStephen!"

Two figures approached over the top of the mound that FitzStephen and the seer sheltered behind.

"Told you to leave us alone!" FitzStephen yelled. He massaged the back of his still throbbing head, and blinked into the harsh light at the crest of the mound.

"It's de Prendergast sir. He's back." One of the figures waved FitzStephen hither. When FitzStephen didn't move they started down the hill.

Above the men, framed against a patch of blue sky between two towering banks of clouds a murder of crows turned through a slow arc, then flapped off growing smaller as they flew into the west.

"Sire, look," the old man said pointing to the birds. He stood, mimed the shape of their flock with his hands, and made an expansive gesture. He clasped his hands, beseeching.

"The fates are with you. Your enemies will fall," the man jingled a purse. He held out his hand. "A kind and generous king you will become."

"Which enemies?" FitzStephen turned. Small knife still in his hand, he grabbed the seer and shook his frail shoulders. The old man in his green shawl seemed one with the scrubby bushes and trees. The briar crown on the mans head shook and fell to the ground. "Who are they?"

The seer held up a finger, begging a moment to speak. FitzStephen released him, and cleaned the other of his knives — a long fighting blade — on the grass. He dried it on his tunic and replaced it in his boot. The man gave a shaky smile, tentatively held out his hand.

"Some silver, sire," the old seer said with a lop-sided grin. And he insistently held out his hand again. "For more about your enemies. And to make it sure, to keep our secrets."

FitzStephen slashed the mans throat.

The old man's frail body fell to the ground. At that moment a gust of cold sea wind moved the mists which covered his corpse, to become one with the dock, arrow-grass and sedges.

"Captain FitzStephen. He's waiting for you," one of the soldiers said, walking down from the mound. A third man approached over the hill. It was d'Courcey.

You'll keep our secrets now.

As the men walked down to join him, FitzStephen moved in front of the old man's body.

"What is this?" d'Courcey said, arriving and looking at the mess.

"Good fortune, d'Courcey," FitzStephen said. He jutted his chin out, and stroked his stubble, as he looked into the west. The crows in flight were small black ink marks against the white cloudy sky now. He pointed with the small knife to the portentous flight. "Good fortune, for us."

"What about de Prendergast?" asked d'Courcey, jerking a thumb over his shoulder back toward the camp. "You said you wanted words with him."

"He is a dead man," FitzStephen said. He slapped d'Courcey on the back.

He puzzled for a moment that the seer's blood did not mark the blade. But he sheathed his knife at his belt, walked back toward the camp.

❖

"Sergeant, what do you think he's going to do with Captain Prendergast?" the page asked in a whisper, nodding at the silhouette of FitzStephen trudging ahead of them.

"Don't know," the barrel-chested man gruffly said. He slapped his hand down on his sword hilt. "Nothing, I hope."

"Sergeant, you must promise me you won't speak of what you saw, not to the men," said the young page, catching at the cuff of the bald-headed man as they strode a few pages behind FitzStephen, around the base of the rise, toward the camp.

"Well, I *saw* nothing," the Sergeant said.

The page smiled nervously.

"And that's a problem," the Sergeant pushed with a finger and cocked his helm to expose the quizzical grimace on his face. He squinted at the page. "Aye?"

"I know, I know," the page said. "A five year hell in a Welsh prison. With nothing but shadows and ghosts for company. But look! He weathered it, a great man! You should see Cardigan Sergeant."

"I don't care about his castle back home. I care if he can lead. There was *nothing*, son. No-one," the Sergeant said, then he jerked his thumb behind. "Back there. Him and his ghosts."

"He is a great man. I don't know if we can be sure of what you say you saw," the page said.

"Yon 'great man', he was talking to thin air! A great old conversation with no-one at all!" the Sergeant said.

The page bit his lip and nodded slowly. "Not so loud! Captain was practicing his speech, no doubt."

"Oh, aye? Well I saw him slashing away with his knife at the mists," said the Sergeant. "Practicing that too, was he?"

The sergeant's brow furrowed and he shook his head. He glanced at the page.

The young man pulled his helm on firmly and hurried to catch up with FitzStephen.

❖

A group of noisy starlings flew down from the rafters of St Mary's church, fighting over a beak-full of twigs. Hilde looked away from the priest as a pair, mother and fledgling perhaps, fought off an interloper and settled back into a crevice in the dark recesses of the thatch.

"My saints, how long have we been talking," Father Stephen said. He leaned back against his pew.

"Sorry Father. So much has happened," Hilde said.

"Thank you child for everything you've told me. But I'm still not sure how I can help. Your friends at the Priory or the Chief seem your best chance," the priest said. His face fell, a cloud across his eyes. "I really must get back."

Back to the vestry, to his quarters to clean up the mess. To see what kind of state his wife was in.

Why would Alice side with Jezabel, or with the man in black? This had been the question, the despair, the feelings of betrayal hovering over Hilde like a dark cloud since her mother was accused and taken.

But the puzzle of Alice's testimony, her story of the devil she had seen by Duncormac Hill, took on a whole new light now Hilde had heard the woman's drunken ramblings at length. If Jezabel had wanted Alice's help a good jug of fortified wine likely would've won her over. Her lush turn of phrase only needed a small urge and her anxiety would push it the rest of the way. Unfortunately the Brehon might not listen long enough to understand this.

And the damage Alice'd done, now written up in the witch-finders parchments, was lost on her addled mind, floated off in a sea of strong wine. What point would there be in trying to get her to recant her story, so strangely specific, of the cloven hoofed demon and his wicked liaison with Bronach?

"Hilde?" the priest was on his feet now, gesturing toward the door.

She looked up, scooped up her bag and donned her boys hat, and reluctantly stood.

"Father, what did you think of what I said about the man in black?" Hilde asked, as she turned to the door.

"What do you mean?" Father Stephen ushered her along.

"I mean taking in what the Reverend Mother said of him and his fakery, what if I can find a way to nay say him? What if I can bring a counter to each of his tales? Would you stand with me then?" she said. She paused by the door, blocking him from opening it.

"If the Priory supports you, yes I will," he said. "But this Ahearne is dangerous, I can't oppose him alone. I will help Hilde, if the time comes and I can."

"Promise?" Hilde said. She relented from the door, and held his hand instead.

The priests eyes grew moist and he put a palm to his forehead. "Yes, Hilde. If you can do that, let's see."

It was the best she could hope for. Hilde pulled her cap down over her eyes, and walked down the church steps.

18

The Battle of Slaney Fields

Scudding dark clouds pushed by gusting chill winds from the north-east crested the a range of mountains. In their lee a road wound through a wide river valley. From those hasty clouds rain trailed lashes of dull grey-blue that washed a army of men on that road from the head of the column to the tail.

A quilt of green pastures and brown fallow fields spread lush in the verdant curve either side of the column of marching men. Great old oaks bordered the road in places and in this grim winter reached their craggy leafless branches into the sky.

Arran Blaine took off his ill-fitting helm and ran a hand over his face. He grinned at his brother-in-arms, Dónal O'Rourke, and tipped his head back as he drank in the rainwater.

"Slake your thirst now, man! Still a long march before we ford the Slaney and get to fill our water-skins," Arran said.

He spluttered when the storm over filled his mouth. Dónal laughed bitterly.

The closer they got to Dublin, the northern reaches of Leinster, the more danger they were in. No time for jests.

Arran shoved the rangy, sullen man at his right. "Donegal, cheer up man! You're the actual soldier."

"Yea. I know what's ahead my brother," Dónal replied. He kicked a clod of dirt that lay in his path. The soldiers in front of him scowled and cursed. "If you knew you'd nay be so cheerful."

"Talk to me, Donegal," Arran said. He slogged along for a bit, hand resting on his sword hilt. At last he drew it, and sighted along the blade. He gestured to the road, to the other soldiers in the column, then to themselves as he spoke. "We have no choice to be on this road. You can choose not to be a sour old wretch."

Dónal gritted his teeth, a muscle working in his jaw. His padded canvas jacket, studded with iron, had no sleeves, only ripped armholes where he'd torn the garment to fit his rangy frame.

"You could not call me that," he answered.

"Annoys you does it?" Arran answered, a boyish grin on his face, as the rain streamed down it. "Donegal?"

"We are from the same place both of us! But I get stuck with the name!!" Dónal shouted. "You're the one with the skill to make silver. I've nothing to distinguish me but the dead end town I came from. At least you of all people could leave it out."

He glanced at the other man. The silversmith ignored him, and played with the sword like a toy, a bauble. Arran's smaller finer hands so expressive when he spoke, unmarked by working in the fields, his jacket failing to hide that his slender muscles were only used to fine work. For Dónal years on a plough as a youth before soldiering gave him coarse hands, but ones that gripped strong.

"Seems a true enough workmanship. No idea beyond that!" Arran said, a last gambit to get some friendly words from his countryman. "At least tell me how to hold the damn thing."

"Tightly," the taller man said, reaching to close all of Arran's fingers around the hilt. Begrudging words and a shout from a sergeant riding to the side of the column came at the suggestion of them breaking ranks. The sergeant pulled his sword a short way from his sheath until Dónal gave a placating palm.

"And high," he said, once the sergeant had taken his attention off them. Dónal's eyes that had been kind once, misted. His long neck and prominent Adam's apple showed when he swallowed, as now. "When the blood and sweat flows, hang on to it tightly. Put it high and swing it down hard at anyone who might harm ye."

"Sounds easy," Arran grinned. He experimented with the movements.

"Ye won't win a fight with a sword," Dónal said. He blinked at Arran, shaking his head. "It's a numbers game. If there's more of you, kill them. If there's more of them, run. Run my brother, and fight later."

They slogged on through the sodden mud of the roadway, and to their right the Slaney got closer. Here and there the road cut through hillocks, with stretches of earthworks and stone perhaps from the Romans, maybe the vikings. Whomever had built it for their armies, now it made easier going for this army.

The rises of Baltinglass lay a dim shadow due south behind them. Home lay further south again, a distant fond memory. Soldiering had seemed so much better a purpose than the plough. But the fickleness of Kings put paid to those feelings of pride in Dónal. A sour expression passed over his face like a shadow as memories rose unbidden of the King's regal image.

To their right hand over the Slaney, the Wicklow Mountains reclined, a sleeping giant in the mists. The country raised in rolling hills around them. Grumbling, slogging, and half-marching half-stumbling the men pushed on.

Around them pastures lay and dwelling houses stood, filled only with those too young, too clever, too old or too broken down to fight. The press gangs of King Diarmait had spared few in their quest for more bodies to fight the rising power of Ruaidri Ua Conchobair and his allies.

"I'm not a fool," Arran said. The tone of him, the comments about swords his brother, the taller man made not lost on him. As a rank recruit, pulled into service against his will with no more than a half-day's training, the silversmith's chances in a fight were gloomy. He looked at his toes, slogging along the rutted roadway.

"Hah. You were still a boy when I came back from my first fight," Dónal said. "Still no much more than a lad now. King Diarmait's men should never have taken ye. You were a damn fool to stay with me, and try to stop them."

"I nearly ran when we passed Ferns," Arran said.

"Should have run," Dónal said. "The sergeant's fat. They'd have never caught you."

"But we're brothers," Arran said. "My little girl would not want to hear how I'd left her favourite uncle to fight a battle without me."

"You're the damn fool Arran," Dónal said.

"You'd not run."

"Aye, I would. But for yon man there, ready to put a pick through my hand if he caught me."

"You'd not leave me. Same as I'll not leave you," Arran said. He punched the taller man on the arm, and made fists, as if to fight Ruaidri's Munster men with his bare fists.

"You know this High King that Diarmait calls us to help?" Dónal asked. The road headed a small rise now and bent toward the east. The slog became harder and up ahead some shouts of protest were met by clangs of weapons and shields. Men tired and hungry.

"Do tell," Arran said. He'd heard the story before but at least the cynical soldier was talking.

"High King Mac Lochlainn swore on the Bachall Ísu! He swore in front of the Bishops that he'd restore Mac Duinn Shlébe to his throne. But instead this great king, this mac Lochlainn blinded him!"

"Terrible! Kings cannot be trusted!" Arran said with a laugh. Donegal was not buying it.

"It is no joke. Swearing on that holy? I'd run now if I thought I could get home past all these jumped up sergeants. Take their horses from them, and what are they? Some of them look as they got their armour same time you did," Dónal swept his hand in a derisive gesture. Luckily the sergeants who'd looked their way before were dealing with some other dissenters. "I would. I would run all the way back to Duncormac."

Arran's face fell. A cloud passed across his eyes, and he massaged his brow to hide the pain. His eyes filled but the rain hid it. Dónal had known him since their boyhood and he knew there were tears there despite the rain.

After a time they reached the top of the rise and the way became easier. Dónal searched Arran's face but he was quiet.

"If something happens. You know, if I don't come back. Tell Bronach and Hilde I love them," Arran said. His eyes were fixed on his feet. One step after another. "I'm going to miss her tenth birthday."

"Yea. Brother, I'll tell them," Dónal said. He mustered a smile "But how about you go back and tell them yourself, alright?"

Arran smiled back. Dónal was not looking his way any more. Shouts went up.

Now they'd cleared the hill top, in the distance a dark line arrayed across the quilt of pastures by the ford over the Slaney. Soldiers. Ruaidri's men.

Dónal's face hardened. All around them the sound of weapons being readied for real.

And the shouts of battle in the making.

❖

Their detachment from the middle of the column had spread out along a ridge, and whosoever orders they'd followed gave the horn and the drum and the shouts at the perfect time. Dónal and he ran down the slope with hundreds of others of King Diarmait's men right as a detachment of Ruadri's men reached the soggy bottom and started up the other side.

Moments passed, legs like lead.

In a daze Arran followed the shouts of Dónal and a sergeant who led a group of twenty men. They intercepted the remainder of a platoon of the Failghe as they came through a break in the trees. The first one Arran killed was a boy, running with glee that turned to horror when he saw them waiting the other side of the tree line. The second an older man groaning, blood spurting from a wound on his leg, until Arran put his sword gently through the mans heart.

Now all around Arran lay dead farmers, sack makers and millers. Every muscle in his back and neck ached. He was alive but part of him wished he weren't for the evil he'd wrought. The iron smell of blood pervaded everything. The rain had ceased moments before the order to charge. He wished now for it to rain and wash him clean.

Arran raised a weary arm and wiped caked blood from his face. He cleaned enough of his sword so it'd fit in the scabbard. His forearms hurt like fire.

As inexperienced as many of theirs were the other side were worse and with inferior numbers they were cut down in swathes. Bodies lay like discarded rags all over the green and gold fields. Pitiful groans came from some dying slowly. Dónal'd said to watch for ones playing dead and Arran treated every dying rattle as a threat, his nerves firing.

The twenty, now less, stood near a stone wall as high as their chest, where they'd met the High Kings men coming over a stile. The dead arrayed around them. Dónal's shirt was ripped down the sleeve and he had a gash on his shoulder. But his knuckles were white on his sword hilt, his eyes everywhere, breathing like a dog after a fox.

A couple of men were pushing and shoving over a dead body, some trophy or other one had hold of had caught the eye of the other.

The sergeant returned from peering over the wall. He grabbed one of the two by the ear.

"The fight is over that way," the sergeant said in a half-whisper. His eyes flared white, the blood pumping in his neck. "Ruaidri still has hundreds of men. Uí Tuathail, the Uí Broin, maybe some Ui Failghe still. Valley narrows here. We go over, take 'em from the side."

"Best stay this side and back track to the road sir! Join our main column," that was Dónal, pointing to their left.

"Over the wall men! Now!" the sergeant signalled with his sword to the right and up the valley. The two men were still arguing, one pulling at a medallion around the mans neck with one hand, keeping the other man at bay with his other hand. "You, stop! Get over the wall!"

Arran and their squad mounted the wall, and a gleam of sunshine broke through the clouds silvering the rain soaked trees and the water of the Slaney ahead. Stumbling along in the group they moved ahead as the sergeant yelled. But they were going down hill. Which was bad. Brambles and rocks here led them down a slope and that felt wrong.

The men shouted. Dónal's voice was absent. Everything seemed to slow, and in the beams of sunlight become like a dream. Dónal's voice floating. *Run. Run.*

Arran turned and there was the rangy soldier waving frantically from the wall. Behind the wall.

Soldiers from his group pushed him from behind and he stumbled forwards. When he looked back Dónal was gone.

Then the Ui Failghe fell on them like a tide.

"Donegal! Donegal!!" Arran called.

And a sword came down on Arran Blaine's neck.

❖

"Donegal!" the voice called.

The huge hands grabbed his shoulder. Dónal O'Rourke lashed out, his hand striking wildly. Bare fists now, another flailing blow.

"Wake up man! Steady!"

The hands landed a blow on Chief Fiach's thigh. Fiach grabbed his wrist then leaned on his forehead. Pushed back into the grass, Dónal's eyes opened to see the moon through leaves. The shine of red apples.

"Arran!! Where's Arran!" Dónal said. He blinked and bucked, but couldn't move an inch under the bigger mans weight and strength. As skinny and dissipated as he was, the occasional farm work kept him from being a complete wreck, and it was all Fiach could do to hold him down. There was still fibre in him.

Dónal's eyes still stuck in the dream. "Brother!!"

"Dónal. He's dead," Fiach said. He pulled his hand from the forehead slowly. "You're in O'Neill's orchard."

"What?" Dónal sat up, rubbing his eyes. A hot tear formed and he gritted his teeth as the pain of sobriety beat on him. The world spun and he slumped again.

"See all the apple trees?" Fiach said, straightening up. He was so tall and wide he had to stoop under the fruit tree they were under. Fiach kicked at an empty stoneware jug that lay on it side. "There's the only dead soldier."

"What do you want?" Dónal got up on his elbow. He rubbed his head, and took stock of his clothes and surroundings. "What day is it?"

Fiach stood back and wiped his hands on some dock leaves. "Saturday evening. The folk at the Dire Goose told me where to look for you. But listen, I have work for ye."

"There's no work. Not for the likes of me," Dónal snapped. He lifted the jug but nothing came from it.

"Aye there is work Dónal. I've been trying to find sword hands. And there's not many. I've work for ye. If you've strong enough stomach for it," Fiach said.

Dónal rubbed his shoulders. It was cold and he was hungry. "Have to find Jezabel."

"Can't help with your needs man. But I have food," the burly chief said, patting a waxed cloth wrapped piece of roast fowl. Fiach extended a hand toward him. "And if you want to kill yourself, there's a fight I'm going to."

"What fight," Dónal tried to get up. He retched. He knelt on all fours, and threw up at the base of the apple tree. "All the fighters are dead."

"You're here," Fiach said.

"I died on that field years ago. What you see is a shadow," Dónal said. A bat flew over the moon, the flapping of its leathery wings punctuating the still of the night. "I'm no fighter. You talk to a ghost."

"You vomit and whine like a live one. You've fight left," Fiach said.

"What's the work?" Dónal said warily.

"After we eat. Its a fight much nobler than with that bottle. And for a cause better than the vices that woman of yours feeds. Remember Bronach? What would Arran think of you now? Remember your niece? Hilde?" Fiach growled the names in a low voice.

"Get their names out your mouth," Dónal growled, glaring up at Fiach through the spittle and vomit that flecked his face. He struggled to get to his feet. "I'm for hell, nothing surer. But they're best off nowhere near the likes of me. Or you, Ostman."

"That's it man! You have fight in you. Tomorrow we fight and die," Fiach pulled his axe from his shoulder. He swung it lazily but the blade whistled past too close to Dónal's head for comfort. He admired it in the moonlight for a moment, and replaced it in the sling over his back. Then he held out a hand toward Dónal. "But we go now and eat. Join me. Yes?"

"Yes," Dónal said, taking Fiach's hand.

He stood, wiped the puke from his hands, pushed back the ghosts and the two men walked toward Duncormac Hill.

19

The Norman Camp

With evening quiet trammelled only by the sigh of the sea, the laughter of soldiers sharing a joke carried clear across the night air. Most soldiers in the camp on Duncormac Hill were in their tents. King Diarmaid mac Murchada, deposed ruler of Leinster himself, lay in his marquee sleeping off the long march and subsequent carousing. His men slept around him in their kits. No tents for them, left behind before the forced march south. A few Leinster-men played dice by a fire, some sat on a log watching the stars, and eyeing the Norman armies warily.

On the hillside above the camp a ring of men gathered, of both Norman soldiers in armour *and* guardedly beside them two dozen from Diarmaid's army. The latter a knot of soldiers in motley armour nudged forward for a better view. And they all stood almost silent, looks of disbelief on their faces. A few slowly shook their heads, as they all looked on in horrified curiosity at their two Norman Captains who seemed on a collision course.

Etienne d'Courcey reached for his Captain and leaned to whisper to him urgently one last time.

"He's dangerous, sir. Don't do this," d'Courcey said, gripping FitzStephen's sleeve. "Listen to what he has to say."

The barrel-chested, bald-headed sergeant in charge of FitzStephen's personal guard nodded vigorously. "Ye don't have to fight him sir! We have Strongbow's charter!"

"He's lain with the enemy," FitzStephen said, a dark storm behind his eyes. "Young weakling is dead."

"The man bargained! For us!" d'Courcey insisted, yanking on the big man's sleeve insistently. "He says we take Wexford without a fight!"

"Shut up," FitzStephen snapped at his lieutenant. "Traitors!"

The big man's breath rasped from the run up the hill. His face red with effort and emotion twisted into a mask of rage. He wrenched from the lieutenants grasp. FitzStephen's jacket pulled askew, and he looked down at it, covered with the blood of the rabbits he'd mutilated.

FitzStephen tore the jacket from himself and threw it at d'Courcey. He roared a foul curse. The bloody garment flecked the lieutenant's face with red. Gore spattered and shaking, he rolled up the jacket and backed away into the line of soldiers.

The curve of the big Captain's back, hunched like a cornered bear, steamed in the cold early evening air. His hands clenched into fists so tight his forearms shook.

A chorus of whispers ran around the soldiers in the ring. FitzStephen flexed his arms, circling to the higher ground of the circle. Everyone around pressed in to see. Fingers pointing at one then the other. By sheer bulk FitzStephen was twice the warrior of de Prendergast. But by the hushed conjectures a few favoured the younger, nonchalant, blonde-haired captain.

"You're insane," de Prendergast said. He stood at the low side of the circle, facing the top of Duncormac Hill as his opponent circled around to the high side. De Prendergast's eyes flicked from the muscles bunching in the bigger man's legs to the placement of his feet. The younger warrior imperceptibly adjusted his weight.

Behind de Prendergast in the crowd the dark green and black shadow that was Giffard smiled, his teeth showing white in the moonlight like a demonic presence. He looked at FitzStephen, the rising moon over his shoulder like an ill omen. Giffard measured him with the eye of an undertaker.

"Traitor," FitzStephen said, his face shrouded in moon shadow. "Traitor!!"

FitzStephen lunged, snatching a knife from his belt. The huge muscles in his legs bunched like the hocks of a raging bull and his arms went wide. He crossed the circle in a trice. Gasps ran around the crowd drawing more from their tents.

The smaller man dove down to the right, away from FitzStephen's knife hand. And he plunged head first to the ground. The ground he chose, rocky and dry. But instead of splitting his skull, to the gasps of onlookers he tucked and rolled over his forearm and shoulder like a circus performer.

FitzStephen's flailing arms came up empty. His knife blade slashed through thin air. Bodily he crashed into the circle, scattering men left and right.

De Prendergast came to his feet in a crouch, twitching like a cat, eyes everywhere. He ran his tongue across his teeth. His right hand clenched around a long knife that had come from nowhere.

FitzStephen tangled with the men on the lower side of the ring. A few scrambled away, eyes crazed. FitzStephen's slashing steel had been inches from their faces. A gaping private shook as he distanced himself from the steaming flanks of the big fighter.

"Last chance. Stand down," de Prendergast hissed. He pointed the knife at FitzStephen.

FitzStephen shook his head at the sound of de Prendergast's voice and turned, looked for him, shaking off the soldiers like insects. The burly Captain, face covered in blood, bared his teeth, and growled his displeasure at finding de Prendergast still alive. He pulled his own long knife.

He sprang.

But the advantage of the high ground had gone. FitzStephen's charge came slow. And de Prendergast read his movements like a map. The smaller man feinted to the right, and FitzStephen's knife hand dutifully lunged in that direction. But next instant, de Prendergast twisted away to the left, his left foot sweeping around to stand at a vantage outside the big mans curving thrust. The blonde whirlwind pushed FitzStephen's knife blow even further off course. De Prendergast tossed his knife from his right hand to his left, all the time in the world.

Wild cat. Snake.

The men whispered, talked in gasps. Pointing at de Prendergast. Giffard just smiled. FitzStephen blinked, and turned.

De Prendergast moved, his right arm a blur as he circled FitzStephen's forearm. The big man's knife trapped, de Prendergast lifted, locked out the big mans elbow. A gash opened in the big man's bulging neck muscles as the smaller man's knife flew up, reverse grip, left handed then slid around to lie at FitzStephen's throat.

"Coward," FitzStephen said. His eyes bulged. Continuing to turn his head bought the knife hard up against the turgid veins in his throat. His greater strength useless against the slighter man's leverage.

De Prendergast, a head shorter than the burly captain, tightened the elbow lock and pushed FitzStephen's chin skyward with his fist as he bought the knife up even higher. FitzStephen tried to speak but only a gurgling sound came.

"What was that?" said de Prendergast, as he cocked an eyebrow. He bought the chiselled planes of his face close to FitzStephen's lantern jaw. The big man struggled but could not move without pushing the knife further against his throat.

"Sir," Giffard quietly called. He gestured to the crowd of FitzStephen's men in the circle, becoming more agitated by the moment. "Discretion."

"Oh, really? He says he will kill me, and I'm supposed to be merciful?" de Prendergast said archly, to the gathered crowd. He turned to his captive, and shoved the left fist hard under FitzStephen's chin again. "I really want to kill you. Now I see how truly mad you are. But you can serve me yet."

Ah!! Aaaagggh!!

FitzStephen cried out as de Prendergast stamped on the side of his knee. With a sickening crack the big man slumped to the ground, leg folding unnaturally, the big Captain screaming in pain.

De Prendergast turned his back on the tragic figure, and walked toward the large group of soldiers Giffard nodded to.

"D'Courcey, why don't you give the orders?" De Prendergast smiled, but his eyes stayed hard as flint. A few feet away FitzStephen howled again as he tried to put his weight on his right leg. "Just until Captain FitzStephen is back on his feet."

D'Courcey nodded and numbly started to dismiss the men. A babble of voices erupted. Men pushed this way and that, leaving the circle in all directions to disavow what had passed, but all gave de Prendergast a wide berth. The lieutenant went to his defeated Captain and draped the jacket over his shoulders.

"Tonight we eat and rest. All of us! Then we fight for our King!" De Prendergast shouted above the din. "Come on, let's cheer for the King of England! Long live King Henry!"

Giffard dug a few of the men in the ribs. The cheer spread. At first only de Prendergast's men followed, but then FitzStephen's joined in.

Long live King Henry! Long live the King!

After the cheer was done, the blonde haired man swept a hand through his hair and straightened his tunic. He strolled uphill to the higher point in the camp, then turned to address his seventy men.

"Tonight we eat and rest. Tomorrow we march to victory!"

❖

From the cover of a thick copse of hawthorn, briar and elm Chief Fiach Caton and Donegal O'Rourke looked through the leaves, down the slope of Duncormac Hill toward the sea. Firelight flickered in the gloom, wisps of smoke drifting in the still night air up to cross the new moon. An owl cried its eerie challenges nearby, and the rustle of bats in nearby hideaways echoed across the pastures.

Whatever entertainments the Norman soldiers had on tonight, it seemed to be keeping them occupied. Another night, another blessing. Chief Fiach parted the branches again and peered into the gloaming. For a time there was quiet. But something was happening.

A big disturbance broke out below, followed by a man — who looked Norse, but slight, not tall — walking to address the men. The words were french and english, hard to discern.

"Donegal, what did you make of that?" Fiach whispered. "They getting tired of waiting?"

"Bastards," said the rangy man hidden nearby. He spat out gristle and but kept chewing on a bone of roasting fowl. He peered out the gap. "Attack at dawn, sounded like? Don't like the look of that light-haired fellow."

"Dawn? Aye, I reckon," Fiach said.

The rustle of bats in the trees around them was unnerving. Fiach put his hands on the rough bark and peered up into the branches but no winged creatures were there.

He pulled the Norman horseshoe from his pocket, and ran his fingers over the odd curved nail holes. Strangers with strange ways.

One more still evening before the town he had given his life to protect was sacked and ripped apart by invaders. The group was bigger than ever, as yet another smaller army — maybe 400 men — had arrived that morning. Surely today was their last reprieve, before the horde crossed the bridge over the Muck and tore apart Duncormac.

Dónal was right. They'd come at dawn most likely. That's what Fiach's ancestors used to do. Stealing up rivers in their boats in the dead of night, arriving with swords and axes in the first light. Simple, brutal and effective.

But waiting here, they'd not surprise him. They'd march and he'd be ready.

Duncormac was not kind to outsiders, and it seemed no matter what he gave it was never enough. If these foreigners marched into their town, to trample over Riane's grave, it would be over his dead body. If, after they sacked it, there were any in Duncormac who cared for Fiach Caton they might write on his grave that he gave his all for the village that called him Chief.

"We meet them on the bridge," Fiach said, after a time. The stars had moved across in the sky. "If we come out of the trees, they won't have their archers ready until there's too many of their men there to loose arrows."

"Oh aye. Aye. Good plan. You said 'we' Fiach?" Dónal wiped his hands on his tunic.

"Donegal. Not going to lie man," Fiach took his axes from his back and ran a thumb along the edges, holding it up to the moon. "We is me and you. Us ghosts."

The other man came up to him, and Fiach saw there were tears in his eyes. "Aye, 'we' then."

Then Dónal looked down the hill. Something caught his eye.

A big man, limping came up from the crowd. He headed around the curve of the hill, to their right.

Three bats took to the wing, black shapes against the starry sky. Something — fox probably — had scared them from a clump of trees and rocks. The big man stopped, and looked up at the flying creatures passage, and made the sign of the cross on his chest.

"I tried to raise some men, but the High King didn't leave many," Fiach said. "So will ye fight beside me? Dead men, side by side?"

"The bridge then," said Donegal. "Dawn."

"Can you use this?" Fiach asked, passing the other man his axe.

"Aye. Ye've nay got a sword? It'll do."

"Good man."

"Going to lie down here and sleep for a bit. Wake me when its time. Give it to me then."

"Dawn then," Fiach said. He slid the axe back into the sling on his back and moved back into the cover of the tree canopy.

The smell of food wafted up from the camp.

Hiding in trees was not his way. His hands, resting on the bough of the tree itched for the fight. Even though dawn was a long time hence, Fiach did not feel like sleeping. He parted the branches and leaves again.

The soldier from the camp, his right leg lame, still stood head tilted back looking up at the flight of the bats.

These strangers, what did they believe? How many had planned to come to Irish shores to die here? Not many like as not.

Perhaps when he, Fiach, stood on that bridge in the morning the enemy would turn. They might turn, rather than one of them die. Had they made their peace with their Gods? He'd see how many had.

The big man limping, reached the pile of rocks and trees, sat and rested.

Fiach slumped over the bough of the tree and rested his eyes.

❖

Hilde walked along the main road of Duncormac away from St Mary's as the sun lowered in the sky, brightening a red band of cloud to the west along the mountain tops. Saturday evening meant normally there'd be a crowd gathered at the Dire Goose, but strangely the roads were bare.

There was the small round house. Attached to the front of Padreg's and with its high window. Where she'd nearly been caught by the harridan Jezabel. And her lackwit husband, Uncle Donegal. "Uncle" didn't even seem right, as he'd never visited since Da never came back from the war.

Was Mama still alive in there? Were they feeding her? The O'Neills must feed her surely. It was getting so cold. Up and down the Main Street it was quiet, but the risk of Jezabel appearing out of nowhere like she had last time was too great.

Ahead the bridge led to the west, out of the place she'd grown up. West, away from home. It was best to hide outside of town. The big willow at the cross roads, where the Back Road led down to Caton farm seemed a good place to pause. So many thoughts careened through Hilde's mind.

Hilde moved into the big tree's shadow and folded her arms tightly. St Mary's had seemed a sanctuary but Father Stephen's words dashed that hope, that childish idea forever.

What was left? Where would she go if she left town?

Was not God all powerful? Why would his house not give her shelter? Why did Father Stephen hear the confession of bad men, and harbour his drunken sop of a wife but not give Hilde succour when she most needed it?

Strangely she could not feel anger or hatred toward him. Hilde pulled her borrowed boys coat around her shoulders tightly. It was getting colder and the coat was not going to be enough if she could not find a place indoors.

There were games adults played between themselves and instead of anger Hilde just furrowed her brow in puzzlement at the images in her minds eye of the good priest and the people he'd made compromises with. Alice, her madness, her drinking. Father Stephen knew of it, but did nothing. Is this what it is, to be a grown up?

The shadow of the tree did not feel safe. Voices coming from north along the main road got louder. The sun completely gone now, a cold moon rose. It seemed ever more unnaturally quiet.

Hilde moved quickly and rubbed her hands against the cold. No-one was around at the bridge, and she paused briefly to look back on the town before walking over it.

The windows were shuttered at the Dire Goose, candle light gleaming through cracks there. It looked welcoming with its almost comical sign of the giant bird outside, but it'd been made clear she was not welcome there. Would Jezabel be inside serving well-heeled travellers? The O'Neills would take Viking coin from the Kings of Dublin or cows from locals, but Hilde had neither.

Her stomach rumbled. Hilde laid a hand on it and ruefully thought about food again. She groped around under her coat, in the drawstring bag with her few things. And came across something hard. She drew it out and a chain swung from it.

Her heirloom. The beautiful silver cloak pin her father had made. Mama must have put it in there when she packed. Hilde hung it around her neck, ran her fingers around it's curve, along the pin. Arran Blaine, Silversmith of Duncormac. What far flung field did you lie in? The part of her that knew he was gone was in charge now.

Up ahead lay Duncormac Hill. That was not a place she'd thought to go but it was where her feet were leading her. She and her Da had hunted for rabbit and birds eggs there. They once found a small cave under the bole of a gnarled oak. It might at least be shelter from the worst of the cold. There was nothing more she could do tonight.

Closer to the coast, climbing the hill, even the gentle night breeze was bitingly chill. As Hilde came up the lane, through the copse at the top of the hill it seemed two dark outlines lurked in the shadows under the tree canopy. Two men, one large and the other shorter, thinner.

Chief Fiach!

Hilde nearly ran to him, skipping through the forest. Her Mama had said the Chief would help her. He had named her after all!

But she bought herself up short as she saw the other. She rested and hid behind a tree less than a stones throw from them. It rustled and the leaves clattered. Hilde clenched her eyes shut and winced. The Chief turned but didn't seem to think anything of the noise.

It was Uncle Donegal. He stood with Jezabel, when she'd said her Mama would burn.

What were they saying? Surely the Chief didn't believe any of Jezabel's lies? What would they do if they found her?

Uncle Donegal said something about a sword. The Chief had his axes out. Hilde strained her ears, and leaned on the rough trunk of the tree.

The chief held up the horseshoe she'd given him. He had been around the village with it, called meetings, showed the evidence of the threat. The chief was occupied with whatever dire business had caused him to run from his house with his axes, and leave his terrified son to run the house.

If she approached him again for help, would he just hand her over to Dónal O'Rourke?

There below down the hill to the west was the oak, the clump of rocks and scrub around the cave mouth. A place to crawl into and hide and perhaps to sleep. There might be bats but most would be out in the night. She could find room there.

But what Hilde saw next made her jaw fall open in disbelief. A huge campsite beyond the oak.

For a fraction of a moment she thought it was a circus, but the tents were in rows. A few larger tents but many smaller. Some fires burned, red pin-pricks in the night. And carrying in the night the voices of the occupants, men who spoke in a strange language.

"Saints save me!" Hilde gasped. She clapped a hand to her mouth, and stopped in her tracks.

Soldiers. Hundreds and hundreds of soldiers. From some other strange land. This is what Gáethán feared. These were the ruthless demons her mother and father talked of that came in the night.

Hide!! Hide now! Move!

Hilde gritted her teeth, and clenched her fists, stuffing the fear down inside herself, as she hurried toward the cave mouth.

And one of foreigners, a huge man, walked directly toward her. He held a wicked knife.

Though he walked with a limp his eyes were wild with pain and anger, and he would not stop.

"Hold there witch! Move and I'll kill ye!!"

20

The Cave on Duncormac Hill

The late evening moon hung among skulking clouds.

Hilde ran, saw nothing but the cave. Not the huge man whose words of threat still hung on the night air, his breath mist.

Blood rushed in her ears. Tears bought by cold winds half blinded her. Hilde scrambled faster than she'd ever run toward the dark cleft in the hill.

It must be too small for him to follow. Please.

Moonlight glinted off the leaves of the stunted oak, just a stride or two away. It grew from rock, strangled by whitethorn. As she reached it, worn boots slid on stones that lurked below the tussock and Hilde's ankle turned.

"Aaaah!" Hilde cried out as her feet went from under her, she hit the ground and pain shot up her leg.

The spleen of fear and chase ran through her. Eyes wide and wild she gripped the grass finding purchase. Hilde sprang up and ran the last yard over a red hot fire in her right leg. She paused. He must have heard.

Hilde had to fight down the pain, had to keep moving.

She put a hand on a knotted root and vaulted over the bole of the ancient oak, between a clump of brambles that tore at her jacket. Knees and elbows cracked against stone as she clambered over boulders into the narrow crack of the cave mouth.

It seemed much smaller than when she'd played here with her father just a few years ago. She lay, her heart thumping in her chest for a few moments.

Silence. Where was he?

Hilde screamed as many leathery wings beat against her and past her, then flew upward.

After a few heartbeats that seemed an age Hilde pulled her arms from her face.

A flight of bats clung together in the distance now and getting smaller, the black jags of their wings a vanishing warning written in ink against the twilight sky. The big man stood transfixed watching them, mouth hanging open as though God himself reached his hand down to touch him with awe.

The man was close enough now to make out his face. He stopped, bloodshot eyes casting left and right. He uttered a stream of curses in English or French, then some more words Hilde could not catch.

The big man paused then shouted, his face lifted to the moonlight, "Witch! I see you!"

She saw him. But he did not see her. He gazed wildly. Made no sense.

With his injured leg, his foot dragged along his path. A nasty but shallow gash ran around his neck to the underside of his chin. The man moved like a wounded animal.

He paused and leaned on the tree, seeming defeated, as he gazed up to the sky. His was a profile of pathos. Pale, but red faced, and with wavy light brown hair. He wore armour and a ripped up padded jacket. In the moonlight it was hard to tell, but it seemed stained with blood. His language was heavily accented, brutal sounding, a mix of Welsh and Irish.

He was a huge man, nearly the size of Chief Fiach. But he by his stance and gritted teeth was a man racked by anger and pain, which possessed him like a demon. His threat rang in her ears. But his venom was turned on the sky now. Toward the bats. He shook a fist at them, cursing in terrible stilted Irish.

"Flying away witch? You cannot doom me!!" he screamed, and then trailed off.

His speech sounded more Welsh than Irish. Or perhaps his rage made the words lose their sense. Who was his anger for? He mistook Hilde for another? Either way he blocked the cave mouth now, and Hilde lay as silent as she could.

❖

For a short time there was no sign of the man. His shoulders were so broad and with his limp there was hope he might not be able to pursue Hilde down through the cleft. Then a shadow shifted she'd thought was a root of the oak. He waited still at the approach to the cave, and she redoubled her efforts to stay still and quiet.

After what seemed an age but must've been no longer than to boil an egg, Hilde's leg cramped fit to burst. She moved it carefully. But gasped and then groaned as her sore ankle pushed against a sharp rock, where she lay inside the cave. She bit her fist, breathed through the pain as much as she dared. She watched him for any sign he'd heard. She hardly dared to breath. The bodies of other residents in the cave rustled slightly as Hilde's ears attuned to the damp silence of the cave, and she shivered trying not to think about them.

The wind picked up outside and sighed through the boughs of the twisted oak.

The man was so close now, a stones throw. He moved every so often. He limped heavily, brow furrowed with fury and desperation. What was he thinking? What did he want with her?

His breathing heavy, it caught now with small cries of agony. His eyes turned to the sky, tracking the flight of leathery wings over the trees. But then he looked around him, suddenly on edge, as though a boggart would jump out from a toadstool.

What did he believe, this man from the east? He called her witch. But what could he know of her? Is he possessed by the same poisonous ideas that bought the man in black, the troubadour Bishop to her town? The Bishop was Irish, and this man a stranger, but perhaps they both prayed in the same church.

There was a nobility to him, a square jaw and a proud brow. His cries, even in a butchered Welsh-Irish, with a heavy accent had the strength of a man used to having his way. A petty ruler or local baron.

What had bought him here then, to this blasted hill on an Irish shore?

Hilde peered over a jagged root to watch for more movement, and noticed more men walking up the hill. The injured man would seek their help to get her from her bolt hole. She wriggled down into the cave frantically. And regretted it sharply.

Argh!

She cried out as her ankle raked across a sharp rock.

The man moved. He cocked an ear to the wind. He put one foot, his lame one, up on a rock near the cave mouth, and shook his fist at the sky again.

"Face me! No more tricks! I'll strike you down witch!"

Hilde lay still and hardly dared to breathe. She moved noiselessly to lie on her back, and ease the pressure on her ankle. The sky at the cave mouth became a painting upside down. Like her world but topsy-turvy. Tree branches growing down from the sky, the man's broad-shouldered silhouette hanging upside down, moon and stars on the ground.

It had seemed only this morning that the Reverend Mother at the Priory would take her in, champion her cause, impeach the Bishop and save her Mama. Riding through the town on the donkey cart with Sister Gráinne she'd felt part of something.

Her Mama had thought Chief Fiach would help. Father Stephen too said she was in the right. But before this enormous world changing threat of invasion what were the promises of one or two ordinary men? Duncormac was her home, and Blaine Cottage her birthright. But she and all her accusers too, stood to be swept aside by this force of hundreds of foreign invaders.

Without allies, she was run to ground, hiding in a hole, a hunted beast. Hilde was an alien, robbed of her place in the world. Wings beat. In the upside down world, flying over the starry floor, bats were coming back to roost. Hilde reached to cover her face as the bats swooped in to their home. Leather and talons beat against her skin.

"No!!! Nooo!!" Hilde screamed.

She tried to jam her sleeve into her mouth to staunch the sound. Even as the part of her filled with terror, another part tried to silence it, motivated by the greater terror of the armed man who'd sworn he'd kill her.

After a time the bats roosted, hanging from tree roots and cracks in the roof of the cave, like a crop of eerie fruit.

Whatever weird confusion had held him at bay he found her now. It was too late. The man came. The man's boots clambering over the boulders at the cave entrance. Moon-shadows of his hands reached toward her face.

❖

Moments passed. Others came.

Voices raised and accusations flew. Different languages. Hilde took her hands from her face.

At the cave mouth now, several figures filled the frame. None of their words made any sense. Hilde rolled over, and pressed herself into the darkest part of the cave she could find but still see. Hilde braced her good foot against a tree root.

Two of the men seemed to care for the big man, and tried to persuade him, beseeching him and holding his sleeve. He tried to reach into the cave but his broad frame and sore leg made it awkward.

One man offered him a stick for him to walk with, bound with twine and padded so he could fit it under his arm. That man worked to straighten the big man's injured leg, and bind it to staves made from whittled branches. The injured man cried out with howls of pain. The visitors plied him with drink.

The big man seemed mollified but pointed to the sky and then to the cave, insisting. Whatever he said, it seemed they disbelieved him.

The other men were in two groups and seemed in tension with the big, injured man and his attendants. Not enemies but conflicted nonetheless. Hilde strained to see their silhouettes and catch their words on the night air. Folded arms, stiff bearing and awkward silences.

A smaller man, with light hair, stood beside a man in dark clothes, who when he turned his head Hilde instantly recognised. The dark-clothed man was the one with the cruel smile that she'd seen on the goat paddock hill.

Near those two was a group of four men. One regal in bearing with a fine fur collar to his cloak stood with several who acted as attendants to him. This group stood silently to one side, speaking in Irish. The Irish of Leinster men. They seemed disbelieving, shaking their heads slowly.

All of these men were in the business of killing. It was their stock-in-trade as surely as the Blaine's was silver.

What had Chief Fiach and Uncle Donegal from their vantage hiding in the copse made of these men? They knew killing was coming. But what did they hope to do?

The strangers language was impenetrable, but clearly dressed for war and bent on conquest, what insight could they possibly gain that would help. Did the village elders of Duncormac have any hope of turning the invaders aside?

The conversations finished. The men all moved off, all but four. The man with the fur and the big man with the injured leg, and what seemed like an attendant to each remained.

He struck a pose, the regal looking fellow, one hand braced against the gnarled oak. That forehead and the beard. The man in the fur was King Diarmaid.

As if he had leapt from the painting in the Priory, and stood on the ground in front of her. He put his arm around the big mans shoulders, and looked up to him. The moon light full on his face. Hilde's eyes sprang so wide, and she gasped again despite herself.

Her father had always spoken of the King as if he were a fine man. Mama had blamed the war on the High King Ruaidri who'd won out and whose allies exiled Ma and Da's favoured ruler. It had never been King Diarmaid that was to blame. But Hilde had found as she grew older that others in the village did not think so much of him.

King Diarmaid spoke in Irish slowly, so the big man could follow with his Welsh-English ears. Hilde could almost make out his words. She stretched along the side cleft in the shadows. His voice was beautiful, deep and resonant. But Hilde remembered the thinly veiled disgust her Mama had in her voice the last time she spoke of him.

Was he a captive? It didn't seem so, as he had a retinue with him. Why was he with these foreigners? Curiosity burned Hilde's ears as he she strained to hear.

"...the sidhe, the Tuatha Da'naan come and visit us Irish. Our old ways have us leave out gifts for them," the King said with an expansive gesture. The big man scowled.

"You honour our ways. Captain, I thank you. Your Irish is good, for a welsh speaker. But these omens you speak of. They're good! Not bad!" the King said, holding up a jug to the big man. "Let's not change our plans. Here, put your knife away. You cannot kill fate."

The big man, the Captain, just nodded. His eyes flicked into the cave, right to where Hilde lay.

"Do not go chasing the sidhe, Captain. Very bad luck."

"Make my own luck. With my blade," the big man said.

His knife blade flashed. He plunged it into the oak, inches from the Kings hand. King Diarmaid's minder leapt to his side, but all was well. The King moved his hand and made light as he scratched his head. After a short time he spoke again.

"You say you saw a soothsayer? Read the guts and it was a good omen too?" King Diarmaid said. In return he got only sullen looks from the injured Captain. Diarmaid pressed him with the jug again. "Good omens then! See? Forget this talk. Here. Help the pain."

"Aye," the Captain said. He took the jug with both hands and drank it down in one huge pull. King Diarmaid pulled his knife free and handed it back to him.

"Put aside your grievance with Prendergast. If he has parlayed with Osraighe, it is for *our* benefit. I regain my throne, you become a wealthy baron. Solve it with him after we take Wexford, I beg of you Captain."

The Captain grumbled an unintelligible response.

Begging? Who was this man she'd thought King? Making deals with savages from the east? She stretched up and bent her ear to the Captains words.

The tree root under Hilde's foot snapped and she slipped bodily down into the cave. A flock of bats flew up, their wings in Hilde's face, talons scratching.

Hilde screamed as their wings battered the air leaping toward the cave mouth. At least her wails were drowned by the shrieking of the night creatures as they panicked and flew up toward the night sky.

Jacket over her head Hilde lay whimpering gently to herself. On the bats arrival, and her screams giving away her presence she'd been saved by the intervention of the strangers compatriots. Now she was done for surely.

Why had the compatriots stopped him, and not aided his pursuit of her into the cave? He clearly was some sort of lord? Used to getting what he wanted. He was injured, why didn't they listen to his orders? Surely that is what his words must have been when they arrived?

He had been pushing into the cave, reaching to grab her. Unless they didn't believe him. But why wouldn't they? Curious.

In any case her reprieve was short lived. She had now given herself away *again*.

This time as the bats *left* the cave. Doom was about to descend as the big Captain turned that knife on her.

Hilde took the jacket off her face as the last of the bats flew out. She would face her death.

But the big man was leaping at the bats, slashing with his knife. He winced in pain, each time he landed on his injured leg and shouted curses that would curdle anyone's blood. "She escapes!!"

King Diarmaid seemed with his hand on the mans back to be trying to turn him back to the camp. The two attendants with him the same, taking care to stay clear of his knife.

Captain, its alright.

They soothed while he railed. Among the Captains wild language Hilde heard one word, one name she knew.

"The Morrigan."

<h1 style="text-align:center">21</h1>

The Morrigan

The night thickened, and wisps of cloud gathered. At times they covered the crescent moon. The sighing sea, and the low croak of a sleeping crow punctuated the silence. The two Norman soldiers pushed through the damp grass up Duncormac Hill. Above them sailed the leathery wings of bats, almost silent, marked by inky absences in the field of stars.

"Wait. Perhaps we should just leave him," the head of FitzStephen's guard said. He put his hand on d'Courcey's shoulder.

Voices came from behind them. They paused.

"Cold feet Donellan?" d'Courcey asked with a wry expression on his face. He looked for the source of the voices.

He liked a good sleep before marching. Now it was late. But worse, with the fight between the two Captains it seemed the whole campaign might fall apart like a rotten cheese. D'Courcey did not relish the task of diplomacy it might take to get FitzStephen back in the fight, from whatever sulk he was in.

The entire execution was a complete mess from landing, with that Irish King failing to turn up to his own war, despite a blood promise to King Henry that he would. But Robert FitzStephen could still lead an army. If cajoled.

"Lieutenant, these moods of his," said Donellan. "The men ask questions."

"Merde, is that mac Murchada? Last thing we need is more Irish madness," d'Courcey muttered, looking back over his shoulder, biting back curses.

Donellan, the older man, had poor eyes. Probably could not see the figures approaching through the mist. But he was not an archer, he just needed to see over his shield to the end of his sword.

The strapping mercenary Sergeant lived in Cardigan near d'Courcey's camp, but was of Irish stock. Out of courtesy to him as much as anything, d'Courcey tried to take care not to speak ill of the Irish. But here was a King who was responsible for such a miserable campaign that d'Courcey prayed to God and wished he'd never gotten on a boat from Wales to join. Now late at night, long after he should be curled up in his kit, he would have to test his diplomacy and his halting Irish too. But at least he had Donellan with him.

The King had a few of his retinue with him, Bran FitzPatrick and three others he did not recognise.

"D'you think he's of sound mind? Its all I'm asking," the barrel-chested man said. "I'll fight if I'm paid. But I'm not paid enough to die under a madman."

"You a pious man, Donellan?" d'Courcey snapped back. He put his hands on his hips. They might as well wait for the Irishmen to join them.

"Aye," Donellan cautiously answered.

"Well, is it of sound mind to speak to God?" d'Courcey asked. "You can't see God, can you?"

"But he's chatting to himself!" Donellan said, nodding to the silhouette of the lantern-jawed man up the hill. "And he sees soothsayers, spirits and portents in the wind! Took cook's rabbits from by the stewpot and covered himself in blood… for what?"

"Captain FitzStephen has a great military mind. His years in the Welsh prison led him to think differently perhaps than the rest of us. Spirits talk to all of us in their way, Donellan."

"He's near crippled now. What Prendergast did to him was horrible to watch," Donellan said, nodding toward FitzStephen. "Will the men follow him after that?"

"Will your men follow you Sergeant? Even after that whipping?" d'Courcey asked, turning as the royal retinue reached them to continue up the hill.

Donellan looked down, and muttered to himself as he rubbed the mark on his arm. He turned and uttered a low curse at the sight of the Irish King and his men nearing them.

"They'd better. As you've said, deserters will pay with their lives," Donellan said.

"Sergeant, let's be good allies for the King shall we?" said d'Courcey using his halting Irish, to speak well of the patron King for their small war. "Let's make the best of this."

Ahead on the hillside FitzStephen waved his hands at a gnarled oak. He seemed to be gesturing to the sky, and then to the base of the tree. As they drew closer d'Courcey had to admit it did not look good.

How could he put a good face on this for the Irish King? Would he want to reduce the amount of land they were to be given? That was a joke as he knew FitzStephen planned to take what he wanted anyway. If the King made demands, that was how to fob him off.

The big man clearly in pain, hobbled to a rock and put his foot up on it. Wiping his face as the mist and night air dusted it with moisture, d'Courcey squinted in to the moonlit night. There was a cave at the foot of the tree. FitzStephen seemed obsessed by it.

Perhaps he could be made to see reason. The cold, the night air and some distance from the camp — where de Prendergast was basking in his victory — might have cooled his rage. The fight meant nothing in the scheme of things. It was FitzStephen who had Strongbow's charter.

It was time for some real talk, and FitzStephen could be bought around. The sooner they marched on Wexford the better. The Irish King might even help. It would require some tact and firmness. Both were reasons d'Courcey had been put on this charter by Strongbow in the first place.

D'Courcey turned as the Leinster-men arrived.

"Lieutenant d'Courcey, isn't it?" the Irish King smiled broadly. One of his attendants held out a hand to help the king as he stepped over a knot of slippery tussock to the small clearing below the cave in the hillside.

"King mac Murchada, we are truly blessed you're with us," d'Courcey said in faltering Irish. "This is Sergeant Donellan."

"Evening!" Diarmaid said. Bran and the others touched their helms in greeting.

"He speaks Irish! At least better than I do," d'Courcey said, with his hand on the shoulder of the bald-headed Sergeant. "And we are both so fortunate God has bought us to be fighting alongside you."

King Diarmaid pointed to FitzStephen, as they drew nearer.

"I sense the good Captain might be down on his spirits," said the Irish King. He slapped his compatriots on the back, and held up a jug of liquor.

"We were just going to see to him ourselves," d'Courcey said. The lieutenant massaged the bridge of his nose. Would more strong drink help matters? Most likely it would worsen them. "I'm sure he will be fine. You must need some sleep before the battle."

"Ah! Let's cheer him up!" said Bran, nodding to the King and ignoring d'Courcey. He raised the two jugs he carried and moved toward FitzStephen.

❖

As the mists rose higher Hilde could see tendrils of it picked up by gusts of wind across the hillside. It seemed a thing alive. The tension between the men outside the cave mouth grew, and they didn't seem to notice the wreaths of white.

Racked with hunger and exhaustion Hilde shook herself. Queer thoughts, waking nightmares, faces in the mist reared up. Almost a fever dream with the spleen of fear pumping in her for so long. Hiding, trapped. She had to move.

Darker at times with cloud across the moon, she dared to move to where she could stand up in the cave. The men distracted, the dark, they wouldn't see her. Hilde kept hard up under the roof, head amongst the tree roots and earth that formed a dank lattice there amongst the deepest shadows. It stunk of the bats and their leavings.

She risked peering out as the men's argument grew more heated, looking for a path back up the hill.

In the distance a wall came down along the tree-line and it might provide cover if she could run to it before the men noticed her. They were all drunk, and the mists and gloom gave cover, so perhaps there was a chance.

Wait! Who was that? There on the wall!

A head, looking this way. Hilde strained her eyes into the night. A sentry? One of the invaders or one of her kinsfolk?

No. The head had horns. It was a goat, but not moving.

Hilde wiped the grime and roots from her face. Stared again.

The moon brightened again for a moment. The goats head lay at an unnatural angle. It was dead, a carcass.

Gáethán had mentioned one of his flock had died and was left to dry. Hilde patted her chest, willing her heart to still. She moved back into the shadow, and waited for her breathing to settle.

The Chief and even Uncle Donegal would be welcome, if she could make up to the spinney on top of the hill. She could take her chances with whatever Dónal O'Rourke had planned for her. Anything but this blood-soaked madman. Hilde looked out the cave's mouth again. The King and the madman talked, measuring their distance, but sharing jugs.

They talked of sacking the town! How could Diarmaid do this! How could he.

He the King! Sack his own town!

Hilde's face flushed with shame as she remembered her childish imaginations of his court. And her hopelessly naive ideas about his deeds. No-one got to be King by being a gentle man. Her father had been gentle, now because of this *King* she had no father any more. That was certain now.

How had she believed that somehow Da was just waylaid, and would come home one day.

Uncle Donegal had said something about how he was already dead. Hilde's dad had died there in the North.

It made sense. That's why he was in his cups all day. Uncle Donegal wished he had died beside him, by his tone. Those were their words, dead men the two of them. That is how he saw himself. A dead man walking.

No wonder the villagers hated the King. Her Uncle's nickname too, forever branding him as from the north.

Now she saw it too. How could she have been such a fool.

Anger welled inside her. Like a red curtain, mixed with exhaustion to a delirium.

And in that fury Hilde leapt from the cave mouth.

❖

The night wind freshened. Stars and a crescent moon came and went behind thick cloud like shy actors in silent play. Mist rose further from the marshes, enveloping the camp so the tops and pennants of their tents peeked above. Soldiers slept in rows under a blanket of white.

In the distant sky to the north a shimmer of lightning shot across the sky. Near the top of Duncormac Hill, FitzStephen started, and raised his hand against the flash.

Storms up past the Wicklow mountains. Nothing unnatural.

The stars appeared in places through the clouds, marked occasionally by night creatures on the wing. The mists rose in front of the distant hills, with the clouds becoming one veil in the gloom

It was through the mists that she came from Tír na nÓg. Through the mists was the door. They'd come before.

FitzStephen was half not here, his mind again far away in the long cold night of the Welsh dungeon. So long had he been there. And even pulled from it to once again be a soldier, a cruel part of his mind longed for that exquisite torture. For the darkness.

For FitzStephen the words of d'Courcey and the Irish King all came and went. And the Irishman's liquor was welcome, for sure. He was right, it did soothe the fire in his leg. They were talking but their voices amounted to nothing.

The wind moaned faintly through the branches of the oak, resonating from the depths of the cave. From the Otherworld.

The Morrigan had come.

And there was no-one else. No-one walking this earth whose words he wanted to hear. Not d'Courcey, not this Irish King. Her of Sidhe was near, in one of her forms. That much was certain.

She had more counsel for him. And he would hear it if she would give it. She may've taken to the wing as a crow, be near or far away.

Those who came when he was incarcerated, unjustly, in Wales, had come at his hours of greatest need. Pious though he was, it was beyond his ken why the spirits of the wild Irish and Welsh folk had come to him. God forsaken, behind the thick walls of Welsh castle dungeons, FitzStephen had laid beside Irish, Welsh and English prisoners alike for years. He'd never seen the spirits visit them.

But he, a good Catholic, had been sought out. Irish spirits came and talked to *him* through long nights. Kept him alive when fever should have taken him.

His fellow inmates, had had short lives most. They liked to talk too. Their tales and counsel, and for many their deaths, passed through his warriors mind and soul without remark.

FitzStephen had no argument with any man, save the ones he'd been asked by his King to cut down, and put in the ground. Why they all endlessly wanted to talk, it made no sense. FitzStephen rubbed his shoulders and pulled the collar of his bloody coat up around his neck. The mists getting closer made the cold seep in.

This d'Courcey was pleasant enough, but it was a mystery why Strongbow'd saddled FitzStephen with him. He was not much of a fighting man. A blessing came when finally d'Courcey walked off down the hill, leaving him with the idiot Irish King.

FitzStephen had thought a few times about killing him. Ireland was green and rich. Taking a county or two here to be a baron would be more convenient without the drunken Leinster-man.

Late to his own war. FitzStephen shook his head.

"No more drink then?" King Diarmaid asked. He must have mistook the shake of his head as an answer, but FitzStephen's mind had been far away. Diarmaid shrugged and took a long pull on the jug himself. He leaned against the oak tree. A crow in the trees higher branches cracked open one eye and took a step.

"I ken what you say. Its a good omen," FitzStephen said. Some more of the Irishman's liquor would be a good stead for the empty belly he had, and to staunch the pain and the cold. FitzStephen pointed to the jugs that Diarmaid's attendants had left at his feet. He reached a hand, and the King bent to check among them for any still full.

"I should get back to my men. And get some rest before we march at dawn," Diarmaid said. He nodded to Bran.

"We sack the town first," FitzStephen said. "We blood our fighters."

"Aye. To be sure," Diarmaid said. He coughed, and looked at Bran.

"You don't look sure. King."

"No, I see. It makes sense. The town will have ale, food and women," Diarmaid said. "But Wexford. Stopping by the town, it's delay."

"*You* talk of delay?" FitzStephen pushed the King's shoulder.

Diarmaid swept the hand aside, or tried to, but the big man's arms were like boughs of oak.

Bran drew his sword in the blink of an eye. Faster still, FitzStephen's knife appeared in his hand.

Bran pulled the King back and struck a fighting pose. FitzStephen laughed.

"You have toyed with us too long, *King*." FitzStephen lunged, a feint only. Then again, another feint. He belly laughed as the other two jumped. His maniacal guffaws echoed in the cave mouth like a call from the bowels of hell.

The crow in the tree made a low threatening sound in its craw, then jumped into the air. Bats squealed and took to the wing flapping against the stiffening wind.

"You killed them!" floated an ethereal voice. Whites of eyes against the dust and dirt. An accusing finger pointed at Diarmaid, *killed killed killed* echoing in the cave.

FitzStephen lunged finally with his full weight, knife raised at Diarmaid.

"No!" came a wild shriek. "He *is* King!"

High pitched and piercing. With that voice, mixed the cries of bats and the wings of bats beat and rose from a curl of mist. A figure stood at the mouth of the cave. Perched on a rock. Roots and dust.

"Soaked in enough blood," the figure shrilled, pointed at FitzStephen.

FitzStephen face pale as parchment, stepped back. His hands shaking he dropped his knife.

Bran whispered to Diarmaid. FitzStephen muttered under his breath.

Morrigan. War.

The King tried to back away. His foot caught on a rock and he stumbled. FitzStephen felt his knees go weak, the pain in his leg suddenly overwhelming.

FitzStephen fingered his jacket, wiped ineffectually at the gore on it. She would wash the armour of those ready to die in battle. Doom them to die. Appeared as three, the maid, the mother, the crone. And here he was in the bloody armour. Would this mean his end? Would he die on these Irish shores?

"I am Robert FitzStephen!" FitzStephen growled. His face cast anger and bravery but his hands shook.

"Don't go that way," she said, finger pointing to the bridge to the town.

"Do I die tomorrow?" FitzStephen shouted the question.

"What?" Bran said. He made to move toward the wild-eyed dirt-caked apparition. King Diarmaid nodded to him, pointed to the figure, urging.

They did not understand as FitzStephen did. Do not anger the Morrigan, unless like Cú Chulainn you are warrior enough to kill the witch outright. FitzStephen held Bran back, hissing through gritted teeth.

FitzStephen leaned forward hanging on every word.

"No riddles!" the Captain demanded.

"His armies," she said, pointing to King Diarmaid. "Dead soldiers. Rise to kill you all!"

The figure shrieked at King Diarmaid now. Pointing, accusing. In a language lost to time.

She was the maiden. Silhouette against starlit sky. Her childlike finger nonetheless terrifying as she stood on a rock at the side of the cave mouth, framed against the crescent moon, wreathed in mist.

"Get her Bran!" Diarmaid said.

As Bran moved FitzStephen launched himself at the two of them.

And the Maiden melted into the darkness.

22

The Nightmare

Rage hardened to a solid force at her back, and Hilde's body propelled by it shot out of the dank earth and roots of the cave into the night air, and she found herself scrabbling for balance on top of the rocks at the mouth.

The sea breeze, a cold night wind, teased a low howl from the cave mouth, and rattled the branches of the oak tree.

The men there arguing did not turn. Their foreigners voices hushed on the night air. Rough and accusing. Ready to murder her, but she stood nonetheless, on the rocks, balanced between escape, life and certain death.

Her King was there in his furs, who had ordered her father to die in the North. To not come home. With him aides simpered and nodded, not fine courtiers, not noble captains. Just as gore-soaked.

Another, the madman, jacket covered in blood, stood armed with a knife. His promises to kill her rang no less strident in her minds ear. But Hilde still stood in defiance and rage.

The big man with the crazed eyes, joined by his lieutenants, the foreign invaders bargained with the Irish King and his soldiers. None looked at her. If they did, how could she survive any of them. Even as fear sought to shrink her, delirious anger and cold and hunger railed against it.

The cold moon shone balefully. Her hands now claws in shadows that reached through the night to the awful men arrayed before her. The oak tree by her side with its twisted boughs merged its shadows with her darkness. Its clawing branches and her hand reached as one.

This cave her father, Arran Blaine, had showed her, it was safe land, a known place. Strength came from this rock.

The image of her father's smile, his hands when he gave her the cloak-pin, came clear as day. He put its chain around her neck. Tears burned in her eyes. This fur trimmed King killed many the day he sent Arran Blaine to die. Took him from her home, and others from theirs, without a second thought.

But not killed; his memory.

Why; for greed, for power.

"You killed him!" Hilde screamed, with every measure of air she had in her lungs.

A demon of the night herself now, violent fury ripped through Hilde's veins, whites flaring in her eyes as the distant flashes of lightning reflected off them.

Her words echoed from the cave. The bats there moved as if a single creature. And as voices screamed in her head to run, to hide, instead the heat of fury won out. Her accusing claw pointed and japed.

The King and his men turned toward her. The big man twitched at her words, galvanised. The row had turned violent.

Time slowed. He lunged, knife blade pointed direct at King Diarmaid. The clawing night demon howled in Hilde's head for blood.

He took lives freely! His turn! Rip him apart!

In her heart another voice struggled through the fog of exhaustion. A voice like that of the Reverend Mother reasoned with the demon: *Diarmaid can save lives yet.*

Hilde's thoughts flashed to Chief Fiach and Uncle Donegal a stones throw away, ready to fight and die.

"No!" Hilde screamed. She flicked a glance behind her, up the hill toward the spinney. The head of the dead goat stood watch on the wall. A sentinel in the night. Past that sentinel there was a path to escape.

The men with King Diarmaid pulled him from the knifes path and the King himself tried to sweep the blow aside but the madman's bulk and ferocity kept on. Diarmaid missed skewering by a whisker.

"More blood?!" Hilde shouted. "No!"

"There is no Morrigan!" yelled the barrel-chested, bald-pated man at the knife-wielder's side. "Come on man, drop the knife!"

Invaders. But they know us. Speak our tongue?

But the bald-headed man surely made a mistake. The big madman surely attacked because of his own demons. Not because of the tide of death in Irish wars, and not the Irish Gods of those wars. Not because of the animus that gripped Hilde.

"You are our King!" Hilde screamed, shivering violently in the cold night air. Her pointing hand at Diarmaid shook with hunger as much as fury. "Stop this! Stop! Send your armies home!"

The men all shouted at each other and over them her voice fractured into a screech that joined with the cries of the bats.

The big man slowed, and looked at her, his jaw hanging open. His eyes wild and staring, darted all around. Foam flecked his lip. A madman. In charge of their army.

As the madman paled and looked, the other men saw her too, as if for the first time.

The madman spoke to her, half in Irish. He held up his hands and let his knife drop. He said his name, *FitzStephen.*

His other words were broken nonsense, but his tone a challenge. Would he understand a word she said? Unlikely. Why had he not killed her as he promised?

Kings and generals listening to a dirty rapscallion perched at a cave? There was nothing to lose, her life was forfeit already. As was Chief Fiach's, as was Donegal's, like her fathers.

"Enough! No more blood!" Hilde said. A lull came in the wind, the men quelled as unexpected quiet. Hilde looked back toward the bridge, to the spinney. "Do not go that way! Why should more die?"

The madman said something else. King Diarmaid's and his men gestured toward Hilde.

"A beggar. She pleads for her town," said a man with the King, in Irish.

"Gut her Bran!" Diarmaid shouted, pointing at Hilde. "Find what ye can from her, mind."

"King! Our town died in your armies already!" Hilde screamed, rage filling her again, her dirty finger pointing, first at Diarmaid then the bridge. "Don't cross it! We died to serve you. We will rise to fight you! Will you walk over our dead bodies?"

Diarmaid's men moved toward Hilde. The big man, FitzStephen, shouted in his language and then launched himself bodily at Diarmaid and the man called Bran. His broad shoulders spread and hands unarmed, his reach wide like an avenging angel. Bran drew steel and then others followed suit as he crashed into them.

The rock Hilde stood on moved. She lost balance, tumbled backward and landed on the side of the cave mouth. The wet grass slapped her face, and the gusting wind blasted her with cold. Her body shivered violently.

Brigid save me, give me strength.

Hilde picked up her coat-tails and she ran. Her breath steamed in the cold, and her legs felt like lead. The frigid air seeped into her bones. Ahead was the wall, the sentinel's horns like a guide. She fixed her eye there and ran for all she was worth.

At the wall, Hilde folded and leant on the stonework lungs racked with the cold. Her whole body shivered. A dark thing inside her wanted her to lie down, and succumb. For the last heat in her body to leave. Hilde fought. She straightened up and there was the carcass of the goat, hollow sockets staring. It had been gutted, and left to dry, but mocked her still with its death mask face.

She rounded the wall, and tugged at the goatskin. She lifted and shook it, ichor falling from it. It had stiffened, and stunk awfully, but made a passable cloak. She pulled the thing over her head and the shivering lessened. Hilde's mind cleared a little and the darkness retreated.

A noise behind, down the hill. Hilde jumped. A bolt of fear sharpened her resolve even more.

Back at the cave the big man gesticulated after Hilde, leaning on his wooden crutch, his ruined leg slowing him in his pursuit. He waved his minders to follow him and they though trying to mollify him, made ready to follow his orders.

Hilde ran again. Headed for the cover of the tree-line.

❖

The spinney was a canopy of overgrown hawthorn that clung to the branches of an old, burned and lightning blasted rowan tree, surrounded by ragtag clumps of smaller elms and undercroft. Older townsfolk referred to it as 'the copse' but farmers had cleared it back where the ground was arable.

In the middle where Donegal hid, hunched over, gloom pooled. Stars shone in a few cracks through the dark leaf cover.

A stick cracked as Hilde approached, and her breathing was laboured. Too tired for stealth. The moment lost where she'd hoped to regard her Uncle for a time, before speaking.

"Hilde, I am on watch, while the Chief sleeps," Dónal O'Rourke said as she approached. He held a finger to his lips. "It's alright. Not going to take you to Jezabel. Don't look so scared."

"Not scared. Mad. I hate you," Hilde said. Her words slurred with exhaustion and hunger.

The older man was rail thin but wiry, standing upright now, his deep-set eyes and curly dark hair made him the quintessential Irishman. But the ravages of drink showed on him despite his current sobriety. He had on a stout coat, and wore a sling over his back with a long-handled axe in it. The same as the ones Hilde'd seen the Chief take from his house.

He walked closer to Hilde, one hand held up as she flinched.

"I'm sorry, that is all the food we have. I was saving it," Donegal said, passing her a small package. "But you look on death's door."

Hilde's shaking hands gripped the waxed cloth Donegal had given her, gulped the contents and scraped the last crumbs of roast fowl from it. She gobbled it so fast, face first. And then regardless of the dirt wiped what fell on her lips into her mouth. No wonder the soldiers had thought her wild, she felt little more than an animal.

The soldiers.

"Uncle Don, what I just saw and heard, you won't believe! Gods truth! This man with a knife! And the King is there! Saints be! And I got so angry! I spoke to the King! And the man! Told them off!" she said, tears swelling in her eyes. She eyed the weapons and armour. "What are you and the Chief doing? You can't fight them!"

"Not if I can't figure out how to use this!" Donegal said with a lop-sided grin, jerking a thumb at the axe over his shoulder. "I'll do my best though. Tell me Hilde. Slowly."

Hilde stood, a dead animal draped over her, and her face caked in mud and roots in her hair, which all seemed to compete with her tumbling words to pique Donegal's curiosity.

"Slow down!" Dónal O'Rourke whispered, slapping his forehead in exasperation. He gestured at Hilde, palm upturned. "Can't make sense of you! Let the food settle, ye making no sense at all."

"Please Uncle Donegal. Wake the Chief!" Hilde insisted. "I need to tell him too."

Hilde and Donegal crouched amongst nettles that the Chief and he had trodden down and laid their coats over. The Chief lay there, huddled like a baby, snoring gently.

"He hasn't slept for days," the tall, dour man said. "Leave him. Tell me."

This was a new Uncle Donegal. She could believe he was a soldier. There was no sign of the drink-addled sop, hanging off Jezabel's every word.

Death waited for them all, a final end, in the tents down that hill. And Dónal O'Rourke, perhaps done with shirking, stood ready for it.

Hilde sighed.

"How can I trust you?" Hilde eyed him warily. She folded the cloth, and gave it back to him. "Aunt Jezabel and you both, stood outside Pádraig's and said Mama would burn!"

"No-one can trust me. I let down everyone. You don't know anything about me, Hilde," Donegal said. "You think to judge me?"

"I hate you!" she blurted. She punched him on the arm, and then wound up for another punch but the older man caught her fist in his hand. She eyed him huffily. "Are you even my Uncle?"

"I'm your Uncle. Who else you do you have Hilde," Donegal said.

Hilde's brow shot up, and her mouth opened in a silent oh.

"I'm sorry Hilde," Donegal said, a slant to his eyes, a mote of regret. "Look, what did you hear? And what in Saint Brigid's name is that dead goat on your back?"

"I'm freezing! And it's - I need it," Hilde said. She pulled at the skin over her shoulders, and pouted at him. "And I'm so hungry."

Hilde bit her lip and stared at him. He hardened again, now no fear and no shame in his eyes. She rubbed her shoulders. Although the spinney was at the very top of the hill, it was warmer than the exposed hillside. The shivers that had been racking her body began to still.

"What possessed you to go running down to the invader's camp?" Donegal said. "That was brave or stupid."

"Father — your brother — showed me a cave there," Hilde explained. "I was going to hide."

"Hide? Right next to a camp full of foreigners?" Donegal arched an eyebrow.

"Well, I didn't know about the camp full of soldiers! I just wanted to hide in the cave. But a crazy man with a sore leg was there," Hilde said.

"I heard them fighting among themselves, one seemed to come off worse for wear. A big fellow, this crazy man?" Donegal asked.

Hilde nodded.

"Why are you hiding in a cave Hilde?" Donegal asked. There was genuine care in his voice. "Go and stay with the Chief, or at the Priory. Surely…"

"I have nowhere to go! I have no-one!" Hilde said. She held her face close to his and began counting off on her fingers. "The Chief is here! Gáethán can't keep me. I went to the Priory but they told me to leave."

"The Priory kicked you out?" Donegal said.

"I fibbed to them. Because of the man in black staying there. But Uncle, did you know that that Bishop is a fraud? The Reverend Mother is going to work against him! She hates him!"

"Oh, aye. A fraud? Well he seemed full of it. The man makes no sense to me. Not surprised," Donegal said, shaking his head slowly.

"Why are you following what he said then!" Hilde said, accusingly.

"Hilde, you'll need to talk to Jezebel about that," Donegal said. His jaw tightened and he looked down. "Tell me what you heard."

Slowly, and with some suspicions at first, Hilde started talking.

❖

Hilde related the whole story, including the tension between the King, and the man who called himself FitzStephen. She talked breathlessly for several minutes, until Donegal began nodding slowly, and clasped his hands together with pursed lips.

"Uncle, some of them speak our language. Do we have to fight?" Hilde said. "Can you or the chief not speak to them? Parlay?

"I know these men," Donegal said. "When I fought the Failghe, such as these were amongst them. Come across from England. They're fast and ruthless. There for gold. And for what they can take besides."

"But you could try!" Hilde protested, wringing her hands.

"Try and die. After they got what they could from me. Where the ale is kept. Which houses had women. King Diarmaid is a fool for trusting them. When you told me he was with them I couldn't believe my ears," Donegal looked Hilde in the eye.

"King Diarmaid said he would question me too! He is a horrible man! I can't believe I wanted to go to see his castle. Siding with foreigners to get his throne back. I hope Ferns burns to the ground with him in it," Hilde said.

"You'll find your thoughts change, Hilde. You can hate me. Hate me all you want. Maybe one day your Mama will tell you everything, but for now just be glad you're still young," Donegal said. He clapped a hand on her shoulder, and pulled a wry expression at the goat skin cloak she wore with its gruesome horned head. "How do you feel about King Diarmaid now?"

"He's a monster!" Hilde said, putting her hand on her Uncle's arm.

"There's a fine case of your mind changing, then," Donegal said, with a wink.

They stood like that for a time. Donegal looked out through a gap in the foliage a few steps from their sheltered spot and then returned. The Chief stirred but stayed sleeping.

"Can I stay?" Hilde asked, insouciant expression on her face. She folded her arms. "I just want to sleep."

"You can't be here Hilde," Donegal said. "There'll be fighting, and dying soon."

"I don't care," Hilde said. She pointed to spot a few steps away under the hawthorn. "I'll just lie there."

"If the Chief wakes he'll have to take you back into the village. Try to help you. He's not slept for days. He's been helping the whole village all his life. Got little thanks," Donegal said. He looked at the big man, lying on the ground chest rising and falling slowly. "And come dawn my captain here'll lay his life on the line for them."

Pride appeared in the watery brown eyes and the thin, lined face of Dónal O'Rourke again. The look became that of a soldier protecting his comrade-in-arms. Hilde barely remembered it, but now looking at him, he could well be the spritely, affable man who left Duncormac, marching alongside Arran Blaine. When she was young, and things were good, and much simpler. Hilde scratched her head, and rubbed her face.

"I'm on watch. I know what you being here, looking like death would do to him. And I can't allow that. They will attack any time," Donegal swept a hand in the direction of the camp.

"What do I do?" Hilde asked. She shrugged, her face a picture of abject misery, swaying slightly with sheer exhaustion. Donegal sighed.

"I am going to tell you to do something the Chief would never tell you to do. Go to the Dire Goose. They never lock the door at the back. If you're quiet Thomas and Emma won't even wake up," Donegal said.

"Alright," Hilde said. "Will you be... here? Will you be alright?"

"Truth is it'll be over for me fast. Just need to stay out of their archers sight until I take a few of them invading shites," he said. He experimented with the axe, taking aim at the bough of a stout hawthorn.

"No!" Hilde's eyes were too dry, and her chest too tired for tears. But her heart was breaking despite all her words of spleen against Donegal. How could he be a partner to Jezabel's attacks on her Ma and then be like this?

"This might be the last time you see me. Won't ask for a hug, but know I'm sorry. I'm the sorriest man there ever was," Donegal said.

"Uncle!" Hilde said, forgetting to keep her voice low. She raised a hand, but then didn't move toward him. "You could go east!"

"Done running," Donegal said. "Get to O'Brien's. Find something to eat. And if ye hear the soldiers come, then you hide."

"Uncle," Hilde's eyes brimmed with tears and heat rose in her throat. Donegal went to look through the crack in the trees toward the Norman camp.

"Take care Hilde," he said over his shoulder. And he turned his back.

23

A Night Demon Rests

The moon high in the sky now drifted beyond the banks of cloud that hung blocking the stars at the horizon, over the Blackstair Mountains, over the distant hills. On the path to the Inn Hilde paused to look for anyone seeing her approach. The wan crescent clear of the clouds cast moon shadows around Hilde's feet.

A finger of cloud crossed the moon's face. More cloud moved after it, and soon would obscure the moon again, to bring dark shadows, a perfect friend for a thief such as she.

Crows hung malevolent, pretending to sleep, exposed by the moonlight in their black deeds, hatching dread schemes. One moved a claw. It revealed itself in doing so, where it had been just a black shape on the craggy claws of a dead tree marking the foot trail down to the road that led west. Another of the black cloaked fiends let out a low warning garble as Hilde paused there by the tree. Yet another echoed it.

Arrrk.

Arrrrk. Arrrk.

But Hilde was a night demon now too. Her breath on the night, now the mists of Tir na nÓg. Her goat hide, not a cloak now but a second skin. She wore a magic spell. She walked in the Otherworld now, not alive, not dead. The crows let her pass.

Running past the wall from the cave, a half-remembered skein from the accusations she'd witnessed while hiding in the pear tree had led her to stop at the horned sentinel. She took it as her skin. But there was something more than that, a plan she'd had, but her exhausted mind could not grip on the quicksilver thread. When she needed to run, and needed to staunch the killing cold. She just acted now, almost animal. The way she'd eaten the morsels Donegal had given her, as though reason had abandoned her and something of the wild night had replaced it.

There had been plans, perhaps unlikely to succeed but a chance. Pieces of a salvation that might have come within her reach if she kept striving but now none of that mattered. Things she'd dared hope for at the Priory, alliances with Gobnait and Gráinne gone now. Just surviving was a chance. If she could put one foot after another, through the cold, wet blanket that rose between the tussocks and whitethorn.

Hilde's legs so leaden, baulked at every step she ordered them to take toward the distinctive dark silhouette of the Inn's roofline. From the dead tree Hilde followed the foot trail down toward the bridge. Mists rose to meet her as she neared the chattering currents of the Muck.

Along the dark foliage marking the course of the River Muck, dimly in the moonlight, thatches peeked through the willow branches, marking homes of families that were soon to be put to the sword. Those sleeping there ignorant or hopeless but in either way powerless to stop the army that Hilde had seen on Duncormac Hill.

Had the Chief in his quest for sword arms told them of their dread fate? One that waited politely on the towns doorstep? Had they run and abandoned the homes under those thatches, or had they stayed hoping their God would spare them with a miracle? Left the big Ostman to defend the village by himself and still hoped to be rewarded with mercy by their Saints?

The cloying grey enveloped her legs. Hilde's foot turned on an unseen stone, and she reached a hand toward the trunk of a scrubby tree. It had been rudely hacked back but now grew stubby branches obstinately out over the trail. She paused bracing on the tree. The horizon and night sky spinning dangerously as weariness and hunger preyed on her vision.

How had Uncle Donegal slipped from her roster of hated enemies? Anger and indignation had been carrying her plans forward, but now survival made for coarser choices. Simpler calculus, food and warmth. Animal needs.

He was her Uncle too. A memory arose.

His nickname, spread from her family to the whole village, might even have been a result of Hilde's early young days of talking. Yes, that was a memory. And she not saying his name right.

Hilde swayed at the tree, willing her leg to move, still throbbing from the pains inflicted in the cave. She gritted her teeth, gripping the branch, but succumbed to memories just a moment longer. And a grim smile curled the corners of her mouth slightly at the images of Donegal and her Pa together at Blaine cottage.

But why was it him at this day of all of their deaths in her mind. Had he really again became that soldier she dimly remembered as a child?

Unc'el. Dom'gal.

The two men laughing, her mother shaking her head. A tiny Hilde clapping her hands.

Get to O'Brien's. Find something to eat.

Yes, Uncle.

He was right, she had to eat, and get warmer or likely die in her sleep. Right here on this slope, beneath this ignoble bush. That was an end of choices, an end of chances.

Hilde's foot came free, and dreamily she wondered how it had done so. And she stumbled on down the trail through the deepening mists.

❖

Curls of grey masked everything here, a shroud for the village of the damned, a veil through which would pass those who fell before the swords of foreign invaders. Those who were dead but did not know it.

Under the eaves here at the back of the Inn, Hilde moved, a thing of the gloomy mist. She was a ghost already, a phantasm, the aching hollow in her belly, the claws of her hands marking her as of the Otherworld. She was not of the solid walls and oaken doors of the Inn, and would pass through them like the mist.

Moonlight cast the horns of her cloak against the lime walls of the Inn for a moment then the crescent went behind cloud again. She and the sentinel one now, her bones animated by the magic of the world beyond.

Goats and a cow moved and steamed inside the barn attached to the Inn. Hilde pressed her eye to the crack and saw not much more than the beasts long lashes, the whites of their eyes as she startled them out of sleep for a moment. Then the steam from their nostrils caught a chance moonbeam. Warmth. The barns back door was barred from the outside and pegged in place so she could open it. And moving in with the warm animals was a temptation, though loosing the door was a risk. The goats would likely spook and give her away.

Hilde eyed the wooden back door of the Inn warily. Not barred at all. As Uncle Don said. She could do this. A few steps more.

Despite everything she'd been through Hilde'd never stooped to burglary. But now as the entire town stood to be sacked and gutted by the very King who she'd thought to be the upholder of order, the champion of the ordinary folk, such concerns seemed trite. Hilde hardly touched the door and it seemed to open but perhaps she was already a spirit, the door opening to her infernal presence. Horned beasts of Tir na nÓg need not worry about the law of Kings.

Ethical concerns dispatched, this otherworld demon would follow the call of her aching belly. The door to her criminal trespass did open easily as Uncle Donegal said it would. The innkeep would not awake. Although she left the ethereal mists behind, Hilde's delirium born of hunger and fear, followed her as she stepped over the threshold.

A faint red glow there in the bar room emanated from the coals in the fireplace, picking out the wooden furnishings in hellish outline. Hilde struggled to grip any reality in this red-tinged dreamscape.

She blinked and coughed at the woodsmoke, kept inside by the wooden front window shutters barred now for the night. With the back door ajar the fire sparked up slightly and she moved inside before the snap and crackle bought unwanted attention. Hilde crept further inside and pushed the door shut behind her.

In a sack at the end of the bar among some broken tankards, Hilde found a heel of stale bread. She fell on it like a mad thing, regardless of what adhered to it, spitting the foreign matter out as she wolfed it down. A battered wooden crate of empty earthenware jugs, sat on the floor near the front door. Hilde crept along behind the wooden slab that comprised the Dire Goose's bar top.

The floor here made of planks echoed a footstep, and Hilde stooped in a panic. She hid behind the bar, then after a time of silence from upstairs, she crept on tip-toes like a demon thief in the night.

Boards on the floor here told of the O'Brien's cellar below and a possible hiding place.

But no. It was gloomy now, dark over the bar shelves, away from the fire, but with the doors open there would be light. And when the soldiers came that would be their first port of call. No good hiding there the ale was kept.

Hilde shook a few of the discarded jugs, and found two which still contained sludge of the grains the ale had been brewed with. She poured it into her palm, and ate that too, pulling a face at its sourness.

With the food in her belly and the warmth of the room, Hilde felt the tug of sleep, pulling at her eyelids, weighing her limbs almost too much to bear.

❖

Crows who lurked in the branches of an old oak, but they are Donegal and Chief Fiach watching the armies of the invaders. They came from fire, those hell crows, climbing out of the inferno of a demonic netherworld. Donegal turned to the chief, his feathered cloak spread and he promised to fight the enemy soldiers with his wicked beak. The Chief crow, eyes closed in enchanted sleep croaks quietly.

Hilde floated nearby, she of the mists, now orange and red with demon light. And now she flitted down and hung at the mouth of the hillside cave, curling with the mists through the boughs of the twisted oak. The King of Ireland stood there, and with him a hulking madman jumped to his bidding, ready to attack her town on his command.

The town will have ale, food and women.

The moon shone down an accusation on his face, and his fair looks and golden tone twisted to that of an evil monster. He was an abhartach, a sickly creature who lived to suck the life from others.

And Hilde riding in the mists had believed him a charming regal figure once. Never again. How could his ugliness ever leave her eyes, it was burned there now. Flickering around in red. She lashed at him with her demon claws, shadows arcing in toward him but his minions yanking him to safety.

Sister Gráinne called to her, entreating her to not kill the King. And the Reverend Mother's voice too joined, chiding her for being a night demon, for telling lies. The Reverend Mother raised her cross and Hilde buckled to it.

Hilde ached, and her gut heaved. The food, too much on an empty stomach.

She lay on the floor of O'Brien's with a table leg digging her in the ribs. The fire she'd crawled closer to, semi-conscious, now burned down almost to ash, and a log that had finally dropped its coals into pieces glowed its last. Hilde blinked, and wiped the dust of the floor from her face. The stink of the goat skin reached her nostrils now, but she still held it close.

Outside on the moor it'd been tolerable for its warmth, but it was not yet cured and in the enclosed spaces of the Dire Goose bar room its odour became acrid, biting. Hilde rubbed her nose and pulled the horrible thing over her shoulders.

Hilde shifted to find a place on her body that could bear the hardship of the floor. She began to drift off into the Otherworld. There was a faint warmth in her body now that came not from the fire but the liquor she taken, the dregs of the jugs by the door, and it felt fine.

That was brave or stupid.

Her deeds now paraded before her like text in one of Sister Gobnait's books, arms length, little ants. None of it had been brave, it was all fear and anger, that at times shook her from head to toe. But that had been her. She'd taken the King of Leinster to task, and she'd faced the huge man, a mad knife-wielding commander who shouted after bats. None of those exploits made sense now and as Hilde descended back into sleep her dream scape refused to accept them.

That Hilde was mad too. As mad as the bats. Dancing like a shadow in a jaunty lamplight shadow play along with the King and the mad commander.

Was she hiding?

Uncle Donegal had said to hide. Hilde cracked open an eye. She'd found her way under a table near the fire, near the dying light. Her bones felt too sore now to struggle for a better place to wait. This would do.

This seemed as good a place as any to await the invaders.

Death might come quickly. Best not to know. She'd already closed her eyes again.

Hilde slept.

24

The Small Hours

Through the gap in the trees the rows of tent peaks stuck up in the moonlight like the teeth of a baleful creature. Dónal couldn't face Hilde, but he could face that. A sure death, it would come quick and hopefully clean. The big man, the one Hilde'd described as a madman, moved slowly back to his tent and disappeared inside. The slender, youngish lieutenant at his side began an animated discussion, judging by the gestures, berating those with him. But then soon he too was gone inside and only the sentries remained.

They'd get a few hours sleep before strolling into Duncormac to desecrate and pillage. To massacre them all. The big mad-man had the blood lust. Dónal knew it, he'd seen it before, on both sides.

The sounds of Hilde's passage from the trees had dimmed and Dónal went back to where the Chief lay, curled up in his coat in a soft patch of nettles, nestled under canopy of the spinney.

"Why do ye call me Donegal. Even that is a lie," he whispered. Dónal looked up from the sleeping man, and back toward the North. From whence he and his half-brother had come as very young men, seeking their fortune. They hadn't come from Donegal though. Not as far north as that. Bréifne was a swear word in these parts, and given Uí Bhriain ran the local general store that'd seemed a fair region of the North to claim as home. A little white lie that had stuck.

And now Arran was dead, and he Dónal the liar, stood to inherit it all. He wanted none of it. It was ashes in his mouth, the very thought of it. Death was too good for him, Dónal Ua Ruairc.

As cousins of Tigernán Mór Ua Ruairc, King of Bréifne, escaping the lot of his other family seemed like the beginning of a new life. Had he stayed, it would have meant fighting and beating all to become a cruel ruler; or losing, disappointing the family, and being given away as a hostage, held by a cruel allied king to motivate loyalty, or by an enemy as a chip in a bargain. Maybe even losing his eyes, blinded in retribution for some royal sleight, all for power.

He and Arran had wanted none of it. Dónal's skill at fighting had bought him nothing but a life of fear. And Arran's skill with silver could be a path to a new life. But it turned out being pulled into soldiering was a constant, a danger no matter where you ran.

Worse, after his lies, his running, cruel fate left him alive to rue his days.

But somehow Jezabel was always there with a drink for him, and those eyes of hers, like river pools to drown him.

Forget it lover. Have another taste.

Arran had it all, skill with his hands, a wife who loved him, and a daughter bright as a button. And he Dónal was doomed to betray Arran's memory, betray them all.

And now the final disgrace descended. He lacked the courage to go and end it.

Donegal held up the axe Fiach had given him, his hand on the haft below its blade. His hands trembled. As they did when he was off the liquor for long enough. He ran his tongue over his lips. The water-skin lay empty beside the chief. He'd given the last of it to Hilde.

He closed one eye and tilted his head, the silver of the faint moon catching the axe's edge, as he tried to imagine himself in battle. He recalled a time when battle had seemed a game, and he beat his brothers time and again, lanky arms and long sword, always finding a mark on their armour. The axe trembled and Dónal grabbed it with both hands, snorting in disgust.

He hung his hand by his side. Why was he the one to come home? Stupid Arran, stupid man. Now he was dead and his loving wife was locked in a small round room. She'd never get to tell Hilde of their past.

His mistake was thinking about such things.

Have another taste.

Sobriety, and self loathing were losing their grip on him, on Dónal Ua Ruairc. He closed his eyes, and stood head hanging, let the axe fall from his hand. He'd be no use with it. It landed almost noiselessly in the nettles.

"Is it time?" the Chief mumbled. His captain, who would soon die for his village.

"No mate, not yet," Dónal said. He is a good man. Not like Dónal Ua Ruairc. "Get some more sleep."

Silently Dónal Ua Ruairc walked toward the Inn of the Uí Bhriain where the back door was always open.

❖

The old pear tree's bough hung over the infernal scene, a cold dead arm holding Hilde in a chill embrace. Below, the Bishop, his capes flowing, raised his fist and unfurled a parchment from which fiery symbols leapt, each one a damning indictment of Bronach Blaine. The villagers at his back held aloft torches whose flames leapt at the cadence of his words, orange and red glow rising higher and higher, to the thatch of Blaine Cottage.

Brave Emma's testimony!

Try as she might Hilde could not see her Mama's face, and as she strained the spy nest drew all the heat from her body. She could not move, could do nothing to stop the mob below. She cried out but no words would come, her plea stuck uselessly unsaid in her craw.

Fergus Keenan, the blacksmith! You see me!? Save us!

Father Stephen! Save us!

She tried to call for their help but the acrid smoke of the torches seized her throat shut.

Jezabel and Alice stood either side of the witch finder. The man in black, he grew taller, his fancy hat near to the eaves as he stood above Emma, hand on her shoulder. Hilde gripped the tree, as the mans eye slid slyly in her direction.

He would have his revenge against her for working with the Reverend Mother against him. Chasing her across the cloisters was over, now she was a little bird stuck in a tree, her Mama soon to be roasted alive. Her home to be forfeit. The decisions of the Brehon foregone.

Emma. The work of demons.

The man in black laughed, an ugly barking sound. Accusing Hilde of her futility. Her Mama's voice raised.

"No!" Hilde croaked, out loud.

The cold surface beneath her hands, as she pushed herself up, not the pear tree, but the cold hard floor of the Dire Goose Inn. The fireplace now filled with darkened coals, a few faint glimmers of orange in their depths. A wisp of smoke rising, the culprit for her dry throat.

The words and callous laughter were those of the innkeep and his wife, coming down the stairs. Still exhausted after a few bare hours of rest, Hilde desperately shook herself from the dream. No light through the shutters, it must be not dawn yet. A lamp coming down the stairs, threw the light she saw.

"Emma!" Thomas said, out of sight up the stair, continuing whatever argument it was that'd entered Hilde's dreams and awakened her. "Ye mad if you expect me to believe that!"

"Thom, forget that. What was that noise? D'ye hear it?" Emma said, her steps halting. "Sounded like a voice, but strange."

"The enemy already?" Thomas said. There was a clank of steel. "The Chief said they'd be on us any moment."

"Nay, there's been something getting into the scraps and jugs," her steps started again, she appeared at the foot of the stairs. "Thief maybe."

Hilde got to her knees and drew her goatskin about her shoulders. She cast about for a weapon. Just to hold them off long enough to escape.

Thomas O'Brien, stocky and red-faced moved down the stairs, sword in hand, and lifted his lamp to hang on a hook behind the bar. His wife Emma, in a nightdress and woollen robe joined him, face like a haddock on a slab, fuming and eyes flinty.

A poker, a long bar of iron stuck from the fireplace. Hilde grasped it without thinking and instantly regretted it. The handle seared the flesh of her hand. She screamed.

Aarrrgh!

The poker came free of the coals, as Hilde dropped it and glowing logs tumbled from the fireplace, breaking open with a shower of sparks. A red glow lit up the end of the inn where Hilde had lain between two rows of tables, and she jumped to her feet. Glowing coals spread over the floor.

Aieee!!

Hilde howled in pain as her hand throbbed with fire.

"Demon!!" Emma let out a blood curdling scream.

Hilde, stood adorned with horned head and rotting skull, dirt and roots, whites of her eyes staring. An apparition, she faced the two O'Brien stalwarts. She the night demon hoarsely howled again.

Aieee!!

Emma clung to her husbands forearm, jaw working, not able to speak. She pointed at the creature of the mists lurking at the other end of the room.

"It's… It's…" Thomas stuttered, holding up a tarnished short sword, his arm shaking as his eyes grew as wide as soup plates. He held the sword with a decent grip, and bought it to bear but its tip wavered betraying his lack of courage.

He swallowed, shook his head and blinked. The pair of them side-stepped down between the rows of tables.

"Alice warned us!" Emma finally cried out. She feverishly grasped the small silver cross at her neck.

These brave two. Armed and outnumbering her, but terrified of a thirteen year old girl. Monsters in their minds, making them creep and fret like infants. All while the Chief and Uncle Don faced a real threat. Thomas had a sword, he could have stood with them. Damn them both.

Aieee!! Aieee!!

Hilde let out another smoke scratched screech. She raised her arms so the cloak lifted high behind her, fanning the embers into a last orange glow. Like wings the tails of skinned beast outlined in orange.

Emma jumped, and grabbed Thomas so hard he dropped his sword, and fell to his knees frantically scrabbling for it.

"Ye daft stupid wench!" Thomas said, turning his fear into anger against his long suffering wife.

Hilde leapt over a chair, and sprang down the side of the room. The front door was barred inside. A night demon she might be, but the iron straps and heavy timber would take too long to move. Hilde vaulted a stack of jugs in timber crates, knocking a couple flying in the process, and slid behind the bar toward the back door.

Thomas grabbed up his sword, and struggled over his ample gut to his feet. The two of them spun around looking for her. With the light of the lamp hung near the bar, she was an easy target.

"Ye fat bastard! Get it!! Kill it!!!" she urged. Thomas brandished his sword, and snorted like a charging bull as he came for the unarmed girl.

Hilde jumped on the crate she'd knocked over. There on the wall near the lamp hung a sword on brass hooks. Strung to the sword by a cord of sisal, a leather helm with bronze inlays rested on a ledge. Hilde grabbed the weapon, and ran for the back door, the helm trailing after on its cord.

As she cleared the end of the bar, Hilde tucked the cord and helm under her arm, and gripped the blades's handle as she'd seen Thomas do. Just enough of a threat to get her through the door and away. She swung the blade up, meaning to raise it high. But the blade was heavy and her hand hurt from the burn of the poker. It pointed at the charging man's midriff.

As he tried to run to cut off her exit Thomas near ran onto the sword's point. He stopped in his tracks, gawping like a salmon out of water. He overbalanced and near dropped his own sword.

The back door was not barred, as Hilde'd left it. She kicked at the door and rushed outside.

Where the banks of the Muck sloped down behind The Dire Goose Inn, a small clearing stood, cut into whitethorn and bracken. Mists stirred listlessly in the night around it, and stars shone in the blanket of the night above, framed by the foliage around the clearing.

It was the Inn's midden pit. The smell here was masked a little by natural wild thyme and tended bushes of lavender. But surrounded by low walls of sods, the funk pooled, and the midden pit reeked especially foul near its centre, where Hilde crouched.

Loosing the barn doors was a clever move, and it'd come to Hilde before she even realised her own genius. The sounds of the O'Brien's rounding up their sleeping beasts and searching the barn to see if she was in there bought a smirk to her face. Hilde balanced the stolen weapon on her thighs as she squatted, the helm trailing, rested on the ground. They may still come after her so she hung on to the cumbersome thing for now.

The cold still bit at her hands, her nose and cheeks. The goat skin still gave some warmth, and the cheer of the Inn still had not faded. She'd only tried for what she needed to stave off starvation.

She'd only taken leftovers but the Innkeep acted as though it was a crime to take even those pitiful scraps. The fear of a pair of mean-minded grown adults at a thirteen year old girl with a dead goat and some roots in her hair was a sight that would never leave her.

Aieeee. The demon's cry.

Hilde held her nose at the midden's stink as she chortled into her sleeve. Her hand throbbed where the poker had burned her. A small harm in the scheme of things. If her luck held she'd outsmart them a bit longer, enough to sneak through the undergrowth toward the bridge.

The two of them were still looking around the bush and scrub behind the Inn. She'd hoped they would assume the path of escape for fleeing demons followed the main road, but unfortunately they now were very close to her hiding place.

Hilde moved behind a pile of discarded and stinking earthenware right at the back of the midden. To avoid being betrayed by the sound of breaking pottery, she carefully pushed aside a few pots to find spot to crouch in, out of the moonlight.

And there it was.

The sickle and the skull. Indrechtach's mark, on a long necked flask.

It was completely intact and after her scraping lay cast in the silver glow of the crescent moon.

The voices of the Innkeep and his wife faded as though they came down a long hollow. Hilde watched her hand reach out and take the vessel.

Under it lay a mud stained bag of black muslin, with a drawcord; also with Indrechtach's sigil. She grabbed that up too. Finally reality slapped back, her legs came alive and Hilde stooped to sneak off. She put the vessel in the bag, and in a pocket as she threaded between the willow boughs along the river banks.

Through the mists she wove, back toward the bridge, with a little chuckle, and a little grim smile on her face.

A few minutes later Hilde emerged from the thickets and scrub on the eastern banks of the Muck, by the Duncormac bridge. She kept low, out of sight from the front yards of the

Dire Goose, though from the sounds of it the Inn's proprietors were still beating the bushes at the rear.

The calls of the O'Brien's grew fainter and a donkey brayed. It seemed the animals from the barn hadn't been so easy to round up. If Hilde was lucky they'd have their hands full long enough for her to get over the bridge unseen.

On the bridge was a figure. The mists wreathed the legs of the tall, rangy man silhouetted there, head hung, gazing into the water.

It was Uncle Donegal. Why was he not on watch? Why was he not with Chief Fiach?

As she approached he started, twitched. His axe. It was gone from his hand.

He was a ghost, hollow cheeked in the moonlight. He looked left and right, and gripped his right hand into a fist. He looked unwell. His chest rose and fell. A sigh.

His eyes tracked toward the Inn. He clasped a fist to the side of his head, and the expression on his face looked that of a man on the rack. Bones ripped apart by a force that tormented his very human frame, eyes full of despair as if will paled and hope escaped.

His hearing was astonishingly good, it'd always been. He'd be listening to her breathing as she walked through the undergrowth toward him. He'd have heard the O'Brien's calling out.

She spoke softly even though she was more than a stones throw from the bridge. His eyes now were fixed on the water flowing under the bridge.

"Uncle Donegal, wait there," Hilde said as she approached, a slip-shod, moonlit, goat-skinned demon ragamuffin, slogging up out of the mists on to the embankment. She stepped up to the bridge.

"Guess what I found," she said.

25

The Mists of Tir na nÓg

The dew hung heavy on the wild thyme, dock, nettles and whitethorn by the bridgehead. The night nearly spent, paled a touch now at the horizon, clouds there swelling as their curves appeared from the black into the beginnings of the false dawn. A sea mist stole along the waters of the Muck and rose around the ankles of the two standing there by the bridge.

Donegal gripped his hands into fists, and his eyes flared at the sight of Hilde standing stock still in the wet grass, looking toward him accusingly. He for his part, seemed fixed in his tracks on the bridge road. The surreal ombré of pre-dawn light, the exhaustion, the enormity of a huge foreign army on their doorstep, all of it conspired to freeze them both in a tableau.

Hilde frowned, snapped from her reverie, and shaking her head slowly, began to approach him. Through her coat, she fingered Indretach's flask, the slimy prize reeking of midden-filth in her pocket. The surprises she had, the things stolen from the Inn, she kept now held firmly behind her back. This was not the Uncle Donegal of just a few hours ago she'd hoped to share her news with. Dónal Ua Ruairc stood before her, shifty and unremorseful.

"Hilde, why aren't you at the Inn?" he said. He stamped his feet, and backed away from her onto the bridge. "I told you to get somewhere and hide. And why are ye still wearing that revolting goat skin? No-one'll take ye in like that."

In the face of his chiding, Hilde eyed him. She'd have none of his petulance. Her head kept slowly moving from side to side. She widened her stance and flicked the tails of the goat skin out wider.

"I am the Morrigan. Who are you to question me!" Hilde said accusingly. She straightened the goat skull and raised it on top of her head. His eyes moved to the inn, over Hilde's shoulder as she came up on the bridge.

"I'm doing what anyone would do. And you can join me, get safe. Or not," Donegal said, wiping his hands on his front. He ran a shaking hand through his hair. He nodded toward the inn, and took a step.

"You face a demon! Witch's spawn! Safe? I am afeared by all!" Hilde said. She raised her hands again, and side-stepped in front of him, planting herself in the middle of the bridge.

"Hilde, I'm done playing," Donegal said. He rolled his eyes. He moved to push her aside but the tremor in his hand was so bad he cursed instead. Suddenly angry, he scowled. "Get out of my way."

Hilde tensed, and swung up the sword that she'd held at her back, did not yield. She pointed it at him, and just as with the Innkeep, Donegal found himself walking on to its point. He gasped.

"The Morrigan has stepped from the mists to find you. No more running," Hilde said, a haughty expression on her dirt-covered face. "Leaving your watch? Your captain? What of your brave words?"

"I've no stomach for your stories today, Hilde," Donegal said. He took a step back from the sword point.

"And what about the Bishop? Calling Bronach Blaine a witch. You'll take that story, though?"

Dónal Ua Ruairc hung his head.

"At the Priory, I told you they wouldn't let me stay for telling stories. But everything they do there is stories! Gods, saints, angels. All their books are full of stories!" Hilde lowered the sword, as the weight of it became too much. "You're a liar! You're all liars!"

"Hilde. I'm going," the man said, one fist to the side of his head, as if trying to quiet the struggles of his angels. He went to move past Hilde.

"You are a fighter for this town!" Hilde raised the sword again.

"That man is gone. There's no fight left," Donegal paused, as the blade blocked his path. He bowed his head low, and his hands hung toward the ground, fingers trailing in the mist.

"You fought in the field next to Arran Blaine. You fought the Failghe. And the foreigners," Hilde protested. She let the sword drop slowly.

"I ran! I left Arran to die! Know the truth! Your uncle is a wretch, not a fighter," Donegal said, his voice cracking. "Let me go. War is not a game. Arran died in vain. Please. Please."

"I'll fight them. And I don't need this sword to do it," Hilde said. She walked to the side of the bridge, where the broad stonework of its arch came to her thigh. She placed the weapon there, and pressed a hand on it, eyeing her Uncle as she did it. She let the helm trail on its cord to rest on the carriageway, where its details were lost in the carpet of mist.

"Hilde," the tired soldier pleaded. His hands hung at his side, his voice quivering. "Ye shouldn't have taken that sword. It belongs to the O'Briens."

"The Morrigan knows fear when she sees it," Hilde said, a smirk on her face. "The O'Brien's hung it on a wall, because they were too gutless to heed the Chief's call. The Morrigan took it from their undeserving hands. You know what to do with it."

Dónal quietly sobbed. "Ye don't know who I am, Hilde."

"Show me. Fear is in you, but fight anyway," Hilde said. "That is what courage is."

"Where did you hear that story? Courage?" Dónal shrugged and held up his palms. He looked left and right of Hilde's feet, but could not bring himself to face her or push past her. "Hilde, have you gone mad?"

"The Morrigan will fight them. The witch's spawn, the Bishop named me," Hilde said. She held her hands high to each side, making claws of her fingers. "It won't be Hilde. Don't worry yourself for a moment."

The curly haired Uncle, eyes full of wet, mouth cast in an anguished curve, clutched his hand to his head as though the grip of his thirst pained him exactly there. He let out a low moaning sob.

"You don't have to worry about Hilde. Or Arran. Or Bronach Blaine," Hilde said.

Dónal's sobs grew louder and he pushed his fists against his eyes. "O Lord have mercy on me. Strike me down."

"It's the Sabbath day today. Careful or the Lord might give you what you pray for," Hilde said. "I am going to visit Mama. I have something to show her. Uncle Don."

Her Uncle Donegal crumpled. He kneeled at the side of the bridge, clasping his hands in front of him. His voice now a soft whisper, through spluttering, wracking sobs. "Oh Lord."

"The Chief believes in you. Go," Hilde said softly over her shoulder. He would hear that. He twitched, as if to flinch at her words.

She kept walking past him toward the town, through a carpet of white, still under a star-studded black blanket of night.

❖

Ahead the roundhouse attached to Padraig's store gleamed in the moonlight. The thatched eaves of the old store over hung it, and the willows nearby played moon shadows across its curved surface. It seemed an impenetrable tower in miniature. Like a Kings tower mocked.

A figure, huge like a bear, hung in the shadows in front of the gaol. Hilde gasped as she approached and held a hand to her mouth. She stopped, her heart in her throat.

Someone come to kill her Mama? Now with the Brehon due tomorrow already, would they visit their own view of justice? Hilde's pulse hammered in her neck.

She fought down the bodily weariness. And the exhaustion of so long running at a fever pitch of dread. Pushed it down inside. The Morrigan does not tire, the eternal ones of the Tuatha Danaan do not fear a bear. Or a Sluagh.

Hilde shuddered. She drew her goat skin around her.

Hilde walked on. A gleam showed, a lamp covered with a cloth. The hand of a man, not a bear.

"Fergus!"

The shape turned from the gaol window. Hilde drew close and the blacksmith grinned.

"What on earth! Hilde?" the burly smith asked. He rubbed the top of his head, his shaggy mop of hair thinning there. His eyes sparkled as he looked her up and down. "Ye need a good cleanup, girl!"

"The man in black took Mama. I can't go home, its forfeit," Hilde said.

"What's all this?" Fergus asked, gesturing up and down at Hilde's strange attire.

"I'm the Morrigan!" Hilde said, raising her arms so the goatskin flared. She clawed her hands and bared her teeth.

"Oh, aye," the blacksmith said. He beamed at her. "Would the goddess of war like some roast fowl? I've been sneaking some food in to your Mama."

"Ohh! Yes please!" Hilde said. She walked up to him. He held out a wax-cloth with some still-warm roast bird, and a small cake of boiled barley.

Hilde went past the outstretched hand and hugged him. As tall as Hilde was for thirteen years, she only came up to his chest. He went bright red, and pushed back on a goats horn that'd near taken his eye out.

Hilde stepped back, smiled, took the parcel of food and wolfed it down. She tried to be more demure, picking bits with her fingers instead of shoving the whole parcel in her face like before.

"In here, just in case," Fergus said, pulling Hilde off the roadway's edge and into the shadows under the eaves. He cupped a hand to his mouth and called in a whisper up to the high window. "Bronach, I have Hilde with me!"

"Hilde?" a woman's voice floated through the dark portal. It seemed she was in another realm. But it was her Mama.

"Mama!" Hilde called. Fergus gestured to his knee crooked up against the side of the gaol. He boosted her up and she stood on top of his leg, bracing against his broad shoulders. "Mama! Are you alright?"

"I'm fine. Hilde are you alright? You sound tired." Bronach floated, from the blackness behind the stone.

"Mama! I found some things!" Hilde said, trying to staunch the croak in her voice.

She nodded at Keenan's smithy which lay just next door to Pádraig's. "Mr Keenan, can you let Mama out? Your tools! You can surely open the door?"

"Hilde, I'm the one that drove those spikes in to keep it shut. I'm sorry. Its just until the Brehon come tomorrow. The village council decided. I can't just let her out. Much as I'd like," the blacksmith gave a wonky grin, and massaged his brow with one hand.

"But, you must know! The invaders! What if Mama is still in there?" Hilde asked.

"When they come she's as safe in there as anywhere," Fergus Keenan said.

"Mama!" Hilde called. "I miss you."

"Quiet!" Fergus said in a stage whisper, raising his finger to his mouth.

"It's alright sweetheart," the voice floated from the inside of the round house.

Hilde looked at Fergus. She was desperate to tell Mama about the goat and the flask. Fergus was an old family friend, but he also did what the village council said.

And what the Chief asked.

"Why are you not fighting!" Hilde said, suddenly accusing. She gestured toward the spinney, toward the bridge. "What did you say when the Chief called on you?"

"Hilde, I have a wife and child to keep safe," Fergus said.

"So did my father! My father is dead, and here you are comfortable and happy?" Hilde's eyes blazed.

"What can I do!" he protested. "They have armour! And horses!"

"You said nowhere's safe. I thought you'd be brave," Hilde said. "I can't believe you said 'No' to the Chief. I'm going to fight them myself."

"Hilde, no!" Bronach's voice came through the dark slot high in the round house wall.

"That's nonsense," Fergus said, as he scratched his head again and blinked at Hilde.

"I am the Morrigan now. Don't worry about Hilde, she will be fine," Hilde said, cupping her hand to direct her voice toward the slot in the wall. She moved out of the shadow.

"Oi! Who is that!" a voice came down from above their heads. At a window in the thatch of Padreg's Goods, a hand pushed open a shutter. "Patrick, its some kind of beast!"

"Fergus, stop her!" Bronach's voice echoed from the round house. "Hilde!! No!"

Hilde marched off into the rising mists, her head held high.

Up ahead on Duncormac Hill the canopy of the hawthorn and the old rowan tree formed a tangled silhouette against the steadily rising rim of the false dawn along the far horizon.

Hilde pulled the goat skin around her shoulders against the cold and gazed up at the sky. The real sun would emerge very soon, unleashing a radiant glare. The retreating night sky seemed completely devoid of cloud. It would be a bright Sabbath day on which to have their town put to the sword. Hilde pushed harder, breathing raw now as she neared the spinney with no sign of the Chief.

The narrow track, used by Gáethán Caton when he'd bought his goats up here, wound its way into the bush just a stones throw ahead. Could his father, the Chief, still be sleeping?

Below, behind the stone wall, and beyond the trees, torches played. Dots of orange light, flame held aloft as soldiers prepared to march. It looked perilously like the force, a black and grey line of helms and torchlights, were aimed at the bridge. There was a low mumble of voices, as tents tops came down, and the invading host worked in the dark to strike camp.

Donegal had said the Chief had been awake for days, trying to raise arms, but surely he'd wake for this? It was colder as she reached the top of the hill and pressed into the undercroft of the spinney. Hilde's breath steamed on the cold morning air.

A great hand reached around Hilde's face.

She stumbled.

Bodily she went backward, with no idea where. Feet dragging. Someone tall and strong pulling her.

She flailed and tried to bite, but though it shook the hand was too strong. Hard, as if from the plough. Then she was under the tree canopy and the starlight dimmed.

"Quiet!" said a voice. In Irish.

Mmmmph!

Hilde struggled and tried to cry out.

"I'm taking my hand away. No screaming, alright?" the voice seemed far too reasonable to be the madman or his cohort.

Hilde ceased kicking. She turned, and there was a quintessential Irishman. Her Uncle Donegal. He wore an old cracked leather helm, with pieces of tarnished iron in its straps. His eyes were moist but he looked at peace.

Hilde let out a sigh of relief. Damn, he was stronger than he deserved to be. Working in Bolan's fields must've put muscle on those skinny bones. "Uncle Donegal!"

"Shh, girl. Not so loud," he said, a wry grin on his face.

"Not your girl. I'm the Morrigan," Hilde protested quietly, as she stood back from him and wiped her face where he'd muzzled her. She folded her arms and stared at him dolefully.

"Listen. I'm sorry. And thanks for..." Donegal began, but a crack from a branch broke their whispers.

"Donegal," came a deep voice, from inside the spinney. Feet crunched over sticks, as the chief appeared, pushing aside a bough of whitethorn. "Thought I'd lost you."

"Oh, you're awake then Chief?" Donegal said. He managed a toothy smile.

"Where the hell were you? What happened to being on watch?" the Chief spluttered. His tone was angry but under it was immense relief. One axe stuck from a sling over his back, and he gripped another in his hand. He gestured with it to the hillside below. "These rabble are nearly about to march on our town."

"Oh, I just thought I'd pick this up," Donegal said. He raised his hand, and in it flashed a sword. He slashed back and forth with it a few times. A smile stole across his face. He nodded at Fiach's axe. "You can keep that thing."

Hilde grinned. Fiach pulled an apple out of his pocket, split it in half with a twist of his hand, and munched it. He spat the seeds out at Donal's feet.

"Hmm. What are you thinking bringing Hilde here?" the chief asked.

"Bringing? She came here. Besides, this is the Morrigan. Isn't that right?" Dónal said.

Hilde nodded, and accepted the other half apple from the chief. She patted her stomach, still full from the barley and roast bird that Fergus had given her. She gave the fruit to her Uncle.

"Stay in the copse. You'll be safer here," the Chief said, as he turned and grabbed Dónal by the earlobe.

"Oi!" Dónal said, laughing and half-choking on his apple.

He slapped the hand away and fell in beside the big Ostman as they walked toward the bridge.

There was no chance of Hilde staying here. She walked behind them, catching snatches of their strategy talk, as they descended toward the bridge, into the mists.

26

The Battle of Duncormac Bridge

A blue-black sky stretched its dome out from a pale line in the east behind the tree tops on Duncormac Hill. Opposite, the stars and moon made a full retreat with the last of the deep black of night. Spectral false dawn light showed up the tops of helmets, last of the striking tent poles, the captains marquee, and a few thin streamers of smoke from doused fires. What had been pasture abiding next to a road down to the sea lay trampled, dug up, and littered as the near thousand men here struck camp.

The bulk of the army stood in rows, around three detachments of several hundred men each. A regal figure in a fur-lined cloak attended at one strength of men, near five-hundred in motley leather armour, bearing an assortment of weapons. Drips of dews shook from nettles and sword grass as stragglers of men and horses pushed to join at the rear.

A blonde-haired man strode and rousted another unit of well armed men with pointed shields, long bows and distinctive helms. The man carried a whip at his belt. He pointed into the east, and made a sweeping gesture. A small group of knights nodded and cheered at his pronouncements, and his men followed suit. Nearby a man in black and green, on a small dark horse watched on.

A third force kicked over fires, and loaded horses, desultory in their movements. Sea mists snaked among these last men closer to the bottom of hill. In dribs and drabs they joined at the back of the formation. Their breath steamed, and that of their pack horses joined them in the mists, all a water colour tableau of misery and subdued voices. Sedges and salty mud stuck to them, conspired to suck at their feet.

As the blonde haired man, and the King finished their speeches, the lowest status soldiers made their lot obvious. They picked their way through the semi-dark, and boggy ground to find their place, all while avoiding their commanders ire.

But higher up the hill, a small detachment of thirty-five Norman soldiers, bowmen and their sergeants assembled on the seaward arm of the crossroads, on the approach to the main road. Two horsemen rode up toward the crossroads, toward the mounted standard bearers already waiting at the small columns head. Stone walls and rows of trees cast deep shadows forcing their destriers to pick their way carefully through rocks and ditches alongside the narrow roadway bearing the waiting knights, archers, and swordsmen.

With a drawn sword raised to catch the light, the lantern jawed figure, a captain, sent his countryman to the back of the column, and walked his horse out onto the roadway. With booming cries, he directed the first unit of men along the main road, and over the small rise. The group of soldiers in the front headed by a solid older man in sergeants epaulettes marched forward, their formation tightening up into six-abreast as it left the laneway. A few dared to exchange querulous words and one them copped the flat of the big mans blade at the back of their head. The man struck, stumbled, then adjusted his helm, the nose piece apparently blocking his vision, biting back a curse.

At the rear of the detachment four men on horseback chafed. The man who'd been with the captain was one. He, with high cheekbones and an aquiline nose, joined them but stood his destrier apart from the other three. A lieutenant by his helm, he counted heads and pursed his lips while the other three — all knights — prayed to their gods and tightened straps on their armour.

"Lieutenant!" called one, eyeing along his sword.

"D'Courcey!" muttered another holding his palms up, when the lieutenant feigned disinterest. "What is this!"

"Scouting party," D'Courcey snapped, his eyes flashing. He added some curses to his answer. The knight slowly shook his head.

"Thought yon Prendergast'd knocked our Captain off his perch," the knight said, a disbelieving smirk occupying his face after d'Courcey's terse answer. But the lieutenant kept on with his accounting. "We indulging his paranoid insanity?"

In answer d'Courcey turned his head, and studiously looked up the small column to continue his count.

"He's really back, is he?" said one of the soldiers at the rear of the column. He nodded toward the lantern-jawed captain and whispered to his countryman.

"Aye, looks like," said his mate. They both hitched their pack straps and strained to see what was ahead.

❖

On the main east-west road just the other side of the crest a small laneway branched off up toward the top of Duncormac Hill. Not much more than a goat track.

The formation of men snaked through the crossroads, over the crest and neared the junction. The noise of the small army, despite attempting quiet, reached the small Inn, just the other side of the roads crest, and shutters already fast, were battened. Fires extinguished. Lying doggo, fooling no-one.

Just as the captain, his proud jaw held high, cantered his destrier into the entrance way to the roadside way-stop. There'd be no troops making a detour there. The Captain rubbed his thigh, to assuage an injury. He surveyed the way they lay in front of them.

Ahead was a bridge, just faintly visible through the mists. Snaking left from it up into the countryside, willows and brambles marked the line of a river, its chattering course quietened somewhat by the thickness of the sea fog, and the lushness of the undergrowth. The mists caught in places by slow morning breezes that moved over the rise of the hill ticked up in wisps that writhed in mystic dance.

The sun moved to show a sliver of its brilliance over the tree tops. But that cast the mist covered bridge crossing in deeper shadow. The mists more impenetrable than ever glared where will-o-wisps darted up to the sunbeams, caught in the breeze, before diving below the willow boughs. The mens voices quietened. The eerie sight, a portal to another realm.

The proud captain shivered, and looked back to his army.

D'Courcey pulled at the reins of his mount. Not able to see what FitzStephen was looking at, D'Courcey eyed a piece of high ground nearby.

"My sword arm is all we need! Take the village!" a tall knight said, striking his saddle with the heel of his palm, causing his mount to buck and step as d'Courcey moved behind them. "Then Wexford! Let's go!"

"Aye, what are we stopping for?" another knight said. He laughed. "The sodding Irish High King got his forces hiding in the apple trees over there?"

"Our Captain is cautious. Bad portents. Omens. Costs us nothing to be careful," d'Courcey said. He walked his horse past the three knights, around the rear of the detachment.

"He's mad! Jumping at ghosts?" muttered the third knight, a young strapping lad with broad shoulders.

At the back of the column, FitzStephen's page led a fresh horse, and he turned his head, wincing at the comment. That man had been down on the moor, when the captain had gutted a rabbit and talked with spirits. "Not so loud, sir!"

The tall knight held his finger to his lips, and shook his head at the young knights boldness. The young knight mimed frustration, but the taller man drew a finger across his own throat in reply.

D'Courcey bought his mount to a halt on the high ground opposite the Inn. He raised his hand to his eyes and peered into the fog, squinting at the rising dawn.

Something moved there. Among shadows.

Horns, dead eyes.

D'Courcey blinked, removed his helm to wipe his eyes.

"Archers! Take a position here!" FitzStephen called.

He pointed to the open main road, opposite the Inn where it sloped down toward the bridge. The other side of the bridge, dimly through the mists in the dawn half-light the rooftops of houses lurked, faerie refuges in a cloud-land. From his horseback the Norman captain shaded his eyes and peered into the mists.

"Move forward twenty paces! And down!" a sergeant said. His small porcine eyes, and pink cheeks puffing up with the effort of his shouted commands. His sword drawn, he shouted his order again. "Twenty paces! And down!"

The soldiers moved forward, and as a man dropped to one knee. The sergeant red-faced with the effort, braced to the ground then massaged his bandaged hand, sore where de Prendergast had used his whip. The archers moved down behind the infantry, readying their bows.

"Nock!" screamed FitzStephen. The archers eyes turned to a wiry sergeant with iron grey hair, flints for eyes, and a soft cap in place of the usual helm.

He repeated the captains command. "Nock!"

He pointed to the bridge, where the parapets loomed through the white. D'Courcey peered into the gap of the trees where for a moment a figure seemed to stand.

Horns. Arms, no wings.

A score of bows tilted to the sky. FitzStephen nodded to the archer's sergeant and slashed downward with his sword.

"Loose!" the sergeant called.

The arrows rained down on the carriageway, caromed off the stonework and into the mists.

Ah ha ha ha!

A tinkle of laughter echoed up from the trees. Or was it the chattering of the stream.

"Again!" FitzStephen called. His eyes wild, he stared into the mist. His hand clawed at his face.

This didn't look good. The men could not see what they were firing at. A few grumbles arose from the ranks as they drew more ammunition.

This looked to be a waste of arrows. D'Courcey turned to head back to his Captain's position but there behind him, was Giffard. Damnable man was near invisible in the trees. The infantry, got to their feet again.

"How's the scouting party going?" Giffard said, in his broad Languedoc accent. Was he himself one of those heretics?

"Just seeing what we can flush out from these trees," d'Courcey muttered.

"My captain speaks with the Irish King. We think it best to just go around," Giffard said. "If we want to take the village we can do it from the south, without having to cross the bridge and trip over whatever might be in this mist."

"Ground is soft south. Why ford the river, when there's a bridge," d'Courcey said. "We have made this decision."

"Your Captain thinks there is a risk at the bridge. Yes?" Giffard smiled, his thin lips stretching over yellowed teeth. "Who is he firing at?"

"It's covering fire," d'Courcey said. He sniffed, and furrowed his brow.

"Or is this bravado? Him proving he is not afraid of *faeries*?" Giffard asked, spitting the last word, gimlet eye piercing the lieutenant.

"Get the hence Monsieur. Go spy someplace," the lieutenant said, dismissing the Frenchman with a wave of his hand.

Giffard shrugged, as d'Courcey moved a pace or two away from him. The lieutenant made a show of surveying the battle field. Over the other side of the road, FitzStephen raised his sword in the air, and dug his heels into his mount. It reared up as he shouted.

"Again, damn you!!" FitzStephen screamed his order, cutting a heroic figure on his destrier.

"Nock!" called the sergeant of archers.

The red faced man at the head of the small group of infantry signalled to his men, and shouted "Down!"

Bowstrings tightened.

"I believe him. He sees what others do not," d'Courcey said, as much to himself as Giffard. He guided his horse past Giffard's and toward his captain.

And I saw something in the mists too.

In the deepest part of the mists Hilde could barely see her hand in front of her face. The cloying white on her legs made her shiver to her core.

The stone and earth of the bridge felt solid beneath her feet, but the first dawn light behind them filtering down through the trees illuminated the mists, creating a fantasy land where dim shapes moved into view, and only the chattering of the river over its course left and right gave them a sense of where they stood.

"Where is Donegal?" Hilde said.

"Damned if I know," Chief Fiach said. The two of them stood in the centre of the bridge. It seemed likely death would be very quick, but also unlikely that they'd see it coming. "He said he was trying to see where they were."

"Can I get on your shoulders?" Hilde asked.

"Ha. Surely," Fiach chuckled. He held out his hands, and she climbed to put her legs around his burly neck. "Tell me how many hundreds."

"I just want to see like Uncle Donegal," Hilde said. Through the mists ahead the road sloped up, and there on top of the roadway not more than two hundred yards away, stood rows of men in strange metal helmets. The man, the big madman who called himself FitzStephen, he was there too, on a horse, just outside the Dire Goose.

A loud thump and a grunt came.

"Get down! They're about to loose arrows!" a voice sounded, muffled through the mists just behind them. "Get under the bridge!"

It was Donegal. He appeared, grabbed Hilde under the arms, and rushed her to the end of the bridge.

Hilde giggled uproariously, as the rangy soldier thrust her over the parapet. They ducked under the arch just as a hail of arrows descended.

"What's so funny, ye daft girl!" Donegal said. "We could have died!"

"It tickled! Your hands! I didn't mean to laugh, I can't help it!" Hilde pouted. "Uncle, thank you though. I guess you saved me!"

The clattering sound of many shafts ricocheting off the bridge ceased after a short time. They moved quietly and quickly back onto the bridge. The sun slightly higher in the sky made the mists brighter but no less easy to see through.

"Chief, hold me up again! Please!! That man is there!" Hilde whispered.

"Ye crazy?" Fiach asked. But his tone recognised that they all had taken leave of their senses, for standing in front of certain death.

Hilde strained her neck and peered toward the figure on the horse outside the Inn.

"Hilde, keep still!" the Chief said.

"Trying to catch his attention," Hilde said. She stretched up and waved her arms.

"Oh my, they're firing again. Run."

An arrow sizzled past. It was too late.

27

Blood in the Water

Donegal stood at the side of the bridgehead by the time Hilde and Chief Caton got to the rear of the carriageway but the arrows already fell hard. The Chief picked Hilde up and threw her to Donegal, then dived himself over the parapet.

A hail of shafts collided with the carriageway they'd stood on only a moment ago. This time the volley was less disciplined, a few wayward shafts had signalled the onslaught.

"Cannot believe we are still alive," Donegal said, a lilt to his voice. His hand rested against the solid stonework of the bridge arch, his lungs heaving from the sprint.

"Told you! The Morrigan is with you!" Hilde said in a sing song.

"They'll likely send their army. Those men bending to let the arrows past? You have to leave Hilde," the Chief said.

Hilde folded her arms and stuck out her bottom lip. She rolled her eyes so much that the goats horn hood and cloak she wore circled with her.

"I'm getting up in the tree again," Donegal said, and he moved off.

Hilde's eyes tracked his departure, a hand pausing on Hilde's shoulder as if he wanted to add to the chief's warning.

After a moment his voice came through the cloak of white, almost as if from the spirits themselves.

"Hilde, the Chief's right. If the invaders don't take me, I'm sure your Mama will kill me in this life or the next for not keeping you out of harms way."

But Hilde followed the Chief as he walked forward across the bridge, a few more paces to where the mist thinned.

"Chief, hold me up again. I can hear their voices. It's that man from the cave, the big madman," Hilde said. "If I can somehow just reach him."

Fiach gave an anguished expression, but had seen how Hilde steadfastly refused to retreat to the village. He boosted her onto his shoulders again.

"I see him!" Hilde whispered.

"Careful Hilde!" Fiach warned.

"Captain FitzStephen!" Hilde called. "Captain FitzStephen!"

"Hilde stop!" Fiach said. "Ye can't parlay with these people!"

"Captain FitzStephen! Captain FitzStephen!" Hilde called again. She waved and stretched up. Then to the side.

"Careful! I'm losing you!" the chief stumbled to his left and Hilde reached out as it seemed she might fall. Hilde jumped down.

"Chief! They're sending warriors!" Hilde said, as she ran to the parapet. If it came to it, she could jump in the river and escape perhaps.

Fiach moved to the other parapet. There in the mists ahead a burly shape appeared. It was just one man. No neck, a scar down his face. Strong. A fighter, his helm with its nose piece marking him alien, bizarre. An invader.

Straining up from her perch on the parapet Hilde saw a couple more slowly coming down the hill. Eyes furtive below their helms.

What were they doing?

"The army's on the move!" hissed Donegal from somewhere above.

The Norman fighter appeared right in front of Hilde. She gasped.

The Chief moved, half-crouched, the curve of his huge back arcing as the axe in his hand flashed, a blur in the mist. For a fraction of a second it seemed he'd missed, the man who'd come would kill them.

The Norman's blade sliced inches from Hilde's neck.

But the man's head toppled and bounced across the carriage way. Hilde shook like a leaf. She raised her arms to balance and leapt back, far too late than would have saved her had it not been for the Chief's blade.

Like a huge beast now, the Chief's entire body seemed to shake as though lightning had struck it. The axe gripped in his fist, a conductor and the mists a field of lightning magic. He shouted a booming ear-splitting cry, the whites of his eyes blazing as Hilde had never seen him.

The whole army of the invaders advanced on them down the slope.

❖

Half of the disc of the sun rose above the horizon now. Arrows loosed in the second volley littered the broadway and stuck in trees. Among the men in the detachment voices raised slowly, querying tone, and whispers carried on the breeze. A whinny sounded from the mount of one the knights at the rear.

As Lieutenant d'Courcey reached FitzStephen's warhorse, the big Captain leapt from it. He landed awkwardly on his sore leg, but on the opposite side of his mount from the scouting party. No more reputational harm done.

"What are you doing Captain!" d'Courcey said as dismounted and tried to help the man. FitzStephen straightened and as he rounded his horse to the sight of his men held his chin up.

The Captain cupped a hand to his ear and paused.

"D'you not hear it d'Courcey?" the captain said. His eyes flared, daring the lieutenant to counter him.

Captain FitzStephen.

D'Courcey was about to shake his head in disbelief when again the tinkling voice floated through the cold dawn air.

Captain FitzStephen.

There in the mists, a yard above the ground, a horned figure floated just barely visible in the white. It raised its arms but they bore leathery skin like the wings of a demon.

"Morrigan!" FitzStephen shouted. It was a strange word. Learned perhaps in the Welsh prison. The burly captain walked forward, raising his sword and doing all in his power to hide the agony of his injured leg. "I will kill you!"

"Captain, no!" d'Courcey hissed. He flicked a glance to the opposite side of the army. Giffard still sat there in the shadows, shaking his head slightly.

Did he see it too? This Irish sorcery?

Captain FitzStephen. Captain FitzStephen.

The sing-song voice, high as birdsong whispered through the trees. The figure appeared through the mists again below them, its raised hand pointing downstream toward the sea. The dawn sun lit the fingers of mist with magical fire.

"Sergeant, take your men and kill that… Go!!" d'Courcey yelled to the red-faced man. He tried to restrain FitzStephen.

Captain FitzStephen.

"With me!" the stocky sergeant yelled, pointing at two men, and headed down the hill. The bridge was too narrow to fight more than three abreast. But after a few strides he saw he was alone. He stopped and turned, pointing at the two men, their faces pale. "You and you, now! Or be hanged!"

They were the ones de Prendergast had whipped, and a more sorry pair d'Courcey had not seen before. The sergeant cursed, and strode toward the bridge. A couple of men shouldered past the cowering pair and moved to catch up to the sergeant.

"Captain, stay here," the lieutenant said, clearing his throat and straightening in his saddle. "We'll deal with your Morrigan."

He'd meant the word to be said derisively but somehow he choked on it.

Despite himself a shiver ran down his spine as he said the strange Irish word. He rubbed his shoulders, suddenly feeling a chill. The word ran through the ranks, whispers and turned heads carrying it.

Morrigan.

The burly sergeant reached the parapets of the bridge but the horned figure had melted into the mists.

He quested ahead, shield up, with his sword held high. He went ahead two paces. The two soldiers behind quickened their advance. The rest of the detachment moved down the slope.

"It's alright! Nothing here!" called the sergeant. "Come on!"

And his head flew from his shoulders. An axe blade from nowhere, from the mists; a huge Ostman bearing it, like a ghost walking, like the reaper of souls himself.

"No!!" FitzStephen yelled. His face pale as parchment.

A handful charged, keen to avenge their fellows, now the enemy had shown themselves. The two sorry men slowed and raised their shields. FitzStephen wailed.

"Stay back!" d'Courcey screamed. The archers would not be able to fire, and the knights could not charge through the rabble.

Two men at the front ran forward onto the bridge, and a slender figure swung from above, bringing his sword down behind a soldier's shield onto the sorry man's neck. The slender figure kicked the dying man out of the way, on to the ground, dropped to a crouch and rammed his blade under the other mans shield, up through his gut into his heart.

As deadly as a tree asp. The figure melted back into the mists.

The two men lay both dead before their cries reached the ears of their comrades.

❖

On the high ground opposite the Inn, Giffard sat, his hands resting crossed at the wrists, reins of his destrier loosely looped through his fingers. He slowly closed his eyes, shook his head and blinked at the sight before him. The mad captain and his lieutenant d'Courcey had completely lost control. A whole detachment of soldiers in complete disarray.

Against, what, shadows? It looked as though there was two of them. A big man with an axe, plus a swordsman. And a third actually, a kind of shaman. Non-combatant by the looks. No troops behind them, else he'd have heard them.

They engaged the next wave of Norman soldiers but the narrow bridge meant no more than a couple could reach them at a time. But the villagers, at least those wielding weapons, were tiring already by the look.

No easy victory this way, FitzStephen's scouting party now looked to be making a full retreat. This would really not do. What a disgrace.

No trouble. Giffard tightened the straps on his greaves and tugged at his gloves. He took his buckler from his saddle.

The damnable luck of the Irish. They must've taken cover when the volleys of arrows came down. And somehow used the cover of the bridge to surprise the infantry. These Welsh Marcher lords were too used to fat, and ale, and comfort. And quite mad to boot. Letting themselves be distracted by the ridiculous shaman's antics marked them as amateurs.

The damn knights, even if only three of them, would be able to take however many of the poorly armed villagers were on the bridge. Villagers'd be no match for mounted and armoured knights. Giffard shaded his eyes and looked for the knights at the rear of the scouting party.

But the knights were caught up in the retreating rabble of soldiers.

This could not be left to rest. From the high ground here a perfect line lay to the right hand bridge head. Prendergast would not be happy to hear of an early loss.

Giffard was a knight still. He styled himself that still even though he now was more a fixer of problems. And still there were only two small problems on that bridge.

Giffard did like a fight when he was certain of winning.

He'd take the swordsman first. Then the one with the axe. And two Irish heads would make a nice message for the men.

Giffard spurred his horse, pulled his helm down into place, and charged.

Ducking into the mists and out again, the Chief cut down another invader. Donegal swung his sword like a man possessed, a grin spreading across his face. He braced off the parapet of the bridge, and sprang to get behind their shields. Their screams filled the narrow space of the bridgehead. Hilde found a branch like the one Donegal had been on and crouched, looking on, open-mouthed at the bloodshed.

The army that had been descending now turned. One or two still pressed on, but as the score of infantry men retreated the horsemen and archers in the rear scrambled to clear a path.

Hilde squatted on her bough, hugging her knees. It was horrifying to see these invaders' blood spurting from grievous wounds, injuries toppling them, ending their lives. But more chilling it was the Chief, her Uncle Don, men she'd known all her short life, taking them. Heroic tales from books was not the same as gore and death on the muddy ground.

But fear and exhaustion still addled Hilde's mind and everything that passed before her became like a dream. The axe now stitched itself into a tapestry. The bright crimson spurting from the invaders neck flowed as the stroke of a brush, red ink on a page in one of Gobnait's books.

From her perch on the parapet of the bridge she saw a man ran in from Uncle Donegal's right. She saw herself, heard herself call out to him, her words black ink, joining the red running against the white mists. Don's blade flashed. A man fell over the parapet, his blood a red streamer in the water.

Then to her left thundered a dragon.

Hot breath flaming in the dawn sun, a dark man on a big horse bore down on them, too fast. He moved so quick, in a second the heaving mountain of beast, his huge destrier was upon them.

The Chief made a powerful sweeping blow like that which'd fallen deadly to all comers in the brief heartbeats of the battle so far. Hilde's heart leapt into her throat.

Against the horseman the blow was for naught.

The Chief's axe though cold truth for footmen could not reach to a mounted warrior sword held high, on a rearing barded horse. The black and green knight struck downward from his saddle. The Chief fell against the parapet, groaning, a wound down the side of his head, ear hanging by meat.

The man in black and green, like Donegal was not big, but his moves came fast and none were wasted. Donegal turned, glanced at the Chief, and leapt to meet the towering threat. Don jumped on to the mans stirrup and grabbed at his saddle to pull himself in striking range.

Striking up against the horseman's armour rendered Donegal's blows weak, and the man snapped out with his small shield, pushed aside the Irishman's sword and caught the side of Don's head in a wicked blow. He worked to right his saddle, canted off from the Irishman's weight.

Hilde felt sick. The illusion of the heroic parchment page evaporated. Donegal was down, his head saved by his old helm, but the brittle leather was now in two. His sword lay just beyond his hand on the carriageway.

The Chief blinked, struggling to orient himself, streams of his own blood flowing in his eyes. There were no more of Duncormac left to raise arms.

The man in black and green came on. A man with a mirthless smile. He sprang from his horse, blade and body in unison, every move planned. He landed lightly a pace from the prone soldier. The foreigner, as certain as the falcon to a mouse, there to end Donegal's life.

The Irishman turned his head up from the mud of the carriageway, and there was no fear. He reached for his sword, to be sure he'd die with it in his hand. A trickle of blood ran from Donegal's mouth. The mirthless man's blade descended, his armoured shoulders, forearms and sword all of one piece in the dawn light.

28

Dawn

A hammer came from nowhere. Flew out of the white. Hilde gasped and held a hand to her mouth.

Saint Brigit save us.

It struck the invader in the stomach, and he frowned. As if an insect had bothered him.

The knight in green and black, and his downward sword blow, folded like a bedsheet. The billet of iron thrown with the force that makes legend, would have downed many. Winded, the knight bent as if to look at the hammer as it tumbled to the stone. The man stumbled back two paces, and raised his head, looking for his next sword blow.

But Fergus Keenan strode from the mist, long legs closed the gap, more hammers at his waist, and another long handled one in his raised hand, its pointed end flying down toward the invaders head.

With that uncanny speed, the man in black and green, snapped out his small shield, and braced his stance, moving at the same time toward his horse.

The blacksmith's bulk and height all lay behind that hammer blow. And the pointed end of the metal piercing the shield drove the invaders hand down, forcing his whole body off balance. Keenan raised his boot to kick the mans head like a pigs bladder at the May fair.

The man's other hand groped, reached his saddle, and yanking hard, pulled himself clear of Fergus' boot with no more than a hairsbreadth to spare him. Hilde jumped from the parapet and ran to Donegal. The trickle of blood from his mouth flowing stronger now, his eyes fluttered then shut.

The Chief groaned, cried out, tried to move onto his hands but collapsed on the carriageway. The invaders horse skittered a few steps as the chief's axe landed with a clatter on the stonework next to the beasts legs. Fergus raised his hammer again, advanced, but the man in green and black half-ran, half-dragged to keep up with his mount, slipped further away.

The invader vaulted onto his horse and urged it on, his left hand a mangled mess where Fergus' hammer had caught it. He cursed a bloody oath in his language as he hunched over his injury, urging his destrier in a canter back up the slope.

Hilde squinted now as the sun climbed fully out over the eastern horizon and the main road glared in its rays. The man in green and black bent over his horses neck, screaming commands at his compatriots headed over the crest of the hill. Whatever his orders were they apparently fell on deaf ears.

Hilde took a few steps out into the light. In front of the Dire Goose Inn the big madman sat alone on his horse. Hilde raised her arms then strode forward to take a stand at the edge of the bridge.

❖

D'Courcey swivelled in his saddle. *This is madness.*

There is no Morrigan. It's just mist.

"Stay in your ranks!" the thin faced lieutenant screamed.

Archers strained, some trying to see through the mists, others stretching their bows. A couple of arrows flew, went wide. One hit a Norman infantry-man in the shoulder. No shaft found its way to the figures fighting in the mist.

"Stop firing!" howled the sergeant with the iron grey hair. He balled his fists, tore off his cap, cursing a bloody oath, and threw it on the ground. "Who told you to fire!"

"Get back, get back!" screamed FitzStephen. "Doom is upon us!"

A score of soldiers turned and retreated. They'd seen their countrymen cut down by figures that leapt from the mists, from the trees. An eerie horned figure that presided over all of it impervious to their arrows.

A pair of crows flew out from a bush, disturbed from their torpor by the men crashing up against their perch.

Arrk, arrk, ark.

One soldier screamed, pushed his countryman over in panic. Soon they were all running. One man, flecks of foam on his lips rushed into a boulder and fell. Another man turned, saw his fallen comrade, and sunk to his knees making the signs of the cross. A stray arrow caught him in the face and he too fell.

Other men kept their cool, snarled and cursed, glaring and gesturing at FitzStephen, as they moved back up the hill. The captain on his horse now sat resolute, impassive. The archers sergeant cuffed several of his men around the ears with his own bow of yew, and threatened to shoot others himself if they would not stop firing.

But now the infantrymen had all withdrawn, or lay dead. The field of battle cleared, but the archers sullenly put arrows back in quivers, and turned to follow their colleagues up the road.

Down in the mists, the Morrigan stood, on the bridge head. Unscathed. A hundred arrows, and the demon stood untouched.

The waters ran with our blood. The bridge is cursed.

D'Courcey walked his horse over the crest, to put the small valley forever behind him. To never speak of it again.

After a time FitzStephen followed.

❖

Hilde stood there akimbo.

You will not come this way.

The big man for the first time since she'd seen him hung his proud head. He turned walked his horse back over the crest of the hill and out of sight.

"Don't try to move Fiach," Keenan said, bending and wiping the blood from the chiefs face. "I'm sorry I did'nae come earlier."

The smith looked at the chief's loose ear, and pressed it back into place. The smith tore off his shirt, and wound it twice about the Chief's head, then scooped the big Ostman's arms under his. The muscles in the smith's arms and back bulged under the strain as he lifted the big man clear of the road. There would be no-one for miles around that could have made that lift.

Hilde wiped her Uncle's forehead. He was cold. She laid her goatskin over him. His eyes blinked open. "Ach, Hilde, that thing stinks."

Hilde grinned from ear to ear. "They've gone, Uncle! You beat them!"

282

Keenan shot a glance toward the main road, but bent to his task of getting the leader of their village to safety. "Ye weigh as much as a heifer, man!"

"No dying on me Caton. They're not done with us yet," Donegal said wryly, as he heaved himself off the carriageway. He rubbed his head, and ran his fingers through his hair. He gazed at his hand, fingers in front of his face as if counting them in disbelief. "Still not dead, hey? And you, my she-devil. Ye'll never listen to me will ye?"

"Are you alright Uncle?" Hilde asked, helping the rangy soldier to his feet. "Your eyes went funny."

"That knight in the black. He rung my bell pretty hard," Donegal said. He kicked at the old leather helm, now split in two. The pieces rolled across the carriageway to rest against the parapet. He sighted down his blade, its edge dented and surface caked with blood. "I'm still on my feet."

Hilde extricated herself from her Uncle's arm. He swayed back and forth, blinked, and nodded to her. Then moved out to the light to gaze up the main road.

"But Hilde, we haven't won. They'll regroup. The best soldiers fight when they know they can win. That man in the black and green, he'll be reporting back."

Hilde moved over to Fergus Keenan's side, and looked over his shoulder. He wore just a woollen singlet, his shirt wrapped around the Chief's head.

"Fergus, is the Chief alright?" Hilde asked. A tear snuck out of her eye and rolled onto her cheek. The smith held the Chief clear of the ground, but the big ostman could not take steps on his own without collapsing. A trickle of blood ran down his head from under the gore-soaked impromptu bandage.

"Let's get him back to Pádraig's. Missus O'Neill can tend to him," Fergus said, a catch in his voice.

Fergus, Fiach, Donegal and Hilde arm-in-arm, moved down imping, half-dragging, off the bridge, back toward the village. At the Dire Goose Inn a shutter opened a crack.

"Uncle Don, the chief will live won't he?" Hilde gripped Donegal's arm hard.

More from the pain of her pulling on his arm, he slowly shook his head, but then realisation gripped them all. Especially the soldier.

The pain. At coming away from yet another battle where he was alive. And the good man who he'd joined battle with did not leave with him.

He began to sob. And shake. The grip of drink turned on Donegal with a vengeance in that moment. He looked back at the Dire Goose. "Ye head on now, I have to go give something back that doesn't belong to me."

The sun rose above the horizon, and the gulls screeched in the distance toward the sea.

On an early Sunday morning.

❖

"It's only waist deep sir! Right here!" the scout said, standing dripping in front of de Prendergast as he pointed back behind himself at the bend of the Muck River. "Water's clean too."

"Here!" shouted de Prendergast, signalling the young infantry scout back to his post on the other bank. The chiselled planes of his face remained impassive, as he turned and stood in his saddle to the columns of men behind him. Archers, infantrymen, Normans and Leinster-men restlessly waiting for his order. A lieutenant, a grizzled veteran with a bad leg but a stout arm, stood next to a standard-bearer with de Prendergast's flag. He raised his hand to his brow in a salute, and to see his Captains face as he gave the order.

"We march! Single file! Bring up the wagon!" shouted de Prendergast. The lieutenant, nodded and shouted orders down the line.

The sun rose up over the horizon now, and with it the prospect of fording the river became more pleasant, as its depth could be clearly seen as trivial in the good light. The scout, a young welshman with a crooked nose and a cauliflower ear, nodded, saluted to the orders and waded back across the watercourse.

Below this spot the ground became marsh, sodden and treacherously soft. Above it the trees and lee of the hill tightened the river into a deeper and much more challenging channel of rapid water. Just here they'd found a good crossing. Whatever happened at the bridge, de Prendergast hoped it didn't further delay an already tardy campaign.

The young welshman hitched his pack on his back, and as he reached his post stood with his flag raised, there on the opposite bank. Two men on horseback stood further up the bank from him, casting about, looking into the east, into the rising sun toward the low hills for their direction. Down the column a squad of men responded to shouted commands from their sergeant and to a count of three lifted a sturdy wooden cart onto their shoulders.

De Prendergast tugged on the reins of his barded warhorse, kneeing it forward down the bank and into the waters of the Muck River. The sky above clear and blue, home to wheeling gulls, corvids and honey eaters, lit even brighter as the sun climbed into its cerulean dome. The distant hedge birds chattering in the nearby rows of trees mirrored the chattering of the men, all seeming to gossip about the promise of a new dawning day.

It'd been too long for fighting men to be stuck on this damn hill. Moving felt good.

Ahead over the dawn horizon in the east lay Wexford, and an easy victory. FitzStephen's fall from grace would be to de Prendergast's great benefit. Always a place for killing, and murdering, but always its best done selectively and quietly. Staying on the right side of the populace cost less in terms of soldiering.

The wedding with the King of Ossary's daughter a brilliant stroke of statesmanship in that regard, while also a service to his loins. As de Prendergast's eyes were leagues away, on the bustline of Éadaoin, the smell of her lavender on his mind, he allowed the big warhorse its head as it crossed the river.

The warhorse picked over the stones in the middle of the watercourse, then as de Prendergast dug his heels into the big mare's flanks she galloped the last few paces up the riverbank, before any chance to sink into the soft ground. But from this higher ground in the distance, an ill-ordered gaggle of helms, horses and riders rounded the hilltop.

FitzStephen.

His unmistakeable profile on the skyline there, his scouting party a rag-tag group of infantry and archers, half-running, milling about as they moved around onto the lane toward the sea.

It'd been crystal clear that the scouting party was a pointless exercise, but would the big buffoon make an issue of the fact that de Prendergast had already marched the men east? Not if he wanted another embarrassment, but then he barely seemed in control of his own mind, let alone his actions.

Another great scene would not help morale.

"Get that cart across dry! Sergeant!" shouted de Prendergast. The young welshman moved a few paces down the bank, and shouted advice to the men shouldering the wooden wagon, and they sought a better footing. "Stay single file!"

As the group rounded the bend from the crossroads onto the lane and all of their strength could be seen, de Prendergast's mouth dropped open. There was a dozen men missing.

And there was Giffard, slowing his horse as he emerged from the trees. He hunched over his horse, nursing his left hand.

"Lieutenant. Get me a report! What the blazes happened at that bridge," de Prendergast shouted, pointing at the sorry detachment of fighters filing down the lane toward the back of the army. The lieutenant followed his gaze, but lacking the vantage of his captain, furrowed his brow. He exchanged some words with a sergeant and looked for his horse.

The man from the Languedoc, rode with his saddle not quite straight on his horse. Giffard, his face like thunder, looked up at his captain across the hundred yards and the river that separated them and mouthed the bloodiest curse de Prendergast'd seen. The Frenchman's cast was so black even at this distance de Prendergast saw that he had murder in his eyes.

"Get that report now lieutenant!" de Prendergast said, in a tone that made his man abandon the thought of asking any question. The lieutenant sprang onto his roan destrier and galloped up the lane.

29

The Ire of the Witch

"I'm telling you sir, there's something with this village," Giffard said. "Devils, they're devils."

"Don't be ridiculous," de Prendergast said. The column of men, horses and equipment filed past behind him and up a lane that led toward the east.

They stood in front of a small farm, at a junction between the lane, and the bigger road that led from inland down the eastern bank of the river. Through fruit trees and stone walls the rooftops of a small village peeked perhaps a few hundred yards away. The farm looked abandoned, the front door ajar. No doubt the knights had already ransacked it for spoils.

"Just one detachment of men, that is all I ask," Giffard said, gingerly wrapping his mangled left wrist with his neckerchief. He jerked his head in the direction of the village. "Kill them all, burn the place to the ground."

"What's the fastest way to Wexford?" de Prendergast asked. He signalled to the welsh scout holding the flag to join on the end of the column as the last of them forded the river, then acknowledged the lieutenant who galloped to a stop nearby.

"What?" Giffard said, as he finished binding, pulling the knots tight with his teeth. He pointed east with his good hand. "There, over that hill."

"So, my loyal advisor, why should we go into the village?" said de Prendergast walking his horse closer to Giffard's and jerking his thumb in the direction of the village.

The frenchman's face reddened, his eyes full of tears of rage and pain. His usual detachment and calculation replaced by cold hatred. De Prendergast grabbed the man's left hand, and lifted it. "Can't hold a shield. What use are you to me?"

Giffard bit off a curse, then clenched his jaw, biting his lip until it bled. He refused to cry out with the pain of his hand, but his eyes filled with tears anyway.

"Who did this?" de Prendergast said. He let the ruined hand go.

"Witch," Giffard said, through gritted teeth. He hunched over his horses mane. "Ostmen."

De Prendergast held the reins of his mare, bringing it a few steps up onto the narrow road. He dug in his saddlebag, and pulled an earthenware flask. He pulled the waxed cork stopper with his teeth and drew a mouthful of the liquor before handing it to Giffard.

The frenchman looked up at him, and wiped his eyes. He drained the flask and sucked his teeth. "Merci."

De Prendergast pointed east, and slapped Giffard's horse on its rear and it took a few steps. "Go."

Giffard took one last look at the village and mouthed off another curse, before following de Prendergast's orders.

Witch.

Ideas like that were dangerous.

❖

Hilde sat on the bridge parapet, in the shade of the willows, the last of the morning mists pooling in the river bed below. The dawn sun now glared low in the eastern sky, a damning yellow eye. At the western end of the bridge a patch of bright sun played across bloodstains and the bodies of fallen warriors.

She daren't shut her eyes for the images of the Chief caked in blood that pushed into her minds eye. What Uncle Donegal had said started to become clear at last, how the world continuing on made no sense when others who were so much more than you had lost their lives.

As Fergus dragged the Chief into Pádraig's, Donegal had slunk off, and Hilde knew where. She'd followed for a short time, and upon seeing him go into the Dire Goose she realised she did not know what she could possibly say. How could she ask him to give any more. And now she found herself here on the bridge. Among the blood of the foreigners and the blood of her people.

Her Mama, still imprisoned in the round house at Pádraig's, had been spared any of this. Hilde always went to her with every question and now, how could Mama know anything that was more important that this mortal truth? It all seemed futile. She'd talked to Hilde always of the grace of Saint Brigid, told her she must listen to the lessons from the sisters at St Moragh's. For what?

Had those dead soldiers a god they prayed to? For what?

Hilde's hands were chilled through from gripping the stone of the bridge, and she crouched now, like a raven knees tucked under the goatskin, hands under her arms. She felt stuck half-way between Hades and the waking world. The watercourse of the Muck chattered from the distance, past St Moragh's, past the trees that crowded the banks and down through the stone arches underneath her.

The long bough Donegal had crouched on to gain a vantage in the battle over this very bridge wavered in a gentle morning breeze, a yard from the bridge. The leaves of the willows filtered the sun draping its bark in patterns of green dappling. Hilde pulled her goatskin cloak closer about her. The day warmed but a core of cold settled in her gut.

It seemed an outrage, a devastation of everything that the bible held about good and evil, about a powerful god who saw all. It felt like the saints had abandoned her as too unworthy for mercy, and that from now her existence would be tragic, bereft of blessings.

❖

"He's not making any sense sir. Keeps talking about a Morrigan," the lieutenant said. The sat astride their horses, on a lane just the other side of the river. "Captain has lost twelve men. But I agree it sounds like madness."

The old lieutenant had been giving the report de Prendergast'd asked for some moments already. He was not given to fancy, but the events he related made less sense with each one he related. He'd grilled FitzStephen and d'Courcey but none of what they said made any sense.

"Twelve men dead?" de Prendergast asked. He walked his horse slowly up the road toward the village. In front of him, flanking left and right two mounted knights walked, their swords drawn, and shields up. Both good men, de Prendergast had had them on raids before. "Of a detachment of twenty to thirty? Archers and and infantry?"

Both men's gaze strayed now, and checked the tree line for ambush, traps, ballistae and other trickery. Welsh-Norman hard men all, who knew a smattering of Irish. One, Montaigne, shared De Prendergast's Flemish ancestry and pragmatism.

This shaman and their tricks must be shown as nothing for the men be afraid of. They had to be ready to win a siege at Wexford if it came to that. Just a short deviation to put down this witch nonsense, then they'd catch the army with no time lost.

Twelve men dead. Not good for morale. If they could not find and kill this "witch", a few villagers head's do instead.

"Aye, these Ostmen 'came up from the dead'. That's what the captain said," the lieutenant pulled a face as he relayed the words. He shook his head, as the blonde captain stared at him. He pointed to the river where mists still clung to the tree line. "They rose up from that Irish mist."

"Dead men?" de Prendergast asked rhetorically, one brow raised. He spat on the ground. "Dead men stay dead. How did two dead Irishmen kill twelve of ours?"

"Some were shot by our own bowmen, a couple more somehow… were taken by the river mists. Found dead by a rock."

"Mists?" de Prendergast asked. Éadaoin *was* full of fancies. He'd heard talk of the mists before from her.

"Aye. They hold that the Morrigan lives there. The dead are there, in the other land behind the mists."

He tried to remember some of the stories Éadaoin had told him. Tales that she'd heard as a child. These Irish, a beautiful people at times, but so dim. Like cows. "Mists cannot hurt a man, lieutenant. What's this Morrigan?"

"Not sure sir. Some kind of witch goddess," the lieutenant peered into the trees and undergrowth a long the river on their left as if something would leap from it. Despite the sun rising higher in the east, the mists clung stubbornly to the low ground between the raised banks of the river.

Crows on the branches of a nearby willow tendered their thoughts.

Arrk. Ark. Ark.

The left most of two knights in front jerked his reins and his horse reared, taking him a moment to bring it under control.

"Alright, that house," de Prendergast indicated a thatched roof and small barn just ahead in the orchard. "Kill everyone in there. Find someone to tell us where this witch is."

The Normans walked closer to the lane leading down to the house and through the willows the bridgehead hove into view through wisps of mist. Here the taller trees shaded the sun, and the night chill clung. As his knights went to the house, bashed the door down and went inside, de Prendergast walked a few more steps up the road.

"Lieutenant," de Prendergast whispered. He moved his horse back along the road a pace.

"Oui?" the lieutenant said, turning from watching the house.

De Prendergast pointed. Hovering above the bridge's parapet, a horned figure stared at him from the mists. Staring black eye sockets. Arms that were leathery wings. Despite himself he shuddered.

The lieutenant trotted his horse to where de Prendergast stood and pointed still. The lieutenant followed his gaze.

"Can't see anything sir. What am I looking for?"

"Idiot," said de Prendergast. "There!"

But the figure was gone.

The lieutenant looked at his captain and blinked, he opened his mouth once, ran his tongue across his teeth.

"Damn it all man. Get those men out of there, follow me," de Prendergast said. He cantered his horse toward the bridge, and dismounted. He looped the reins over a branch. "It was there, I swear."

"Yes sir," the lieutenant said. He pulled his horse up to the same tether and then ran a few steps down the lane to bellow orders to the knights inside the house. "I'll get them."

Meanwhile de Prendergast drew his sword, and flexed his hands inside his grieves. He walked toward the bridge.

There it was again. The horns resolved through the river mist, and a light breeze cleared the wisps away. She stood on the bridge parapet, hands on hips. Not floating, not flying, just standing up on the parapet. A trick.

The figure looked like a young girl, draped in some kind of goatskin cloak. Face caked with dirt. Not a devil at all.

A mortal. Who could die.

As de Prendergast approached, he examined the tree canopy, and checked all the approaches. The mists were retreating. The intelligence had been they used mist cover to attack, but there was no attackers left.

Let's get poor Giffard his scalp.

De Prendergast swung his sword, circling it to warm up his arm. But there would only be one stroke.

The girl began screaming, some Irish gobble. A spell perhaps? Summon the dead?

A smile curled at the edge of de Prendergast's mouth.

There is no-one coming.

Let this be the last we hear talk of witches.

"Ye trying to sell back to me my own property now, Dónal O'Rourke?" Thomas O'Brien said. He set his hand on the blade that lay on the pockmarked timber of the Dire Goose's bar.

Some days he might have been joking, with a comment like that, but today, when a foreign army marched outside his door anger and fear made his leering face even uglier than it usually was.

He pushed the sword away as if it were a bent penny. O'Brien wrung out the rag he had in his hand in a bucket and wiped down the bar. Over by the fire Emma, glanced up from cleaning with a stiff brush and shovel, where a mess of spilled coals and ash stuck to the dirt floor.

"No, no. Its your sword, Thomas. And I'm sorry about the helmet. She only took it because it was all together," Donegal said. He rested his hands on the bar, to stop the tremors. The smells in the Inn, so familiar. His body so ready for the sweet taste.

"She? That damn witch spawn niece of yours?" Thomas said. "Well I'll be taking it, and you'll be having no ale from me, unless you have payment!"

Donegal rubbed his head, the beating he'd had still surrounding him with stars and lights in his vision. Thomas set a taper to light two more lamps. Thomas moved to bar the door again. He'd taken an age to open it after Donegal's knocking.

"Nothing for the fact I just fought for the village!" Donegal said. Hilde was right, the damn man was craven to the core. "They're not gone you know! Still a threat!"

"My lord, look at you! Covered in blood!" Thomas said, tucking a rag in to his apron string. "That injury looks bad man. You should go up to the priory."

"Its not my blood and guts. The Chiefs and a few of them invaders. I told you. I saved the village this morn!" Donegal protested.

"Ah tosh. The last of them marched through the fens. As if a drunk like you got anything to do with them leaving. They're up through the goat paddock on the three hills now. Away with ye. Not have the walking dead in my Inn," Thomas said.

"Thomas, please. Please man," Donegal said. His body quivered with the pain of existing. The shame of standing on his own two legs, the walking who should be dead. He closed his eyes. The face of Chief Fiach Caton looked down on him. The face of Arran Blaine. Tears streamed down his face.

"Ye pathetic shite. Saints save me. Wait here by the fire and I'll get ye summat to eat at least, we have some scraps," Thomas said. He started toward a bucket of barley and shooed away the vermin from it, but then stopped.

Thomas cocked an ear. "Wait, ye hear that? Sounds like your heretic girl calling now."

"Her names Hilde. A wee girl who's got more bravery in her little finger than your whole fat body, Thomas Maine," Donegal said. He straightened. "And I'll be having my sword back."

"Your sword!" Thomas spluttered. He raised the piece of wood that he looked to bar the door with as if it were a shillelagh, to strike him. His face soured and he gritted his teeth as he rounded the bar toward Donegal.

"Shove yer scraps up yer backside," Donegal said. He snatched the sword and shouldered past Thomas out the door. Outside the cries of Hilde were loud, then they stopped.

Last time I ever come here to the Dire Goose.

Donegal ran for all he was worth toward the bridge.

From the roadway voices floated, and Hilde turned, walked a few steps along the parapet. A man in Norman armour. Not a speck of dirt on him, fine breeches, his blonde hair stirred by the breeze. Like a knight from a book. His movements so precise, a pleasant smile on the hard chiselled planes of his face. He looked directly at her, pointing.

Hilde called out, but only a croak came out of her mouth.

The blonde haired man issued some orders to his countryman in his tongue, pointed again, peering in her direction with his helm under his arm. He was a captain then, like the madman. But his very manner chilled Hilde to the bone.

Nearby him several horses stood. The blonde captain called toward Pádraig's homestead which lay behind him in the orchard. The countryman nodded and walked back in that direction.

The blonde haired captain turned back looked right at Hilde and kept walking, that same even smile on his face. As if he'd found a ripe peach unattended on a tree. The sound of his boots crunching in the mud and leaf mulch of the bridgehead snapped Hilde from her stupor.

Hilde screamed her Uncle's name at the top of her lungs. The invaders smile spread wider.

She couldn't move, her legs failed her. She willed herself to run up the bridge into the west. Surely the soldiers who'd gone that way were gone now, she must run. But against that was the cramping cold, the exhaustion; but also she froze inside.

Hilde clasped her hands to her head.

Save me.

She called inside, shouting soundlessly to her gods, to the old ones. That day she'd left home, her Mama had left the statuette of Saint Brigid to look after her, that was the time the rain came. The feeling that came over her was as then.

The god of the sisters of St Moragh, of the Bishop had no power over this man who walked toward her. As if he had all the time in the world, as if his cool blue-grey eyes fixing her to the spot, as if the sword he moved in patterns was as inevitable as the seasons, as this day.

Hilde turned, sprang upward, reaching for the bough with her toe across a gap as wide as a man is tall.

It was a leap greater than any she'd made playing in the pear tree. No time to think. It happened before she could know what she was doing. And for all she'd willed her legs to move, now they exploded with this crazed leap she scrambled to reach for handholds in the branches above as well. All limbs flailing as though with enough work she might walk on the air itself.

And her toe landed, above a hand gripped, the tails of her goatskin flapped and she skidded on the bark, nearly falling as her body spun around the hand-hold, just finding another grip in time. Hilde found herself staring at the man two yards away, shaking his head slightly.

He sprang as though his feet had wings, and landed lightly on the parapet. Now just a yard away, he took a swing and Hilde screamed.

The blade passed within inches, as Hilde swung away, her feet flailing out six yards above the rocky riverbed, hands clinging desperately to the branches above.

❖

"Hie! Invader!!" a clod flew between Hilde and the blonde man.

He turned, leaning back easily out of the projectiles path. He jumped back onto the carriageway and picking his every footfall, walked toward the sunlight, where Donegal stood.

The Irishman, two hands on his sword, moved sideways, and kicked one of the dead bodies. He drew a finger across his own throat and then pointed at the blonde captain.

I killed your countrymen. Now I'm going to kill you.

The blonde haired man lowered his stance almost imperceptibly, the muscles in his thighs bunching. He was a head shorter than Donegal, but he moved like a cat. His speed landing on the bridge was terrifying. The invader tilted his head slightly watching Donegal move in the patch of sunlight.

The Irishman's side was covered in gore and guts, and his tunic gaped from a cut, blood seeping down it slowly. As he stepped, circling measuring his distance from the Norman Captain, it was plain he'd taken a bad wound there. He hunched slightly and the grimace on his face as he took a step that side confirmed it.

Still the Irishman taunted him, he winked at Hilde, even as he clutched a hand at his wound.

Another step on his left side, Donegal's foot turned on an unseen rock, the injury on his left causing him to bend, become vulnerable.

And the blonde captain sprang. He was too fast, covering the ground between him and Donegal in the blink of an eye. His blade aimed with a deadly lunge straight to capitalise on the wound in Donegal's side.

But there was no wound. There was no rock.

Donegal pushed to the side and back off his front foot, with a speed of his own that'd be impossible if he had been wounded. He dropped low on his back leg and swung his sword into the blonde captains path, slashing directly into his midriff with both hands on his blade.

It was a blow that would've spilled guts and dropped any man, but the invader turned his lunging blade over in a move too fast to follow. He parried outward, and Donegal's blade slid up the other man's to its hilt. Donegal's arms quivered and bunched with the effort, but finally pushed his blow past the invaders guard.

Donegal's blow won out, he had two hands on his blade to the invaders one. The man was made of iron, but Donegal's old bloody sword ran up the mans greaves slicing into his elbow. He pushed him, trapping his blade further, trying to unbalance the blonde-haired man.

Donegal shouted and spat. His eyes flared. The ruse was clever, that of an old warrior. Donegal was fast and used every ounce of his strength, but this invader was a man of iron.

Hilde stared, both hands shoved in her mouth with horror. The man struggled to free his blade and turn it on the Irishman. But at the same time as his bodyweight moved through the lunge, he spun and moved to sweep Donegal's front leg.

"Merde," the captain said, in a matter-of-fact tone. He hadn't expected the ruse with the faked injury. None of this was to plan, and he clearly didn't like that.

Donegal saw the leg coming from below, and dove into the carriageway, pushing his opponents blade overhead, and denying the blonde captain's kick its target.

The Norman captain feinted a lunge, and then again, skipping with his front foot. Donegal's eyes were everywhere even though his body was relaxed, and he ignored the captains distractions. Then suddenly a lunge turned into a vicious cut from above, the captain raising his blade at the last minute to bring it down on Donegals right shoulder so fast his sword was a blur.

Donegal moved slowly but his shoulder was not there when the Captains sword whistled past, and instead the Irishman's looping, gangly kick that snaked out of nowhere aimed straight for the captains exposed ribcage.

It nearly struck home.

"Hilde, run!" Donegal yelled. The cocky expression gone, he circled looking for any mistake. The captain made none.

Hilde backed along the parapet. She could run to Fergus for help, but he was in the house where the blonde captains compatriots had gone.

She looked back up the main street. Over the crest of the Priory hill a large black shape. It resolved, a group of two dozen figures in black, walking toward them.

The Priory. They'd be too late to help. Hilde backed away up the street toward them.

Donegal sprang, braced off the parapet wall and aimed a cut down behind the captains buckler. The blonde invader braced, pivoted and turned the blow aside. Landing, Donegal aimed a kick at the mans legs.

The captain swapped his sword to his left hand and flung his right hand out to the rear for balance as he danced to stay out of the kick's way. Donegal lashed out with a chancy blow at the man's chin, but only landed a grazing punch. The Irishman pushed through the blow, and hit the invader hard in the shoulder with his elbow.

Donegal was trying to drive the man away from Hilde. If only her legs would work. The figures in black walking up the road did not seem real. What did it mean?

The blonde man choked back a shout of surprise. He spat in Donegal's face, blood and spittle dripping down the Irishman's forehead. Donegal was tired. His movements slowing, with the heavy weapon.

If the punch to his shoulder from the sword's guard hurt him he showed no sign, two slashes in quick succession followed by a kick aimed at Donegal's knee. The Irishman pulled back but came up against the side of the bridge. He used no shield and stood off balance, no way to defend himself.

The Norman grinned. He twirled his sword. Donegal closed his eyes.

"Leave him!" Hilde screamed.

"Morrigan!" the Irishman said. He meant Hilde, it was a warning for her to be quiet. "Take me!"

"Silence!" The Norman screamed the foreign word, and pressed his sword up against Donegal's throat. "Il n'y a pas de Morrigan!"

The Norman's words made no sense but Hilde understood the fury on his face. This was not battle. It was vengeance.

"I'm ready. Spare the chief. Take me," Donegal said, his voice hoarse as the Norman sword pushed at his throat.

The steel hot like a poker burned through Donegal's flesh, blood pulsed over the blade.

"No. Uncle! No!" cried Hilde.

30

Into the Mists

All the world slowed. A breeze that blew from the cold tops of the Blackstair Mountains stole on tiptoes through the willow branches along the Muck. Birds hung in the air. A fine mist of rain began to fall, but each drop glided, sliding down silently. Hilde no longer breathed. Her eyes could not open any wider, and her grip on the branch froze solid.

Death that crept about the bodies on the road whispered grey hushing words that nipped at Hilde's ears. She rose out of her body.

Her icy hands clung with their own disembodied will to the branches of the tree that overhung the bridge. From above herself, she saw the players around her on a silent stage, her Uncle Don, the blonde haired man of iron from over the sea.

In the breeze the mists roiled so thick now, curls of white writhing up afresh to tease the tree boughs.

Drawn from her body she willed herself to care but the horror of the invaders blade at her Uncle's throat, a red gout of blood on his tunic occupied all that she was.

In the river behind her, there knelt a figure. It was the mist. Come real.

A woman washed rags at the waters edge, blood streaming from them. Blood that never stopped coming. Not rags, but armour, a tunic. Now the shape became mist again, and the shape rose, and without turning Hilde knew the figure regarded her. Voices raged in Hilde's head to move, to run, but everything was frozen and she floated above herself.

Hilde's body shook, but risen above it as she was the tremors did not reach her mind or her eye. The wail of pain that surged against Hilde's throat had no outlet as she floated so distant from her own frame.

The blonde man, the angles of his cheeks bunched with fibres of muscle as he screamed at Donegal, commanding him in words Hilde did not understand. But the invader too moved so slowly, his words a drawl, jaw working in lazy arcs.

There was only one word the foreigner said that Hilde knew. *Morrigan.*

Then the foreigner did no longer grip his prey. The Irishman became mist for a moment and slipped away from his sword, from his locked arms, slowly falling.

The goddess of war, the fate, her fingers of fog, arms of rain, body of bridge-stone and mist, hair of bloodied battlefield grass now received Dónal Ua Ruairc. The Irishman's face shone serene, even above the bloody red gash on his throat, as he fell like a leaf from an autumn tree over the parapet of the bridge.

He fell into the mists, the chattering invisible waters below, and was gone.

❖

At the tail of a long column of armed men that wound over the Broken Hill, riders in Norman armour moved east in sullen silence. The lane they travelled up narrowed to a goat track between black stone outcrops that rose up through the grass. Horses and men at arms strained at a cart with supplies and it too passed up the defile. Jittery Norman archers peered into the rocks that stood like rotten teeth along the crest of the escarpment, but found only crows that mocked their passage.

A young goatherd wrestled a group of his unruly charges in a paddock at one of the hilltops and planted his crook to watch the column march by below. He rested both hands and his chin on the handle of the wooden staff which bore a carving in relief of Saint Brigid.

The sun gaining height in the morning sky cast soldiers shadows harsh on the rock, jagged alien figures, strange helms, pointed greaves, invaders who did not belong. The goatherd made the sign of the cross on his chest.

One of the men at the rear of column bore a heavy burden. By his posture, a commander of men, he sat pained in the saddle despite no injury apparent. He fixed his eyes far ahead as the army marched through the jaw of the mountain.

Just four days ago the army had touched land on Eire, boots and hooves, eager. Now that army was twelve men less.

It had come to pass that Irish soil pushed back. He had lost men.

The goatherd sighed deeply, as the column of soldiers moved into the east. The horseman assuredly a leader, even at this distance, by the gestures he snapped at the others he rode with. If so he could've with a word, a wave of his hand ordered slaughter of the goatherd and his goats.

But it seemed the man had had his fill of strife. He removed his helm, hung it from his saddle, squinted his eyes shut into the morning sun. The horseman ran his hand over his forehead and smoothed his strange blonde hair. The goatherd, a tall Irish lad, swatted away flies that swum up from the scat his flock left, as he urged them further along the escarpment. If the army passed he could lead them toward fresh pasture. He tugged at the ropes used to control them, and rapped a few with his crook.

An early lone gull circled in the sky above the men, as if hoping for food in the army's wake. As it circled higher it let out a raucous cry.

The goatherd slowly began untethering his charges to graze, and tilted his head to watch the gull. The back of the army neared the tree-line now.

Another knight rode back, out of the forest, to the rear to meet the commander. The goatherd shaded his eyes, and paused untying his goats.

This knight, in green and black, almost merged with the forest. He rode with one hand on his reins, and called to the blonde haired man, but the distance and the wind again took his words away.

A breeze stirred the commander's perfect hair, as he slowed to a walk. The knight hunched over his left hand, snarled again at the commander as his warhorse drew closer to the rear of the column. White cloth at his left hand. A bandage.

The knight remonstrated, angry gestures with his good hand, shouting more words. Words lost to the wind. The blonde man did not meet the other's gaze, but slowly shook his head side to side.

And eventually the two rode side by side, in sullen silence, into the forest and out of sight.

❖

Saint Mary's church steeple bore a simple white-painted wooden cross that stood this Monday morning against a brilliant blue cloudless sky. Its shadow fell across a crowd of villagers arrayed along the Main Road who craned their necks toward the vestry. The group had swollen to near fifty as the sun climbed higher in the sky. It would soon be noon.

Swifts darted and swooped along the line of willows and elms that marked the ridge and the Main Road, disturbed by the clamouring throng. The smithy, where on any other Monday morning a column of smoke would rise, was quiet. Its hearth unlit, several villagers used the forge's front wall as a vantage point.

Their gaze fixed, and speculation centred on an area of open ground between the church and the vestry, where on Sundays the wagons of the faithful would draw up, but which today hosted an unlit pyre. Roped to a cross on top of the stacked timber hung Bronach Blaine, and by their voices every single person in the village had an opinion on her guilt and her fate.

At Pádraig's the window shutters lay open and the O'Neills crowded out on to the roof top, conjecturing and nodding along as they waited for the delegation meeting in the vestry to emerge.

Hilde, Gáethán and Fergus Keenan walked up the path from the Caton farm to face a wall of eager questioning faces. The hubbub of voices, met by a raised hand from the big blacksmith, quietened to be replaced by earnest whispering. Their tone changed, and the crowd turned back to the steps of the vestry.

Father Stephen occupied the entrance to the vestry, the building which Hilde had snuck into only two days ago. From the top of the steps he called out above the ruckus, holding his palms up and nodding at the calls from the crowd. One or two most impatient of the crowd pointing at the room through the entrance behind the priest looked to be on the verge of crashing in there to precipitate events.

Hilde, Gáethán and Fergus reached the back of the crowd and the big smith helped them clear a path toward the churchyard. Hilde wore fresh clothes, but still ill-fitting as they belonged to Gáethán. The boy carried a large woven basket of Hilde's things.

"Our beloved chief who fought for us, would have called this tingmote! But today I stand in his stead. The Brehon have been meeting this morning!" shouted Father Stephen above the din, waving an hand at the door behind him. He waited until the voices quietened. A muffled cry came from Bronach, whose mouth was gagged.

Father Stephen's face looked like thunder. He stabbed a finger accusingly at the unlit pyre. "The church of Saint Mary does not support this outrage. Bronach's fate is *not* foregone. The Brehon meet in the hall behind me! But they still must hear from the aggrieved, from the witnesses! People of Duncormac! Who among you are witnesses? Who is aggrieved?"

A cacophony erupted. Shouts and waving fists. Whichever direction emotions headed in became impossible to discern.

Tingmote. Ostmen. Invaders. Witch. Witch. Witch.

Tiernan O'Rourke stood on the church steps, and shouted a curse, waving his fist in the air. A few in the crowd hurled stones and rotten fruit at the figure roped in the pyre. Still others made the sign of the cross and muttered to their saints.

Pádraig himself shouted angrily at the mess. Indretach stood in front of the smithy, along with the O'Briens and the northern farmers. After the outrage and guilt of the invaders coming to their doorstep, the prospect of burning alive one of their own united all in their fears and anger.

"Mama!! Mama!!" Hilde shrieked as the pyre and Bronach's head became visible over the heads of the crowd.

"Don't push!" said O'Meara the weaver, as Fergus helped Hilde and Gáethán through the throng.

"I've been here for hours, wait your turn!" said O'Donnell the wainwright. He snarled angrily until he turned to see the height of Keenan behind and above him.

"People of Duncormac! We have faced a grave danger and all of you are worried. But we must respect the Brehon! The life of one of us is at stake," Father Stephen shouted, and eventually the crowd quietened and he continued. "The one before you has served this town as a council member. Bought your goods. I will have no more disruptions! Anyone throwing objects will be asked to leave!"

Two at the back raised arms ready to hurl more rotten fruit in response, when as one looked North.

As Hilde reached the front of the crowd, gasps and turned heads told of a delegation approaching. That way, North, lay the priory.

❖

The hubbub of voices rose again, as speculation ran rife among the gathered villagers.

What had happened to the body of fallen hero Don since after the battle Fiach Caton had been taken there for his final hours. Had he passed yet? Who would take over?

"Any news?" Hilde said, nodding in the direction of the Priory, as she squeezed Gáethán's arm. The goatherd shook his head, and looked away, North toward the Priory, to where his father lay.

The lanky goatherd shrugged off Hilde's touch and stepped away toward the delegation from the priory, their heads distinctive over the crowd by their black woollen habits. They had with them a wagon, several nuns walked along with it, and more rode inside.

"Gáethán," Hilde said, as she went to follow. Fergus put his hand on her arm.

"I have to keep ye here. Sorry Hilde," Fergus said, stepping in front of her as Gáethán darted off toward the nuns from the priory.

Then the heads swung as if joined to one beast all in the opposite direction, toward Pádraig's as a figure all in black with a distinctive tall hat marched forward. Behind the Bishop, Cormac Bolan slid out from the portico of the General Store and took up a position at the back of the crowd, arms folded, rocking back and forth on his heels.

"I will speak! The word of God must be heard!" said the man in black. He strode into the rear of the crowd and they parted to let him through. If he could see the delegation from the priory over the heads of the villagers, it did nothing to dim his fervour. The Bishop loudly cleared his throat as he took up a place at the front of the crowd, and looked left and right as if in hopes of a higher platform for his planned oratory.

The pyre was his arrangement, and by his manner the stage also ought to be his. But the man in black, with his showman's hat had to bear to be interrupted. The door behind Father Stephen opened. Four dour faces appeared, bearded men in long robes, one taller than the others.

"Quiet. Please," said the tall man. He carried a tall staff, which he rapped on the wooden threshold of the vestry, putting paid to the throat clearing from the bishop. The tall brehon put his hand on Father Stephen's shoulder as the priest moved aside to allow the four to move forward.

"You will be heard Callum Ahearne," said another of the Brehon, as he moved out to face the crowd. He — a stout man with flecks of dark in his white beard — smiled but his eyes were flinty. Evidently all the Brehon had excellent hearing.

Behind him the two others nodded in the direction of Cormac Bolan, and the Bishop then exchanged solemn words.

"I will speak!" said Hilde.

"The Witch's Daughter!" shouted Ahearne, an accusing finger extended in her direction. Grumbling curses from Cormac Bolan, echoed from other surly faces in the crowd.

Hilde stretched up to her tiptoes and boosted herself by holding Keenan's shoulder. There at the back with Bolan stood Jezabel. She wore black, and strands of her curly hair stuck out from under a black straw hat. She looked daggers at Hilde. As if Hilde alone had been responsible for Donegal's death.

"You will be heard Hilde Blaine," said the tall Brehon.

A rumble went through the crowd, but as Keenan turned to glare at the faces, a couple of hands held up with projectiles ready rapidly withdrew.

"Quiet, please! Who else will speak!" said the tallest of the Brehon, rapping his staff again.

A voice rose from the priory delegation. It was too weak to hear.

"Quiet!" shouted Father Stephen.

Two black wool clad nuns in the wagon lifted something heavy, and the crowd hushed, moving back from the delegation. Gasps then whispered praises to their saints issued from a dozen throats.

"I will speak," said Fiach Caton. His bandaged head, and sorry figure still larger than life stood in the wagon, propped up by the statuesque nun Maida, on one side, and by Grainne on the other. Hilde had met Maida in the Reverend Mother's office. She never spoke, so why was she in the delegation?

"Papa! Papa!" Gáethán said, his voice rising as if he would burst. He tried to vault into the wagon, but Maida held up a palm, and moved in his path.

"It's alright son," said the Chief. His voice was weak but clear.

"You will be heard, Fiach Caton," said the tall Brehon. He raised a curling brow, and surveyed his fellows. They nodded, one after the other. The tall Brehon rapped his staff. "You come to us from death's door. So we shall hear from you first. What is the justice you seek?"

31

The Brehon

The Chief, Fiach Caton, spoke for a good time. His injuries, head swathed in white bandages, red stained in places, so prominent that they provoked more commentary from the crowd than his words. He rested for a moment then continued.

"And it was then, our brother Dónal Ua Ruairc in his kindness gave his life to defend our town," Fiach said. He coughed, and Maida lowered his head, so Grainne could give him more water. "Don stood up to an army! He beat back and defeated a dozen invaders!"

Unlike before the crowd now stood in almost complete silence. At the rear of the crowd Cormac Bolan, Jezabel and the Bishop exchanged furtive glances. The Bishop held up his hands as if to disagree, to demand his piece, but the stout Brehon furrowed his brow, and held a finger to his lips.

"He lived in shame. You knew him by several names, Donàl, even Donegal, the town he came from. Because he was never accepted here. But you all should be the ones to feel shame!" the Chief shouted.

Chief Fiach held up a palm to the nuns who urged him to sit back down.

"I called on all of you to defend us! But it was his niece, Hilde here. She stood with our brother! Thirteen years. A child," Chief Fiach's eyes searched the crowd now, as a few grumbled calls of *witch child* petered out. "More honour in her heart than any of you! I myself named her, and as an Ostman I'm so proud of her fighting spirit!"

"She is Bronach Blaine's daughter! And she called to our proud Irish tradition, taught to her by her mother. And that belief as much as my axe, and our fallen brother's blade turned away the invaders! As her father's had before. Blaine bravery saved all of you!" the Chief said, an admonishing finger playing over all the crowd until finally a coughing fit near consumed him. His eyes clouded over for a moment, emotion and physical pain bit back by gritted teeth. Maida moved to better support him, and Grainne changed places with Gobnait who stood next to her in the wagon.

As they lowered him to his bier in the wagon, Fiach raised his voice again. "Bronach Blaine and her daughter are heroes of this village. Let them return to their home. I have said my piece."

"Lies! The daughter and the mother alike! Both witches! Heretics all!" shouted Ahearne.

"Ahearne! You may now speak. What is your complaint?

Gripping the lapels of his tunic, the Bishop strode forth and began his oratory.

❖

"Alice?" the Bishop said again.

314

The Bishop's oratory had gone on for some time and while it began impressively soon the Bishops glances about the vestry and church, and frantic gestures at Jezabel began to become obvious.

"I swear we have Alice here, waiting to attest to you of Bronach Blaine and the demons that witch summoned to do harm to this town! Alice!"

The Bishop stood with his mouth open, hand high, holding an unfurled parchment.

A flock of starlings chose the moment to fly from the door of the church, where the shutters had been thrown wide open for the tingmote. Tiernan O'Rourke ducked and shielded himself as they flew past him, his rheumy eyes startled and unseeing as he flailed to keep them from his face.

"Avaunt! Tormentors!" slurred a voice. "Begone demons!"

Behind Tiernan O'Rourke, a woman appeared, hanging on the older man's shoulder. It was Alice O'Connor, the preacher's wife.

"Alice!" said the Bishop.

She stared horrified at the flock of starlings, eyes wide and wild. She struck a dramatic pose, shooing them as they continued their flight up to the church's roof top.

With her stood Father Stephen's old man Fearghal O'Connor, scratching his balding pate, and swaying dangerously as he struggled to take stock of the crowd outside.

"Ach woman, we got a few churchgoers here..." Fearghal said, gesturing with the flagon in his hand.

"Demons tormenting me, with their little wings, Fearghal!" Alice said, as she too began to take in the gathered crowd.

The flagon in Fearghal's hand dripped on Alice's foot. Alice spied it, grabbed it from him and held it up to her mouth. She stumbled as she tilted her head back, lost the grip on O'Rourke's shoulder and tumbled down the stairs, giggling all the way to the bottom.

As the starlings settled on the roof, and their chirping abated the Bishop drew a breath, but the tall Brehon rapped his staff.

"Enough. We have *heard* from you Callum Ahearne," said the Brehon.

"*Bishop* Ahearne!" said he, indignantly.

"Liar!!" shouted Grainne from the wagon. Another figure in black behind her nodded, but stayed seated.

"Quiet!! We do not consider the matters of the church here," said the Brehon. "We have heard you speak of heresy, and of demons. These are matters for you! And perhaps Father Stephen."

"Do you hold yourselves above God?" shouted Ahearne.

"You say the Lord God has been wronged. But is he here among us? Does the Lord God speak today?" said the stout Brehon. "You show us parchments, but bring no-one to attest to them."

"This, this is witch-craft!" said Ahearne pointing at Alice at the foot of the church steps. She struggled to get to her feet.

"You called for Alice, *Bishop* Ahearne. This sorry woman, has her demons, but they come from a flagon. Not from hell," said the stout Brehon. He pointed to Alice with his staff.

"And you speak so much of demons. Why are you a man of God *promoting* these beliefs?" said the Brehon at the rear, who'd not spoke until now. He had a reedy high-pitched voice.

"Alice has testimony for you! Its the witch that is promoting them! She saw the demons, I swear it! Cloven hooves, horns, these markings," shouted Ahearne, pointing at his parchment. He turn at last to Jezabel, but she clasped her hand to her face, then shook her head.

"*Bishop* Ahearne, you are done! We *have* heard from you," said the tall Brehon. "Who is here to tell us that Bronach Blaine summoned demons to harm the village? You admit you did not see that yourself. Is Alice speaking today? And what wrong has Alice suffered?"

"I have said all I can. The church holds that Bronach is a blasphemer and a heretic. She harmed Emma, making her barren, and damaged Cormac's crops. What more can I say? I yield," said Ahearne. He stepped back toward the crowd with a flourish, rolling up the parchment as he did so.

The Brehon with the high-pitched voice walked forward. "We cannot pronounce on matters of the church. If you are the authority of the church then we must defer to you Bishop."

The soldiers and allies of the Chief in the crowd shouted angrily at this, but soon quietened.

"Father Stephen? Can you speak for the church?" the Brehon asked.

"I cannot. The Bishop is my superior. And I stand as village chief. I must remain neutral. I'm sorry," he gripped his hands into fists, and his face twisted in anguish as he glanced at Bronach on the pyre.

❖

There was much discussion amongst the Priory delegation, but no-one stood. The gathered villagers began to grow impatient and cry out.

Witch! Demons!

The crowd shuffled impatiently. The sun shone from directly overhead now, and the shadow of the cross of Saint Mary's fell directly over Bronach Blaine still roped to the pyre.

Two men tried to walk up with burning torches but were dealt with by Fergus and unexpectedly Pádraig Ó Néill and his son who stepped up to help.

The voices grew more subdued. The Brehon conferred among themselves.

"Hilde Blaine, what justice do you seek?" the Brehon rapped his staff as he spoke, brooking no more shouts from the villagers.

Hilde stepped forward, Keenan shadowing her as curious villagers craned to look at her.

"Your great honour! Thank you for letting me speak. But may I see my Chief first?" Hilde said.

The Brehon conferred, nodded, and Keenan helped Hilde onto the wagon. She took from him the bag he carried.

"I am so glad you lived, but Chief...my Uncle. He is gone, isn't he?" Hilde began.

Maida lifted the Chief from his bier, and he squeezed Hilde's hand.

"Yes, Hilde, he is," the Chief whispered. "He came to me. I was dying and he gave himself to the Tuatha Danaan, for me. I saw him at the foot of my bed. He said goodbye and vanished."

"Chief, you should rest," Maida said.

He squeezed Hilde's hand again and lay down. Then the nun who'd been seated at the back of the wagon stood.

"Reverend Mother!" Hilde whispered, and gasped. She showed the old Abbess her bag, and the woman nodded, then smiled conspiratorially. Gobnait showed the Reverend Mother a large book she carried, and they nodded to each other.

The Abbess grabbed Hilde's forearm, and bent to whisper in her ear. The tall nun, the Reverend Mother's aide, put a protective hand on the old woman's curving back. After a few moments the Reverend Mother sat down, and a half smile stole onto Hilde's face.

Hilde turned and put one foot on the side of the wagon. She shouted to the crowd. "This is Ahearne's demon!! Look for yourselves!"

She put her hand into the bag and drew out the goatskin cloak. Holding a horn in one hand, and stretching the hide above her head Hilde turned so the whole crowd could see the mouldering artefact.

Ahearne pushed through the crowd toward her, spluttering in denial. As he drew close Hilde threw the goatskin at him, and it landed square over his head, with the horned skull draping over his back. Jezabel and Bolan rushed up to help him extricate himself.

"There is your demon!" Hilde shouted, pointing at Ahearne, Jezabel and Bolan. "Alice in her cups, saw Gáethán's goat, dead on a fence. And these people took an ill woman's testimony of a dead goat to harm my mother! To take our family home!"

"That home was my husbands!" Jezabel screeched.

"My poor Uncle Don, who gave his life for this village. He too was a victim of this woman. If there is any evil here, it is the demon drink, and it comes from her! You and my honourable Uncle never wed. Get his name out of your mouth!"

"Witch!! Witch!" screamed Jezabel, pointing at Hilde.

"Quiet! Hilde speaks!" called the tall Brehon. "Ahearne, bring that goat skin to me."

"And this!" Hilde shouted. She held up the earthenware flask. "Found in the midden, behind the Dire Goose. Indretach!"

The apothecary nervously looked either side of himself, his beady eyes darting, as Hilde thrust out the flask, but the crowd soon helped him overcome his shyness, and pushed him forward. They eagerly awaited for more drama as exciting as the goat skin.

As the apothecary neared the wagon Hilde threw the flask down to him. He fumbled but caught it.

"It bears your mark! What did this potion do?" Hilde said. Indretach looked at Ahearne, who shook his head frantically.

"Answer the girl!" shouted the tall Brehon. The shorter Brehon with the high pitched voice stepped forward.

"Its mugwart, belladonna and peony. It will bring on the menses," he said, his voice squeaking with nerves.

"Give it to us please!" said the tall Brehon. "Bring on the menses? What would that mean for a pregnant woman?"

"She could lose her child," Indretach said, quietly. "And become very ill, even barren."

"That potion, I found empty at the back of the O'Brien's tavern where Emma lives. So it was not witchcraft that made her barren! It was this!" Hilde shouted, open palm extended toward the sweating apothecary.

"A lie! There's only her word!" shouted Ahearne.

"The witch's daughter! She cannot be trusted!" shouted Jezabel.

"Indretach! Is this the same potion?" the Reverend Mother though small and bent over, had a voice firm and authoritative. Years of commanding the staff of the priory gave her an air of someone not to be denied. She walked to the edge of the wagon, and held out another earthenware flask. Maida handed it to Indretach.

"Hilde Blaine! Do you allow the Prioress to speak?" the tall Brehon asked.

Hilde nodded. She extended a hand toward the Abbess to continue. The canny old woman had allowed the Bishop to think the flask had been lost, thrown in the huge midden heap never to be recovered. Instead she'd kept it.

"I cannot speak, and of course our catechism prevents me from raising my voice above that of a bishop," said the Reverend Mother. She raised the heavy book Gobnait had given her. "But I have a duty to tell the truth when asked in secular proceeding. I must correct this record, so Indretach?"

"Yes, your Reverence," Indretach said, holding up the flask. He began nodding slowly. "Mugwart, belladonna, peony. Same."

"And Reverend Mother, where is the flask from?" asked Hilde.

"*That* flask came from *this* mans room in our priory!" the Reverend Mother strode up and down the wagons bed, gesturing first at Indretach, and then Ahearne.

"What else did you find there?"

"Why *forged* letters, of appointment to a Bishopric," said the Reverend Mother.

"Forgery! Poisoning!!" said Hilde, pointing to Ahearne. "Is he even a bishop? With that hat, I think him more a jester!"

The crowd began to mutter quietly at first then in a more belligerent tone.

Forgery. Poison. Faker, fraud!

"Who was this flask for *Mister* Ahearne?" Hilde's question reverberated through the crowd. "Who else unwillingly carried your seed?"

Grainne sunk to her knees and began sobbing. Her cries so racked her, that Gobnait put her arms around her and draped her shawl on her knees. The Reverend Mother crossed to Grainne and stood beside her. She looked daggers at Ahearne.

"*He* is the one who harmed our town. Set us against each other," said the Hilde, stabbing with conviction her points home to the man in black. The man swept off his hat, and went to climb up to strike at Hilde in the wagon. Maida grabbed his left hand from the side of the wagon and pulled it loose as if he were an unruly child grabbing from the adults table.

Hilde's eyes grew wide, and a lump formed in her throat. The bishop stumbled backward, frothing and spitting. He was as mad as the invader FitzStephen. All these men filled with hatred from their crusader sermons in Europe.

"Hilde, thank you," said the Prioress, and she kneeled next to Grainne.

"I beg you, Brehon brothers, my mother is god-fearing woman, and she has raised me to be the same. To defend our town against enemies," Hilde said. She pointed at the bridge "I was scared but I stood there when our enemies came for us, and our holy spirits answered my call."

A murmur of voices crossed the crowd, raised eyebrows and turning heads. A few eyes with tears.

The tall Brehon stroked his long beard. Behind him his brother Brehon traded whispered words, and held up the potion bottles and the skin of the goat.

"Release Bronach Blaine. It is this man who ought to be gagged, not Hilde's mother."

The crowd erupted in a cheer, clapping and shouting. Straw hats thrown in the air, soared up in to the noonday sun.

Keenan strode up on to the woodpile, and soon Bronach collapsed into his arms. Hilde ran to her.

"Mama, are you alright?" Hilde asked.

"Water," croaked Bronach. Then a weak smile spread across her face, eyes focusing. She saw that it was Keenan that held her.

"Mama, can we go home?" Hilde asked, tears streaming down her face.

"My Hilde, yes. Yes we can."

32

Epilogue

Sheets of grey and white cloud littered the northern skies but over Blaine Cottage the sky opened to let mid-morning sun onto the small-holding. Jackdaws waited in the pear tree while the crows higher in the pecking order dived on worms turned up by Hilde's plough. Sebastien brayed indignantly as she batted his rump with a switch but pulled again as the heavy wood and iron drew through damp soil. Hens gobbled grain contentedly in the coop, but the pigs had already scoffed their breakfast and rooted in their pen for more.

Down the lane towards Duncormac a crowd of starlings flew up from a hedgerow, squeaking their displeasure at being disturbed. Through the fruit trees, obscured by the heat haze, a figure in black trudged there, along the rutted carriageway toward the row of apple trees that marked the bound of Blaine land. A trunk weighed them down, and a broad-brimmed hat shaded their face.

Hilde started, a gasp escaped her, and she set the plough down too hard. Sebastien snickered. Hilde shaded her eyes and peered but the figure walked behind the trees. It was only a brief moment that a memory of her father, and his wares of silver returning down that lane rose up from her childhood. The watercolour recollections arrived less frequently now, but jolted her when they did. Hilde took her hat off and wiped her eyes with her sleeve.

Bronach Blaine walked into the yard, brushing past the ripening apples, and swatting at the flies that followed her from the lane.

"Great work dear girl," Bronach said, pushing her hat up from her face. "Take a break. I have some pies from the Dire Goose."

"Did the man buy?" Hilde asked, a grin spreading across her face.

"He took two of the mirrors I had made, and a set of spoons of your father's," Bronach said, hand on hips. She patted the pockets of her skirt and drew out a purse that clinked solidly as she held it up. "He's a majordomo for a merchant in Wexford. Paid in Norman coin."

"Mama, that is wonderful! I'll put Sebastien in his stall," Hilde said. Pastry and meat scents arose from a muslin bag Bronach carried. Hilde dragged the plough to one side and led the beast to his place, filling buckets for him with feed and water. The aroma of the pies made him strain at his tether as Hilde hastened to follow her Mama to the cottage.

"Hilde, I'm stopping the mending work," Bronach said as she moved inside, dropping the trunk at the kitchen table. "Blaine's silver-mark still carries good weight from Kilkenny to Wexford it seems. And they're not to know or care as long as their mirrors and spoons are bright and polished."

Bronach went through the contents of the trunk, setting aside scales and examining a billet of silver.

"I'm to work this into a signet ring. And we keep what remains. Hilde I need your good eyes to help me. I know we can do this," Bronach said. She held up a parchment, and a small cup with an impression in wax.

Hilde stood at the wooden bench that ran along by the fireplace. They'd need more water soon, and now she did most of the work around the cottage, the question of who'd go to the well did not need asking. Furrows marked Hilde's brow, and she gritted her teeth as her hands leaned on the bench.

She turned, drew a deep breath and set out two cups of water. Her Mama's face though lined and eyes rheumy bore a radiant smile. The pies steamed on the table, cut into halves now. Bronach gestured to Saint Brigid, replete with offerings before her on a small shelf above the fireplace. Next to it stood the heavy book that Gobnait and Grainne had made.

"Hilde, we've been blessed. Saints be praised," Bronach said, nodding in recognition of the concern she'd caught on Hilde face. "Blaine women are strong. I know we can do this. My daughter who has shown me nothing is beyond her."

"Mama," Hilde said, chewing her lip. "I still have nightmares."

"We start on it after lunch. Now, there's news! It's been two bare years since Diarmaid mac Murchada brought that horde to our shores. The merchant told me our Diarmaid *died*! Just a day ago. That's tidings of war for you."

"Died? Of what?" Hilde said, as she sat and started shovelling the pie crust into her mouth.

"No idea," Bronach said.

"I'll ask Gobnait on Sunday," Hilde said, washing down the last of her pie with a swig of water.

"Shall I make us some nettle tea?" Bronach asked.

Hilde nodded, and her Mama put a pot on the fireplace.

❖

The couple walked arm in arm along the banks of the River Suir. She pulled out the combs that held her long curls, and they tumbled down, now flecked with a few silver strands. She smiled at her beau as he smoothed and his similarly grey peppered blonde moustaches.

A few in the crowd at the church they'd departed pointed and speculated. A couple of the matrons harrumphed and turned away, which was precisely the effect Éadaoin had hoped for. The other burghers set to nodding and gesturing expansively at the excitement of a new force in their town of Ardfinnan.

"Where are we going, so mysteriously that we cannot take our carriage, my lord?" Éadaoin asked.

"You waited so long my love, and I wanted to have good news to tell you," Maurice de Prendergast said. He pressed on grinning from ear to ear as they rounded a row of trees marking a bend in the river. "I know how hard it was when my wife passed away and yet instead of my coming to be with you I had to campaign for our good King Henry all those years."

"You explained your faith and mores would not allow another marriage. I was not happy, but it made me more determined that you must be a man of quality worth waiting for," Éadaoin said.

"Do you know its ten years almost to the day that I landed at Bannow Bay with that madman FitzStephen? I had no notion of how I would make our romance work, but the fates were with me," de Prendergast searched her face for a reaction.

"The fates?" Éadaoin asked. De Prendergast kicked at a stick, his fine leather boots marked by it and one of the footmen behind wincing at the polishing task that now lay ahead of him.

"That Irishman. He fought well that day on the bridge, but I had him bent over the parapet and thought to kill him in cold blood," de Prendergast said. He gritted his teeth, flinty-eyed as he turned to gaze across at the rocky outcrop on the other side of the river. "My sword was at his neck. But something gave me pause. And then he slipped away."

"You've never talked of that. I hear bits and pieces of that day from you, my captain. What really happened?" Éadaoin asked. De Prendergast shivered.

"I can't explain it. But darling, Éadaoin, after that day I had a new respect for your traditions. Although my Lord God guides my every action, there is something in the magic of this country. I hesitated. And the Irishman, he was taken. Away into the mists."

"Oh! You mean… he fell into the river?" Éadaoin asked.

"That is what I told Giffard, that I slit the man's throat and pushed him into the current," de Prendergast stared at the river banks of the Suir. A woman there knelt by a basket and de Prendergast shuddered as he watched her.

The woman stood and turned, calling to two young boys who shouted and laughed playing with a kite. De Prendergast rubbed his face.

"I felt that day was the best victory I ever had. And things have gone my way since, my darling. And that brings me to this!"

"What ever are you talking about?" Éadaoin asked. The twinkle in her eyes gave away some of the pretence that she did not have any knowledge of her Captain's plans.

At a discreet distance guards and footmen walked behind. But de Prendergast even ten years on from the landing that had defined his career in King Henry's western expansion had a spritely step and his retinue had to pick up their pace.

Then he stopped, put up his boot on a river stone and held out his hand. There past the row of trees a striking headland jutted out, marked by rocky terrain and today framed by blue skies.

"There overlooking Ardfinnan I will build a mighty new castle. For you and I," de Prendergast said. His enigmatic smile spread and his eyes misted over as he stared at the horizon where new towers would be raised.

"Surely you'll not be spending the proceeds from the sale of your lands in Wales?" Éadaoin asked.

"My new title has yet to be decided, but I will be governor of these lands. King Henry has rewarded me for my successes against the English rebels that so dogged him. The castle is for my domicile and my garrison both, to represent the King here," de Prendergast said.

He put his hands on his hips and scanned the river banks as Sunday's town errands sent folks bustling across the pleasant country by-ways. None washed armour at the riverbanks, no mist rose. The captain linked arms with his lover.

"Lady of the castle at Ardfinnan. I like it, whatever the title winds up to be. And I prefer the weather here too," Éadaoin said with a laugh. "When will we return to speak to my father? He is anxious for the marriage to be proper. And have you decided on how you'll handle Wessex?"

"Tomorrow we go back. I'm not sure how I will handle it, Éadaoin," de Prendergast said. He turned and waved at his footmen to clear out of his way. He muttered half to himself. "But I wish to be a good Norman. That has stood me in good stead and I'll keep to it."

"You wish to be what? What title was that my Lord?" Éadaoin asked.

"Hah. I care not what they say I was. Let my head stone just read 'Here lies a good Norman'."

❖

Text reproduced below of facts about Maurice de Prendergast and of the Aubrey de Vere poem "The Faithful Norman" are drawn from the <u>Kilkenny Archaeological Society article</u> March 2021 by Richard Prendergast.

*The Faithful Norman himself joined the Knights of St John of Jerusalem in his later years. He became Master of the Hospital of Kilmainham their chief house in Ireland, and it seems most probable that **he died**, holding that distinguished knightly office, **in 1205**.*

THE FAITHFUL NORMAN

Praise to the valiant and faithful foe !
Give us noble foes, not the friend who lies!
We dread the drugged cup, not the open blow:
We dread the old hate in the new disguise.
To Ossory's King they had pledged their word:
He stood in their camp, and their pledge they broke;
Then Maurice the Norman upraised his sword,
The cross on its hilt he kiss'd, and spoke.
"So long as this sword or this arm hath might,
I swear by the cross which is lord of all,
By the faith and honour of noble and knight
Who touches you, Prince, by this hand shall fall I
So side by side through the throng they pass'd,
And Eire gave praise to the just and true.
Brave foe I the past truth heals at last:
There is room in the great heart of Eire for you.

• THE END •

Download your *FREE* full-colour maps

Buying this book gives you access — for $Free — to full-colour large scale versions of the meticulously created historical maps of Ireland & Wales and Duncormac in 1169.

You've already seen the small black and white versions at the front of this book. With the restrictions of publishing I've made these as clear as I can. But beautiful high-resolution versions of these maps await you online!

Now, for *free*, you can trace Hilde's adventures and the paths of the invading Normans in highly accurate full-colour maps in electronic form. Download them to your phone, tablet/iPad or laptop and blow them up to see all the details of Duncormac, the Priory and the bridge where the battle happened.

- Your access code is **WITCHS-MAPS**

Visit the companion website at:

- https://www.storybridge.org/thewitchsdaughter

Read the following short story ebooks from Sarah Smith.

Obman's Demon

- https://sarah-jane-smith.gumroad.com/l/zchomv

In Victorian London, Silas Smirke is a pathological liar & ambitious doctor who has a gift land in his lap; the new sensation of x-rays. But he has not reckoned on the patients at Bedlam Hospital.

A turn-of-the-century tale of medical hubris in the mysterious and storied asylum of London, England. The London Tube has just been built, and a new world is dawning. A historical horror you can read in an hour or so.

The Clockwork Heart

- https://sarah-jane-smith.gumroad.com/l/the-clockwork-heart

A Steampunk Story. Inspector Carstairs of the Clockwork Constabulary is on the trail of Romina Hearn. But when she decides to steal hearts from Dr Sbaitho's Factory, a terrible truth could the unwinding of them both.

The Green Door

- https://sarah-jane-smith.gumroad.com/l/the-green-door

A Ghost Story. In the 70's a professor is faced with horrifying revelations about a past student, himself and his own conduct, in the lab behind the green door.

Read short stories and articles by Sarah Smith on the Substack publication "Authentic Writing". There are free and subscription stories to read in different genres, such as:

- Steam punk

- Modern fiction

- Science fiction

…and more!

Authentic Writing

Install the Substack app and search for *Authentic Writing* by Sarah Smith. Or navigate to the publication directly in your browser:

- https://authenticwriting.substack.com

Direct links genre fiction writing:

- https://authenticwriting.substack.com/t/fiction

Steampunk:

- https://authenticwriting.substack.com/t/steampunk

Autobiographical:

- https://authenticwriting.substack.com/t/author

Subscriptions are very cheap and you can read as much as you want! There's a huge back catalogue there available to subscribers.

As a bonus, I communicate often and use Substack as my mailing list, so its the best place to find out about new things I'm working on.